BEAUTY

SLEEP

USBORNE

For Greta Rose Davison.

Those who you keep in your heart, enclosed in love,

will always live.

First published in the UK in 2019 by Usborne Publishing Ltd., Usborne House,
83-85 Saffron Hill, London EC1N 8RT, England. www.usborne.com

Text © Kathryn Evans, 2019

The right of Kathryn Evans to be identified as the author of this work has been asserted by her in
accordance with the Copyright, Designs and Patents Act, 1988.

Cover images: Test screen glitch texture © Shutterstock / Tomertu
Closed eyes © Shutterstock / Dmytro Bochkov. Open eyes © Shutterstock / LUCKY_CAT

The name Usborne and the devices ♀ 🌐 **USBORNE** are Trade Marks of
Usborne Publishing Ltd.

A CIP catalogue record for this book is available from the British Library.

ISBN 9781474954877 05153/3 JFMAMJJ SOND/19

Printed in the UK.

BEFORE

I understood. I really did. This was a chance. Our *only* chance. It was this or die.

In some ways it was a relief. I was so tired of being ill. Worn down from all the puking, from being so feeble, from trying to seem okay when Stacey came to visit, and when Mum and Ima kept their tearful vigils between my bed and Alfie's.

It was so much effort and my head hurt so much, my joints, my skin... I just wanted to sleep. To hand over all this...*trying*...to someone else.

So yeah. I understood.

But what broke me, what killed me, was the thought of Alfie, my baby brother, being enclosed in that pod and sent to sleep until they could wake us and cure us. It was unbearable.

Alfie was so small. He'd only just turned five. We'd celebrated his birthday a few days before we both fell ill.

His bubbly head of curls had bounced with excitement when he'd opened his present, a Fisher-Price cassette recorder.

He'd interviewed us all:

"Lulu, what you gonna be when you grow up?"

"Your big sister, little man. Always."

I could hardly bear it. The thought of losing him was a lead weight pressing down on my chest.

He was going to be first, so he wouldn't have to go without me. They pushed our beds together so I could hold his hand as they sedated him. On the other side of the bed, Mum and Ima sobbed softly, stroking his hair. Alfie's breathing changed from shallow and rapid to barely there. His tiny hand went limp in mine and my heart cracked in two.

chapter one
LAURA

Thoughts came, like fluff, white fluff.

Colds?

No. Clouds.

But I am cold. So cold.

Am I dead?

I can't think…

Is this death?

I am so…so cold.

My head, the thing in it…brain, my brain is…empty.

Who am I?

What am I?

There's nothing to hold on to. I can't…

There is an absence of…everything.

Not a face, not a memory.

I am…blank—

A ragged trail scorched my throat, raw and sore. I retched,

choking, gasping for air. Light blinded me. I screwed my eyes tight shut, tried to turn away, but still the light burned. *I* burned.

"Come on, Laura. You can do this. Your name is Laura Henley. You're in hospital but you're going to be fine. You just need to breathe."

Pain bit through my head as I blinked against the impossible brightness.

"There you are. Welcome back. You've been asleep for a little while. We've just woken you up. You're in Blackhurst Clinic and you are going to be fine. You just need to breathe."

A blurry face hovered above me. I blinked again, trying to clear the fog clouding my eyes. Panic surged through me. I tried to move but I was weighed down, trapped. My heart raced. Where was I? Why couldn't I move? What had he said? Had I been kidnapped? I struggled to sit up but I couldn't even lift my hand. I tried to speak, but all that came out was a husky growl. I blinked again, trying to see, trying to communicate.

I can't move, I can't move...

Someone pressed a damp sponge to my burning brow.

"Shhhh," a female voice said. "Shhhhh."

Terror flooded through me. My body trembled, shuddered, shook violently. I was the centre of my own personal earthquake. My teeth crashed together. I bit through my tongue. Gulping sobs erupted from me and tears poured down my face. Someone held my shoulders as a deep, crushing pain cramped my heart, and flooded into my arms.

"She's arresting. Stand clear."

With a violent punch to my chest, I slipped into oblivion.

chapter two
LAURA

I don't know what they did while I was out of it, but the next time I woke, I felt like I'd necked a few pints of snakebite.

Snakebite and black: half lager, half cider, mixed with blackcurrant. Turns your vomit purple when you puke it up. Which you will.

I tried to catch the thread of memory, but whatever it was, it danced from my grasp. I blinked. Everything was soft with light. A shadowy figure swam in front of me.

"Hello. Let's try that again, shall we?"

I tried to speak and a dry whisper came out: "Where…?"

"You've been through a bit of a rough time, I'm afraid. Your name is Laura Henley. You've been very unwell but you're okay now. You've been asleep for quite a while. There's nothing to worry about. You're at Blackhurst Clinic and we're taking care of you."

I tried to reach towards the voice but my limbs were too heavy – lifting an arm was beyond me.

"Can't see you," I managed.

"Well, I'm not much to look at, to be honest."

Someone laughed at that. It sounded nice. "My name is Benjie Bautista. I'm the doctor in charge of your care here."

Pain gnawed through my brain.

"Head…" I said.

"Hurting?" he asked.

I gave the tiniest nod.

"Mariya, can you increase drug release?"

Someone did something and the pain in my body eased, leaving behind a vague feeling of something forgotten, something important – but what?

Thinking was…hard.

The voice said, "What can you remember, Laura? Can you tell me your full name?"

Name. My name. He had said it earlier. What was it?

"Laura…Henley?" I whispered, searching my empty brain for some hint as to who Laura Henley was.

"Good, good. Do you know where you are?"

What had he said?

"Clinic?" It came out in a muffled lisp, my mouth too dry and sore to form the word properly.

Someone poked a wet stick in my mouth and swabbed it round my lips. I spat it out but my mouth felt better after.

I tried to touch my lips. It was a monumental effort to move my arm and it was so heavy that I dropped it, like a fleshy lump, and smacked myself in the face. I remembered that I'd bitten my tongue when they woke me before. Where was the bite? I couldn't feel it.

The man lifted my hand gently and put it back by my side.

"Tongue," I said.

"Yes. You bit your tongue. Remembering that is an excellent sign, Laura."

I blinked, trying to clear the film over my eyes. "Can't see."

"Try not to worry. There's technically nothing wrong with your eyes; they're just not used to being used. It's been a while."

"Why…?"

"You've been very ill."

I tried to remember something. Anything.

"Punched me…in chest."

A woman laughed again, soft and gentle and very amused.

The man, the doctor, Benjie, said, "We didn't punch you, Laura. I'm sorry to say your heart stopped beating. We had to restart it."

"That's bad."

The laugh again. I liked it, it was…kind.

"Pretty bad," said Benjie, "but it's a lot better now."

In those first few days, I didn't much care who Laura Henley was. I didn't much care about anything. Heat and pain cycled through my chemical-soaked body and it was all I could do to just keep breathing.

I woke and slept and woke and slept for what seemed like for ever. Eventually things began to change. One afternoon Benjie came in with a group of people. I'd just woken up and, as I blinked myself properly awake, I realized I could see his face more clearly.

"Your eyes are crinkly."

He laughed and they crinkled up even more. "They are, and they're going to stay that way. I like my crinkles."

He turned to the group of people and I guess he smiled at them too because they all smiled and nodded back and I could see them. My heart swelled a little.

"I can see you. I can see all of you."

"What perfect timing," Benjie said. "Because I think you're ready to properly meet your recovery team. It's still early days but your test results are looking good, which means it's time to start some serious work."

"Work?" How could I work? I could hardly move.

"Don't panic," Benjie said. "We'll be with you all the way, but we need to step things up if we're going to maximize your recovery. You probably know Mariya, your day nurse, and Stephen who covers nights – he's catching up on his beauty sleep. They're your dedicated nursing team. To get you fully back to normal though, we need a bit more expertise. Edna here will head up your physiotherapy and nutrition, and Vera, your psychiatric rehabilitation." He indicated two interchangeable square women with matching cropped blonde hair and white tunics.

I said, "Hello."

They smiled at me encouragingly. Their teeth were dazzlingly white. Weirdly white. Like light-pinging-off-them white.

I was staring at their smiles when Benjie said, "And this" – he stepped back with a flourish – "is Miss Lilly."

A woman with a razor-sharp black bob stepped daintily forward. She had huge violet eyes, pale pink glossy lipstick and skin like a china doll. She was absolutely stunning and…I know this is going to sound weird…but she smelled incredible. It was like a warm hug of scented air: orange and wood and a hint of black pepper, fresh and warm and spicy. She smiled at me and something in me melted.

"Laura. It is so lovely to see you wide awake and back with us properly."

She offered me her hand, careful to help as she took mine – she must have known I could still barely lift my arms. Her fingers were cool and delicate and held mine like she didn't want to let me go and then she did and I felt cut adrift. I wanted her to take my hand again – so much so I tried to reach out. It was ridiculous. I didn't even know her.

Or did I? The thought came with a grip of panic, both scary and embarrassing: *Should I know her?* That's the weird thing about forgetting everything – it's strangely calm, like sitting in the eye of a storm, in the empty spot where nothing hurts you. Until the storm touches you.

Meeting Miss Lilly was the first brush of the storm, the first real stirring of need. A deep-down, desperate need to know. Who was she? Why did I feel a connection to her?

I looked at Benjie and then back at her.

"Do I know you?"

She leaned forward, placing her fingers lightly against my cheek. That scent enveloped me again and I pressed my face towards her hand. "One thing at a time, sweetheart. Let's get you better. You have the best people I could gather to look after you. They assure me your memory will come back, but it has to be taken gently, okay?"

I nodded.

"And finally, that's Giles, head of media." Benjie waved vaguely towards a man standing behind the others. "But you don't need to worry about him for a while."

Miss Lilly took her hand away, leaving the faintest trace of perfume on my skin and a yearning in my heart.

"Okay, team," she said, "over to you. This young woman means everything to me. I want one hundred per cent from all of you, all of the time. Understood?"

They nodded crisply in reply and she left, taking all the sunshine with her.

I made myself concentrate on Benjie as he said, "Physio starts tomorrow, Laura, but today we're going to begin weaning you off that drip and onto these delicious milkshakes!"

He gestured to a trolley Mariya had pushed in. It carried a single metal beaker with a fat straw in it. Unfortunately, my brain had gone out of the door with my mystery visitor.

"Who was that?" I asked Benjie.

"*That* was Miss Lilly, CEO of the world's most famous

skincare company and owner of this clinic. Now, let's see if we can sit you up."

Edna or Vera, one of them – it must have been Edna, as she was in charge of physio – went around the other side of my bed. Between her and Benjie, they tried to get me into a sitting position while I carried on asking questions.

"But what is this place? Do I know that lady?"

I slumped sideways, so feeble I couldn't even hold my own body upright. They leaned me back, moving some pillows so I was more supported. I was distracted for a minute, because for the first time I could see out of the window opposite my bed. The sky was blue and the tops of trees were visible in the distance. It looked like the clinic was in an enormous park. Did Miss Lilly own the park too? And why was she so kind to me? Why did she feel so familiar? A thought struck me like a lifeline.

"Is Miss Lilly my mum?"

Benjie sat on my bed. "Okay, let's take one thing at a time. Firstly, this place is Blackhurst Clinic, known for providing anything from beauty treatments and relaxation to cosmetic augmentation and addiction rehabilitation. Historically, it's also been at the forefront of some very innovative clinical research. That's why you're here. Secondly, Miss Lilly doesn't have any children. She is the very famous, very wealthy face of Miss Lilly Skincare. She has the money to help you and a generous heart. That's as much as I can tell you. I'm sorry, Laura. When you've started to remember, we'll do everything we can to accelerate the process, but right now, we need to let your brain rewire itself without too much interference from us."

I felt stupid for asking after he'd explained, but the truth was, I *could* have been anyone: a school kid or a spy; a dinner lady or a detective. Probably not a detective actually, given I had no idea how to even figure out who I was. And, for the sake of my own brain, no one was going to tell me.

"Now then, aren't you desperate to try Edna's milkshake?" Benjie said.

I smiled. "Actually, yes, I think I am." All I'd had since I'd woken up was water and whatever was fed into me through the drip in my arm.

Benjie stepped out of the way and Edna picked up the metal beaker and held the straw against my mouth. Some muscle memory told me what to do and I sucked. And sucked. And nothing came up the tube.

"Keep going," Edna said. "You're nearly there. C-plan is specially formulated to build you up and give you all the nutrition you need."

I tried again and a dollop of cold, tasteless gloop plopped onto my tongue and slithered down my throat. I gagged on it, turning my head away, and a memory bowled into me so hard that it knocked the breath from my lungs.

Feeding a little boy with a headful of brown curls. His face turning this way and that, smearing his skin with the white goo on the spoon as he shouts, "No, Lulu. No!"

I clutched the sheets. Sweat chilled my skin. I looked desperately at Benjie.

"What is it? Pain?"

I shook my head, shivering as I whispered, "A little boy."

"A memory?"

"He called me Lulu. Who is he, Benjie? I think I'm going to be—"

Benjie whipped a cardboard dish in front of me as the gloop came back up.

I knew then that I'd forgotten something important, so terribly important, to do with that little boy. I was sure of it and it frightened me. I clutched at Benjie, trembling. "Who is he? I should know, I can feel it!"

But Benjie couldn't help, or wouldn't. He just gently patted my shoulder until I fell into an exhausted sleep.

When I woke up, either Vera or Edna was sitting by my bed. I pretended I was still asleep.

"I'll still be here when you're ready to talk," she said softly.

Talking. It had to be Vera then. With a sigh, I looked at her. "Who is he, do you know?"

"I think you are on your way to remembering that yourself."

That single snapshot of memory had ripped my heart out and put it back in sideways. It scared me. I was comfortable in the clinic, cared for – I felt guilty for thinking it, but it was like remembering threatened that. I wanted to know and, at the same time, I didn't.

"Can I have a drink of water?"

Vera went to the sink. The sky was pink outside.

"Is it morning or evening?" I asked.

"Evening," she replied. "It's beautiful, isn't it?"

I watched her fill a glass from the single high tap. It curved over the sink like a swan's neck. Another memory slammed into me.

A damp day walking by a pond. My hand inside a larger hand. Two swans circle each other on the water, their heads bowed together, forming a heart. I twirl under the person's arm, dancing with them as they laugh.

I tried to grasp the loose thread of memory but it snapped like rotten cotton. As my brain chased after it, I realized something that filled me with sadness.

"Vera," I said, "why does no one ever come to see me?"

chapter three
SHEM

It wasn't the rat running over my sleeping bag that woke me up, it was the blinding sun streaming through the shed window. I scrunched my eyes up against the light and rolled onto my back, feeling for Scrag. He was out already. I sat up, scratched my itchy head and whistled. Within minutes he'd wriggled past the broken plank at the back of my shed and was wagging his stubby tail in front of me. He dropped a bag of stale bread in my lap.

"You clever boy! Been down the park robbing ducks, have you?"

I rubbed his scruffy head and pulled a crust out of the bag. I gave one to him and took one for myself. It was bone hard. I couldn't even bite through it. It had been a baking night and sweat trickled from my pits to my pants. I should have got up earlier and gone down the beach for a swim, freshened myself up a bit. It was too late once the sun was properly up. People would already be spreading towels over the pebbles, getting their picnics sorted. Showing off their perfect little families.

Screw that.

At least I had my shed. I loved it. It had everything I needed. A door, a roof and an army of cockroaches. One scuttled across the floor and I crushed it with the hammer I kept near my bed.

Crunch.

I was invincible.

I rubbed my thumb on the warm wood of the hammer's handle. It was one of the things Bert had given me when we still lived in the squat. He had this idea that I could be a carpenter or something. Fat chance of that with one hand and no proper training, but still, I liked making stuff, and I loved working with wood.

We used to go along the shoreline when everyone had gone home – or before they'd arrived – and pick up bits of driftwood, sea-glass if we were lucky, all sorts of flotsam. Then we'd make things together out of what we'd found. Pecking seagulls, little bobbing boats, seaside scenes, that sort of thing. I'd sold all his long since and made a few quid from my own. They weren't as good as Bert's, but I was getting better. It was harder to find the wood in the summer – other people took it. It was easier in the winter but then I was tempted to burn it for the warmth. I always regretted it after. Like when I burned the complete works of Shakespeare that Bert had nicked from a library. It wasn't like I ever needed to read that again – I knew those stories inside out

– but once they were ashes, I felt colder than ever.

I'd been proper lucky Bert had taken me in. I don't remember a time before him. There were a few versions of how he'd found me. The one he told me most often was that I was wandering down the side of a main road when I was maybe four or five; just striding along with a screwdriver in my good hand and the blankest expression he'd ever seen. I don't remember anything about it – or about life before Bert – and Bert used to tell stories for money, so who knows what was true?

It was me and Bert against the world for at least ten years, maybe twelve. Most of that time we were in hiding. And by most of it, I mean all of it. We never went out together in the day. He said the authorities would take me away if they found out how we were living and that he wasn't my proper dad. But he *was* a proper dad to me. I couldn't have asked for better. Even after he got ill, all he thought about was what would happen to me when he died.

So he found this place for us. An undisturbed shed, in an undisturbed garden of an undisturbed house. One day someone would buy the house and do it up, but while there were rats in the roof, rot in the floorboards and rumours someone had died in there, people stayed away. My shed was a gazillion times better than sleeping in a doorway and getting a kicking from some drunk or trying to find a sheltered spot that didn't have spikes sticking out of the floor.

Nice touch that, the spikes. Treating homeless people like pigeons. Who came up with that idea? Is there no part of their brains thinking, *Sleeping on the streets must be pretty awful. The least we should do is let people who have nothing at all lie on a bit of pavement at night.*

Scrag slurped at his old ice-cream tub full of water. I was raging with thirst – my tongue was sticking to the roof of my mouth. Time for a drink. Might even be able to squeeze another cup of tea out of my teabag.

chapter four
LAURA

I lay awake that night, filled with a strange, empty grief for a life I couldn't remember. Fear and need made a sickening soup in my stomach. I clutched at the idea that the swan-necked tap had triggered such a vivid memory. I could remember the feeling of that larger hand around my smaller one and I realized that my body wasn't just a thing dealing with pain and learning to move again; it held physical memories of its own – if I could find a way to access them.

I felt my face with my fingers. My skin was smooth, my eyebrows thick and bushy, my ears rubbery and complicated. I squidged my nose – it was like a playdough blob in the middle of my face. Great. I was Mr Potato Head.

Mr Potato Head.

In pieces on a wooden floor, one of his ears stuck down a crack in the boards... My fingers scooping it out with a long match and it flicking through the air and landing...on a fluffy

black cat. The cat looking at me with disdain and sashaying out
of the room, Mr Potato Head's ear still stuck in its fur. Somebody
laughing, an absolute bubbling-over of joy.

Was it the same boy? The one who called me Lulu?

I smiled.

I had a memory that made me smile, and I'd found it by
poking my own face.

By the next morning, I'd had a genius idea. If I could see
what I looked like, surely I'd remember everything? I don't
know why it had taken me so long to think of it. Other things
on my mind, I guess. Like trying to stay alive. When Benjie
came in, I said, "Could I have a mirror?"

Edna bustled past him before he could speak.

"You've got a mirror, Laura. You just need to get out of
bed and walk to it."

She pointed to the one by the sink. On the other side of
the room. It might as well have been on the moon.

"I'm afraid I'm with Edna on this one," Benjie said.

I looked across at the mirror. It could be the key to
unlocking my memories but... "It's miles away. Couldn't you
just tell me a little bit more about who I am...?"

"We could, but then there's a danger of laying a false
memory trail – something you'll think you've remembered
yourself, but is actually something we told you."

"I'll risk it."

"Well, I won't. Your mind needs time to re-form its own

neural pathways. There are things that will help nudge it along, and seeing yourself might be one of them."

"Fine," I said, prickling with irritation. "I'll walk to the stupid sink."

I tried to get up and fell forward, crumpled in half, my face muffled in blankets.

"It's not going to be quite that easy, I'm afraid," Benjie said. "Edna starts your proper physio today. Work hard at it, and you will get the rewards."

"I thought you were nice," I mumbled into the bed.

"I am nice," Benjie said, sitting me back up. "This is for your own good."

"Blah, blah, blah," I said.

"I'll leave you to Edna," he said, with a wink.

I wanted to throw something at him.

Edna was not like Vera after all. Vera, the psychiatrist, was all forced calmness and soothing words. Edna was a ball of ferocious energy, determined to torture me with physiotherapy – stretching, pulling, pushing, twisting, rolling. She came twice a day and between her visits I had talking therapy with Vera, which mostly involved trying to "immerse myself" in the Mr Potato Head memory and mentally follow the cat out of the door.

Between them, they drove me crazy. Days went by, and no new memories came.

One day I snapped.

"Just tell me! Tell me who I am!"

"You're Laura Henley. You're in the rehabilitation phase of your recovery—"

"I know, I know that, but tell me who I AM. Tell me about my brother!"

Just like that. There it was.

That little boy was my brother. My baby brother.

Vera smiled but I felt like I had my skin on inside out. I couldn't picture him, but I *felt* him. The absence of him.

"Where is he?"

Vera's face went blank. I felt sick to my stomach.

"This is cruel. Please, just tell me."

But they wouldn't.

A new determination to reach that mirror spread through me. I had a brother and I didn't know where he was. I didn't even know his name. But I had a brother. That thought coiled around me, driving everything I did. And I did it all. Whatever they asked. I offered up my arm for blood tests – there was a tiny needle inside a cuff that made it easy for them to monitor my vital signs and extract what they needed. I didn't complain. I practised the exercises. I drank the C-plan milkshakes. I did everything, but not happily.

I refused to speak to Benjie. He was in charge. He was the one who was stopping them from just telling me. He was the one who was making Edna torture me. And he was so annoyingly nice about it.

"I know you're mad at me. I understand, but I have to do what I think is best for your long-term recovery."

I scowled at him.

Then one morning the whole team arrived. Everyone except Stephen, who'd gone off shift, and Miss Lilly, who I hadn't seen since her first visit.

Edna spoke first. "I think we're ready to see how you do standing up."

"Now?" I said, as Mariya came in with an old-lady walking frame.

"Edna thinks you're ready," Benjie said.

"Do you?"

She nodded. "You've worked so hard, Laura."

I took a good look at the mirror for inspiration, then pushed the blankets back. Edna offered me her arm and, inch by inch, I worked my way to the edge of the bed. Mariya placed the frame in front of me. All I had to do was shuffle forward, take hold of the frame and let my feet drop to the floor.

"You're doing so well," Benjie said.

"You are," said Mariya.

"Not much further," Edna said.

I got to the edge of the bed pretty much on my own. I was sure I was going to make it to the mirror. I reached over the frame, placed a hand on either side and felt for the ground with my feet. When my toes touched the cool floor, I soared with victory. What was standing up? Nothing.

I slipped forwards and...my legs buckled underneath me. I landed in a heap on the floor, trapped inside the stupid frame with my feeble arms looped over the top.

I was a baby. A bruised and battered jelly baby with jelly legs and a jelly head.

"Not bad for a first go," Benjie said.

"You'll get there," said Edna.

They scraped me off the floor and put me into a chair by my bed. Frustrated tears bit behind my eyes but if I wanted to fill in the empty space in my head, I *had* to know who I was, what I looked like.

"I want to try again."

"And you will, but rest first. I'll come back this afternoon," Edna said.

"No. I want to try now."

She nodded and set the frame in front of me. I steeled myself, clenching all my muscles to lift myself out of the chair and stand. It was harder than sliding off the bed, but as sliding off the bed had ended with landing in a heap, I thought this might be the better way round. My entire body trembled with the effort.

It was all I could manage that day, but I stood.

The next morning, I took my first steps. Hesitant, shuffly, old-lady steps, but it made me laugh with joy.

"I'm doing it, I'm doing it!"

Then, inevitably, my legs buckled and I slid down inside the frame. But I'd done it. I looked up at Benjie and Edna and said, "I walked."

"You sure did," Benjie said, a big fat tear rolling down his cheek.

I forgave him for the torture. I was so close now and so sure that seeing myself was the key to it all. Twice a day for three days I tried, and if my legs had held up, I would have done it more. It was exhausting but exhilarating. I could feel myself getting stronger. On the fourth day, I walked over halfway before my legs started to buckle.

Edna said, "That's enough for this morning. We'll try again later."

"No. I can do it. Just give me a minute."

I closed my eyes, saying to myself, *I'm going to find you, little brother.*

I breathed deeply and pushed myself on, one step at a time, until finally, I made it to the sink.

I'd done it. My legs were wobbly and my arms were shaking; I felt sick and dizzy; but I'd made it. I hesitated before I looked up. I felt kind of shy about what I'd see. *What if I don't know my own face? What if it means nothing to me?* I looked at Benjie and he nodded, encouraging me. I turned back to the mirror and there she was. I was. Me.

There was no blinding flash of recognition but I was relieved to see I wasn't Mr Potato Head. The nose that had felt so huge was just a nose. The eyebrows were thick and dark but looked nothing like hairy slugs. I had a pointy chin, sharp cheekbones and light brown eyes. Thick dark hair spiralled from my head. I wanted to touch it, but both my hands were taken up by the walking frame. It looked dry. Parched.

Gentle fingers combing conditioner through my hair, teasing it into ringlets.

Mum? My mum? I concentrated on the memory, the feeling of that gentle touch. Someone loved me.

Darkness grew in my chest. So much worse than the absence of everything was the absence of *something*. I had a family. I knew it. *I felt it.*

"Benjie," I said, my voice pitiful, cracking with hope. "My mum…"

"You remember?" he said.

I didn't want to admit that it was only a fraction of a memory in case he just repeated that I had to remember in my own time. I said, "Why doesn't she come? Where is she?" I could feel the sobs building in me. "You're so worried about protecting my future, but what about my *now*?"

Benjie said, "I'm going to fetch Vera. Edna, can you help Laura back to her chair?"

When Benjie returned, he sat beside me and took my hand while Vera hovered nearby. I was light-headed with fear about what he was going to tell me. If you have to say a thing that gently, it's bound to be really bad.

"Laura, we think you are suffering from something called dissociative psychogenic amnesia – a specific type of memory loss. There is no cure. Treatment varies, but the current mode of thinking is that we need to allow your memory, with encouragement from us, to rebuild its own library from foundations that you can already access."

There was no cure? And he was never going to help me?

Not ever? I couldn't bear it. "So I go crazy trying to work out who I am, when all the time you know? My family are in here." I pulled my hand away from him and tapped my skull. "I can feel them. It's driving me mad not being able to reach them. You could help me – you just won't."

"It's not that I won't. It's that we don't believe it's the best thing for you."

"You don't know that though. Not for sure. And what about me? What about what I think?"

I let the tears fall. Didn't even try to stop them. "You said you could give me encouragement, so do it. Give me a scrap of something, anything to work with. Please, Benjie. Vera? Please."

I was practically begging.

Benjie sighed. "Maybe you're right. Maybe if you know the basics, it might help your recovery. But maybe it won't. Maybe it'll make everything worse for you..."

"How can it be any worse? I can't forget any more than I have!"

"It might stop you remembering accurately."

"But you can help me with that." I looked at Vera. "All of you. You're the best in the world, aren't you? That's what Miss Lilly said. Please. Help me."

Benjie glanced at Vera, who gave the tiniest of nods. He stood up. I thought he was going to leave, but he said, "Your kind of amnesia is usually caused by violent trauma. And in a way, that is what has happened to you." He rubbed a hand over his face.

"I don't understand."

"You were very ill, Laura. Your family were desperate. At the time, there was no conventional treatment that could save you. This clinic offered to take you on as a cryotherapy patient."

I frowned at him, trying to figure out what he was saying. "Cryotherapy?"

"Strictly speaking, cryogenic therapy. You were placed in a cooled gas suspension chamber until a remedy could be found for your illness. You were dying, Laura. To give science time to find a cure, you were frozen."

"What? That's not a thing, that's…"

"It is a thing. You were—"

My stomach turned over. I held up a hand. "I remember."

I am lying in bed, so weak, crushingly tired. Someone is trying to explain…it's cancer. There is no hope left except this, to go to sleep for a while, to buy some time. Two people are crying – who…?

With an electric jolt, I remembered: Mum and Ima. My heart squeezed as I pictured them. Mum, tall and elegant with a mass of black curly hair; Ima, short and broad and solid. My two mums. My shelter, my warmth, my safety.

Love and loss swamped me.

"Benjie…Mum and Ima – why don't they come? Don't they know I'm awake?"

A look passed between Vera and Benjie before Benjie spoke. "A lot of time has passed since you were frozen, Laura."

My heart galloped. "What do you mean? How much? Benjie, how much time?"

"A few...years."

"*Years?*" I gasped. "Years? How many?"

No one answered. I said it again, forcing each word out. "How...many...years?"

Finally Vera replied. "Just over forty."

chapter five
LAURA

I was winded by it.

"Forty? *Forty years?*"

"I know it's a shock," Benjie said.

It was impossible. Completely impossible. I tried to process what they were telling me, but my brain couldn't cope.

"How…what…how…?" Then my head snapped up. "Wait, is it gone, the cancer?"

Benjie smiled. "We began treatment as soon as you were revived. You slept through most of it, but you responded well. You'll need a lot of monitoring, but we're confident you are on the road to a full recovery."

I wrapped my arms around myself, as if I was checking I was whole. "So what…when…what year is it?"

Benjie paused, then said, "2028."

It was impossible. It couldn't be 2028. That sounded so far in the future – it was science fiction.

What was the year I went to sleep then? I wracked my brain, frustrated again by my lack of memory. Then I remembered sticking something into a scrapbook – a picture of Prince Andrew and Fergie getting engaged – and writing the date in bubble letters. It was March. March, 1986.

I shook my head.

How could I remember that and so little else?

Forty years?

Benjie held my arm. "I'm so sorry. We weren't sure… We didn't want…"

I pulled my knees up to my chest and curled into a ball, turning my head away from them. I closed my eyes. I wanted to shut him out.

I wanted to shut everything out.

They didn't leave. I could hear them whispering. Still I kept my eyes closed.

Forty years.

A lifetime.

No.

No, it wasn't. It was a *long* time but it wasn't a *life*time.

How old would Mum and Ima have been in 1986? I searched my patchy memory. Early forties? Maybe? A spark of hope ignited.

I opened my eyes. "They could still be alive, Mum and Ima. Do they know? Can't you find them? Tell them I'm awake?"

Benjie bit his lip.

"I know they'll be old, it doesn't matter, Benjie. I just

want to see them. I need to see them. I can cope, I swear."

He wouldn't look at me. Cold crept over my skin.

"Where are they, Benjie? I'm not asking for a memory. You can't influence my brain by telling me something I never knew."

His hand tightened on my arm as he said, "I know. It's just going to be very hard for you to hear. I'm so sorry, Laura, the last known data imprint of your parents was a hire car they'd picked up in France."

"Data imprint?"

"A sort of recording, of where they were. It showed that the car was in a fatal collision just south of Calais."

It was like a sledgehammer to my chest. I couldn't breathe. Somewhere deep inside me, I started shivering. I was dimly aware of Benjie trying to hug me. I clung to him, drowning. It wasn't fair. I'd worked so hard to remember. I'd only just got them back and they'd been snatched away.

The hand I'd held, the arm I'd twirled under when we'd seen the swans – it was Ima's.

Going out for a walk, pulling on yellow wellies to leave the house, bursting with excitement because it was nearly Christmas. Mum needing a nap, her tummy round and fat…

Oh God.

Oh God, oh God…

Alfie.

The little boy.

My brother. My baby brother.

Panic bloomed in me, flowering into shuddering shock.

"Alfie! Where is he? Benjie, my brother, he has to be here. Alfie has to be here. He was with me, he was sick too, he was put to sleep before me!"

Benjie held on to me, but I struggled against him, as much as my weak limbs would allow.

"Where is he? We were together!"

I had to find him. I tried to grab for the walking frame. I was gabbling, I knew it, but every inch of me was screaming for my brother.

"Laura, please…"

Tears cascaded down my face. I was making a noise like some kind of injured animal, but I didn't know how to stop.

Benjie whispered something to Vera. She said, "Not now, it's too much."

And I knew. I knew.

I looked at them, and their grim faces told me everything.

"He's dead too, isn't he?"

My world collapsed.

I shut down.

Utterly broken.

chapter six
SHEM

I was full of beans. Not literally. Literally I was full of water and dry bread, but that was a whole lot better than nothing, which was quite often what I had for breakfast. The sun was shining and Scrag was trotting along next to me, weeing on anything that stayed still long enough. Bert used to call them p-mails. Little messages for his doggy pals. It made me smile, remembering that. I'd always say, "Nah, he's a modern dog. They're Status Pupdates."

I missed Bert. Since he'd gone, I'd been a bit braver about going out. I'd had to be really. It was impossible to get food otherwise. Bert had always done the food runs, leaving me strict instructions not to go anywhere until he came back. Food hunting had to be done in the day cos shops locked everything up at night, including the bins. I'd been nervous about it at first, but it was all right. I was careful, and we did okay, me and Scrag.

We headed for a little supermarket by the seafront. On a

sunny day, it was always full of people buying stuff they'd forgotten to pack for their jolly day at the beach. More people meant less chance of me getting caught borrowing stuff. It had been a few weeks since I'd been in there, so I reckoned it was safe to give it another go.

When we got there, I said to Scrag, "Right-o, little feller, you stay here. I'll be two ticks." I smiled at myself. Sometimes I sounded more like Bert than Bert. I liked how I could still hear him in my own voice – it made him feel closer.

I went inside. It wasn't busy. Damn.

"Oi, you."

I looked up, knowing full well that was the tone of voice reserved for scumbags and maggots. Me, in other words.

A huge hairy shop worker called over, "I'm watching you."

"I'm getting some food for my dog."

If you're a bit scruffy, people automatically think you're a thief. I found the dog food and picked up the cheapest can before heading back to the door, where Hairy Face was stacking some floppy lettuces.

"Just getting a basket, if that's okay with you?" I said.

He grunted and when he turned back to his rabbit food, I slipped an apple in my pocket. At the cheese fridge I tucked a tiny block of Cheddar up my sleeve. I didn't say I wasn't a thief. I said people shouldn't *assume* I was one just because I was a bit scruffy. Anyway, I planned to pay them back when I had money. I was good at making stuff. Like an inventor. One day that would pay. One day.

I grabbed a pint of milk, put it in the basket and headed for the checkout.

"Can I have a bag?" I said.

"They're fifty pence."

"Oh." I counted out the coins I had, enough for the milk and Scrag's tin of food, with twenty pence over...

I said, "Will you take twenty?"

"It's fifty pence, and if you're paying with cash it's ten per cent extra. Come on, there are people waiting."

I looked behind me. A queue had grown. That was perfect. If I spent enough time searching through my pockets and asking questions...

"Ten per cent extra? That a new poor tax, is it?"

"I don't make the rules, mate. It costs them more to bank it or something."

"Well, how much is another ten per cent?"

"Didn't you go to school?"

Someone huffed behind me. Excellent. Just a few more seconds...and...

"Oh here, take it."

Bingo. I took the bag, gave him the coins and left him muttering to himself as I stepped outside.

Sometimes small victories meant the world.

I made a fuss of Scrag for a minute and then we sneaked round the back of the store, me mentally crossing my fingers that the bin would be open. Yes! I glanced quickly behind me, in case I was being watched – believe it or not, people don't like you taking stuff from bins. Honestly, I really don't get that – I'm doing them a favour. They have to pay to get rid of the waste, so really, taking stuff from the bin probably paid for the apple and the cheese.

The bin was a treasure trove – yogurt, doughnuts, more cheese, even a packet of ham that was only a day out of date. I shoved what I could in the carrier bag seconds before the back door of the shop opened and out came Hairy Face.

"Oi! You! I knew it!"

"Thanks," I called, legging it. I knew he wouldn't chase me. Far too much effort for no good reason. I'd just stay away for a few weeks, then there'd be someone new behind the till and I might get lucky again.

I let the heavy bag swing beside me, enjoying its satisfying weight. "We'll have a feast today, Scraggy Boy."

I whistled as we walked. I was thinking the day couldn't be more perfect when I spotted a huge black car coming towards me. My heart flipped over. It wasn't the first time I'd seen that car and every time I did it gave me the creeps. The last time I saw it, it slowed down like it was checking me out.

I was relieved when it drove past me, but it came back. This time, it slowed to a crawl beside me and the driver's door slid open. The guy swivelled in his seat so he could properly intimidate me. Definitely the same ugly brute in a suit I'd seen a few days ago. His car alarm went mental: *"Driver's side door is open. Please close the door."*

"Hello again, boy."

I wanted to run. I tried to get out of his reach, but the

pavement was too narrow. My heart was starting to hurt, it was thudding so hard.

"Aren't you going to say hello, then? That's not very polite, is it? I'm pretty sure you were brought up better than that."

I flicked a panicked glance towards him. What did he mean? Was he talking about Bert?

His car said: *"Please close the door. Driver assist will close the door."*

The car kept pace with me and the man's big gorilla arm reached for my carrier bag. I snatched it back as the car door began to slide shut with him inside. He forced it back open and the car said, *"Locating safe place to stop."*

"You've got the wrong bloke, mate," I said, walking quickly away as the car slowed.

I could hear him behind me, yelling at his car: "Just drive, will you? I decide what's safe for me, you pile of…parts!"

"I'm sorry, I do not recognize your instruction. Would you like to return to the main menu?"

I didn't hang about to listen. There was an alleyway ahead. I scooped Scrag up and ducked down it.

chapter seven
LAURA

I wouldn't speak to any of them. Actually, that's not entirely true. I *couldn't* speak to any of them. They all tried – Benjie, Vera, Mariya – but it was as if my throat was full of hard dough. I could barely breathe, let alone speak.

I lost count of the days. I stopped drinking the milkshakes and doing my physio exercises. I gazed out of the window, over the tops of the trees, wishing I could just disintegrate into it all.

I think I must have collapsed after a while of refusing the C-plan, because one minute I was in my chair watching a cloud drift across the blue sky and the next I was back in bed, and they were reconnecting me to a drip. The cold liquid chilled my veins.

I let my mind wander, picking up and sorting memories. It was so painful, so exquisitely painful, but I couldn't stop.

The day Alfie is born: Mum and Ima so proud – having obviously needed a bit of help conceiving, and it having taken a while. I am eleven and it is the happiest day of my life. Mum lays Alfie on her hospital bed and I put my arms all the way around him like a nest – a sister nest. I notice a little mole above his right eye. I kiss it and whisper, "I'm going to look after you, always, I promise."

Tears made a wet pool on my pillow.

Alfie stealing ham from the fridge for our fluffy black cat, Pickle Cat-Chops. Alfie trying to push me on a swing. Alfie's first day at playschool. (I'd been more nervous than him or even Mum and Ima. "What if he doesn't like it?" "What if the other kids pick on him?" He'd been completely fine, but I'd spent the whole day at my school with a feeling of dread in my stomach...)

Wait.

School.

Metal gates – black blazer, yellow-and-blue striped tie, backcombed hair, black eyeliner... Stacey.

Stacey.

My best friend.

Hanging out behind the netball courts at school.

Stacey, super-cool Stacey, the girl who made me laugh every day. Every hour.

I had a friend. A best friend.

Stacey and me, miming in front of a mirror, singing, singing... to what? A band. The Cure, Robert Smith. A tape deck. The first time we hear "The Lovecats" on the radio in Stacey's kitchen... making cheese-and-jam toasties and bouncing around, easily picking up the lyrics. Stacey bites straight into her toastie, forgetting the volcanic-jam risk. She burns the roof of her mouth so badly she ends up with her face upturned under the kitchen tap swigging cold water, like a human waterfall, for a good five minutes.

My heart hiccupped. Maybe I wasn't entirely alone. Maybe I could find some reason to live in this place, this *time*, where everything else had been taken from me. Maybe I could find Stacey. I could call her. She'd come, I was sure of it. I'd move heaven and earth for her…even if I was… how old would she be? Older than I remember Mum being… But people didn't change, did they? It didn't matter how old she was.

"Laura?"

I vaguely heard Benjie speaking to me.

"Laura? Miss Lilly is here. She wants to speak to you. Can you wake up?"

There was that scent, that warm spicy scent. I opened my eyes and turned towards it.

A cool hand rested on my arm.

"I am so desperately sorry for all your losses, Laura. I can only imagine the pain you are going through. If there is anything I can do to help – anything at all – you only have to ask."

Her voice was so soft, something about her calmed me. I struggled to sit up, and forced the words out.

"There is something. Someone. I had a friend."

She nodded.

"My best friend. Her name was Stacey Flowers. Could I call her?"

Something flickered across Miss Lilly's face, something like worry – or disappointment. It was so fleeting I couldn't tell which.

She nodded. "I know who you mean. Look, Laura, there's no easy way to say this—"

I couldn't bear to hear terrible news again, I just couldn't, so I interrupted her, shaking my head. "Don't say it – she's dead too, isn't she? I have no one. No one at all."

"As long as I am alive, Laura, you will never have no one. I will always be here for you. Always. Do you hear me?"

She said it with such passion I was stunned.

"I have looked after you for years. I don't expect you to understand how much you mean to me – how could you? You were asleep all that time. But I wasn't. I was working on a reversal process that would revive you successfully. On a cure that would clear your body of the cancer that almost killed you. I was determined we wouldn't lose you – the loss of your brother was devastating to everyone here. I couldn't let that happen to you too."

Silence hung in the air, but it wasn't awkward; it was like a warmly scented cocoon I wanted to curl up in. I felt guilty for thinking it, but part of me wished I hadn't started remembering, that all I knew were the kind people around me. Maybe that was the real reason they'd refused to tell me anything – to protect me. Maybe they'd secretly hoped I'd never remember and they wouldn't have to tell me all the terrible truths.

Miss Lilly looked down at her perfectly manicured hands.

"Your friend isn't dead, Laura. I'm afraid she…well, she's behaved rather badly over the years. Initially, I am sure it was because she was upset by what had happened to you, and of course, she was very young back then. She no longer has that excuse."

"What did she do?" I asked, trying to reassemble what I knew of Stacey. She was always wildly defensive of me – having two mums made you a bit of a target, but pretty much no one called me Laura the Lesbo after Stacey had kneed Mark Wright in the nadgers for saying it.

Miss Lilly studied my face, as if deciding how much to tell me. "There were a few things. She wouldn't stay away from here for a start. Understandably, she wanted to be near you. But she upset a lot of my clients, people who came here for rest and recuperation from a harrowing world. I tried to help her, but I was afraid of what she might do next."

"What do you mean?"

"She broke in a couple of times. Destroyed some equipment. A client sued me for distress caused due to my lack of security. I had to get a restraining order."

An almost complete story came back to me. Stacey had gone out with this punky kid from the boys' school. He'd got off with another girl at a party and when Stacey found out, she went mental. Whenever we saw him in town she'd make me follow him, close enough so he'd know we were there, but not so close that he could do anything about it. She'd make silent calls to his house. She even designed a poster of him and scrawled *LOVE RAT* across his face. We'd printed copies and stuck them up on lamp posts around town.

I saw him one day when I was on my own. He looked so miserable. Even after what he'd done, I felt sorry for him. I told Stace she'd punished him enough and I was getting bored with following him about. She didn't involve me after that, but I know she kept ringing his house because his mum complained to our school and our whole year group had to listen to an assembly on "appropriate post-break-up behaviour". Stacey could be pretty relentless in her pursuit of justice.

I was sorry she'd caused Miss Lilly trouble, but I also knew she'd done it for me. My heart ached for her.

"That sounds like Stacey," I said. "She was pretty fiery when she was upset. She'd be different now though. If she knew I was okay."

Again, that look flickered across Miss Lilly's face, as if she was judging how much she could tell me.

"Laura, there were other things. Things I don't really want to tell you."

"What things?"

She looked at her hands again and said, "She didn't always have your best interests at heart. Laura, I don't want you to feel badly about your friend, but I'm afraid if you contact her…"

"What did she do?"

Miss Lilly hesitated for a moment like she didn't want to tell me. "The accident your parents were in…" She sighed. "The reason they were in France was to escape the press.

At the inquest, it was suggested their minds might not have been on their driving because of all the stress they'd been under. Stress caused by Stacey Flowers selling a horribly embroidered story to the papers – a story about you."

I stared at her, open-mouthed. No. Fiercely loyal Stacey? It wasn't possible. She loved Mum and Ima. She'd never do anything to hurt them. Would she? I sifted through the jigsaw pieces of memory that were slowly sliding back into place.

Stacey round ours for dinner, helping with the washing-up, decorating the Christmas tree.

I shook my head.

"I don't know what her motivation was," Miss Lilly said. "People do all sorts of things for all sorts of reasons. I'm sure it won't just have been for the money."

Money? Stacey had sold us out for money? The disbelief must have shown on my face because Miss Lilly went on, "Laura, your parents gave you the greatest gift they could. They wanted you to live. They gave everything to make that possible. Don't throw it away by letting yourself slide into a black hole. I will do all I can to help you. But you have to try, okay? You have to drink the horrible milkshakes and do the horrible physio…"

I smiled sadly at her. I didn't know what to say. Everything I'd known. Everyone. It was all dust. Dust and ashes.

"I know you must be feeling lost right now." Miss Lilly touched my arm. She was gentle, kind, everything I needed her to be. "There is so much for you to adjust to. What happened in your past, and dealing with the present. But I want you to look forward to your future too, the future your parents gifted you. A lot has changed in forty years. Some of it is quite exciting, Laura. In fact, I hope you don't mind, but I've brought you something. Can I go and get it?"

What could I say? She was trying so hard and she was right – Mum and Ima had done everything they could to ensure I'd survive.

I owed it to them, to everyone, to try. I nodded and said, "Yes, thanks. I'd like that."

chapter eight
SHEM

I kept running. Too hot in my coat, the carrier bag slicing into the fingers of my good hand while I tried to hang on to Scrag with my stump, curling it under him like a hook. What if it came to a fight? I was so scrawny I'd be useless. Scrag would be better than me. I didn't want to test that out though, so I kept running, even when my chest screamed for air.

I didn't slow down till I hit the beach and the crowds. Bert used to say that the loneliest he'd ever felt was in a crowd but, I've got to be honest, they have their uses. I mean, I prefer walls, a roof and a door with a lock, but in the absence of that, people make a pretty good defence against the dark arts.

I glanced behind me. I thought I could see the car again, but it couldn't follow me onto the pebbles so down I went. I was near the pier, where the promenade was too far above the beach to jump down. I headed for the ramp instead.

I tried to stay calm – it was a sunny day, lots of families out – no one was going to try anything much in front of hundreds of witnesses. Even if I was only a homeless kid.

I picked my way towards the sea, stepping between coconut-sun-creamed bodies as fast as I could, trying to think what I'd do if he followed me onto the stones. I risked another glance back, but before I even had a chance to focus, I'd walked into someone.

They gripped my arm and said softly, "Oops-a-daisy."

I held on tighter to Scrag and turned round, hoping it was just some dad I'd teed off by treading on his kid's towel.

No such luck. It was another man mountain. Not one I recognized but one with exactly the same air of friendly menace as the pig in the car. I tried to run for it, but he gripped my arm harder and said, "Bit rude of you to run off when my friend wanted a nice chat with you."

He nodded up the beach and I could see the other dude now, arms folded, watching from the promenade.

"Someone we know has been looking for you. You've been quite hard to pin down."

I said nothing.

"Why don't you come with me now? You can bring your little doggy if you like. Nice and easy, no fuss."

"Why? I ain't done nothin'."

"Well, that's not entirely true, is it? We heard you helped your friend Bert out quite a lot when he was sick. And sometimes that help wasn't exactly legal, was it?"

"I don't know what you're talking about."

Although I knew exactly what he was talking about. Bert had smoked a bit of weed to help with the pain when he was ill. But that had been over a year ago. If they were police, why would they bother with me now? Could they be dealers? But Bert had always been so careful to pay his debts.

"And then there's the new vagrancy laws."

"What?"

"Haven't you heard? They're cleaning up the streets, sunshine. No one wants people like you bringing down the tone of an area."

"I don't live on the streets," I said. "My dad's over there."

I pointed at some random stranger down the beach and the idiot turned round to look. I took my chance, yanked my arm free and legged it. Scrag gave a little whimper – I think I was hanging on a bit too tight. I said, "Sorry, feller," but didn't stop leaping over bodies on the beach. I didn't look behind me until I got near the arches beneath the promenade where I couldn't be seen from above unless you leaned right over. There were little shops all along and a lot of people. I walked fast, melting into the crowd, then headed up and out. I needed to get away, but I didn't know how or where to go. If I went back to my shed now they might follow me.

I wracked my brains, trying to work out who they were. Had Bert done something I didn't know about? I walked up a main street – there was a one-way system, so the man in the car wouldn't be able to follow. I didn't dare check to see if they were after me on foot. I had to assume they were.

The street was busy with VR gamers and coffee drinkers. There were a few clothes shops and one that sold books.

The bookshop! They had a back door that was quite often open when it was hot.

I might be able to duck inside and through to the back alley and hopefully lose the pair of them. I walked as quickly as possible without drawing attention to myself. I could see the shop ahead, but it had a great long queue outside.

As I got closer I saw a sign:

Are you still a Belieber? Meet Justin here at an authorized automated signing! First come, first served!

A bunch of over-excited thirty-year-old pop fans blocked my escape.

I gritted my teeth and pushed my way into the shop. "Sorry, sorry, sick dog coming through."

The queue led to a table where a holo projection of some guy with swept-back hair and too many tattoos looked utterly bored. An autopen printed his signature on whatever was put in front of him. The queuing people were so wrapped up in paying for a computer to pretend it hated them that no one took any notice of me.

I went straight through the second-hand book section and, with relief, saw the back door propped open with a broom. I stepped through and out into their yard. I opened the outside gate, peered up and down the street, then headed off.

I walked for ages, trying to shake off the feeling of being followed by doubling back and weaving a weird trail. I was drenched in sweat and Scrag was panting his head inside out by the time I felt safe enough to go back to my shed.

Safe? What was I thinking? Bert had warned me: people like us were never safe.

chapter nine

LAURA

When Miss Lilly stepped out of the room, Benjie ventured, "Are you okay?"

I nodded, knowing full well that I'd probably never be okay again. Not really. But also not wanting to upset him – he'd done so much for me. They all had.

Miss Lilly came back in and handed me a neat white box. I took off the lid. Inside was a square of pale pink metal nestled in tissue paper. I stroked a hand over it. Colours swirled together on the surface until they made a face behind what looked like prison bars.

I looked up at everyone, astonished.

The metal square said, *"Hello, you are not currently an authorized user."*

I looked again and realized the face behind bars… "It looks like you, Miss Lilly."

She smiled. "It does, but it can be anyone. It could be one of your mums if you like?"

Despair edged up to swamp me and I grabbed for the thing that had made me feel better. The person.

"No," I said, "I like it being you."

She looked so touched, tears shone in her violet eyes, and I felt like I'd done something good. Some small thing to repay her kindness.

"You had computers at school?" she asked.

"Sort of."

"Well this is a 'sort of' computer."

This did not look like any computer we'd had at school – those had been like giant typewriters you plugged into a television.

"How does it work?" I said.

"Benjie is itching to show you, so I'm going to let him, if that's okay? Try and have fun, and if there is anything you need, or want, please let one of the team know. I'll be back as soon as I can."

She leaned forward to gently kiss my cheek and her soft smell swept around me. I watched her leave like I was under a spell.

Benjie touched my arm and said, "Ready?"

He swiped his fingers through the bars hovering over the computer and they disintegrated. Then he made a pinching gesture and the face that had sat behind the bars transformed into a tiny, upright Miss Lilly wearing a white coat. Its minuscule mouth said, *"Hello, Benjie, welcome back."*

"Hello, Notitia, please map new primary user."

"Are you sure you want me to map a new primary user?

Please touch my hand to confirm."

Benjie placed his enormous hand on hers and her body split apart in a scattering of colour. It was beautiful. She re-formed and said, *"Hello, new user. My name is Notitia. Let me take you through the set-up process."*

Benjie whispered, "You have to answer, so it can map your voice."

"Okay."

It asked what language I wanted, what time zone, if I required disabled-access functions, then finally if I accepted the terms and conditions. Loads of text scrolled across the space where Notitia had been. I got bored of reading it after the first paragraph so I just said, "Yes."

The little Miss Lilly said, *"That's it. Now please touch my hand."*

I aimed a finger at her tiny palm and she said, *"Mapping biometric detail, please wait. Facial recognition complete. Isolating DNA. New primary user profile complete. Hello, Laura."*

I looked at Benjie. "How does it know my name?"

"It just mapped your DNA. It knows everything about you."

"DNA?"

He said, "It's like a code that only belongs to you. Everyone's DNA is kept on a government database. It's used on computers so no one can access your account without authorization."

"But you can."

"Yes, but only because I've already been mapped. You can delete me if you want – I'll show you how."

"No, no," I said. Deleting someone sounded worryingly permanent.

"Where shall we start?" Benjie asked.

I shrugged. Given that I'd paid zero attention in computer studies, I didn't have a clue.

He said, "Notitia, display Google Earth."

The tiny computer lady stepped aside and a spinning globe appeared. It was...magical. Benjie squashed it with his hand and an image appeared on top of the metal plate, just like a TV screen.

"Pinpoint Blackhurst Clinic," he said.

The thing zoomed in through clouds, over countries, to fields and houses, until it was hovering over a large H-shaped building set in a huge park bordered by trees.

"Is that here?" I said, astounded.

Benjie nodded.

"That metal plate has aerial photographs of the whole world?"

"That metal plate is more usually called a slate – and yes, it does. And a lot more besides. Notitia, load –" he paused – "YouTube."

Notitia said, *"What content are you looking for?"*

Benjie laughed and said, "Cats. Cats doing crazy things."

It was, literally, amazing. Like a TV and a library had been smooshed together. Only better. And with more cats.

Cats sleeping in weird places, cats falling off window ledges, grumpy cats, funny cats. And dogs. Thousands of dogs. I lost myself in it. It was so easy to jump from video to video. It was numbing and comforting and Benjie decided to leave me to it.

"I'll come back later, show you some more things…"

I hardly noticed him leave.

I stumbled on music by accident. I'd said, "Notitia, find more cat videos. I love cats."

"Do you want me to find the video for 'The Lovecats'?"

"Yes! Yes, you clever thing, yes!"

My head bobbed along to the music as the video for my favourite ever Cure song plinked its way past a milk bottle falling over, through a gate and up some steps to Robert Smith pretending to be a tiger. I was swept back to Stacey's front room on a Thursday night – the big box telly showing *Top of the Pops*, her mum and her sister both smoking up a fog, while we sat on the sofa, sucking Vimto out of bottles.

Stacey used to dress like the wild-haired, black-eyelinered Robert Smith. She had a horrible black-and-white striped mohair jumper, just like his. It got fluff in her eyes all the time – not good when you're wearing half a chemist's worth of mascara.

Mariya checked in on me just as the video finished. She leaned over and wiped a tear from my cheek. I hadn't even realized I was crying.

"You okay?" she asked.

I nodded. "Yeah, actually, I am. Do you want to see?"

I was watching the flat screen on the slate. I wanted to make it 3D again, so I did what Benjie had done – put my hand over the screen and sort of pulled it up. It did exactly what I'd hoped.

Mariya was impressed. "Wow, you're really getting the hang of it."

I allowed myself the tiniest smug smile.

When it finished, Mariya said, "Have you heard of a band called Duran Duran? My sister threw an eighties party for her thirtieth, and she had the holo-band – they were incredible."

Duran Duran. John Taylor, the most beautiful bass player ever to have been born. How had I forgotten him? I'd been in love with him for ever. I said, "Notitia, play 'Girls on Film'."

My heart squeezed when John Taylor appeared and then disappeared too quickly. I stopped the video and went back a bit so I could freeze his gorgeous face. It made me smile, remembering how Stacey claimed she hated Duran Duran and their *pretty pop* but listened to "Planet Earth" with me whenever she came round. We'd lie on the floor of my room reading *Smash Hits* and I'd drool over John Taylor while she obsessed about The Cure.

The video looped around and played again, a half-naked girl and a sumo wrestler filling the screen.

I smiled. "Ima hated this video. She said it was sexist claptrap." I was caught off guard by a flood of emotion. "I never saw them play. I always thought, if I ever met John Taylor, we'd have a special connection. He's probably married or something now."

I cried. Properly cried like a spoiled kid. It was utterly

stupid. I knew John Taylor wouldn't have felt a special connection with me, that it was just a crush, but it was one more thing I'd lost. In that moment, I'd have given anything to have my dream back, to have Ima roll her eyes at me as I stuck up another poster of Duran Duran on my wall. I wished I had those posters. I wished I had something, anything, that would connect me with my family.

I told Mariya and she said, "But you do. You have your time capsule. It's ready for you whenever you want to see it."

As soon as she mentioned it, I remembered packing the box.

Alfie and me, growing weaker all the time, but Mum and Ima making it seem like we were going on holiday.

Alfie saying, "I don't have to pack Blankie?"

"No." My heart crumbles. "You want to keep Blankie with you, don't you?"

"I'm a big boy."

"I know, I know you are, but you don't want Blankie to be lonely in the box, do you?"

Alfie hugging Blankie to his chest, a grey rag that had once been a pale blue, satin-edged blanket.

"I keep it…"

My chest throbbing as I nod.

I couldn't bear to see my box and I couldn't bear not to.

I asked Mariya to fetch it.

chapter ten

LAURA

It felt kind of ceremonial. Benjie, Mariya and Vera came in pushing a trolley. On top of it sat a metal box the size of a small suitcase. It didn't look right.

"It was cardboard," I said. "A cardboard box."

Benjie nodded. "The tape that held it together peeled away, plus we had to sterilize everything."

"Sterilize?"

"Just a precaution. It's always better to be safe than sorry. Our immune systems evolve along with germs, a throwback to a twentieth-century bug would not be good. The contents are all there though."

I looked up at him, his soft brown eyes blanketing me in kindness.

"Will you stay?" I asked.

"Of course."

I lifted the lid.

On top was a grainy photograph of my family on a

windswept beach set in a papier mâché frame. It was decorated with pasta shapes and painted dark blue. I caught my breath. We'd made them together, one for each of us. Alfie was weaker than me, but he'd stuck all of his shapes on, with just a little help from Ima. The pain nearly swallowed me. He hadn't known what I knew. That the end of everything was coming. I traced the pasta shapes with my fingers, whispering, "I wish you were here."

A fat tear splashed on the frame, turning the blue paint a different shade. I squeezed my eyes shut, holding back the building sobs. I stood the picture by my bed. I didn't want to cry all over it and turn it to mush.

Next was a watch. A Jelly Fish Swatch to be exact. I smiled as I picked it up. It had been a birthday present. I'd wanted it so badly; it was just so cool – clear plastic with all the workings visible and in primary colours. The plastic had gone a bit yellow. I shook it, trying to make it tick, then turned it over. The battery was crusty inside.

Not much chance it would ever work again. I put it on my wrist anyway, feeling a bit more connected to Mum and Ima.

Then there was Scruffy, the teddy I'd had since I was a baby. He was full of holes.

"Sorry about the moths," Mariya said. "They got in before we transferred everything to the metal case."

Tiny cubes of foam tumbled from his cheeks and paws.

"Oh, Scruff, you poor old bear."

I kissed him gently and placed him carefully on my pillow, leaving a crumbly trail of foam on the bed.

Underneath Scruff was my scrapbook. The one I'd remembered sticking an article about Fergie and Prince Andrew in. On the cover was a picture of John Taylor in a wet T-shirt, gazing up from a bright blue pool. My heart beat a little faster. I remembered cutting it out, smoothing it down so carefully and kissing it. I squirmed with embarrassment, but batted away the feeling by flicking through the book.

It was full of pictures of bands I'd loved: Japan, Soft Cell, Wham! I turned another page and there was a cutting about Prince Charles and Lady Di's wedding and a picture of her in her fairy-tale dress.

I showed Benjie the picture. "Are they King and Queen now?"

He said, "He is. She died."

I pressed my lips together. She was nothing to do with me, but it felt like another piece of my life torn away. I put the scrapbook down and pulled a cassette from the box: "Stacey and Laura's Mega-Mix".

It rattled in its plastic cover and I was taken right back to the afternoon we'd made it, listening to the charts in Stacey's room – it was so hot we'd had the window wide open, her net curtains blowing softly in and out. Whenever a song came on the radio that we wanted to record, she'd pounced on the tape deck, her backcombed hair flopping slightly to one side where her hairspray had given up in the heat.

Would she really have sold a story about us? Part of me wished I could read what she was supposed to have said.

I just didn't believe she would say bad things about my family. Mum and Ima had practically treated her like another daughter. It made no sense. I threw the tape onto the bed. I wouldn't need it anyway. I felt like Notitia could probably find me all the music I wanted.

There wasn't much left in the box. Two copies of *Smash Hits* – one with David Bowie on, the other missing its front page because I'd stuck it on the scrapbook – and some clothes. A pair of dark blue skintight jeans with white piping down the side, a white boxy T-shirt that said *Choose Life* in big black letters (I smiled a bit at the irony of that), a pale yellow off-the-shoulder sweatshirt, and a sky-blue cable-knit Benetton jumper. Stacey's mum had bought that for her, to try and get her out of the horrible mohair sweater. Stacey hated it.

"It makes me look like a dork," she'd grumbled, and given it to me.

Finally, at the bottom of the box, was a strip of photographs. I remembered getting them done in the booth in Woolworths. Me and Stacey blowing kisses at the camera.

My eyes filled with tears.

That was it. All that was left of my life.

I felt weirdly exposed in front of Benjie, Mariya and Vera. Ashamed, almost, of how pathetic it all was. "Could I have a minute on my own?" I said. "I'm okay. I just need a bit of time."

Vera nodded. "That's understandable. I won't be far if you need to talk."

Benjie gave me a quick hug, Mariya squeezed my arm gently and they left.

I rummaged through my stuff again. It felt like there should be more. Something from Mum and Ima. A letter that they'd sneaked in my box – like they did when I went away for the first time with school. A card that said they loved me, that even though they weren't there, I'd be fine. I was flooded with dismay. It was just too little. How was I supposed to start again with a pair of jeans, a couple of jumpers and a few photos? I mean, I had nothing. No money, no exams, nothing. What would happen when I didn't need to be in the clinic any more? Where would I go? What would I do? How was I going to turn these few scraps of existence into a future worth having?

Mum and Ima had wanted me to live, but how?

I closed my eyes. Tried to still the trembling tears that filled me. And I heard them. Even without a letter, I felt them.

"It's going to be okay. You're a fighter, Laura. You can do this."

Mum and Ima had poured love into me and Alfie. I knew what they'd have written. They didn't have to put it on paper. The lessons they'd taught me were tattooed across my heart. They would not expect me to give up.

I had to start looking after myself properly. I pulled Stacey's jumper towards me, thinking getting dressed would be a good place to start. It was a decent plan, but the days of refusing food and physio had taken their toll.

Benjie stuck his head around the door. "Okay?"

I nodded. "Yeah. Benjie, I'm really hungry. Could I have some C-plan?"

His face broke into a massive smile. "Coming up, madam. Strawberry or banana?"

"Both."

For the next few days I did everything I was told, and I felt myself growing stronger. Eventually, after a morning session with Vera, I opened my box of things again. I took off the hospital pyjamas and put on my own jeans. They hung like a sack from my hips. They were meant to be tight! I was way too skinny, my boobs had disappeared and you could count my ribs. To think that once I'd been worried I was getting fat; my scrawny body was living proof of how ill I'd been. I wanted to fill it back out and show the world I was mended. At least in body. I pulled on the yellow sweatshirt. It was also huge on me, but it felt good to be in my own clothes.

I was exhausted from the effort, but there was one more thing I wanted to do.

I knew I couldn't stay in that room for ever. The thought of Benjie turning up one day and telling me I was well enough to leave the clinic was terrifying enough – the thought of him doing that without me even having stepped into the corridor brought me out in a cold sweat. I wanted to be the one in control of it.

I opened the door and clung to the frame. What would

I find? I was forty years in the future. I peered down the corridor. There were no robots. It was just like my room – pale green walls and glossy white floor. There was a window at one end and at the other I could just see the edge of a curved glass desk snaking around a corner. There were two more doors on my side of the corridor, and three opposite. They all stood open.

I took a step out.

Come on, Laura. You can do this. One foot in front of the other.

With a hand on the wall, I walked towards a murmur of voices that came from the direction of the desk. As I passed the first open doorway, I looked in. The room was similar to mine but empty. I lurched a bit past the opening until I made contact with the wall on the other side. The next room was empty too. I was nearly at the desk when Miss Lilly swept around the corner.

"Laura! Look at you, up and dressed. Aren't you adorable in mufti?" She was beaming with delight and something in me lifted.

I smiled back. "What's mufti?"

She laughed. "It's what we called 'home clothes' when I was at school."

"They're a bit big," I said, looking down at my outfit.

My heart twisted as I suddenly remembered Mum holding up my black military jacket, asking me if I wanted to pack it in my capsule. Before I'd got ill it had been tight across my shoulders, so I'd shaken my head. I was tired by then, bone-tired, and she was trying so hard not to cry. Ima had taken hold of both our hands, struggling to keep control herself. I'd just wanted it over.

I wished I could tell them I was all right. That they'd saved me.

Miss Lilly put her hand on my shoulder, sensing the dip in my mood. "Hey, come on. You're doing so well. Chin up."

I forced a smile.

She carefully took my arm and led me round the corner. Benjie, Edna, Mariya and Vera were standing by the desk, almost as if they were waiting for me. They were all smiling, like an advert for dazzling white teeth. Was straight, white and shining the new normal? I closed my mouth, conscious of my less-than-perfect smile.

Miss Lilly called over to the team. "We'll catch up later. I'll walk with Laura to the lounge, if that's okay?"

Benjie said, "Of course."

Mariya said, "I could bring tea?"

Miss Lilly said, "Wonderful."

I felt…safe.

We turned another corner into a bright open space with white leather armchairs and a glass coffee table.

"Let's sit down, shall we?"

My legs were grateful for the break.

"I'm so glad you're making progress again, Laura. Is there anything else we can do for you?"

I shrugged. "I don't know. I don't think so."

She touched my arm gently. "You know, if you ever need someone else to talk to, you could try me? I mean, if you'd find it easier than talking to a professional. Sometimes, what we really need is a friend – don't you think?"

I didn't know what to say.

Miss Lilly looked out of the window and went on. "I know how it feels, to lose your family."

"You lost yours?"

She bit her lip. "Guilt is the worst part, isn't it? That you're still alive. That they're gone when it could so easily have been you."

I thought of Alfie, who'd barely had a chance to live. And Mum and Ima, who had tried so hard to make things right and now would never know that I was okay.

Guilt. Yes. I'd hardly realized that's what it was, but muddled in with all the sorrow and the worry was guilt.

"What happened to your family?" I asked.

Miss Lilly opened her mouth to answer but closed it again. Then she said, "Laura, I've been thinking. I'm not sure what your plans are when you leave here…"

Little spikes of anxiety prickled my skin. Was she going to tell me I had to go, that my recovery time was up?

I tried to speak, but all that came out was, "I…"

"It's none of my business, I know, and you barely know me. But I've watched over you for so long it's like you're a part of my life. A part of the Blackhurst family. I feel responsible for you. Look, there is absolutely no pressure at all to say yes, but I have a huge apartment attached to the clinic here, right next door. When you're well enough, maybe, if you wanted to, you could stay with me?"

It was so unexpected, I just blurted, "Why?"

She shook her head. "I'm so sorry. What a silly idea. Of course you'll want your own life. There'll be family you'll want to stay with. We must help you find them."

I shook my head. "No. I didn't mean that. I don't even think I have anyone. Mum and Ima's families didn't approve of them being together. They sort of cut us off. And I never knew my dad – Mum said he was a friend who'd donated the…you know…necessary. No, what I meant was, why would you do that for me?"

She didn't get a chance to answer, because Mariya arrived with the tray of tea.

Miss Lilly poured. "Do you have sugar?"

"Erm, I'm not sure."

"You still have gaps in your memory?"

"Some. They catch me by surprise sometimes – the things I don't know."

Something dropped into my mind, bittersweet.

The four of us, Mum, me, Ima and Alfie, having afternoon tea in a posh hotel – tiny cakes and finger sandwiches and sugar in a bowl in crumbly cubes. I beg them to let me stir some into my tea and eventually they relent. I drink the sweet tea and it's disgusting…

I laughed and said, "Actually, I do remember. No, I don't have sugar, thanks."

Miss Lilly handed me a cup. It was the first tea I'd had since I'd been revived. I sipped it and the rich taste warmed my insides.

"There is something I could do for you, whatever you decide about living with me," Miss Lilly said. "I'm a primary stakeholder in a school. A very good school, the top girls' school in the country – I used to go there actually."

"A private school?"

"Yes. They'd be delighted to have you."

I flushed with shame. "But I don't have any money."

"I own the school, Laura. You wouldn't be expected to pay."

"I'll be so behind with everything. I'd embarrass you."

"You would never do that, and you don't need to worry; they'd make sure you have all the help you need to catch up."

The thought of going back to school, without Stacey. A posh school too. I wouldn't fit in. They'd never accept me. "What about my old…?"

"Your old school? Of course, if that's what you want. I'm not sure you'd recognize it now though – it's got very run-down."

It had been bad enough when I was there.

"I'm sure you've lots of happy memories…" Miss Lilly said.

I shuddered as I remembered Kelly Knight. She volunteered for gate duty every day and if Stacey and I were late she would yell, "Come on, you two, lesbi having you."

Stacey lost it one morning and punched her right in the face. "We're not lesbians, you stupid cow, and even if we were, at least we're not dickheads."

Stacey was suspended from school for a week, but Kelly never said another word about my mums.

Stacey. Stacey. Stacey—

"Laura?" Miss Lilly said. "You don't have to do anything you don't want to. We could maybe get you tutors instead? It's a lovely school though, it really is. And you'd have a much better chance of success at a school that has time for your individual needs."

I knew that. Everyone knew you had a better chance in life if you went to a better school. And I had to build a good life for myself now. I had no one else to help me. Only I did, didn't I? Miss Lilly was sitting right next to me, offering me everything. A place to live, a good education. Why was I even hesitating? What other option did I have?

Seriously, what possible reason could I have for saying no? To any of it?

"Can I see it? The school?"

Miss Lilly beamed. "Of course you can. Where's your slate?"

"I can look at it on my slate?"

"You can look at anything on your slate. On the internet. The World Wide Web? I thought Benjie was going to show you how to use it?"

He'd shown me Google Earth and YouTube. I didn't know there was more.

"I'll get it," I said and stood up too quickly and with no regard for my stupidly weak body. I collapsed onto the tea things, smashing a cup, and sending a sliver of china deep into my thumb.

"Ow! OW!" I pulled it out; blood beaded rapidly in the cut and dripped on the floor.

Miss Lilly leaped to her feet. "Mariya! Mariya!"

"It's fine," I said, sucking on it. "I just need a plaster or something."

Mariya appeared and Miss Lilly snapped, "Laura has hurt herself. Clean it and cover it up."

Miss Lilly looked panicked. Properly panicked. Like she really, deep-down cared about me.

And I thought maybe, just maybe, everything was going to be okay.

chapter eleven

SHEM

I felt like I had a target on my back. Like, if I didn't move fast enough, someone was going to grab me. That business on the beach had done my head in. Eventually, I returned to my shed. I didn't know what else to do. I hung back before going in. When I was as sure as I could be that no one had followed me, I dived though the overcoat of brambles that hid the door.

I wanted to get inside as quick as I could but when your only hand won't stop trembling, it's a bit hard to stuff a key in a lock. By the time I got the door open, I'd nearly suffocated myself holding my breath. I relocked it and drew the bolt across.

Scrag went straight for his water and lapped and lapped, splashing it everywhere. He didn't seem jumpy like he would if someone was sniffing around outside. That calmed me down a bit. I took my coat off and sat next to him, feeling hot and sick. He gave a little yip and nudged at my hand with his wet face.

"You hungry, Scraggy?"

I opened the carrier bag and fished out a yogurt I'd got from the bin what seemed like hours ago. I dipped the stale bread Scrag had brought back earlier in the yogurt and gave it to him. My stomach was in too tight a knot to eat anything.

I huddled in the corner of my shed, nodding to the spider that sat vigilantly waiting for its dinner to arrive. I was a popular kid, wasn't I? A dog and a spider were my best pals and I was pretty sure the spider would eat me if it could. I tried to be positive but sometimes I hated my life. I wished Bert was still here.

He was one of the good guys, Bert. Seriously, he didn't need to take me on, but he had – he even gave me an education of sorts. He taught me to read from library books. I'd hide in the squat, waiting for him to come back with treasures. Bert loved these books about a kid wizard called Harry Potter. We read them over and over. When we found Scrag, shivering in an underpass, Bert wanted to call him Fang, after a big dog in one of the stories. He looked like a Scrag to me though, so Scrag he was.

Bert was brilliant at reading stories. And telling them. I knew he made stuff up because the stories changed so often. Once he said he'd found me under a gooseberry bush when he'd been out rambling. And once he said I'd been given to him by an emperor penguin during an expedition to the South Pole. I don't even know if that's where emperor penguins live. The worst story he told was that I'd come from the kitchen of a crazy chef who'd chopped my hand off with a meat cleaver.

That one gave me nightmares for a while.

I gave Scrag another bit of yogurty bread. He chomped through it then flopped in a dusty beam of sunlight that had found its way through the grimy window. I made a pillow out of my coat and lay down next to him, scratching the top of his head. He licked my hand.

"You're a good boy, Scrag," I said.

It was so warm I dozed off. I was woken by a buzzing noise near my head. In my sleepy haze I thought I was being attacked by bees, but as I came round properly, I realized it was coming from the plastic bag of stuff I'd nicked. I rummaged through.

It was a phone.

I hadn't nicked a phone.

What would I want with a phone?

Who would I call?

I dropped it like it might burn me and it carried on buzzing against the floor.

Someone had planted it on me.

It had to be that idiot in the car, when he'd tried to grab my bag. Or maybe that one on the beach. The one I'd bumped into.

I went cold. You could trace a person with a phone. They might be on their way right now.

I leaped to my feet. "Scrag. We've got to go."

I'd walk somewhere – anywhere away from here – and dump it.

I picked it up and it stopped ringing. A message flashed up:

Answer the phone, Shem. There's a good lad.

He knew my name.

How?

How did they know who I was? What was I to them?

Bert had told me about kids disappearing off the streets. He'd always warned me to stay close to him or the Death Eaters would get me. I thought it was because he was so paranoid about the authorities taking me away, but I was pretty much an adult now. Wasn't I?

One way or another, that phone meant trouble. I dropped it back in the bag, grabbed my rucksack and said to Scrag, "Let's go."

The further away that phone was from my shed, the better.

chapter twelve
LAURA

Mariya made a massive fuss of cleaning up my cut and wrapping it in a ridiculous comedy bandage. By the time she'd finished, Miss Lilly said she had to go but that I should look up the school on Google.

"It's called Whitman's. I think you'll like it – it's by the sea."

She leaned forward to kiss me goodbye and I was briefly lost in the cloud of soft scent that surrounded her.

Mariya took me back to my room and left me with a beaker of C-plan and my slate. I asked Notitia to find Google. A blank page popped up with the word GOOGLE made of interlocking coloured letters, twisting in and out like a Rubik's cube. I wasn't sure how it worked, so I just said, "Find Whitman's School."

The slate flattened down and a list appeared. I poked at the top result and it took me to a page for the school.

Girls of every skin colour smiled warmly at me. Behind

them sat a building like a block of vanilla ice cream crowned by a caramel-wafer roof. I wanted to pinch it up, to make it 3D, but my big bandaged thumb got in the way. There were links to pages about everything the school did – sport, drama, music, science – and videos of girls from all over the world talking about how much they loved it there. Nerves crawled through me. It looked a million miles away from any school I belonged in.

I rolled my shoulders, trying to shrug off the tension that was building at the thought of trying to mix with the beautiful, talented, rich girls that went to Whitman's. I wondered if I could ask Google about my old school. Then, like a bolt of lightning to my stupid brain, I realized I could ask Google about Stacey. Maybe even find the story she'd sold about us?

Before I could do anything though, Benjie came in.

"Your heart just had a little flutter. Is everything okay? You're due some blood tests; we might as well do them now."

I groaned. He must have seen a spike in my heart rate through the stupid cuff on my arm. For the first time since they'd woken me up, I longed for a bit of privacy. They could literally see my pulse race when something rattled me *and* they could walk in and out of my room whenever they wanted.

I covered my irritation with a joke. "Are you sure you're not a vampire, Benjie? The amount of blood you've taken from me makes me very suspicious."

"Cheeky monkey."

I pulled up my sleeve, muttering, "I'm fine. I was just worrying a bit about school."

"Better safe than sorry," Benjie said.

I looked out of the window while he took a few vials of my blood.

When he'd gone, I stared at my slate. Was I ready to read what Stacey had said? And would Benjie be in and out every two seconds if I did? Some instinct meant I didn't want him to know. Or maybe I didn't want Miss Lilly to know. She'd made it pretty obvious she didn't approve of Stacey.

Instead, I distracted myself. I said, "Notitia, how do you get white teeth?"

There were thousands of results – from natural methods with lemon and baking soda to actual bleach – and there were horror stories too; enamel stripped off teeth, gums so damaged that teeth fell out and a kid who'd burned an actual hole in his throat.

Grim.

I could maybe have a go at the lemon thing though. I didn't want to look like a total dork at the new school. *If* I went. I wanted to have another look at the school but the stupid bandage was making it hard to navigate the pages. My thumb didn't even feel sore, so I pulled it off.

And there was nothing. No cut, no blood, nothing. No sign that a shard of sharp china had been buried in my skin less than an hour before. Maybe there was something in the cream Mariya had put on that helped it heal? I mean, I was in the future. They were bound to have made some advances.

I smiled at the over-the-top bandage. Seriously, they couldn't have cared for me better if I was actual royalty.

I made sure I put the bandage back on properly after I'd finished with my slate. I didn't want them to think I was ungrateful.

chapter thirteen
SHEM

I walked and walked – right across town into Hove. I walked until I found a street where it was bin collection day. Perfect. They could take the stupid phone and incinerate it. I lifted the lid off someone's bin and the thing bleeped another message. I'd been ignoring them ever since I'd left the shed and I didn't want to read it now.

I dropped it in the bin. *Trace that, pigs.*

Scrag was really panting. The walk had worn him out. I knew he needed a drink but I didn't want to go home. I mooched about a bit and spotted a little fish pond in someone's front garden. I opened the gate.

"In you go, boy. Fill up."

The dumb dog jumped in the pond and within seconds a woman was out the front door and yelling at me, "What do you think you're doing? Keep your dog under control! Get out of my garden!"

Yada yada yada.

"I'm so sorry," I said, doing my best impression of Draco Malfoy's dad. "He momentarily slipped his lead. Do come along, Scrag, there's a good dog."

He climbed out of the pond and gave himself a good shake all over the woman's nice dry legs.

"Well!" she said, but we were already gone, so I didn't get to hear the rest.

"Scrag, my friend, you are hilarious."

He yipped agreement.

We were fine, me and Scrag, totally fine. If people would just let us be. It wasn't like I ever bothered anyone. I never had much to do with any other humans. I knew you couldn't trust them.

As we walked, I remembered something I'd buried deep down.

Bert had come back from the beach one day. He'd sold a couple of wooden seagulls and he was in a really good mood. "Come on, Shem," he'd said, "let's go down the pier and get fish and chips."

It was so rare for him to take me out, even when it was dark, that my stomach had hiccupped with nervous excitement. When we'd got down there, there was a massive queue. Bert was a bit jumpy, his eyes darting all over the place. I could tell he regretted bringing me with him, so I looked around for something to distract him.

I saw a kid on his own, maybe ten or twelve – about the same age as me. He was scruffy too. I thought he might be a street kid. He was hanging out by the slot machines, waiting for some drunk to leave his winnings in the bottom. I pointed him out to Bert.

As we watched, some man grabbed the kid by the elbow and steered him out of the arcade towards a black van. A side door slid open and an arm came out and dragged the boy inside. No one but us seemed to notice.

I looked up at Bert, whose face was as white as the chalky cliffs. "What's he done? Why have they taken him? Were they Death Eaters?"

Bert nodded sharply, pulled me into his side and quietly left the queue. We headed back to the squat without our chips.

I tried to ask him about it later, but he said nothing, just clammed up tighter than a rich man's wallet.

Maybe they weren't all stories, Bert's tall tales. Maybe those same people were after me. Only it didn't make any sense. There hadn't been laws about vagrancy then. Or had there? I was such an idiot. I didn't know anything.

The sun beat down. The heat was making me feel ill. I wanted to get out of the glare for a while, so it was a proper stroke of luck when I came across a library. There used to be quite a few libraries when I was little. I hadn't seen one in years. I never got to read unless someone left a book in a bin or on the beach. I looked inside the building. I had a vague idea they had public computers in libraries. Maybe I could do a search for the vagrancy law? That way at least I might know what I was dealing with.

It was lovely and cool and quiet inside. A small bank of

computers sat in a corner, so I headed over to them. Someone coughed. Not a normal cough, an attention cough. I looked around and smiled at the librarian. She raised her eyebrows and nodded at Scrag. I groaned inside – she was going to kick us out. Or Scrag anyway. I didn't want to be separated from him, not after the morning we'd had.

I whispered, "He won't be no trouble. It's too hot outside for him."

Right on cue, Scrag lolled his tongue out and started panting his head off.

"Sorry," she said. "I don't make the rules."

She wasn't going to budge. So much for checking the computers. I dug in my bag for an empty bottle and said, "Can I fill this up at least?"

I knew she had to let me do that. All public places were legally obliged to let you fill a water bottle.

She took it off me and went into a little room behind the desk. When she came back, she tried to hand me half a pack of biscuits as well.

I stared at the biscuits, thinking it must be a mistake. She pushed them into my hand and said, "Have you got any money?"

I shook my head.

She rummaged under the counter and pulled out twenty quid. "It's not much but maybe it'll help a bit."

It had been a long time since anyone had been that kind to me. I felt my eyes filling with tears. And then I wondered what she wanted in return.

"Just take it," she said. "I have a son about your age. I hope someone would look out for him if he was in trouble."

"I'm not in trouble," I croaked past the lump in my throat.

She raised her eyebrows and looked at my shoes. They were a bit broken. And mismatched. One was a tennis shoe and one was a trainer. Neither of them were very pretty.

"Thanks," I said.

"You're welcome, but you can't stay here with the dog. Take care now. Stay away from the main streets and be careful who you talk to – not everyone's nice."

"Yeah, I know." Then I had an idea. Instead of the computer, I'd just ask her. "Do you know anything about a new vagrancy law?"

Her face clouded over. "An absolute disgrace if you ask me."

So it was true: there was a new law. That *must* have been who those idiots were – government thugs. I flushed with relief that I'd got rid of the phone but then had a new panic. Was that the sort of thing a government employee would do? Plant a phone on someone? I bit my lip. Maybe it was. What would I know?

I had absolutely no plan for how to keep me and Scrag out of trouble. I wanted to stay in the nice, safe library with nice, safe walls and the nice, safe librarian but she said, "You take care of yourself now."

And I knew we had to go.

I felt better though. Little acts of kindness do that to you. Also – twenty quid. Twenty whole quid. I could buy us a

chapter fourteen
LAURA

As I drank my C-plan the next morning, I gazed out across the acres of grass to distant trees, and remembered that I used to run. I'd been in the school cross-country team. Not because I was good at it, but because no one else would do it. It was the one thing I did without Stacey.

I put my hand on the cool windowpane. I hadn't felt the sun on my skin, or the wind in my hair for months. If you counted all the time I'd been asleep, it was *years*. I used to love filling my lungs with fresh air, my feet pounding the pavement, thudding new thoughts into my head. I knew my legs weren't up to running yet, but I was in a gorgeous place with beautiful grounds – just to walk in them would be amazing.

I got dressed in my own clothes again and went to find Benjie. I asked him if I could go outside.

He hesitated. "I'll have to check. There are press about and I know Miss Lilly thinks it'll be best if your first dealings with them are under her supervision."

"What do you mean, press?"

Benjie looked at me thoughtfully. "Laura, you're a scientific wonder. The first known survivor of cryostasis. Or, if you prefer some of the more sensational headlines, a real-life sleeping beauty. The world's press are very interested in you. Miss Lilly has done a pretty good job of keeping them under control, but you'll be far more exposed outside. Miss Lilly absolutely won't want any unauthorized photographs leaking out."

I stared at him.

"You're famous, Laura. Everyone knows about you."

"Famous?"

He nodded. "Since you were revived, only Miss Lilly's most celebrated clients have been allowed in – the ones who truly understand the need for privacy – and even those she's only let back in recently. She's turned everyone away to keep your recovery private."

"She did that for me?"

He nodded. "You're very special to her, Laura. She'll do whatever she can to protect you from press intrusion."

"Wait…you said *everyone* knows about me?"

"Pretty much. Unless they live under a rock."

"So if I go to that school, will they know about my family?"

"Quite possibly… Laura? Why?"

I hated myself for it, but embarrassment crept up my cheeks in a blush. The ghost of Kelly Knight loomed its horrible head.

I whispered, "Benjie, I didn't have a dad. My parents

weren't… I had two mums. They were gay."

He looked completely confused.

I said, "Lesbians."

"Yeah, I know what gay means, Laura. Why are you worried about that? Oh! Wait, I get it."

He shook his head and then laughed. "Oh sweetheart, sorry, sorry. You're worried what other kids will say at school? About you having same-sex parents?"

I looked at the floor.

"People don't really care about that any more. We've had equal marriage laws for years."

"What?"

"This is the twenty-first century. Most people aren't worried about who you love. Anyone with any sense is far more worried about who you hate."

"Really?"

"Really. Our prime minister is married to a man."

I didn't see how that was relevant. Margaret Thatcher was married to a man. And then the light dawned.

"The prime minister is a man? Married to a man?"

Benjie winked. "Doesn't stop him being an idiot though."

I felt a sudden surge of respect for this new decade. A spike of hope. It made me want to explore more, and if I couldn't go outside, maybe…

"If there's no one else here I could walk around the hospital then? Edna wants me to do more exercise…"

"Laura! For someone so tiny, you're a bit of a bully. Okay, you can walk, but Mariya goes with you."

"I don't need a chaperone, Benjie. Besides, you've got your little needle spy in my arm. I'll just walk up and down the corridors. Please?"

"Hmmm, all right, but on two conditions: the second you start to tire, you come back; and this floor only, young lady – that should be safe enough. Promise you won't try to get through any locked doors, okay? You'll get me shot if you go AWOL."

I grinned at him. He rolled his eyes.

"At least give me time to make sure it's all secure."

Later that day, I went for a walk.

My room must have been in a medical part of the clinic because there was a different feel when I left my corridor. It had carpet, for a start, and framed paintings hung on the walls. Fat vases of white lilies stood on polished tables, filling the place with a heady scent. Everything screamed luxury hotel, not hospital.

It was quiet. There was no one else about. I walked to a window at the end of the corridor and looked out, trying to see the press Benjie had warned me about. All I could see was neat green grass stretching to the line of trees way in the distance. I stood on tiptoe so I could peer down the side of the building. There was nothing but a drainpipe disappearing into some gravel.

My limbs were getting a bit shaky but I was enjoying myself. I went to the opposite end of the corridor and looked down from the window there. Below was a patio the colour of sand and two people in white dressing gowns lying on sunbeds.

I had an urge to eavesdrop. There was a key in the window lock, so I turned it and eased it open. I could hear every word, as if the sound was being funnelled up the wall.

"...I'm amazed really, given what that awful woman did."

"Stacey Flowers?"

"Yes. I can't believe she was released so soon. She'd only been in prison six—"

They were interrupted by a man in a white coat coming out. I shut the window quickly and then realized my heart was galloping. Benjie would know something was wrong from my readings. I tried to calm down. But...prison? Stacey had been in prison? What for? What hadn't Miss Lilly told me?

I headed down an empty ward, trying to steady my heart rate. But as I walked towards the window at the end, breathing deeply, I got a worse shock: a hand crept over the window ledge and a man pulled himself into view. He stared right at me, seeming as startled as I was, before bringing a camera up to his face. I spun away, charging straight into Mariya and Benjie, who'd come looking for me.

Benjie instantly spotted the man through the glass and yelled, "LOCKDOWN!"

Mariya put an arm round me and ushered me away as an alarm sounded and shutters came down over the windows.

She tried to act normal but I was creeped out.

"Who was that?" I asked.

"No one for you to worry about."

"Was it someone from a newspaper?"

"More likely a freelancer. You've probably just made him a small fortune. Miss Lilly won't be happy. Someone will be for the high jump."

I'd barely got back to my room when Miss Lilly came to see me. She looked very serious. I was worried she was going to be cross with me but after a few questions about how I was feeling, she said, "I'm so sorry about that intruder, Laura. Had I known Benjie was letting you stroll the premises, I would have done a wider security sweep. As it is, it's pushed me into making a decision. I think we should do a deal with the press. You do a conference for them, and they agree to leave you alone. It would take the heat out of your first appearance and you might be able to make a clean start at Whitman's without them hounding you. What do you think?"

My stomach dropped to the floor. Firstly, I hadn't agreed to go to Whitman's yet and secondly…

"Speak to them?"

She nodded.

What if I said something stupid and it was broadcast to the whole country?

I said, "When?"

"As soon as possible. If we can get something out today, our intruder is less likely to make anything from his stolen images – if he managed to transfer anything before he was caught."

What could I say? I felt like I didn't have much choice.

I had three hours to get ready. Mariya washed my hair and conditioned it with this amazing stuff Miss Lilly had given her. She teased it into dark spirals and when I looked in the mirror, it shone. I stroked a hand over it. A delicious smell of coconut reminded me of sun cream and holidays.

Mariya said, "We'd better do something about that bandage on your thumb as well."

As she took it off, I waited for her to make a comment about it healing so quickly. She didn't say a word, so neither did I. I guessed I was right about the cream.

"Do you want to wear the clothes you've got on?"

Good point. Did I want to make my debut in the twenty-first century, in public, on the actual telly, in jeans and a sweatshirt that were half a century out of fashion and three sizes too big for me? But what else could I wear? I didn't even know what was in fashion. And it was definitely too late to go shopping.

"Will I look like a goon?"

"I have no idea what a goon is, but I know you will look lovely. You *are* lovely." Mariya smiled at me.

I was dizzy with nerves.

I wished Mum was with me. She'd say the right things to calm me down. Or Ima, who'd tease me until I was laughing and relaxed. Thankfully, Miss Lilly arrived. She was wearing a different perfume – Turkish delight and roses – a scent full of summer.

"Laura, you look adorable – your hair is gleaming and your skin is absolutely glowing."

She smiled and I was super-conscious of my not-white teeth. "What about my teeth?" I said. "You all have perfect smiles and my teeth are like big yellow tombstones."

Miss Lilly wrinkled her nose. "They aren't that bad. Your eyebrows could do with a tidy, but it's too late for that now."

My hand flew to my face. What was wrong with my eyebrows? I looked at Miss Lilly and at Mariya – true enough, their eyebrows were neat, dark little arcs framing their eyes.

Miss Lilly said, "Nothing to worry about. Everyone will be much more interested in what you say than what you look like. Now, Laura, if they ask anything you don't want to answer, just say 'I'm not sure' or 'I'm not ready to deal with that right now'. I'll be there and so will Giles and the rest of my media team. I'll go down first, then Benjie and Mariya will bring you, okay?"

I nodded and she swept forward and kissed my cheek. I relaxed, just a little bit.

Benjie and Mariya took me down in the lift to the conference room. I noticed two buttons for levels below the ground floor. I asked, "What's down there?"

Mariya said, "Just storage, I think."

Two levels of storage? What was it, a bank vault for a small country?

When we left the lift, I tried to peer in the few doors we passed, but Benjie and Mariya were walking too fast and it was all I could do to keep up. And then we were there. At the doors of the conference room. I could see through a sliver of glass in the door that the room was rammed with people and cameras. RAMMED.

"Benjie, I feel sick. I think I'm ill. I need to go to the bathroom."

"You're just nervous."

"But I haven't seen this many people since, God, since for ever. What if they breathe on me and give me germs? You said germs evolve. I…"

"You've had every vaccination under the sun along with immunity boosters – you'll be fine."

"But…"

He took my hand. "Look through the window. Can you see Miss Lilly?"

I looked. She was sitting behind a large desk covered in a white cloth. Three microphones perched on it. I nodded.

"She's been doing this kind of thing for years. She'll make sure you're okay."

Miss Lilly smiled at me and beckoned. Other heads turned my way, and cameras went up in front of faces. I gripped Benjie's arm and said, "I can't."

"Yes, you can. Go on – in." He gave me a little push in my back.

I resisted but the door opened and Miss Lilly nodded at me encouragingly. I didn't have a choice – I stood as straight as I could and walked into the room.

Cameras popped and flashed and dozens of voices called out my name:

"Laura, Laura, look this way."

"Laura, how does it feel to be in a different century?"

"Laura, you're our very own Sleeping Beauty. What's it like living in a fairy tale?"

For a minute, I went right back to the day they brought me round, my eyes burning in the bright light. I shrank back, but Miss Lilly stepped towards me. She caught hold of my hand and pulled me behind the table. I sat between her and a man I recognized as Giles. I felt safer there and slowly a hush came over the room.

"Thank you," said Miss Lilly. "Can I remind you all that Laura is very young and has been through a lot. We'll answer questions in order of your tickets only. Giles?"

Giles looked down at a little slate and said, "Okay. Number one, please."

A woman in a pale blue suit smiled at me. "Sameera Susts, World News. Hello, Laura. Welcome back to the world. Thank you for taking my question."

I nodded at her, my mouth so dry I didn't think I could speak.

As if she read my mind, she said, "This must be nerve-wracking for you, there's a glass of water there."

And there was, right in front of me. I picked it up and gulped.

"How are you feeling, Laura?"

"Nervous." The whole room chuckled like I'd said the funniest thing in the world.

"But you're completely well now?"

I nodded. "I think so. I'm getting stronger every day."

"It must be hard adjusting to a new life without your family?"

"I..."

The brush-off words Miss Lilly had given me had disappeared from my head but Giles saved me.

"Thanks, Sameera. Number two?"

"Jim Coxhall, Gossip Lines. What do you think of the new fashions, Laura?"

A ripple of laughter mixed with shaking heads went around the room, but I felt safe with this one. "I don't know yet but I can't wait to go shopping."

"And what do you make of all the new technology?"

"I'm only just getting to grips with it but the computers are really cool."

And on it went. I was quite enjoying it until someone said, "Sandy Limehouse, Online Enquirer. My question is for Miss Lilly. Are you still pursuing your civil action against Stacey Flowers?"

Shocked, I looked at Miss Lilly to see what she'd say. She smiled serenely and Giles said, "That question is outside the bounds of this conference."

"But are you—?"

Giles cut her off and said, "That's it, I'm afraid. Time's up. Thank you, ladies and gentlemen. As agreed, we hope you will now leave Laura alone to settle into her new life. Any further questions should come through me."

I was ushered out. Benjie was waiting. I gave him a hug and asked, "How'd I do?"

"Brilliant. Born to be a star."

When we got back up to my floor, the excitement fizzled out. It had been good to be away from my room. Good to be with other people. I picked up the picture of my family. I missed them so much. But beyond that, I realized I missed *life*.

There was a whole world outside the clinic. I was stronger now, strong enough to cope. However much it scared me – and it did – I couldn't stay in my safe little room for ever. I had to take the next step into a new life and I'd already been offered the easiest way to do that. I'd be an idiot not to take it.

I said to Benjie, "Can you ask Miss Lilly if she meant it, about me living with her? If you think I'm ready?"

Benjie beamed at me. "I am absolutely sure she meant every word – and it's not like you'll be far away from the clinic if you need us. The apartment is right next door. I'll message her now."

I stood the picture back by my bed. My stomach twisted with guilt. Miss Lilly would never replace Mum, Ima and Alfie, but they were gone and I was still here. What else was I going to do? I had to live. I owed it to them.

chapter fifteen
LAURA

The day after the press conference, Mariya brought me in a small suitcase and some fabric plasters.

"I thought Mr Ted could do with a bit of attention before he leaves the hospital."

I packed the case while she patched up Scruffy's moth holes. When she'd finished, he looked like he'd been in a battle for his life. I clutched him to me, looking at my abandoned bed, the place where I had battled for *my* life. I wanted to go, but I was also sad to leave. My room had been like a womb, nursing me back to health.

Benjie came in. "All packed?"

"Yep. Thank you, Benjie. You've been so fab, all of you. I'm going to miss you."

"We'll see you for regular check-ups, until you go to school." Benjie picked up my suitcase. "Come on, let's go wait for Miss Lilly."

My team were all by the main desk. Edna had a floating

silver balloon and said, "This is you, flying high!"

Vera handed me a book called *How to Be Calm in the Midst of a Storm*.

Mariya gave me a small bag. "There's a card in there from Stephen and me and some bits of make-up and tooth-whitening toothpaste until you're old enough to get your teeth done properly. I'll do your eyebrows too, if you want."

I should have been offended but I was really touched. Even with everything Ima had taught me about being true to myself, I still wanted to look right. I wanted to fit in. I hugged her tight.

"My gift is arriving later," Benjie said. "I had to clear it with Miss Lilly."

I got a bit tearful when Miss Lilly arrived. I had to remind myself I was literally going next door.

"Ready, Laura?" she said. "We can get home through the clinic, but I thought you'd rather walk outside, now we've dealt with the press."

Benjie came with us to help with my stuff. There were some people about on the lower floor – smiley medical sort of people. I saw patients too, I think. We walked past two glossy women dressed almost identically in tight white jeans and pastel-coloured blouses that flowed around their tiny waists. Their *weirdly* tiny waists.

I turned for another look as they passed and caught them staring at me. I looked quickly away.

We arrived at a set of glass doors that led outside. Miss

Lilly handed me a pair of sunglasses. "I brought you these, as you've not been in direct sunlight for a while."

I put them on. The doors opened automatically and the smell of cut grass wafted in. Somewhere a mower buzzed – and there were birds, so many birds singing. I stepped into the sun and my heart sang with them.

It was a beautiful day – hot and bright with the gentlest of breezes. The grounds were glorious. A huge expanse of green was divided by a butter-coloured drive curving away to a distant road.

As we walked on that drive, the crunch of the gravel took me back – I'd first heard it as we'd arrived at the clinic: *Alfie lying next to me in the ambulance, barely breathing, his little chest fluttering up and down.* I gasped.

Benjie caught my arm. "Laura?"

"I...I'm fine."

I mentally anchored myself with one of Vera's tricks: *touch something, smell something, see something.* Benjie's sleeve, freshly-mown grass and...I turned back to look at the clinic. It was lovely, like a posh country house. Roses clambered up the front. My heart steadied.

We walked around to a smart red door on the other side of the building. Miss Lilly looked up and the door unlocked.

That was pretty cool.

She said, "Facial recognition. It's not that sophisticated but I like it."

Inside, everywhere was painted a gleaming white, like crushed pearls. It kind of glittered. It wasn't homely but it was beautiful; cool and beautiful. A white staircase curved around the entrance hall. Even the carpet was white. For a brief moment I imagined Alfie running up those stairs, planting mucky handprints up the walls.

Would that ever stop? Would I ever not think about him?

There was a buzzing noise somewhere. Miss Lilly stopped for a moment, as if she was listening to something, then she said, "I'm so sorry, Laura. Something's come up. I'll ask Annie to settle you in. I'll be back as soon as I can."

Benjie put my stuff down as a very familiar woman came through a door leading off the hall. I did a double take.

"Mariya?"

Miss Lilly said, "Oh no, Laura, this is Annie. Annie and Mariya have had some of the same facial surgeries. Annie, this is Laura. Can you show her to her room and make sure she has anything she needs? No food yet, C-plan only."

Annie nodded and picked up my case.

"I'll come and find you later this evening," Miss Lilly called as she left.

I smiled, suddenly nervous.

"I'd better be off too," Benjie said.

"Wait. Not yet. I need a hug."

I hugged him like I was six not sixteen.

After he left, I followed Annie up the too-white stairs to a room at the end of the landing. My legs were like jelly by the time I got there – it had been a few decades since I'd climbed a staircase.

Annie stopped in front of an open door. The room beyond was huge, bigger than the whole downstairs of my old house. Annie put my case on an enormous squishy white bed. It faced a wide window that filled the room with light. It seemed to bounce off the walls – they had the same ice-crystal look as the ones downstairs.

"Do you have a favourite colour?" Annie asked.

"Maybe green?"

She keyed something into a slate and the walls shimmered and shifted and settled into a soft pale green the exact same colour as my room in the hospital. Asylum green. That apple colour that is meant to keep you calm. I put a hand on it. "That's awesome."

She indicated a door in the corner of the room. "Your bathroom."

"Oh, wow, thanks."

Then she crossed to the opposite corner and said, "And for your clothes…"

It was a walk-in wardrobe. A WALK-IN WARDROBE. It was pretty empty but there was a copy of everything I'd packed in my box, hanging up, waiting for me. I put a hand on the T-shirt. "How…?"

"Miss Lilly had these made until you can choose more clothes of your own. They're smaller than the originals so they shouldn't hang off you quite so badly. Your uniform is packed in the trunk."

"Uniform?"

"For school."

A brand-new dark blue trunk with brass clasps was tucked against the wall. "But I haven't agreed…"

Annie went on. "Last thing." She held a small card against a glass panel set in the wall above the bed and a screen rose up at the foot. I tried to be cool about it.

"It's an old TV," she explained. "It doesn't have holograms, but it'll sync with your slate, and your phone. The panel controls the lights too but you can just tell the room if you like." She handed me the card.

"Erm, okay. Great. Thanks."

"That card will open all the doors you need, so don't lose it. I'll bring up refreshments but if you need anything else, just call me."

"How?"

"There's an app on your slate."

"Oh, right, okay." I had no idea what she meant but Annie didn't exactly invite questions. I'd figure it out. Somehow. "Can I leave my room, if I want to?"

"Of course. This is your home now, Laura. I believe there are still some minor concerns over security, so it may be best to stay in the building when you're alone, but you can move around the apartment as you wish."

She shut the door as she left. I sat Scruffy on my bed, feeling a bit overwhelmed. I opened my case. Next to my slate was the pasta-shapes frame with the picture of my family. A different life, a different time. The deep ache in my heart was so physical I pressed my hand to my chest.

Would it ever get easier?

For all my chats with Vera, I wasn't okay without my family, not yet. Maybe not ever. But somehow, I had to get on. Blubbing over what I could never have back was not going to help me. I set the picture on my bedside table and picked up my slate. My little electronic pal said, *"Hello, Laura, how can I help you?"*

"I don't know," I said. "Maybe you can tell me how Laura Henley is supposed to survive in the twenty-first century."

"Sure. Here is what I found."

Unbelievably, Notitia showed me a list of entries all about me. At the top was a thing called Wikipedia. I poked it and a page appeared.

Laura Henley is the first known person to survive a prolonged period in cryostasis.

There was an old picture of me and Alfie snuggled on the sofa at home. I caught my breath – I felt the space beside me where he should be like an open wound. I wanted him there, hugging his blankie while we watched *Thomas the Tank Engine*. The pain was crushing. Stacey's name was near the picture with a bubble next to it: More information. Maybe all I had to do was pinch it up and I could find out what had happened to her. If she'd really been to prison and—

There was a sharp knock on my door.

Annie came in with a glass of C-plan. "Miss Lilly asked me to tell you she's charged a pay account on your slate so you can buy a few new outfits."

I looked blankly at her.

"On the internet. The slate. You can buy some new clothes."

She looked at me like I was an idiot. "Ask Notitia. She'll guide you through it. You really can't go wrong."

Notitia was my new best pal. How sad was that?

Annie pointed at the page I was looking at. "I don't advise reading about yourself on the internet, not until you've had social-media training."

I flushed with embarrassment. "I wasn't. It…"

I swiped the Wikipedia page closed. I'd only been gone from the clinic for a couple of hours and part of me wanted to go back.

"You never know who is watching what you read online."

"Watching? What do you mean?"

"All sorts of people track what you do on the internet. That's how they target advertising. Just…be careful. Giles will explain more."

She sounded genuinely concerned, which was worrying given she hadn't exactly created the impression she cared about me. "You should really think about getting ready for your new school," Annie said. "You'll need more than a single pair of jeans and there's not much time."

A chill of anxiety crept over my skin. "How much time?"

"Term starts in early September. Just under three weeks."

That wasn't so bad. It wasn't, like, the next day or anything.

When Annie had gone, I almost went back to that Wikipedia page, but she'd worried me a bit.

"Notitia?"

Up she popped, with Miss Lilly's smiling face. It was weird it being her, like I was ordering her around. Or like she was watching me. I said, "Notitia, can I change your appearance?"

"Yes, Laura. You can choose from a list of avatars or you can specify any person whose image might be in my database."

"Can I change you to John Taylor from the band Duran Duran?"

"Choose your image."

I picked out John in a grey suit with a white ruffle shirt.

Within seconds, there he was, smiling like the Mona Lisa of the New Romantics. I laughed out loud and turned around to say something to…Stacey. How strong was that muscle memory of sharing everything with my best friend? She must have felt it too. She must have been lost without me. Deep inside I still couldn't believe she would have betrayed my family – and prison? Really? What had happened to her? I had to know, the pull was just too strong.

"Notitia, can you search for Stacey Flowers?"

Before she'd even answered, Benjie's face popped up in the middle of the screen.

"How are you settling in, Laura? We got a spike in your readings a moment ago – just checking all's okay?"

My hand went to the cuff I was still wearing on my arm. "Benjie, have you any idea how creepy that is? You are literally spying on my insides. And yes, I'm fine. Just…"

I felt like I'd been caught out doing something I shouldn't.

With a sigh I said, "I was just shopping."

"I guess the price of clothes is enough to get your heart

pounding. Don't forget to divide everything by four to account for inflation."

"Okay, thanks, I will."

"Enjoy!"

He vanished, leaving me with a horrible feeling that I'd never be able to keep anything private ever again. The twenty-first century was getting on my nerves a bit.

Fine. I'd do what I'd been asked. Shopping.

Besides, if I was going to go to that stupid posh school, I needed clothes. I didn't want to get my head kicked in for having the wrong jeans.

"Notitia, can you find Topshop?"

"Are you sure you want Topshop? I can recommend clothing outlets more suited to your style?"

Was my computer judging me?

I said, "I'll decide what suits me, thanks. Notitia, find me Topshop."

"Here's what I found."

Up came a shopfront complete with an assistant saying, *"Hi, what are you looking for today? I can recommend some tooth-whitening products."*

Seriously? Was there a conspiracy to make me even more worried about my not-white teeth? How did it even know? Had Notitia been listening to me talking to Mariya? I shuddered. The assistant continued her sales pitch: *"We also have some great offers in uplift bras."*

I looked down at my nearly flat chest. It was like being twelve again and back in Chelsea Girl with the snobby assistants looking at me and Stace like we were scum. Only now I had no Stacey and no idea of what to buy or even HOW to buy. How did you even try anything on?

The assistant read my mind again. *"Order now and we can deliver in two hours. All returns are free."*

Two hours? "All right, tiny psychic shopping woman, show me some jeans."

Up they popped, picture after picture of jeans in all shapes and colours. Adverts ran down the side. I smiled when I saw one with Miss Lilly holding up a pale green bottle:

Try my new skincare range for young adults – made
with you in mind.

The picture rolled away and was replaced by a new one. It was me, at the press conference, with a banner splashed across it:

Get Laura's Eighties Style!

An arrow pointed to my too-big jeans and my yellow sweatshirt. I poked at the image and it took me to another page.

Laura Henley, 1980s dream queen and self-confessed
shopaholic, inspires one of this season's key trends –
BIG. Big on Hair, Big on Size, Big on Colour! One of
the first things Laura said when she was revived after

They were using me to advertise their products! Could they do that? That quote made me sound so shallow. It was totally out of context.

Well, I didn't need Laura Henley's style, thanks. I already had it. I'd deliberately choose something different. Black black black.

I poked at a pair of tight black jeans and then I saw the price. Even when I divided it by four it was ridiculous. But I needed *something* to wear and I could always send them back if Miss Lilly said no. I wondered if there were any normal clothes in the school trunk. I put my slate down and went to have a look.

The trunk was neatly packed with brand-new uniform. I lifted out a dark blue woollen blazer. It was itchy – expensive – not like the polyester thing we'd worn at my old school. There was a kilt too, purple and blue. Was that uniform or – what did Miss Lilly call it – mufti? I dug deeper. There was another one. And a tracksuit in the same shade of purple. Uniform then. Okay, weird but okay. I smiled. Miss Lilly had packed stationery – a plain black pencil case stuffed with everything I might need and an A4 pad with a leather cover. People still used paper then.

I put them back in the case and pictured Mum's haphazard approach to a new term – a last-minute dash to get school shoes and then a desperate sort-out to see which felt tips hadn't dried up over the summer.

Mum...

I shut the trunk.

I couldn't dwell. I couldn't. I'd buy the stupid jeans. Miss Lilly clearly had loads of money and she wanted to help me.

I said to my slate, "Notitia, how do I pay for these jeans?"

"Would you like to return to Topshop?"

"Yes, yes I would."

The shop assistant reappeared. *"Hi! Welcome back. How can I help you?"*

I asked again how I paid for the jeans, aware that I was making an entire friendship group out of two imaginary computer people. At least, I assumed they were imaginary. Maybe they were real people somewhere out there.

The Topshop lady said, *"We have no size on record for you, would you like to be scanned?"*

"No thanks." I'd had quite enough of being examined. I looked down at my scrawny frame.

Hopefully I'd put a bit of weight on, but right now... "Try extra small."

"Okay, that's ordered for you."

"That's it? How do I pay?"

"We've charged your Airpay account. Thank you for your custom."

"But how do you know where I live?"

"I'm sorry, I do not understand the question."

I guessed it didn't matter. It must know where I was or

surely I couldn't have placed the order.

Tight black jeans.

I hoped I hadn't just made a massive fashion mistake. Was Topshop still cool? What if they were all wearing flares? Or long dresses? What if Laura Henley was the only person NOT dressed like Laura Henley? I'd only seen people in uniform. No, no I hadn't, I'd seen the press people. But they had been old. What would they know? They all had shiny white teeth though. Oh God.

"Notitia, what's fashionable?"

"Fashionable is anything representing a current popular style."

"That is not helpful."

"I'm sorry. Please ask me another question."

I didn't and the slate powered off.

Was it sulking? For real?

I'd had enough of computers so I went for a wander around the house. There was a bedroom next to mine, almost identical except the walls were the same white as the rest of the house and the bedding and curtains were a shimmery silver-blue. It looked tidy but lived in and it smelled amazing – it had to be Miss Lilly's room.

I crossed over to the window.

"Having a look around?"

I turned towards the door with a start.

Miss Lilly was smiling from the doorway. I wasn't sure how she'd feel about me being in her room. "Was it okay to come in? It's a beautiful room."

"Of course it's okay. I haven't got any deep dark secrets.

Though there might be the odd sock that didn't quite make the laundry basket."

I laughed.

"Are you hungry?" she asked. "I have permission to try you on some solid food? If you want?"

I was across the room in seconds.

Mashed apple. That's what my solid food was.

White cloth. White china. Silver cutlery.

Baby food.

We sat together at one end of the table.

"You're disappointed," she said.

"No, I…"

"It's okay. Baby steps, Laura. Your system has a lot of adjusting to do."

I put a spoon in the apple. It was lumpy-looking but the smell was yum. It reminded me of Sunday lunches with crumble and custard and all the family chatter. Mum always made extra in case Stacey turned up, which she usually did – her mum didn't do Sunday lunch.

I looked at Miss Lilly. I wanted to ask her about Stacey, about what she'd said to the papers, but she smiled at me and I just couldn't do it. The way she'd reacted when I'd mentioned Stacey in the clinic… I got the feeling she'd be happier if I didn't even *think* about Stacey.

I took a spoonful of apple and tried to swallow. It stuck in my throat with all my unasked questions.

chapter sixteen
SHEM

As I headed back to Brighton, I prickled with sweat and worry.

Vagrant.

Why was it so stupidly hot? It was always stupidly hot, or stupidly wet, or stupidly cold.

Vagrant.

What if they knew where my shed was? What if the phone had been in there long enough for them to pinpoint it?

Vagrant.

I wanted to scream. I felt for the sharp corners of the twenty in my pocket.

Maybe we should just get on a train and leave. Go to London where nobody knew us.

That actually wasn't a bad idea. I could find a job or something. We could start from scratch.

I made my way to the station. I didn't know how far twenty quid would get us but I could buy a ticket as far as it would stretch and then stay on the train until they chucked us off.

The station was busy. I'd never caught a train before so I watched. People just walked through a gate. It looked like you didn't even need a ticket. I picked up Scrag and tried to follow someone through. They passed through fine but the barrier stayed shut in my face.

I pushed at it but it stayed firm. I looked to my left; someone else just walked through. They weren't doing anything special; the gate was just opening for them. My heart started to race a bit – it was embarrassing, like everyone was part of a club and I was excluded. Someone tapped my shoulder. I flinched against the barrier but it was a young mum with a baby in her arms.

"You need to charge your Airpay," she said.

"What?"

"On your phone. You must have run out of credit."

"Oh, yeah, thanks."

I stepped back and she walked through.

There must be some other way. I looked around for a ticket machine and spotted a sign:

AIRPAY ONLY. CASH IS NO LONGER TAKEN AT THIS STATION.

I wanted to punch something. It wasn't fair. I was shut out of everything because I was poor.

I kept hold of Scrag, tears building at the back of my throat. I sniffed and headed away down the hill. Maybe we could hitch to London. Or walk. I didn't feel safe here, all my places seemed contaminated. The thought of leaving my shed though, my home, it was unbearable – I should check first, to see if anyone had been there. That made more sense.

Scrag caught a whiff of the sea and began to yap and wriggle in my arms. I tried to keep hold of him but he'd got the devil in him and squirmed until he was free. He raced off towards the beach.

"No! No, Scrag! Come back here."

Great. Now I'd have to go and get him.

I followed him down, on high alert for anyone taking too much interest in me. I was a nervous wreck by the time I got to the stones, and Scrag had properly disappeared. I scanned the beach, searching for him, until someone tugged at my sleeve and I yelped like I'd been scalded.

"Hello."

It was a little kid. He looked harmless but I knew you couldn't trust anyone, no matter what size. I braced myself to run, then saw Scrag, who was bounding towards me at last, soaking wet and full of joy. The boy dipped a hand in his pocket and brought out a handful of coins.

"I got all these pennies."

Scrag leaped up at me, wet and full of mischief now he'd cooled down a bit. He started running round me and the boy in a figure-of-eight. The kid thought it was hilarious. Scrag rolled on his back, his stubby legs in the air as the boy gave him a belly rub.

The boy looked up at me with wide eyes. "Are we friends now?"

"What?"

"The man asked me to make friends with you."

I stiffened. My heart did a horrible little dance as I searched the beach, twisting round to check they weren't behind me.

It was all just normal beach people – except for a woman about six beach towels away who was standing up and looking for something. Someone. I said, "Is that your mum?"

The boy shrugged. "Yeah. She won't get me an ice cream."

"Get straight back to her and don't talk to no one else. Didn't she teach you not to talk to strangers?"

With a sulky pout, he headed back towards his mum. I looked again. Harder. They had to be here, watching me.

Scrag got to his feet and shook water off his coat. If I left the beach, they could be waiting to pick me up, but if I stayed where I was, eventually everyone on the beach would go home and they'd come for me. I wanted to puke.

I was a sitting duck. I looked out to sea. There were a few boats bobbing about.

I was seriously, seriously thinking about swimming for one of them. What other options did I have? Call the police? Say I was being harassed? For all I knew, those men *were* the police. Or at least worked with them. The police weren't for people like me.

The little kid was coming back, and he was dragging a man with him. Now if I ran for the sea, *they* were going to cut me off.

I made a noise that sounded like crying. I bit my lip hard to get myself under control. I had no idea what to do next.

chapter seventeen
LAURA

Miss Lilly was clearly so happy to see me eating that I forced the whole bowl of apple down. It got easier to swallow but it sat in my stomach like a heavy blob.

She said, "I am so proud of you, the way you're dealing with everything. You are a very mature young woman."

Annie came in with a cup of coffee for Miss Lilly and a parcel for me. "Topshop delivery."

"My jeans? Already?" And then I blushed, embarrassed that I'd been spending Miss Lilly's money.

"If you need to return them, let me know. I'll summon a drone."

Foreign. Language.

"What's a drone?"

Miss Lilly said, "It's a kind of small flying robot."

"Oh. Okay." I wasn't sure if I was being teased.

"Shall I bring the other thing now also?" Annie asked Miss Lilly.

Miss Lilly nodded. "Why not?"

Annie came back with a wicker basket. Looking up from it, with the most beautiful blue eyes, was a tiny Siamese kitten. She had a matching blue ribbon around her neck.

"From Benjie," Miss Lilly said. "Annie will look after her when you're at school – that's if you want to keep her?"

I picked her up, tears in my eyes.

"Oh yes! Of course I want to keep her – she's adorable! I love her. Hello, little one. What big ears you have, you look like Batfink."

She put a paw on my chin and said, *Meow.*

Deep inside me, a very small bubble of real happiness popped into existence.

"Shall we take her upstairs and you can try on the jeans?" Miss Lilly suggested. "Maybe we can order a few other things together?"

I carried Batfink, her warm little body nestled up close. My legs were still heavy with tiredness, but somehow I didn't feel like collapsing when I got to the top of the stairs.

"We need to sort your schedule out for the next few days," Miss Lilly said. "I want Giles to go over some social-media stuff with you and you need to see Edna and Vera every day, don't you think? Do you want them to come here?"

I wanted to see Benjie too so I said, "It'll be good exercise to walk to the clinic."

"That's true. Okay. I'll get Annie to walk with you."

"I could go by myself."

"I know. I'd just feel happier if someone was looking after you."

I was too distracted by Batfink chewing my hair to argue.

I took my new kitten into the wardrobe with me while I tried on the jeans. She pounced on the old ones as I took them off and then clung to the new ones as I put them on. I was giggling when I came out and for a stupid moment, I forgot where I was. My heart twisted with sadness that it was Miss Lilly sitting on the bed and not my mum smiling at me. And then I felt so guilty, because she'd literally done everything she could to make me feel at home.

I took a deep breath and said, "Do they look okay?"

"They look great."

"Is this what people wear?"

Batfink climbed onto my shoulder. I plucked her down, into my arms.

"Anything goes these days, Laura, honestly – if you like them, keep them."

"Sure?"

She nodded.

I said, "Thank you. For this. For everything."

"It's entirely my pleasure – shall we get a few more things? One pair of jeans isn't going to get you very far."

I started up my slate and Miss Lilly laughed when she saw what I'd done to Notitia.

"I see I've been usurped already."

I blushed and she laughed again, putting a hand on my

arm. "I'm teasing you, Laura! I'm really pleased to see you making things your own."

I got Notitia-John to show us some Topshop tops. There were a lot of T-shirts with logos on. One of them was white with *Choose Ice* in big black letters. It was very familiar.

I said, "Is that copied from my *Choose Life* T-shirt? Are they making fun of me?"

"Of course they aren't! People love you, Laura; they love your story. It's an iconic eighties design, so not hard to guess you had one. You've started a bit of an eighties trend. They're celebrating you. Let me show you something. Notitia, open Laura Henley's Instagram."

Notitia loaded a screen full of pictures of me. I'd never seen most of them. There were pictures of me with the old-lady walking frame, grim determination on my face. Pictures of Mariya teasing my hair into ringlets. There was even a picture of me asleep in my bed.

"What is this?" I said.

"I hope you don't mind but I asked Giles to create an official account for you. There were so many fake ones, I felt we needed to give a truer picture of your life."

"But what is it? Where did the pictures come from?"

"Giles took them remotely – we didn't want you to feel self-conscious. Instagram is just a place where you can post photographs and interact with your fans."

Giles took them? In secret? I felt stripped bare. It was a horrible feeling. *Horrible*. And then I realized what else she'd said.

"Fans? What fans?"

I poked at a picture of me at the press conference. The caption said:

My first press conference, I was super-nervous but #MissLilly took care of me #sleepingbeauty #girlofice #girlfromthepast #vintagefashion #laurahenley

"But I didn't write that."

Miss Lilly laughed. "Most celebrities have help with their Insta accounts."

I squirmed inside. "Sorry, I'm not sure I understand – other people can see this?"

She said, "Anyone who likes your page – it's public. If it really bothers you, we can close it, but people will just pretend they're you and you'll have no control over what they post. If you like, you can take over the account – Giles will show you what to do and he can vet your posts until you get the hang of it. What I wanted you to see were the comments."

I tried to shrug off my discomfort. Miss Lilly obviously felt like Instagram was something you just had to have and she knew a whole lot more about this century than I did.

I read the comments as Batfink leaped about my bed, jumping on imaginary mice. There were hundreds of messages:

You're so brave!
Good luck, Laura!

Welcome to the 21st century!

We love you, Laura!

I'm glad I lived to see this day! I've watched your story
since the day you were frozen!!!

It was lovely to read them – my heart swelled with
warmth. And then I read:

What are those teeth? Didn't you have toothpaste in
the 20th century?

I felt like someone had slapped me.

Miss Lilly pulled the slate away from me and said, "You
see? People are excited to have you back."

"They said I have horrible teeth."

"One person, Laura – a troll. Everybody else said lovely
things. I'll get that comment removed."

"A troll?"

"Not an actual under-the-bridge troll. A bored idiot being
mean for the sake of it. Take no notice."

I knew it shouldn't matter what a stranger said. But it did.

"Seriously, Laura, internet trolls are just trying to get
attention. Ignore it. There is nothing wrong with your teeth.
You know, I think we should take a trip out, to Brighton
maybe? We could do a bit of old-fashioned shopping. It's
probably a good idea, before you go to school, to spread your
wings a little. Why don't we go tomorrow? I'll clear my
schedule for the afternoon."

I scooped up Batfink and held her close. I had mixed feelings about facing the world beyond the clinic and this apartment, but I knew I had to do it. I couldn't put it off for ever.

I nodded.

I didn't sleep much that night. Batfink wanted to sleep under the covers with me. Between nightmares of squashing her and of arriving at school with everyone pointing and laughing at my teeth, I felt pretty horrendous the next morning. Batfink woke me up by patting my cheek and meowing in my face until I got up.

"You're as bad as Pickle Cat-Chops," I said, surprised to find the memory of our old cat didn't come with a bolt of hurt.

I put on my new black jeans with my actual, genuine, original-article *Choose Life* T-shirt. My legs were aching from all the walking I'd done the day before, but I knew from cross-country that the more I did, the stronger I'd get.

Batfink didn't want to be carried, preferring to tumble down the stairs and give me a minor heart attack.

There was a cat litter tray in the kitchen and by the time I caught up with her, she was already using it.

"Clever Batfink."

I rooted around in the cupboards to see if there was any cat food. Of course there was. No supermarket-own brand for my little princess either – there was some posh-looking stuff called Organicat next to a little stack of china bowls. Someone

– Annie, I guess – had put a bowl of water down. Batfink threw cat litter all over the floor in a useless attempt to cover up her wee and then skidded over to me, demanding food.

While she was eating, I looked about for a broom to clear up her mess. One wall was decorated with large poppies. I trailed my hand over it and found a crack down the centre. I stood back and tried to work out if it was a cupboard. I spotted a small black button in the middle of one of the poppies. I pushed it and a pair of doors slid open. It was a lift. I stepped inside. There was a button to go up and two buttons to go down.

I was tempted to go down and see if there really was a bank vault for a small country down there but Batfink came hurtling in after me, followed by a small, round whirring thing that was skidding across the floor, picking up the cat litter. A robot vacuum cleaner! Batfink did not approve – she climbed up my trouser leg, her little claws digging into my skin as she scrabbled to escape. I squealed as she hit bare skin and carried on climbing, tearing a little ragged trail up my arm. I put her on my shoulder and sucked at the bloody scratch on my wrist.

But when I looked at it, there was nothing there. No mark at all. I had definitely sucked off blood – there was no way she hadn't torn my skin. There'd been no magic cream, no bandage.

A cut on my arm had healed itself in less than twenty seconds. Just like that.

chapter eighteen
LAURA

Miss Lilly had already gone to work, and Annie wasn't exactly approachable, so I didn't mention my miraculously unscratched arm to anyone and then it was time to go to physio. I didn't want to leave Batfink, but Annie said she wasn't allowed in the "clinical environment" so we shut her in the kitchen. I made Annie turn off the vacuum thing so it didn't scare her again.

We marched across to the clinic so quickly, I was almost running to keep up with Annie. The team were all waiting for me. I gave Benjie the biggest hug.

"Thank you so much. I adore my kitten."

Benjie said, "She's got an excellent pedigree. Her name is Sasha Spectacular of Saxon Princess."

"Not any more, it isn't. It's Batfink."

I nearly said something about the weird non-scratch when Benjie took my blood, but I really didn't want to be put through any more tests. It wasn't like it was a problem and really, I wanted to stop all the monitoring so I could start feeling normal again, not get them to do more. I saw Edna and Vera, who were both pretty happy with my progress, and then Mariya appeared, snapping a pair of tweezers.

"Want to tame those eyebrows, Laura?"

If I'd known waxing and tweezing my eyebrows was going to leave me with two red, puffy slugs over my eyes, I'd have said no. I mean they looked neater. Neater but more like slugs and REALLY, REALLY sore. As I gazed in the mirror, the puffiness began to disappear. Was that the same healing thing that had happened to my arm? I touched one of my brows.

"Don't rub them, Laura! They'll get infected. Here, take the tweezers and pull out any stragglers as they come through."

I took the tweezers and mumbled my thanks. I didn't feel very grateful, to be honest – I felt like she'd just punched me in the face a few times.

"Or come back and I'll do them again."

I said, "Oh look, Annie's waiting for me, I'd better go."

As I hurried to keep up with Annie's super-fast walking down the corridor, I nearly collided with someone coming through a side door. He was in a white bathrobe with a towel wrapped around his head and he was drop-dead gorgeous. Chiselled cheeks, strong jaw, brown skin, brown eyes.

"OMG!" he said. "You're Laura Henley, Ice Princess. We have got to have a selfie, my followers are going to love this."

He put his arm around me and held up a tiny slate.

Annie turned around and the look of horror on her face properly scared me. I wriggled free of his arm just as I caught Miss Lilly's scent, and she came striding towards us.

"What is going on here?"

No one said anything. It was like we'd all been caught doing something we shouldn't have.

"I think you may have taken a wrong turn, Mr Savage," Miss Lilly said. "Perhaps you could delete that image and return to the cosmetic wing? Annie, please see Central Control and find out why the door lock sequence I requested has been overridden. Thank you so much."

Miss Lilly put a hand in the small of my back and steered me down the corridor.

"I am so sorry, Laura. He's a valued client but…well, that is exactly why I didn't want you wandering around the clinic on your own."

She didn't say anything else but it was obvious she was furious. I wondered why she was so mad about it. Was he press? Had he broken her deal with them? Was that why?

Once we got back to the apartment, her mood changed completely. She seemed as excited as I was about going to Brighton. We headed out straight after lunch.

The sun felt delicious on my skin but I was disappointed with the car. I thought it might look a bit space-age, or at least a bit *Back to the Future*, but it looked like a normalish white car. It was parked in front of a wall of dark glass with a sign that said *Caution, parking plate* and had a zigzag of death running through it, like you get at an electric power station.

"Solar," Miss Lilly told me. "It's wirelessly charging from the sun. One of the few benefits of climate change."

I nodded. Yet again only half understanding what she'd said.

A burly guard was standing by. He didn't look happy when Miss Lilly told him she didn't need him to come with us.

"I would like to spend some time with Laura alone. I am perfectly capable of deciding the parameters of my own safety."

I got in the car and as soon as my bum hit the seat the car said, *"Fasten your seat belt."*

I did as I was told.

Miss Lilly said, "BN1 1EA."

"Thank you, Miss Lilly. Traffic is moderate. Journey time is approximately forty-seven minutes."

A map appeared on the dashboard and I watched a blue line snake across it, tracing a route. Miss Lilly smiled at me. I was just adjusting to the fact that she'd had a little conversation with her car, when it backed out of its space BY ITSELF.

I looked back in a panic, sure we were going to hit something.

Miss Lilly put a hand on my arm. "It's fine. This car has hundreds of sensors – it's safer than having a human in charge."

I gripped the seat, unconvinced. Not only was it driving itself and following its own map, it was also completely silent. Well, I say silent – there was no engine noise but it was surprisingly chatty, for a car.

The car manoeuvred until it faced the gateway and said, *"Estimated arrival time is 2.35 p.m. Would you like me to continue driving?"*

Miss Lilly said, "Yes."

"You are kidding me? No way. You can't, not seriously?"

Miss Lilly shook her head, clearly amused. I gripped my seat even harder as the car accelerated away.

"It's not funny."

"It is a bit funny," Miss Lilly said. "Your face is a picture. Trust me, Laura, it's completely safe."

I relaxed a bit, eventually. There was a lovely, calming smell in the car – sort of cakey with vanilla.

"So what have you decided about school?" Miss Lilly said. "Do you think you'd like to go to Whitman's?"

I shrugged. "I don't know. Do I have to?"

"No, I told you, if you want to go back to your old school, we can arrange it, but I think you'll like Whitman's. I loved it when I was there."

"I don't know anything about boarding schools. Is it strange, being away from home?"

Her face froze for a moment. "Of course, but my parents were very busy. My father established this clinic, it took up a lot of his time."

"What about your mum? Was she involved?"

"What a lot of questions."

I felt like I'd overstepped an invisible mark. "Sorry. I didn't mean—"

"Actually," Miss Lilly interrupted, "it's quite nice not to talk about business for a change. What can I tell you? I suppose Mother was my father's muse – a lot of the therapies he developed were with her in mind. Shah Jahan built the Taj Mahal to preserve his wife in death; my father wanted to preserve my mother in life. The cryogenic programme was all about her, really."

"What was she like?"

"She felt...overlooked. She was easily as clever as my father, but her beauty was always seen as more important than her brain. The aromatherapy content of our products was all developed by her – some really very complex chemistry – but while Father was alive, none of it was attributed to Mother. He called the brand *Dr Crisp's Scent Therapy*. Isn't it awful? I tried for *Scentsation*, but he wouldn't even give on that."

"How old were you then? Were you involved in the business quite young?"

"I suppose I was."

"And then you took over and ended up looking after people like me."

She smiled. "Nobody is like you, Laura."

"Really, though? There must have been others in the programme, apart from me and Alfie?"

She shook her head. "I don't think it's healthy for you to

think too much about that, Laura. Let's just be grateful we have you. Shall we put some music on? You can choose."

I grinned. "Madonna! 'Like a Virgin'?"

The car started playing and Miss Lilly joined in. "I know this one!"

Soon we were both singing and then she said, "Wait, listen, you'll love this – play Madonna, 'Vogue'."

I'd never heard the song but it was unmistakably Madonna. "I love it! Can we play it again?"

We put it on loop and Miss Lilly said, "I'm going to teach you the moves."

She started framing her face with her hands and posing as she sang. She was completely different away from work – funny and cool and relaxed. Her posing face was hilarious – I was still laughing when the car said, *"We have reached your destination. Would you like me to park?"*

Miss Lilly said, "Obviously. Yes."

The car turned into a tiny gateway in a narrow street and pulled into a space.

"Shall we?" Miss Lilly said.

We were near The Lanes. I'd been there before. It looked exactly as I remembered – a jumble of shops, too many people staring in the windows and not paying any attention to where they were going, including me. We passed a shop that specialized in vintage clothes. I was shocked to see the window display full of clothes I'd dreamed of owning before

I got ill. A dummy wore a short grey ra-ra skirt with an off-the-shoulder white T-shirt and a black studded belt double-wrapped around its hips. My cool was today's vintage.

I lingered by the window and Miss Lilly said, "We can go in if you like?"

I shook my head. I needed to work out what was cool *now*. "Can we go to the high street and see what they have there?"

She tucked my hand through her arm and said, "Your wish is my command."

As soon as we emerged from The Lanes, heads began to turn. People pointed and whispered. Miss Lilly kept a tight hold of me and then a girl about my age stuck her arm out towards us.

"OMG, Miss Lilly! I love your Super Skin – it smells so nice – will you sign my arm – I think you're amazing…" She practically pushed a pen into Miss Lilly's hand and said, "I'll get a tattoo over it so I never lose it!"

Someone else shoved between them with a small slate and held it up like that guy had done at the clinic. She took a picture of herself and Miss Lilly and showed her friend. People seemed to gather from everywhere. Then they noticed me.

"It's Sleeping Beauty!"

"It's Laura, the frozen girl."

They pressed in closer and closer, and I started to panic. Someone tugged at my hair. I twisted round. All I could see were faces coming at me and hands grabbing and clasping.

I shrank back but they were behind us, in front of us – everywhere. We were surrounded. I couldn't breathe and then, from nowhere, half a dozen huge people in suits slipped between us and the crowd.

I clung to Miss Lilly, gulping for air. Her arm was around my shoulder like a lifeline. She was apologizing: "I'm so sorry. How stupid of me. I'm so sorry."

We were shepherded back to the car by the suited people. They formed a barrier between us and the crowd that had followed. We were practically shoved into the back seat and one of the suited hulks got in the front.

Terrified, I asked, "Are we being kidnapped?"

Miss Lilly shook her head. "He works for me."

The hulk reversed the car out of the little parking space. The others held the people back but they were still there, waving scraps of paper and mini-slates. A few of them followed the car – I could see them through the back window – but eventually we were away and driving out of the city.

I said, "What…why…what…?"

I couldn't even form the question. We had just been mobbed. I stared at Miss Lilly. She wasn't just well known. She was truly, madly, properly famous. Benjie had told me, but *seeing* it, being in the midst of…*that* – it was mad.

Miss Lilly pressed her fingertips to her eyelids and said, "I'm a fool. It's been so long since I went out like that, just out, walking down the street. I'd forgotten what it was like. I thought I'd been so careful, that I'd managed the press. I forgot about people in general."

"It was like they wanted a piece of us – of you."

"I put you in danger. I am so sorry." She swallowed and her eyes welled with tears. "Do you see now though, why I think you need to be in a place like Whitman's?"

"But wherever I go people will know me, won't they? Or think they do…"

"Probably." She smiled. "But you'll have people like Giles to help. And my security team. And at Whitman's, most pupils are used to mixing with high-profile people. You won't be that unusual amongst the more elite of society."

We drove on in silence. I stared at the back of the man driving, then I realized something. "You told the guard not to come, so how did they know where we were?"

"Somebody didn't take no for an answer. I shall probably have to promote him."

I calmed down and began to feel a bit flat that our afternoon out had been snatched away.

As if she sensed it, Miss Lilly said, "Why don't we get the beauty spa to clear some appointments for us? Hair, nails, skin – the lot?"

"At the clinic?"

She nodded, smiling. "It'll be fun."

"Can they do my teeth?"

She laughed. "Okay – I can see the teeth thing is a big deal. You can have some UV lightening but no bleach. You're too young – they'd shut me down."

* * *

When we got back she said, "You go and check on Batfink while I organize everything."

Within twenty minutes we were walking into the spa. It was amazing. The walls seemed to be made of bubbles that cycled through different shades of blue. Open archways led to different areas, each with a neat white sign: *Georgian Steam Room, Infrared Room, Celestial Relaxation Room, Ice Chamber*. I stopped dead. Miss Lilly followed my gaze. Her hand flew to her mouth.

"It's not what you think! It's a beauty treatment to prevent ageing. It's not..." It was the first time I'd seen her really flustered. "You just sort of dip in the ice, it helps regenerate damaged cells. Oh, Laura, can you forgive me? I am such an idiot."

She took my hand and pulled me towards another archway. I could feel the chill curling round my legs as we passed that ice room. Who on earth would freeze themselves for a beauty treatment? Were they mad?

We walked into a softly lit area that smelled of lavender. Miss Lilly had arranged for us to have calming massages side by side. The spa was otherwise empty and the stress of the visit to Brighton slowly faded into a surreal bad dream.

My new life was so different from my old one. It wasn't just the change in time and place; it was all the craziness that went with being Laura Henley, the girl from the past. Miss Lilly smiled and held her hand out to me. I took it, so grateful that I had her to look out for me.

chapter nineteen
LAURA

Later that evening, we sat in the living room to watch the telly. There were two big white squishy sofas but we sat together, and Batfink, having flung herself around the room like a mad thing, had fallen asleep between us.

The news was on and I wondered if what happened to us in Brighton would be reported. I was relieved when it wasn't, but then the reporter said, "Finally, Stacey Flowers has defied the court order limiting her interactions with the Crisp Estate by once again applying for a freedom of information request."

They cut to a film of a woman coming out of a police station holding a slate up in front of her, completely hiding her face.

"Miss Flowers, who served sixteen years for the fire that almost destroyed Blackhurst Clinic in 1989, will appear in front of Brighton Magistrates on Monday."

I froze. My jaw dropped open and I turned to Miss Lilly,

who very deliberately didn't look at me. She stroked Batfink's head.

"What's that all about?" I asked.

"You don't want to know." Her voice caught on the words. She looked up at me, her violet eyes tremulous with tears.

"But maybe I should," I whispered. Something terrible had happened and it involved two of the only people left in the world who I cared about. I had to know.

"Please tell me."

Very softly she said, "There was a fire here. That's how I lost my parents."

"What?"

"It was arson."

"Stacey? Stacey did that?"

She pinched her lips together and nodded. I was shaking my head without even meaning to. I wanted to crawl away. How was it possible that someone I knew so well – someone I loved – could do that? Selling a story was one thing – maybe she'd been pressured into it, maybe she'd been tricked – but starting a fire where people got killed?

"Was it an accident?" I managed to ask.

"The courts didn't think so."

"But why? What was she doing here? Oh God, no... It was because of me, wasn't it? She was here because of me! Your parents died because of me."

I felt sick but Miss Lilly shook her head.

"No. Don't ever think that. The cutting edge of science has always had its critics and some are prepared to do anything to stop progress. Your friend Stacey got mixed up with a group of activists. Blame lies entirely there."

A tear landed with a soft splash on her blouse.

I didn't know what to say.

"They're like cults, those organizations," she went on. "They manipulate your thoughts to get you to do what they want. They probably used her connection to you to get your friend even more involved."

I shuddered as a memory surfaced. Stacey had once shown me a leaflet about bears being farmed for their bile. The bears were alive but they had tubes stuck in them to suck out whatever it was the farmers wanted. Stacey had been so upset and angry.

"How could people do that? We don't even need the bile! They can make, like, fake stuff that does the same job."

I agreed with her that it was grim but I wasn't thrilled when she dragged me into town to meet the people who were handing out the leaflets. I signed their petition but I didn't like them much. They were a bit, I don't know, intense. Those bear pictures haunted me for months.

Stacey, though, she'd been a zealot about it. She liked one of the guys from the group, but I thought he was a creep. That had fizzled out after a while, but maybe she stayed involved with the group. Maybe it was them who attacked Miss Lilly's clinic?

Miss Lilly said, "I admire people with conviction, but their methods…" She bit her lip.

The worst thing was I could imagine Stacey getting

caught up in the drama, the passion – especially if she was angry about what had happened to me.

I said, "I'm so sorry."

Miss Lilly smiled sadly. "It was a long time ago now. There's no point in being bitter. Apart from losing my parents, the worst thing was the damage to the cryo-pods. So many failed in the heat. It was awful, so much loss. If my father had lived, he'd have been devastated. Those poor people – they'd put their trust in us and we failed them."

"You didn't fail them! You didn't start the fire."

She gave me a sad smile, full of such intense sorrow my heart ached.

"I feel like we did. My parents should have designed a better evacuation plan. The pods were too big to move and there was no way to protect them from the water used to put out the fire. The support systems crashed in almost every pod and we had no way to save the people in them. I think about it every day. You survived by sheer fluke. There was an airduct over your pod that diverted the water away. You were the only one not affected – the last link from my father, a human legacy and our last chance, Laura. I was terrified we'd fail with you too."

Like a dart through my chest, I realized what that must mean. Alfie died because of that fire. Because of what Stacey, or at the very least her activist friends, had done. The horror must have shown on my face, because Miss Lilly said, "I shouldn't have mentioned anything. I've ruined our lovely evening."

My jaw was so tight with anger I had to force the words out. "No. I had to know. And you have to know, you are not to blame. None of it was your fault."

I hugged her and we cried together. I didn't know what to think about Stacey. It should have been utterly unforgivable, but I couldn't quite believe she'd have deliberately done anything to hurt either of us. I needed time. Maybe I needed to talk to her.

Miss Lilly patted my back gently and said, "Well, I sure know how to put a downer on a day."

I sat back and wiped the tears from my eyes. She was so kind. So generous. And we shared so much history. What had happened had cost the lives of her family and mine. I wouldn't let it ruin anything else.

There was a celebrity dance show on the telly. I pointed at the screen. "Okay, subject change. How many of those people have been here?"

She laughed out loud. "Pretty much all of them! See her in the silver tassels? How old do you think she is?"

I shrugged. "Twenty-five?"

"Forty. She's one of mine."

"No way."

She winked. "Way. Tummy tuck, rib removal, butt lift and so much stuff to her face I've lost track. She's actually an ambassador for our skincare range."

"Wow."

"It's the product range that made us famous really – skincare, scented candles, aromatherapy oils."

"What is aromatherapy exactly?"

"When you use certain scents to help your mood."

"Is that why it always smells so good around here?"

She smiled. "We have an entire wing for celebrities who are suffering burnout, addiction, stress, that kind of thing. It can help keep you calm. Anything that aids their recovery is important."

"Who was the man I met in the corridor?"

"A minor celebrity who I suspect was deliberately planted here to try and get some footage of you. He won't be returning."

"I've caused you a whole lot of trouble, haven't I? You've been so kind to me, letting me live in your house and everything. I don't know how I'll ever repay you."

"You repay me every day you get better. You've been part of my life for so long, silently waiting to be cured and revived – there hasn't been a day when I didn't think about the moment I'd be able to talk to you. I can't begin to tell you what you mean to me. In a way, you are the only family I have. Believe me, Laura, you have nothing to repay."

In lots of ways, that evening marked the beginning of my new life. The apartment began to feel like home and the days passed quickly in a blur of clinic visits, playing with Batfink and sessions with Giles trying to teach me how to use Instagram. One day we put a picture up of me smiling with my new UV-whitened teeth. I hoped I'd get loads of nice comments and I did – but one person wrote, *Nice try, Tombstone Teeth* and my new-found confidence was ripped from under me. After that, I only let him put up pictures of Batfink. She always got lovely comments.

In the evenings, I watched movies with Miss Lilly to fill what she called "gaps in my cultural knowledge". Some of them were quite good. I liked *Forrest Gump* (I loved how he just kept going even when things were so confusing – maybe *because* things were so confusing) and *The Martian* (bit of a theme here; that guy just wasn't going to die however bad it got) and *More of Me* (yeah, yeah, same again; that girl had an even weirder history than me). In return, I made her watch *ET*. I couldn't believe she'd never seen it. When it got to the classic line from the film, I insisted we pressed our fingertips together and croaked, "Phone home."

Those evenings on the sofa were the closest I came to contentment. I knew they weren't going to last, that I'd be going off to school, and it gnawed at my insides. One night, as if she'd read my mind, Miss Lilly said, "I'm going to miss you when you're at Whitman's."

I'd never actually agreed to go there, but it seemed like somewhere along the line I'd just accepted it. And I was going to miss her too. And my team. And Batfink.

"I'll call you," I said.

"You'd better." She held up her finger for me to press. Together we said, "Phone home…"

chapter twenty

LAURA

The morning we left for school, Benjie came to the apartment to remove the cuff from my arm.

"Promise to report to the school nurse so she can keep an eye on you."

"I promise."

My arm felt naked without the cuff. It was a bit scary – the beginning of doing things on my own. Miss Lilly seemed to understand. She'd helped me painstakingly choose my outfit – denim shorts, baggy white T-shirt tied at the waist – all pretty plain and anonymous. I hugged Batfink within an inch of her life and gave detailed instructions to Annie on her likes and dislikes. The car was packed, I'd said my goodbyes, there was nothing else to do but leave.

Miss Lilly and I sat in the back with two security people in the front. She wasn't risking any kind of repeat of our last outing.

In no time we were passing through the streets of Brighton

and driving along the coast. The sun burned white off a flat calm sea as the school I'd seen on the internet appeared on top of a cliff up ahead. In real life it still looked like a giant block of vanilla ice-cream with a caramel-wafer roof.

As we approached a pair of large ornate metal gates, I spotted a couple of photographers outside.

"How did they even know we'd be coming today?" Miss Lilly said. "I deliberately didn't bring you on the first day of term." She reached for my hand.

The driver slowed as if unsure what to do.

Miss Lilly was firm. "I'll deal with them later. Just drive, the gates will open for my car."

The photographers pushed their cameras up against the car's tinted windows, but they didn't follow us in as we drove through and the gates slid shut behind us. The road snaked round to a car park.

Miss Lilly patted my hand. "Come on then. Let's get you sorted."

The second we stepped out of the car, a warm wind whipped round us and my hair was thrown about my face. I caught as much of it as I could in my hands and held on to it.

"I should have warned you about the wind!" Miss Lilly called. "Annie has packed plenty of hairbands in your trunk."

It was all I could do to stay upright as I followed her across a courtyard and towards a large wooden door. She rang a bell and a smiling woman answered.

"So lovely to see you, Miss Lilly. Come in, it's a bit brisk today! This must be Laura?"

I nodded.

"We're delighted you've chosen Whitman's. The girls are very excited to meet you – Miss Lilly is an inspiration to them. Any ward of hers will be welcome here."

A shiver of panic rippled through me. My relationship with Miss Lilly might just as easily make me a target. I could already imagine the comments: *"Think you're special, do you? Well, you're nothing special here."*

"Laura?"

I snapped back to the moment. "Sorry?"

"Please take a seat while I let your housemistress know you're here," said the woman, indicating a pair of velvet armchairs under a wooden panel covered with a list of names painted in curly gold lettering. Miss Lilly's name was right at the top: *Miss Lilly Crisp, Benefactor.*

She put a hand on my arm. "You're going to love it."

I smiled weakly. This place was so different from everything I'd known – how could I possibly fit in?

I looked around. It was beautiful. Stone steps led up to a hallway with a gleaming wooden floor. There was an old wooden staircase too. You'd think all that wood would make it gloomy but the whole place shone. It didn't even smell like a school – no old gym shoes and cabbage. It smelled of furniture polish.

I felt odd, like I was outside myself, watching things happen to some other Laura. My old school was made of concrete and plastic. It was loud; full of life and noise. This was the opposite. This was calm and sort of…homely.

A door creaked open somewhere and I heard footsteps. Two girls – one very tall with super-straight shiny black hair, and one very short with Afro hair pulled into a pair of fat bunches – were coming down the staircase, deep in conversation. I watched them round the bottom of the stairs, oblivious to everything but each other. They looked nice. I craned my neck to see where they'd gone. With a little jolt of shock, I realized I wanted to follow them. Life flickered inside me. I wanted to be part of this place. I wanted them to accept me.

I hadn't expected to feel like this…like, I don't know, a bit excited.

The instant I realized it, I felt guilty. Alfie would never have this. Never have the chance to make new friends, to learn new things…

The front door opened and a blast of sea air whipped through the hall. The security people who'd driven us here lugged in my trunk. I stood up to help but a voice behind me said, "Laura Henley?"

I swung round.

A pale girl, with hair the colour of dried grass and a smattering of freckles across her narrow face, thrust a hand towards me. "I'm Marsha. I couldn't wait for Madam, had to come and meet you for myself. We're so thrilled you chose Whitman's."

She had a strange accent, Russian or something. I shook her hand. She was tall, nearly a foot taller than me.

"Hello," I said, trying to look her in the eye like Ima had

taught me. "Are you in my year?"

"And your house – we're in Blue. It's the best for all-rounders."

She beamed at Miss Lilly. "I hope you don't mind me saying, Miss, the girls all love your new range for teens. The spot cream is incredible."

Marsha was blushing and respectful to Miss Lilly, not at all like those mobbing people in the streets.

"Thank you, Marsha," Miss Lilly said, standing up. "It's lovely to meet you. I trust you're going to look after Laura in the true spirit of Whitman's?"

Marsha nodded. "Of course. We were all new once."

Miss Lilly laughed her tinkling laugh. "Indeed we were."

Marsha spotted my trunk. "That is huge," she said. "But we can manage it from here, can't we, Laura?"

I nodded, not at all sure that I could lift it, but determined to try.

Marsha said, "Goodness knows how we'll fit it in your room. Oh well, we'll shove it in somehow. Let's go, shall we? Is that okay?" she asked Miss Lilly.

"Absolutely. Oh, Laura, I almost forgot – here."

She handed me a small paper bag with a ribbon handle. "Mobile phone, my number's in it – one of the girls can show you how it works."

Marsha picked up one end of my trunk as a stocky woman in a tweed suit paced briskly towards us.

"Well done, Marsha," the teacher said. "Always one step ahead. Keep it up."

Marsha raised her eyebrows at me as the tweedy woman offered me her hand.

"Madam Hobbs, housemistress. Heard so much. Lovely." Then, turning to Miss Lilly, "We can handle the paperwork while Marsha settles Laura in, yes?"

Miss Lilly nodded.

"Excellent. Say your goodbyes then, Laura, and Marsha can marshal you!"

She handed Marsha a key, which disappeared into her blazer pocket. Miss Lilly swept forward and kissed my cheek.

"Look after Batfink."

"Of course."

I smiled. "Thank you, for everything."

I didn't want her to leave. Over the last few weeks we'd become really close. She was the nearest thing I had to a parent now. I hovered between her and Marsha.

"It'll be okay, I absolutely promise." She caught me in a quick hug, her lovely scent wrapping round me. "I'll see you soon," she said. "It's exeat in a couple of weeks. Perhaps you could come home? Bring a friend if you want to."

"Exeat?"

"School-speak for a weekend off."

Marsha sighed. "People with families who care love exeat. Maybe I go shopping. Come on, let's take this monster to Blue House and I'll show you where everything is."

She started dragging my trunk so that I had no option but to grab the other end and follow her. It was a struggle to hold the weight but I wanted to manage. I wanted this different life and the hope it seemed to offer.

With one last look back at Miss Lilly, who smiled and waved, I followed Marsha down the world's longest school corridor.

"This is the world's longest school corridor," she said, and a tiny laugh escaped me as she voiced my thoughts.

She looked over her shoulder at me. "It really is. I think. Maybe it's just something they say to gullible new girls." She stopped and said, "That's not a poke, a dig, whatever you call it. We were all new girls once."

"When did you start?" I asked as she began walking again.

"Last term. I didn't want to come. I loved my school in Russia, but now I love it here."

I had been right about the accent, but it was hard to believe she'd only been at Whitman's a few months. "Last term? You seem so at home."

She stopped again, this time in front of a blue door. "It took a few days to settle in." She pushed some numbers into a pad by the door and then shoved it open. "Code is so easy it's pointless: 2222. I don't know why they don't get facial recognition like normal people. They put me in Red House at first but it was full of drama scholars. I couldn't take all the flouncing about. Here, I like."

Through the door was a narrow hallway, thickly carpeted in blue. Lots of tiny rooms sprouted off it all the way down.

"These are study rooms; we share them. And this... Let me just put this down before my arm drops off."

She rested my trunk on the floor and opened a door.

The room beyond was like an old library with a long table down the middle. The back wall was a giant photograph of library shelves.

"Junior Prep Room," Marsha said briefly, before picking up the trunk handle again. "Right, last stop before I take you up to your room – in here." She pushed open another door on the left. "This is the ODR, Ordinary Dining Room. It's just been decorated – nice, isn't it?"

It was a kitchen. A big stone fireplace, lined with blue flowery tiles, filled most of one wall. A couple of pale blue rocking chairs sat by it. A long counter, with a sink and a hob, ran in front of a wall of shelves stacked with mugs and plates and cookery books. It was laid out so you could stand behind it and face the room. Pale oblong tables with chairs in different shades of blue were arranged in front of it. It was like a giant family kitchen.

"Is this where we eat?"

"Only breakfast, tea sometimes, if there's a house birthday. I'll show you the main dining room later. We hang out here quite a bit though."

"Where is everyone now?" I said.

"Oh, there's a 'getting to know you' trip on for the start of term. They've all gone to the Zenathon Aerial Park. You should have had a message about it before you started? I usually TouchTime with my boyfriend on Sundays so I didn't go."

TouchTiming didn't sound like a thing that should be allowed in a boarding school. Marsha read the look on my face and burst out laughing.

"Oh no no! Not that. I forgot, sorry. Okay, so we know about you being from the past, obviously. But we've also been briefed. Madam Bentley totally made an entire history lesson about what happened to you. I guess you've got some stuff to catch up on in this century – TouchTime is like FaceTime but, you know, more real. We're not supposed to use it."

I said, "And FaceTime is?"

"Oh Lord!" She laughed. "You've a whole new language to learn. You'll be nearly as bad as me when I started here only speaking schoolgirl English. Come on, let's go to your room."

I followed Marsha upstairs. I liked her. She hadn't teased me; she hadn't said anything snide about my clothes. She'd been just...ordinary. She reminded me a bit of Stacey. Her confidence, the slight edge of crazy. I bit my lip.

Stacey. There was the past again.

I pushed it away. I didn't want to mess things up with Marsha by being distracted and weird. I felt like I might really, genuinely, actually fit in at Whitman's. Which, given everything that had happened, seemed nothing short of a miracle.

chapter twenty-one
SHEM

The beach noises of families chattering and the sea shushing over the pebbles faded into a single whooshing noise in my ears. I was frozen where I was, unable to decide which way to run.

"This is my dad!" The little kid's voice cut through my panic. His dad was big enough to block out the sun. "I told him you were sad."

"I'm not sad," I managed to say.

"Yes you are. You got tears."

"I'm not sad, all right." I swiped away any possible wetness near my eyes.

"Are you sure you're all right, sonny?" the dad said. "You look like times have been a bit rough."

My mouth was doing a weird puffing thing as I tried not to cry. "I'm not a vagrant."

He held up his hands in surrender. "Sure, sure, whatever. You look like you could do with a bit of help, that's all. Nice dog. So, do you?"

"What?"

"Need some help?"

I looked around again and there they were, the same two dudes from earlier, coming from different directions but both heading towards me, totally out of place on the beach in their suits. I glanced at the dad. He didn't look like one of them, but maybe he was undercover or something.

Could you take a kid with you to do undercover work?

I didn't know what to think. My heart was sending blood to my head so fast my brain was pounding with it.

"You can trust me. I promise."

I knew I couldn't trust anyone. I knew it, but I wanted so badly for someone to help me, so I said, "Some people are following me. They said something about vagrancy laws but I'm not a vagrant, I'm just…"

The man said, "Jeez, I heard about that on the news. I didn't think… Okay, look, come and sit with us and we'll work out what we can do to help."

"I can't give you anything. I've got no money." Which was a bit of a lie; I still had the library lady's money.

"I don't want your money, son," he said, but he wasn't looking at me now – he'd seen the two men closing in on us. "Ah," he said, "I see."

He was going to change his mind. Why get mixed up in my mess? Or he'd hand me over. I tensed, ready to run but not knowing which way to go except towards the water. Could I swim for it with Scrag?

The dad-man put an arm around my shoulder. I almost bolted then, but the kid had got between me and Scrag and I couldn't go without my dog.

I let him steer me back to their spot on the beach, all the way trying to work out my escape. The mum looked up. She was plump and pretty and looked exactly like I thought a mum should look. She said, "What's all this then?"

Dad-man said, "Tobes was right, he is sad. Getting some hassle because of the new vagrancy laws."

"I'm not a vagrant."

"Of course you're not," said the mum. "Sit down, you can share my towel. Do you want a sausage roll?"

"I want an ice cream," said the little kid.

I sat down because I didn't know what else to do. I thought it unlikely the three of them were going to bundle me into a van. Scrag tipped his head on one side as if to ask me what I was doing. Then he yipped and lay down next to me.

"What's your story then, young man?" the dad said.

"Pleeeeease can we get ice cream. I'm meeeeeelting," the boy said. He was pretty funny. And pretty small. Small enough to pick up and kidnap. I looked at the mum and dad, smiling so kindly at me. How could they just let their kid wander up the beach close enough for them pigs chasing me to talk to him?

Close enough for them to snatch him.

I scanned the beach again. They were still there, standing, watching, dark blots amongst the holidaymakers. Trapping me.

The mum handed me a sausage roll. My stomach growled. "Thanks."

Without thinking, I broke it in half and shared it with Scrag. Instead of being annoyed, the mum gave a whole one to my dog and another one to me. Tears snuck up my throat again, making it impossible to swallow. I shoved the second sausage roll in my pocket. The little kid got up and went to wander off again. I said, "Don't…" and looked up the beach, searching for the men. The dad caught hold of the little boy's hand and followed my gaze.

I said, "Just…you should be careful."

He nodded and said to the boy, "Toby, stay here. We'll get ice cream before we leave, I promise." Then to me, "Have you got somewhere to stay? Can we drop you off?"

Lumpy sobs were properly threatening to come out of my mouth. I rubbed the stump of my arm against my eye. I didn't know what to do – these people didn't fit what I knew. Bert had always told me you shouldn't trust anyone, but the library lady had given me money, just given it, without asking for nothing. And these people, they weren't ignoring me, they weren't chasing me, they weren't shouting at me.

Could I trust them? Just a little bit?

More than a decade of only ever relying on Bert was hard to shake off but he wasn't here and I was so tired – to lean on someone else was so tempting.

If I could just get a bit ahead of the men, maybe I'd be okay. I'd got rid of the phone, surely that would lead them miles away. The plan to get back to my shed, check it was safe and lie low for a couple of days seemed the best I had. I wasn't used to asking for help though.

I sort of coughed out, "Can you give me a lift? It's not far." If they just dropped me off near the end of my road, I could go the back way, make sure no one saw me.

He nodded. "Why don't we head off now, get Toby his—"

The little boy leaped up. "Ice cream! Ice cream!"

"All right, you little terror, we'll get ice cream."

I picked up Scrag and stayed close to the family as we walked up the beach. They stopped for ice cream. They offered me one, but I was too nervous to eat and you couldn't keep ice cream for later.

The men were slowly heading towards us but cautious now, less cocky. Was it because they thought they'd made a mistake? Got the wrong kid? That I couldn't be homeless because I was with a family? My exhausted brain was spinning out paranoid thoughts like a candyfloss machine. By the time we got to the car, my heart was hammering. I was as certain as I could be that the family weren't going to kidnap me, but I'd never been in a car. Or any kind of vehicle. Ever.

The mum said, "Hop in the back with Toby. I'll drive – you can give us directions as we go."

I tried to swallow down the panic churning in my gut. But a glance back told me we needed to move. I said, "They're getting in their cars. They're going to follow us."

The dad said, "Maybe I should go and speak to them, Shirl? Find out what they want with the boy? Seems a bit out of order to be hounding him on the beach when he's not even sleeping rough?"

I scrabbled for the door handle. "No. No! Bert said – I can't, don't – I shouldn't have…"

"Hey, hey," the mum said, "it's okay. Ted, let's drive around and see if they follow?"

I said, "You could get in trouble. Why are you doing this? Why are you helping me?"

"Good idea, Shirley," said the dad. Then, to me, "Because, believe it or not, I was homeless once. Everyone deserves a chance. The new laws were meant to get people like you back on your feet, but from what I've heard, the conditions are worse in the detention centres than they are on the street. Strap yourself in."

The little kid showed me how to attach a strap across my chest but there wasn't one for Scrag. I tucked him under mine and he licked my face before laying his head against my chest.

We drove about for a bit, me clinging to the seat, looking constantly behind, feeling sick.

After a while, the dad said, "Looks like they've given up. They must have thought you were with us. I think you'll be all right now, son. Where do you want us to drop you?"

"Are you sure they've gone?"

He looked again. "As sure as I can be."

I reckoned we were about ten minutes' walk from my shed. "Here will be fine," I said. "Thank you."

The mum stopped the car. I double-checked there was no one after us. The dad pulled out his wallet and offered me twenty quid. I wanted to say no, that they'd done enough, but I never knew when I was going to need cash so I took it. I couldn't look him in the eye as I said, "I'll pay you back."

"Don't worry about that. Just pay it forward someday, okay?"

I nodded. "Thank you."

The little kid had fallen asleep, ice cream all over his face. I said, "Those men talked to him. You can't trust no one. Don't let him wander so far."

"Point taken. Look after yourself now."

I was careful heading back and I did a last check before lifting the loose panel of fence to get into my garden. Nothing seemed to have been disturbed. If they'd tracked the phone here, surely they'd already have come? I opened the shed door carefully. Hot air wafted out, but there was no evidence of intruders.

Scrag trotted in and lapped greedily at his water. He obviously couldn't smell anything strange. I locked and bolted the door. It was baking inside. Not a lot of sun came through the window but it beat down on the roof and warmed the shed up like an oven. I dolloped out the tin of food I'd got Scrag earlier. He licked up every scrap and farted loudly as he rolled on his back.

"That stinks, you little pig," I said, tickling his full belly.

I started to calm down a bit. I was as sure as I could be that no one knew I was inside. I pulled out the box where I kept my tools and set to work on a little pecking bird I'd been making. The tools weren't great but I liked how my hand fitted where Bert's once had. I kept them clean and sharp, just how he'd taught me.

The smell of wood shavings always made me think of Bert, before he got ill. I mean really ill, not just the booze. He'd taught me how to make different things – automata, he called them, mechanical toys. And he'd told me which stallholders would buy what. There was a woman with a shop under the arches who liked the pecking birds. I made other things too – turnips that you pulled out of the ground with a winder, tiny figures with hearts that beat when you turned a handle.

Scrag came over and settled down beside me, snuffling in my lap until he found my stumpy arm, his favourite thing to lick. It always made me laugh – I couldn't help wondering if he secretly wanted to gnaw on it like a bone. I pulled him close, rubbed his ears and buried my face in his scraggy head.

"Dog: one – Loneliness: nil. We're all right, aren't we, boy?"

And we were. In that minute we were just fine.

That's what my head said anyway. My stomach was a knot of coiling snakes.

chapter twenty-two
LAURA

Marsha pushed open the door to my room and handed me the key.

"You won't need it," she said. "No one locks their door."

We dragged my trunk in. The room was smallish but nice. A built-in desk stretched from one wall to the foot of a narrow bed. A window looked out onto a glittering sea – it had those little diamonds of glass you can fake with stickers. These were real though, and held together with lead like a crystal jigsaw. It was beautiful.

It was also way too hot and stuffy. I opened the window and the breeze nearly snatched it from my hand.

"Whoops!" Marsha said. "Here…" She tucked a shoelace someone had tied to the handle of the window over a hook in the stone frame. "If you let the wind catch it and it smashes…" She drew a finger across her neck and made a cutting sound. I closed the window, worried it might break, but it had already let in a huge gulp of fresh, salty air. The smell reminded me of holidays with Mum, Ima and Alfie, but instead of tripping me up, Vera's therapy kicked in.

Touch the desk. Smell the sea. See the top of Marsha's head as she bends over my luggage.

I held it together, determined to impress the girl who'd volunteered to help me settle in. No one wanted a blubbing crybaby for a friend.

Marsha opened my trunk and put my blazer on the bed with my slate and Mariya's bag of toiletries next to it. She handed me Vera's book and the pasta-framed picture without a word and started hanging my clothes in the wardrobe. When she got to a long fluffy black thing, she squealed. "I have this exact same onesie. I can't wait for winter – we can wear them together!"

I hadn't noticed it in there. It looked like a rabbit costume. It even had a hood with big floppy ears.

"Really? It's like a giant Babygro," I said, and immediately felt my face go scarlet. Now she was going to think I was horribly rude and an idiot who knew absolutely nothing about fashion.

"Don't stress, loads of people have onesies."

I hoped she was right.

She said, "You'll be okay, you know. Honestly, hardly any girls really hate it here. Come on, if we close the lid, I think we can stand this sideways in your wardrobe."

She tried, and succeeded, in upending my trunk, which we managed to manoeuvre into the cupboard. She shut the door with her bum, then opened it again, tore a sweatshirt from one of the hangers and flung it on the floor.

"That's better. It was way too tidy."

She stood with her hands on her hips and nodded. "Job done, I think. Come on, the others will be back from Zenathon soon. Let's wait in the ODR and surprise them."

I was beginning to feel like I was *properly* defrosting and it wasn't just because the sun was beaming into my little room and heating it up like a sauna. Meeting Marsha felt like the beginning of a friendship. A real friendship.

In the ODR, she put the kettle on. "English tea?"

I nodded. "I'll make it, if you like? Just show me where everything is."

"Oh just root around. You'll learn better that way. Cups are on the shelves. I'll have peppermint, that black stuff is disgusting."

Marsha was so easy to be around. I didn't feel like I was invading her space or anything. She said, "So, are you disappointed we're not all wearing spacesuits?"

I burst out laughing. A proper laugh. It felt good. "Yeah, I guess I am a bit."

I slid her tea towards her. She turned the tap on from the wrong side of the counter, splashed some cold in it then took a sip before saying, "You've got to admit we have better computer games than you. I've seen PAC-MAN."

I smiled. "I haven't seen any of your games but I like YouTube, that's pretty cool. Do most people have computers?"

She nearly spat her tea over me. "You're kidding me?"

I felt my face turn red again. "So most people…"

She tipped her head to one side and said, "Right. You weren't kidding. You have many things to learn, my friend, but fear not, I" – she put her hand on her heart and bowed her head – "volunteer for this difficult task." She looked back up. "I can pretend I'm clever for once. Tell you what, I'll answer one of your questions and you can answer one of mine? So yeah, everyone has a computer – I mean, literally everyone – apart from the anti-tech weirdos. You can't really live without one. Okay, my turn, what was it like waking up in a different century?"

Her face was so openly curious, I just answered straight away: "Weird. Scary. It wasn't the different-century thing – I didn't even know how much time had passed when they first brought me round. It was the confusion. I couldn't remember anything. I didn't know where I was. I didn't know *what* I was."

"You didn't remember anything?"

I shook my head. "Not then. It came back slowly…"

Marsha bent down so her head was lying on the counter and she was looking up at me. "Do you think it's weird? What your parents did? Freezing you like that?"

I stopped for a moment, unable to speak. They'd been desperate. They had no choice.

Marsha said, "Sorry. I didn't mean to offend you. I am a little too direct sometimes. My parents are completely selfish so I assume everyone's are. Maybe yours were lovely. Maybe you had Mr and Mrs Christmas."

I took a deep breath and said, "*Ms* and Ms…"

She shrugged a *whatever* shrug. It seemed like Benjie was right: people really didn't care about that stuff any more. I had that feeling again, of letting go just a tiny bit.

She slurped her tea, her eyes sparkling. "So, tell me, did you have a *special* friend? Hey, how did you even flirt with people if you didn't have the Cupid app? Oh my God, did you write, like, actual letters? That's a cool idea! I could do that. I wonder if Yuri would even open one – he'd probably think it was a bill. Or a bomb. A love bomb."

She was laughing at her own joke when the door opened and a sudden rush of feet and chatter filled the room. Girls aged from eleven to eighteen poured in, along with a giant stuffed chimpanzee and an enormous orangutan.

"The peace is shattered once more," Marsha said, swinging off her seat with a twirl. She clapped her hands. A few heads looked her way but they were clearly all abuzz with their trip, so Marsha picked up her chair and banged it down hard and repeatedly on the floor.

A teacher piped up. "Marsha! That floor is new. Housekeeping will brain me if you damage it."

"Sorry, Madam," she said, sounding anything but sorry. "But look – new girl, well, old girl if you like. It's the girl from the past!"

Everyone turned to look at me. I forced myself to smile. A tall, wide girl with reddish-coloured fuzzy hair – the kind that could be tamed into ringlets if someone showed her how – came towards me. People moved apart to let her pass and, with a sinking feeling, I recognized the type. This was the girl who'd give me trouble if she decided she didn't like me. Or if I was a threat to her. Or… I didn't have time to think about any more "or"s, because Marsha wrapped the girl in her arms and somehow, despite the difference in their sizes, managed to lift her off the floor.

"I missed you, Suki-Pops. I should have come, you were right. Did you buy me a present?"

"Put me down, you crazy Russian!"

"Only if you have Creme Eggs."

"You are squeezing the breath out of me. Right pocket."

Marsha put her down and stuck her hand in the girl's pocket as the girl introduced herself to me: "Suki Phillips. Netball captain. Do you play?"

"Erm…a bit."

"Excellent, try-outs tomorrow. Right then, tea everyone?"

And that was it, no trouble at all. They acted like I belonged. I came from a different world, a different century, but I felt like I might fit in better here than I ever could have hoped.

chapter twenty-three
SHEM

I must have fallen asleep because I snapped awake when rain started hammering on my shed roof. I sat bolt upright, my heart racing. There was a wet patch on my sleeping bag. I thought Scrag had peed on it until water splashed onto my skin. The roof must have shrunk in the heat, cracked enough to let rain in. A bolt of lightning lit up the shed and then tumbled it into darkness with a rumble of thunder. The rain beat down even heavier. Scrag whimpered and huddled close. I put my arm over him while I tugged my sleeping bag away from the drip.

Another bolt of lightning cracked across the sky, sending fingers of bramble shadows clawing across my sleeping bag. I hugged Scrag closer.

"It's all right, lad. It's only a bit of lightning."

Only that wasn't all it was. As the lightning faded, a thin beam of light remained, probing its way into my shed. Searching.

"No!" I scrambled out of my sleeping bag and backed against the wall.

Someone pushed the end of a torch against the window. I pressed myself as far into the wall as I could. The light moved away but then whoever was out there rattled the door.

No, no, no.

They'd found my shed. They'd found me.

chapter twenty-four
LAURA

Once everyone was back, we went to the main dining room. We lined up before a stack of glass lockers dispensing plates of roast chicken, mashed potatoes, peas and gravy. My mouth watered. Then I noticed a column of lockers labelled *Special Menus*. My name was on one of them. I lifted the flap. Banana C-plan and a bowl of pureed peas.

"Mmmm, bogies for your tea. Yum," Marsha said.

I shook my head. It was weird, how comfortable I felt with her. Maybe it was because she was displaced too. I mean, she'd come here, not knowing anyone, and had had to settle in and get on with it. They all had, I supposed, at some time or another. Maybe that made them more accepting?

Curious eyes followed us as we walked across the hall to find a table.

"Keep your sticky noses out," Marsha said to no one in particular. "She's not an alien."

I kind of was though.

She nodded at a table with just two girls at one end. They must have been around eleven, judging from their pigtails and tininess. They looked at me, got a glare from Marsha, and turned their attention back to their food.

Marsha said, "This will be the worst bit. Answer all questions as best you can or they'll start with some mild torture – you know, pulling out your fingernails or something – before they work up to the really mean stuff: teddy-bear kidnap, drawing willies on your luggage."

"They'd have to get at my luggage first."

"That's true," Marsha said, laughing. "I did wedge it in, I am queen wedgier."

I was ridiculously pleased that we had a tiny private joke. The mark of friends.

Suki came and sat with us. "Please tell me that's not some fad diet?" She nodded towards my C-plan.

I shook my head. "I can't eat properly yet – my stomach doesn't like it."

"Thank heavens for that. All that diet nonsense is ridiculous. This obsession we have with looking perfect all the time. Exercise and fresh air. That's all you need."

She sounded like a PE mistress from Enid Blyton or something. She turned her attention to her plate as if nothing else mattered.

Marsha said, "She won't speak now. Not until the sticky toffee pudding has been eaten. Food is her religion and every meal is worship."

Two more girls sat at our table – the tall girl and the short girl with bunches who I'd seen earlier. A stiff look passed between them and Marsha.

"Can we sit here?" the short girl asked.

"Free country," Marsha said.

"You're speaking to me then?" said the short girl.

Marsha shrugged.

I shuffled in my seat at the animosity crackling across the table.

The short girl put her tray down and held out her hand. I shook it. Hers was tiny. She was tiny. Even tinier close up than I'd thought before.

"Keisha Touray. And this is Susan Li."

Susan smiled, somehow managing to look up at me, even though she was about a foot taller than anyone else at the table. I was a bit relieved to see she had braces on her teeth – and I hadn't spotted as many really white smiles as I'd expected. Real life seemed to be a bit different to Blackhurst Clinic and Instagram.

I took a slurp of C-plan. Susan was still staring at me.

"You don't look nearly sixty," she said eventually.

"She's not nearly sixty, you idiot," Marsha said. "She's been frozen. Things don't age when they're frozen."

"Bet it was darned cold," Suki said, pushing aside her now-empty sticky toffee pudding bowl. "Was it darned cold, Laura?"

I tried to shrug the question off. "I was asleep."

"What about when you woke up though – you must have been darned cold then?"

I had an actual physical memory of heat in my skin, the violent shaking, the panic. I pushed it away. In that bright, chatty room, I didn't want to think about it.

"Honestly, I don't remember."

"I bet you miss your friends," Susan said.

An image of Stacey holding her bowl out to Mum for seconds of apple crumble filled my head but was swept away by Susan saying, "And those little boats in the shape of swans you have to pedal."

"What?" Marsha said.

"Pedalos!" Susan said triumphantly. "I'd miss them if I'd come from the eighties."

"We still have pedalos, Susan," snapped Keisha, before steering the conversation back to sanity, sort of. "I'd miss my friends. Did you have friends? Are any of them still alive?"

The question was so abrupt I nearly laughed.

Marsha said, "Seriously, Keisha? Just come right out with it, why don't you? I thought I was blunt. Why would they be dead, you idiot? My grandmother is a hundred and seven."

"She is not."

"She is."

Keisha stuffed a roast potato in her mouth as she said, "Isn't," and earned a scowl from Marsha.

"I bet you played loads of sport," Suki said. "You had nothing else to do back then, did you? None of this pretend sport on a slate. Proper sport. Outside, having fun, like it should be."

She stopped in shock, as if the strangest thought had occurred to her. "Did you have TV?"

"Yes," I said, laughing. "Of course we had TV. It wasn't the Stone Age!"

Keisha, who was eating so fast her plate was nearly clean, asked, "Did you have rationing?"

"No. And we didn't have plague and I wasn't alive in the war. Neither of the World Wars anyway."

Susan said, "You were alive in a war?"

I hesitated before I answered. There'd been the Falklands Campaign, but I doubted they'd even have heard of that, so I said, "No. Not really."

It didn't stop her though. "Did you know Elvis Presley?"

I said, "Sorry?"

"I knew an Elvis Presley. Not the actual singer. My piano teacher's cat."

She was the most completely random person I'd met in my whole life. It was quite reassuring to know I couldn't say anything weirder than her.

Keisha banged her knife and fork together. For a tiny girl, she could really pack her food away. "Hang on…the eighties? Isn't that when Michael Jackson did *Thriller*?"

"I love that album!" I said.

Keisha rummaged under the table and passed me a soft round button. "You know what that is, right?"

I shook my head.

"It's an earphone. Don't make a thing of it, we're not allowed phones at the table."

I pressed it in my ear and heard the creaky door, footsteps and wolf howl that was the start of 'Thriller'. A smile crept across my face. "You like Michael Jackson?"

"I love him," Keisha said, her eyes bright.

"Even if he did bleach his face white," Marsha said.

"He did not. That was a skin condition," Keisha bit back.

"Well, he's dead now so we can all forget about him," Marsha replied.

"He's dead?"

"As a dodo."

I handed the earphone thing back to Keisha with an out breath. "How did he die?" I said.

"It was ages ago. I think he was poisoned or something. Whatever." Marsha stood up with her plate and glass in hand. "I'm done. Shall we go?"

The girls at the next table watched us leave. Actually, I think most people watched us leave, but I was busy thinking about dead pop stars.

"Earth calling Laura!" Marsha nudged me in the ribs.

"What?"

"And we thought Susan was a daydreamer."

I smiled. "Sorry, been a long day."

We headed back to the kitchen in Blue House and sat chatting for a while. I was properly tired though and yawned a bit more obviously than I meant to.

Marsha said, "Why don't we all go to bed? It's nearly lights-out anyway and I want to TouchTime Yuri."

I yawned again – I really was tired. "What exactly is

TouchTime? You never properly explained."

"Just your basic hand-holding, hugging, that sort of thing, over the computer. Depends what app you have."

"You don't have TouchTime, Marsha. You're such a liar," Keisha said, catching up with us. "It's totally blocked at school."

"That's what you think. There are ways around blocks if you know how." Marsha turned to me. "Hey, you should find me on Connexions and I'll send you some links to some cool apps."

I had basically no idea what she was talking about, but I didn't feel stupid. It felt okay to say, "You'll have to show me what to do."

"I will. Tomorrow. See you in the morning. Set your alarm for seven."

"Oh, I don't have one."

"There's one on your phone."

"I…"

She shook her head with a smile. "First lesson. Give me your phone."

"It's in my room."

"Of course it is. Come on then."

Marsha came with me and gave me a quick lesson on what my phone could do. Honestly, it was amazing how much magic was packed into that tiny thing. By the time she left me, I was tired but my head was buzzing. I woke up my slate.

John Taylor's lovely face smiled at me.

"Are you dead too, John Taylor, wet T-shirt king?"

"I don't understand your question. Do you wish to search for John Taylor in a wet T-shirt?"

I hesitated for a moment… "Erm…yes?"

I spent a bit of time following links to ex-crushes, but it got a bit depressing seeing them old enough to be my grandparents. Or worse, reading about their tragic deaths. And there was a niggling temptation itching at the back of my mind. I could search for Stacey. It scared me what I might find. That picture of me and Alfie on Wikipedia had upset me enough – what if I saw a picture of Mum and Ima's burned-out car? Or worse? But I shook my head. It was worth the risk.

I got as far as, "Notitia…" when a brilliant bolt of lightning lit up the window of my room. My first thought was how much Alfie hated storms. Goosebumps danced over my skin.

chapter twenty-five
SHEM

"You gonna let us in, Shem? I've got a nice dry place for you and your little doggy. No leaky ceilings. You could be warm and fed within the hour."

I shivered, ashamed of how my knees trembled.

"You still asleep in there?" The door rattled violently as they tried again. They wouldn't have to try much harder. The hinges were rusty. I prayed they'd go away. Scrag yipped at the door.

"Come here, Scrag," I whispered urgently.

"Ah that's nice," said whoever it was. "At least your little dog has manners."

"Go away," I said through chattering teeth. "I got nothing."

Whoever it was laughed. "But you do, sunshine, that's why we've been looking for you for so long."

I wanted to puke. There was something going on here that I didn't understand. It felt bigger than the vagrancy thing, but I couldn't work it out. Part of my brain was sifting through all the stories Bert had told me, trying to make sense of who these people were, of what they wanted. Another part of my brain was in full-blown panic. I crawled forward and quietly shoved what I could in my bag. Somehow we were going to have to run for it.

"All right," said the man. "If you won't open the door, I'll have to let myself in."

Scrag growled, low and menacing. I slung my bag over my back and picked him up, his little body vibrating with the rumble coming from his throat. With a crack, the man kicked the door and it fell from its hinges, scraping my face on its way down. He filled the doorway. I could *smell* the threat coming off him. Scrag leaped from my arms, straight at him.

"Don't, Scrag!"

He had already sunk his teeth into the man's arm. The bloke shook him off. I heard Scrag yelp as he hit the floor but then he must have gone for the man's ankle, cos the pig yelled a curse and lunged sideways, kicking out and unbalancing as he did. I took my chance, grabbed Scrag and bowled out of the door, running, stumbling through the now smashed-up fence. How had I slept through that? *Not sharp enough, Shem – just not sharp enough.*

I headed to the back of the housing estate. There were woods a couple of fields away – if I could make it there, we might be safe. A sudden smell of fuel and a loud whooshing noise made me turn round. Flames filled the air. They'd torched my shed.

My home. They'd set fire to my home, my last gift from Bert. My heart squeezed – everything I had left was in there. It was the only bit of safety in my life. Why? Why do that?

I gave myself a shake. I'd already wasted too much time watching my life go up in smoke. Something changed in me – anger pulsed down my arms into my legs. I ran, blundering on until my way was lit by headlights from behind me. Blood pounded in my ears. I could hear the splash of wheels in mud but I didn't dare look back. We had to hide, but where?

I bombed across the churned-up ground but my shoes were soaked through and claggy with mud and I fell, still clutching Scrag tight to me with my good hand. I landed on my stumpy arm, folding it in half to take the impact. The ground was so wet and soggy it was like landing in a sponge. I struggled back up and fled again, trying to put as much distance between me and the vehicle as possible. It seemed to be working – the noise was getting more and more distant and when I risked a look over my shoulder they'd stopped moving. Maybe they'd got stuck in the mud. I didn't wait to see if they got out and came after me on foot; I somehow knew they would. I was knackered and soaked to the skin but I kept going.

I made it to the edge of the field, trying to blink the rain away and look about me. I couldn't see anyone following but it didn't mean they weren't. A flash of lightning lit up the posh school on the cliff, then thunder rattled through my chest. Scrag whimpered and started to shiver. The woods suddenly seemed too obvious, so I changed course, pulled my coat round Scrag and aimed for the school, hoping there'd be some kind of outbuilding we could hide in.

I almost walked right into the fence. Thick wire, eight-foot high and topped with vicious razors. I didn't have anything as helpful as wire cutters but I had an old pair of pliers with a snip blade in them. I had to put Scrag down to get them out of my bag. He huddled right up close, his little body trembling. In the dark and wet, I couldn't find a thing in my bag. My chest started to heave in panic.

"Please, just give me a break. Please."

Like a miracle, my hand closed on the pliers, but I'd taken so long. If he'd followed me, I wouldn't have time to cut through a thick fence with a crappy pair of pliers now. The heaving in my chest came out as sobs. I looked behind me and saw a triangle of light scanning the field.

Don't look up here. Please don't look up here.

I picked up my stuff – poor Scrag was soaked through – and went further round the fence, hoping I could hide behind the main school building. I stumbled on through the dark and rain, desperate, confused, angry. Scrag shivered in my arms, feeding off my fear. Once we got round the back of the school grounds, I took a last look to see where the torch was before it was out of my sight. It wasn't coming closer – he didn't know where I was. I didn't allow myself to feel any relief. I dropped to my knees, put Scrag down and set to work.

It was hard-going with one hand and a blunt blade. I had to twist the wire upwards to get enough leverage but eventually the first bit pinged free. My hand ached, I was cold and tired, but I kept going. Sometimes though, sometimes, I just wished things could be a little bit less crap.

There was another flash of lightning. Another roll of thunder. From somewhere, I found the strength to work at that fence until we could crawl through. There was the dark outline of a bell tower. Nobody would be in there at this time of night. Maybe it would be open. My stupid, optimistic brain was already imagining the safety ahead. I jogged towards it.

"Come on, Scrag, let's go get dry."

chapter twenty-six

LAURA

My mood sank as I realized Alfie would never need me to comfort him through a storm again. I heard doors opening in the corridor. There were a few giggles outside and then someone knocked.

"Laura, are you okay?"

I opened the door. My would-be rescuer was tiny Keisha.

"Let me in then."

God, she was bossy. Blunt and bossy. Actually so was Marsha. And Suki. Maybe it was a Whitman's thing.

Marsha arrived and switched off the light as she came in. "No lights or we can't see the sky. Your room has the best view in a storm. So glad you've got it instead of Drippy Issie."

They hadn't come to rescue me. They'd come to enjoy the show.

Keisha whispered, "Issie didn't like this room because of the drainpipe. She thought someone might climb up it in the night."

A flash of lightning split the sky, followed by the most enormous crash of thunder. Keisha squealed and grabbed my arm, giggling.

There was another knock at the door and I wondered where the teachers were. Were we allowed to just wander about at night? Suki came in.

"Knew you'd be in here, Marsha," she said. "Don't mind, do you, Laura? Your room has the best view—"

"In a storm? Yeah, so I'm discovering."

We huddled by the window as the room filled with a silvery flash and then plunged back into blackness. The thunderous crack that followed rattled through my chest. It was rapidly succeeded by a huge crash, much, much louder and very close.

"What was that? That wasn't thunder!" Keisha tried to turn the light on but it was dead. The power was down.

Suki said, "The tower?"

I could feel the excitement flowing from them as they dived for the door. "Come on! This'll be awesome."

Girls were spilling out of rooms, light pooling from torches at their feet. Only they weren't torches – they looked like the phone Miss Lilly had given me. I filed that one for later and followed them to the end of the corridor, where, lit by the glare of a dozen lights, stood Madam Hobbs. She shielded her eyes.

"Back to bed!"

"But, Madam, what was the crash?"

"Was it in your room? Any of you?"

As heads shook, the pools of light from the torches wobbled up the walls.

"We think it was the tower, Madam."

She turned her stare on each of us in turn. "Then you don't need to worry about it, do you? The tower won't be climbing into your beds and bothering you. Back to sleep now, please."

She softened her voice and said, "Are you okay, Laura? What a storm for your first night away from home!"

The girls filtered back to their rooms and I shut the door to mine. I felt my way to the bed and lay down, thinking of Alfie. Despite the beginnings of contentment in my heart, I'd have given anything to have held him tight and told him everything would be all right.

It broke me to know I'd never hold my little brother again. With a shock, I realized I'd never said goodbye. I didn't know where he was buried – or Mum and Ima. What kind of a person wouldn't even think to ask?

chapter twenty-seven

SHEM

The tower, the refuge I'd been heading for, was lit up by a brilliant bolt of lightning, then BOOM…

The whole thing crashed to the ground.

Ten more seconds and we'd have been dust.

I curved my body around Scrag as bits of brick pelted us. Grit filled my mouth, my eyes, my chest. I coughed and spat to get rid of it. Scrag whined and shook in my arms.

Honestly. My life was a joke. If there was any kind of god, he had it in for me.

I was stunned for a minute but the rain kept coming and we needed shelter. I skirted round the collapsed tower as the rubble settled, looking for a shed or something. Anything.

Nothing.

Soon I was trembling as much as Scrag, cold to my bones.

I tried to keep going. To keep looking.

I just…

I was so…

I felt…

Sometimes it was so hard to be me. Maybe I should have given in. Taken up that offer of a roof that didn't leak, no matter what it cost.

Scrag yipped and wriggled up to lick my face, reminding me he was there. I gave myself a talking-to. At least I had him.

I took another look around. The best bit of shelter was the dark shadow of a hedge on the far side of a field. I headed over to it and crawled in.

I was cold and wet but I was alive and I had the best dog in the world snuggled in my coat.

I said, "Who needs sleep, hey, Scrag?"

But he was already snoring those whiffly snores only a dog can do.

chapter twenty-eight
LAURA

The morning after the storm, Marsha was already in the bathroom, fully dressed and applying a thick coat of mascara when I stumbled bleary-eyed to the loo. I hadn't slept for thinking about where Alfie was buried. I finally drifted off after I decided to ask Miss Lilly the first chance I got.

"Not good with mornings?" Marsha said.

"After a night like last night?"

"Hardly Enid Blyton, is it? More like Grimms' fairy tales. Think you can find your own way to breakfast?"

"Yeah, why? Where are you going?"

"Some of us are going to the tower to see what happened last night. Come find us if you like, but don't tell Madam."

I held three fingers up in salute and said, "Guide's honour."

She crinkled her brow at me. "You say the weirdest things."

That was true. I'd never even been a Girl Guide.

I was tempted to follow Marsha, to join in, but I also wanted to avoid getting into trouble on my first school day so I went to the ODR to make tea.

Keisha was waiting for me. "I knew Marsha wouldn't wait for you," she sighed. "Shall we have breakfast here?"

I let Keisha organize me all the way to our form room. The teacher's introduction was brief: "Okay, girls, this is Laura. Some of you probably saw her last night as you were wandering the corridors not sleeping."

A ripple of laughter spread through the room.

"She's one of us now, make her feel like it."

They nodded at me, and that was it. No snarls, no glares. Nothing. I looked around for Marsha, wanting to share the moment with her, but she wasn't there.

She wasn't in our first class either, so Keisha decided to stay with me. She muttered, "Marsha's so unreliable. I don't know why they asked her to show you round. She's always sneaking off."

"How can she sneak off? Where is there to go?"

"I don't know, do I? I'm not the one doing the sneaking."

Marsha reappeared in the ODR at teatime. Keisha nearly bit her head off.

"Where have you been?"

"The health centre, not that it's any of your business."

"It's Laura's business. You're meant to be looking after her. She got completely lost this morning and was really upset, weren't you, Laura?"

"No, I…"

"I can't help having period pain, can I? Not that you'd know – you probably haven't started yours yet."

Keisha looked absolutely furious. Her bunches actually quivered with rage. I couldn't say I blamed her.

I said, "Hey, look, don't argue, okay? I'm fine. Everything is fine. Are you feeling all right now, Marsha?"

"Not that anyone cares but, yes, thank you."

Desperate to steer the conversation in a new direction, I said, "Did you make it to the tower then?"

Marsha nodded. "Do you want to see?"

Before I had a chance to stand up, she pulled out her phone and put it in front of me. Phone. Camera. Torch. Alarm clock. All there, right in your hand. I felt a weird pang of jealousy – the fun we could have had with one of those phones at my school. I literally had to pinch myself under the table. *This* was my school now. This was my reality. I had one of those phones – thanks to Miss Lilly.

I looked at the picture. The entire quad of grass was filled with rubble. Where the tower had fallen it had ripped great chunks of masonry from the surrounding walls.

"What a mess."

"I know! Isn't it awful?" Marsha said, glee in every word.

"Aren't you upset about it?"

"No, you idiot. Who doesn't love a drama?"

As I handed her phone back, it vibrated in my hand. Marsha's face dropped and she pressed the red button, ending the call without even picking it up. I must have looked shocked because she said, "What? It's my father – he'll only tell me what a disappointment I am. Want to come to my room and watch a film?"

Keisha said, "We've got prep in twenty minutes."

"You have. I've got a pass."

Marsha got up and left with a flounce. I wanted to follow her. I felt myself slipping into a familiar sense of friendship. She really did remind me of Stacey – a tiny bit wild, a tiny bit angry. It was easy to picture my life here – watching movies with Marsha, hanging on the edges of her rule breaking. In fact, it was so easy I stood up to follow her. Keisha stopped me by assuming I was heading to the prep room.

"Why not? I'll come with you – let's be early and we can get a head start."

I sighed. I really wasn't bad-girl material. I walked to the prep room with Keisha.

Two hours. Two whole hours of concentrated homework. TWO HOURS. We were allowed music if our headphones weren't too loud, but I didn't have either music or headphones. And you know what was weird? Nobody complained. They came in, plugged their tiny ear buttons in, put their phones face down on the table and worked. Solidly. For two hours.

I hadn't done that much homework in a week at my old

school, let alone a day. And every day. I'd been set some maths, stuff I hadn't managed to do in class – they were way ahead of me, even though I'd been okay at my school.

I tried to focus on the work but the numbers swam in front of me. I was surrounded by the soft patter of fingers on computers, the faint trickle of music leaking from earphones, the turning of pages – the odd sigh of despair, which I suspect came from me. I wanted to slither under the table, but in that hive of brain-bashing I was forced, at least, to try.

The clock crawled round. I got nowhere fast with the maths so I decided to have a go at my English homework. We'd been asked to write an article about why sport was good for you. I stared at the blank slate in front of me. Maybe I could write about running, about being in the cross-country team. More accurately, the round-and-round-the-school-buildings-in-the-middle-of-town team. I made some notes about why I thought it was good for me: fresh air, freedom, power, joy, speed, thinking space…

As I wrote, the urge to actually go out and run grew and grew. They had fields here. And the sea. It'd be proper cross-country. I wondered what the rules were about doing stuff on your own. I could stay in the grounds – that would be safe, surely. Would I be strong enough? My energy levels were still pretty low. But you had to start somewhere.

The door to the prep room opened and a tiny white girl handed a note to the teacher supervising us. She nodded at me.

"Call for you. House office."

chapter twenty-nine
LAURA

The receptionist handed me the phone saying, "It's Miss Lilly's personal assistant. She said it's urgent."

I put it to my ear. "Hello."

"Laura?"

I didn't recognize the voice – it didn't sound like Annie. "Who is this?"

"God, Lu, I can't believe it's you."

The voice on the other end of the line let out a weird little sob. A weird little sob that I would have known anywhere. The same weird little sob she'd made when we watched *The Color Purple* and the two sisters got separated.

My knees gave way. I stumbled against the desk.

The receptionist looked concerned. "Are you okay?"

I nodded and sat in a nearby chair. Turning my face away, I whispered into the phone, "Stacey?"

"Lu," she sobbed, "it's you, after all this time."

I didn't know what to say. All the betrayals, everything I'd been told she'd done, it all fell away. It wasn't like forgiveness – I can't even explain – just, in that moment, it felt irrelevant. I just wanted her back. I just wanted my best friend back in my life.

I burst into tears. The receptionist got up and made her way around the desk towards me.

Stacey said, "Lu, it's okay. It's going to be all right, I promise."

I couldn't speak. She said, "I can't say any more, not on the phone. I'll find a way to get a proper message to you. Oh God, I wish I was with you. Just take care, okay? Be careful who you trust."

Then she hung up. I stared at the receiver. Every instinct in me had responded to the relief of having her back, like the things she'd done didn't matter. Only they *did* matter, and I hadn't asked her about any of them.

"Is everything all right?" the receptionist asked.

I'd almost forgotten she was there. I wondered if I should tell her it was Stacey who'd called. Would she tell Miss Lilly? Miss Lilly might think I wasn't safe at Whitman's if she knew Stacey had tracked me down. She definitely wouldn't be happy about it. I said, "Yes. Thanks."

As I walked back to prep, the initial shock of hearing Stacey's voice wore off. I started to wonder about what she'd said. *Be careful who you trust?* Was there no part of her that felt the first thing she should have said was *Sorry?* Wasn't she ashamed?

* * *

They'd all gone to dinner by the time I got back. I went to the ODR and mixed up some C-plan to take to my room. What did Stacey mean? Who was she talking about? How did she know anyone at Whitman's? And if we were talking trust, what about what she'd done? I could almost find a way to justify her selling her story, and maybe even see what happened to Mum and Ima as an accident. But the fire? She knew we were in that building; she must have known she was putting our lives at risk.

How *dare* she talk to me like none of that had happened? Anger swelled inside me, until my jaw locked tight with fury.

I opened my slate.

"Notitia…" I hesitated. If I said "Stacey Flowers", would Benjie pop up in the corner of my screen to check on me? At least I had no cuff on my arm to tell him my heart was absolutely racing. I didn't want anything to interrupt me this time, so I decided to test it out first: "Find stories about Laura Henley."

"Here is what I found."

A list of articles came up, but no Benjie. I skimmed over the ones at the top – they were all about my revival. Halfway down the page was a headline: Tragic Death of Cryo-Kids' Two Mothers. I felt sick. The first line of the article was visible:

Busty black-haired beauty Isabella Henley and her long-term lesbian lover, Ima McKenzie, died yesterday in a head-on collision… Click here for the rest of the article and photographs.

I retched. There were photographs. I couldn't read it. I took deep breaths, trying to calm down. Benjie didn't appear, even though my heart was running on overdrive, so when I could speak without being sick, I took a risk. "Notitia, find Stacey Flowers."

There was still no Benjie as the list was replaced. Top of the page was an invite to find my real friends in virtual space. So not funny. I needed to know who my real friends were to do that. I scrolled down until I found a report about Stacey appearing in court. It was roughly the same date I'd seen her on telly when I was watching films with Miss Lilly. I skimmed through it.

> Stacey Flowers broke the permanent injunction
> against her designed to prevent all contact with Lilly
> Crisp of Miss Lilly Enterprises. The judge decided that,
> while this was a serious breach, there was no
> intended malice in 58-year-old Flowers' attempts to
> deliver several letters by drone to Miss Crisp's famous
> clinic, Blackhurst. Flowers has been given a
> community order and warned that if she breaks the
> injunction again, the court will have no choice but to
> return her to prison.
> Miss Lilly declined to comment but it's understood
> that she is unhappy with the judgement and is
> considering civil action.

There was a picture of the woman I'd seen on the news.

She was in a horrible grey suit and walking away from a court building. Her face was hidden by a slate but it had to be Stacey. I stared at it, wondering what she'd written in those letters. Maybe they'd been meant for me. It was possible, when she knew I'd been revived. Maybe she had tried to say sorry.

"Oh God, Stacey. What a mess."

My brain felt like it was being carved in two with a blunt bread knife. If she'd really done those things, how could I ever forgive her? And then again, how could I not?

Stacey was the only link I had with my past. Part of me wanted to give her a chance, to hear her side of the story. And part of me was so angry I wanted to forget she ever existed. Only she *did* exist and she'd called me and implied she'd get a message to me. I went back to the list of news reports.

I was so worried about coming across something I didn't want to see that I was super-careful which ones I read. Not careful enough though, it turned out. The next link I pulled up was an archive report on the fire at the clinic with live footage as it happened. Once I started watching, I couldn't switch it off. The fire was horrendous – I could hardly believe it had happened to the building I knew. Smoke billowed in grey clouds against the night sky, flames licked from every window, medical staff were all over the grounds attending evacuated patients. I turned the sound on.

"*Fire crews have been on the scene since two o'clock this morning when several emergency vehicles were deployed to tackle the blaze. We can cross live now to East Grinstead police station where the suspects are being transferred."*

"Thank you, Sarah. We believe all four suspects are from the activist group People's Action for Animals. They waited calmly for their arrest outside the building…"

Four people in handcuffs were being marched into the police station. They were all dressed in black but they held their heads up high and didn't hide their faces. They looked so ordinary: two middle-aged women who could be anyone's mum, a skinny guy, who I recognized with a jolt as the one from PAFA who Stacey had liked, and then there was a young girl with scraped-back black hair and a pale face. I leaned forward.

It was her. Stacey with no hairspray and no eyeliner. I touched the screen.

She looked like a child. Tears were streaming down her face.

"What were you thinking, Stace? What made you do it?" A hot tear rolled down my cheek and plopped onto my arm.

I didn't want to watch any more. My anger had softened into something else, something desperately sad.

I flicked away the video and my slate went back to the list of results. I hovered a fingertip over the link that asked me if I wanted to find my real friends, then I pinched it up.

Notitia said, *"You are not a registered user of Real World Connexions. Would you like me to use your stored data to register?"*

I stared at it for ages; my bottom lip wobbled. Could I bear to make contact after everything she'd done? Could

I really forgive her? I said, "No."

Then, "Wait, yes."

Before I had time to change my mind again, Notitia said, *"You are registered as Laura Henley. You are under eighteen, so you do not have access to TouchTime. All other functions are working properly. You have one contact listed. Would you like me to see if they are on Real World Connexions?"*

That contact had to be Miss Lilly.

"No," I said. "Notitia, find Stacey Flowers on Real World Connexions."

I held my breath but still no Benjie popped up to check on me. Thank God I didn't have that cuff on any more. Notitia gave me a long list of potential Staceys.

Stacey Flowers – definitely a man. Nope.

Stacey Flowers with no picture – maybe.

A blonde girl sticking out her chest and sucking in her very tiny, potentially-devoid-of-ribs stomach. Don't think so.

Then…me.

Well, me and her. Next to Stacey's name was a picture her mum had taken of us on the steps outside their flat. Stacey looked sulky, her hair was backcombed within an inch of its life and she'd got so much black eyeliner on you could barely see her actual eyes. We'd been on our way to the record shop to spy on the lad who worked there. Stace really fancied him and wasn't interesting in stopping for a photo call.

My finger hovered over the image.

Notitia said, *"Is this the Stacey Flowers you want to connect with?"*

After all this time, Stacey chose a picture of the two of us as the face she showed the world. Was it because she missed me and had never got over losing me? Or was it because she wanted to cash in on my fame? She'd done that once already, when she'd sold our story to the press. My head was a mess – anger pulsed side by side with love for my friend. I *needed* to understand why she'd done what she'd done. I needed to speak to her. I said, "Yes."

"We have sent your request."

I stared at the screen, amazed that you could find people and connect with them just like that. The future had brought things me and Stacey hadn't even imagined – and we'd imagined our whole lives. I was going to manage Topshop and have two cats and live in my own flat with all the latest stuff – video player, fax machine, leather sofa and maybe a mobile phone. I let out a snort of laughter. The mobile phones then were as big as bricks.

What had Stacey's life become? I was pretty sure she hadn't married the lead singer of The Cure. She'd always said her dream was an endless life of gigs and parties, but I knew what she really wanted was a happy family, a home, someone to love her. Did she ever find anyone who understood her like I did? Like I'd *thought* I did.

I wished I'd said goodbye properly. The last conversation we'd had, my head had been throbbing so much I couldn't see. She'd held my hand and joked that I was just trying to get Record Shop Boy to feel sorry for me. Then she'd whispered, "Don't leave me, Lu."

My heart turned inside out remembering.

How would I have felt if it had been me left behind? Devastated. Absolutely lost. Who knows how I'd have reacted? What I'd have done.

I was so confused.

I put YouTube on and, very quietly, played "The Lovecats", wondering what I was going to say when she accepted my request. I didn't doubt for a second that she would.

I glanced out of the window. It was dusk and the waves wore glints of moonlight. I opened the window, careful not to let it get caught by the wind. A cool, soft-salted breeze freshened the air. I lay down for a second, but after the night of thunder I was exhausted and I fell asleep, dreaming of the beach, and of Stacey, and of a life that felt like yesterday but was decades ago.

I woke with a start to find the sun already up and an image spinning over my slate. She'd responded.

Stacey Flowers has accepted your request.

A page of posts loaded, all about us. Birthday wishes. Christmas wishes. A lifetime of remembering our friendship. An envelope hovered over the page. I pinched it open.

Lu, I'm not sure this is safe. They say it's encrypted but I've learned to be careful. I can't resist though.

It's you, it's really you after all this time. It was so
good to hear your voice – I can't even tell you.

There was a break and then:

Are you okay? I've missed you so much – I've
practically built a career out of trying to find out what
really happened to you.
I am SO happy. No, that's the wrong word – relieved,
overjoyed, I can't believe you're alive. Really, actually
alive. Message me. Don't mention any names though.
Missed you so much, S xxx

What did she mean, what really happened to me? The
whole world knew what really happened to me. Someone
banged on my door. I quickly typed:

I can't talk now. I'll message later. There are things I
need to understand. Laura.

Marsha stuck her head around my door. "Breakfast,
sleepyhead. Didn't you set your alarm?"

I shook my head. "Give me a couple of minutes."

"What are you doing?" She peered at my slate.

I stood in front of it. "Nothing. Homework. I had to finish
my English. I was writing about running."

Don't ask me why I lied. Stacey's paranoia must have
rubbed off a bit.

"Why running?"

"I don't know. I just like it. It makes me feel good."

"Makes you feel knackered, more like."

As we walked to the kitchen I said, "Would they let me run around the playing field, do you think? The one that goes down to the sea?"

Keisha appeared and said, "Why would you want to do that?"

"Escape," drawled Marsha, yawning widely. "She wants to run away from you."

Keisha said, "You were talking to *Yuri* late, weren't you, Marsha?"

She said "Yuri" in a strange way – I couldn't quite work out what she was getting at.

"Oh do shut up." Marsha slumped at the table. "Someone make me tea."

Keisha made tea for everyone. As Marsha revived, and the kettle boiled for the second time, I asked again, "So can you? Just go running?"

Keisha said, "I should think so. Check with Madam but they'll probably be pleased."

"Oh yes," Marsha said. "They'll wee themselves to have someone vaguely sporty in the house."

"WHO'S SPORTY?" boomed Suki, who'd just bounced into the room. "Oh, you? Netball girl. Why didn't you show up for try-outs?"

I'd forgotten all about them, that's why.

"Sorry, first day and all, I didn't know where to go."

"Not to worry, always the weekend."

"Actually, I was asking about running."

"Running? Runner, are you? Oh well, can't see anyone objecting as long as you don't miss prep. Or try-outs. Right, who's coming to the dining room for porridge?"

Later, as we headed to our form room, Keisha juggled with a massive pile of books. She looked like she might keel over backwards and be squashed under them, so I said, "Here, let me help."

"No, I'm good. I promised Madam I'd get them."

"What are they?"

"Scripts. We start rehearsals today for the house play."

Marsha groaned. "You are such a suck-up."

The whole morning was spent in the drama studio and it galloped by. All the Stacey stuff was in the back of my mind, but rehearsals were very distracting. Also distracting me was Madam Call-Me-By-My-First-Name-Apple (I kid you not, her first name really was Apple) – she had the most astonishing teeth. Not only were they dazzling white, they were pearlized – they actually glistened like snow in sunlight.

I nudged Marsha. "Her teeth!"

She whispered, "And she just had her bum implants removed."

"Bum implants? Are you serious?"

"Yep, it's all about the skinny waist these days."

Madam Apple roared, "Give every man thy ear, but few thy voice!"

We stopped whispering.

Marsha turned out to be really good at drama. I don't know why she'd moved from Red House – seemed to me like she'd fit right in with all the drama bods. Maybe there were too many people just like her. Too much competition.

At lunch my C-plan was waiting next to a bowl of mushed carrot. I forced it down, every last bit, and said, "Right, I'm going to the PE block to ask about running, do you want to come?"

Marsha and Keisha both looked like I'd offered them a bowl of cold sick but Marsha said, "I suppose I'd better."

"You don't have to, I can find it myself."

She sighed and said, "No, I'll come."

The sports hall was tucked behind the main school building. I asked the first teacher I saw. "Hi, I wanted to ask if I could go running?"

"Great!" The teacher practically bounced. "There's a club every Friday."

"No, I meant on my own – could I just run around the school grounds?"

She looked at me like I was an alien, then said, "I cannot think of a single reason why not. School grounds only, though. I'll give you a pass in case anyone asks what you're doing. Top work, Miss…?"

"Henley, Madam."

"Good, top work, Miss Henley. And you, Marsha? Will you be joining Miss Henley?"

"I suppose."

She scribbled a note for us both that said, *Setting an excellent example by running for fitness and fun, permission granted by Madam Hoosier.*

It was almost like I was leading two lives – the one in my head, where I yearned for my lost family and ached over the betrayal of my friend. And the one in the actual world, which was turning out to be a lot easier to deal with.

I sailed through that afternoon, going from lesson to lesson. The work was hard but the teachers were patient – and so were the other girls. Suki was determined she'd get me to try out for netball though and I knew I wasn't fit enough, so before she could start nagging me again I got in my PE kit and slipped out for a run.

I knew Marsha didn't want to come, not really, and I didn't want to be a burden, so I went on my own. I got about fifty yards before I could barely breathe and my legs were a pair of rubbery blobs underneath me.

I sat on the grass for a bit, muscles quivering, and then I lay back and laughed. It might have turned my legs to jelly but running filled the rest of me with joy. I struggled back up, and took a slower pace towards the sea, leaving the beautiful ice-cream school behind. I wished I had a Walkman so I could listen to some music and then realized I could do what every other kid did in this decade if I got an earpiece for my phone. Maybe Miss Lilly would get me one? Maybe I could work for her in the holidays, earn a few quid of my own? I crossed to the hedge line that made up the eastern boundary of the school field and froze. A small brown dog had come racing out of the bushes towards me. I'd been bitten by a dog when I was younger and was always a bit scared, a bit wary. Especially when they were yapping and scruffy and actually, not brown, just really muddy.

"Go away. Shoo. Get away."

It ran round my feet, yap-yap-yapping. I pulled my hands into my chest and stood as tall as I could while peering over my shoulder to see if anyone was near enough to help.

The dog bounced down on its front paws and I was sure it was going to attack me.

"Away. Go on, away."

I walked slowly backwards but it followed me, like it was rounding me up.

"Go away!" I yelled again, throwing my arms out wide, trying to make myself look as big as I could and then I got scared that it would leap up and bite my hands, so I tucked them back in. I was heading for a full-blown freak-out when the dog rolled on its back, throwing its stubby little legs in the air. It wiggled around, tongue lolling out of its mouth, and it seemed ridiculous to be afraid of it.

"You silly thing," I said.

It rolled all the way over and back again, wagging its stumpy tail so hard its entire body moved from side to side.

I took a tentative step towards it and it rolled to its feet. I waited to see what it would do next and then heard a whispered hiss from the hedge. I couldn't make it out but it sounded like a person. I stopped dead.

Journalist.

But why would a journalist be out with a scruffy little dog. Was that a thing they did? Distract you with a furry twit?

I straightened up slowly and stepped away. The dog followed me. I sped up and so did the dog. Well, so be it. If whoever it was lost their dog, it wasn't my fault, was it? I turned and ran back up the field with the dog yapping enthusiastically after me.

The voice from the hedge called, "Come back here, you totally useless fur-faced git."

I ran on. The hedge rustled behind me but the dog still followed and the voice yelled, "Scrag! Come back here, you faithless little mutt!"

He didn't sound like a journalist. I turned back to look. It was a skinny, filthy, completely bedraggled...boy. Man? No. Boy. On his knees and glaring at me. I stopped running and stared.

chapter thirty
SHEM

A quiet space in a hedge. It wasn't much to ask, was it? But no, I couldn't even have that without some posh kid sticking her nose in.

Didn't I have enough to deal with? The rain had soaked through my bag and turned all the bready stuff to mush. I had a couple of yogurts and a bit of cheese and that was it. And then, *then,* like the universe was having a right old laugh at my expense, some rich girl tried to steal my dog.

I was boiling with anger as she looked down her nose at me, Scrag dancing about like he'd made a brand-new friend.

I was sick of it. Just so sick of everything. Why couldn't something go my way for once?

chapter thirty-one

LAURA

He stared back at me. "What? You never seen a dog before?"

He reminded me of someone, but I couldn't place who. It was something about the defiant way he pursed his lips. Maybe it was Stacey. Or Marsha. He had that worried look that he was in trouble but was going to front it out whatever.

"Come on, Scrag," he called, and turned towards the hedge.

"Do you live in the bush?"

I don't know why I was talking to him. It was a stupid thing to do. I was out on my own, talking to a boy who was clearly a weirdo. Even if he was a weirdo with a cute dog.

He threw a look at me over his shoulder. "No. I don't live in the bush, but if I did, it'd be none of your business, would it?"

"It would if it was that bush. This is my school."

He scowled at me and I can't say I blamed him. Who did I think I was? I'd only been at Whitman's five minutes and

I wouldn't have been there at all if Miss Lilly hadn't taken me under her wing.

"Sorry, that was a dumb thing to say." I didn't want to let him go. I honestly don't know why. He was filthy dirty and when the wind stopped battering us with sea air for a second, a smell of unwashed clothes and greasy hair wafted from him. Still, something anchored me to the spot. Maybe it was because he thought I was something I wasn't and I wanted to prove him wrong. "Are you hungry?"

His jaw worked like he was chewing on something. He looked at his dirty dog and then back at me. "Why? You inviting me in for dinner?"

I felt stupid. Like I was playing a game and had been caught out. "I could bring you something later?" Could I? I still wasn't eating properly, people would think it a bit odd if I helped myself to…well…anything that wasn't baby mush. "I could try," I finished feebly.

"Well," he said, "my dog would love a steak and I'd really like a giant pizza with extra cheese and pepperoni. Can I reserve a table for seven? By the window?"

He walked off. As he battled his way back into the bush, I said, "I'll try to come back later, about half nine?"

What was I doing?

Maybe I felt sorry for him. Maybe I just felt like I owed the universe something for giving me Miss Lilly. What would have happened to me without her? Or maybe I just couldn't help sticking my nose in, even when it clearly wasn't wanted.

I walked back to the school building, wondering how I

was going to sneak food out and feeling absolutely knackered, but completely…alive. Benjie and Miss Lilly had been right: I had needed to get out, to live a bit for myself. I tugged my ponytail tighter and headed back to my room.

On my bed was a tiny box with a note.

Dear weirdo, if you must run, at least listen to something cool, M x
PS How to use them:
1. Tap the settings icon on your phone, it looks like a cog.
2. It's obvious from there, be brave.

In the box was a pair of the little ear buttons.

A smile spread over my face. Marsha.

I followed her instructions. It *was* pretty obvious – it was just like a smaller version of my slate. It even asked me if I wanted it to upload music based on my preferences. It was brilliant.

I caught up with Marsha on the way to prep.

"Thanks. You didn't have to do that."

"They're a spare pair. I didn't need them."

"Well, thank you. It's really kind."

Marsha sighed and patted my head. "Anything I can do to save you from your own weirdness."

I smiled. She thought I was weird because I went running, not because I had two mums or had spent almost half a century in a deep freeze. I kind of loved Marsha.

"Have you got your phone?" she asked. When I handed it over, she looked impressed. "You paired them yourself?"

"I was brave, as per instructions."

She laughed and said, "Fastest way to learn is to have a go."

She pressed a camera icon. I knew what it was from lessons with Giles but I hadn't looked at it since I'd arrived at school. She said, "Your Instagram is looking woefully unloved. Hold out your wrist."

She took a picture of my Swatch and showed me. "This is how to put a filter on it – let's make those primary colours pop. Cool. Now hashtags – what is it? #swatch #eighties #sleepingbeauty #girlofice #misslilly."

"Don't…" I said, remembering how horrible those people had been about my teeth.

She gave me the phone back. "Too late."

"Why have you used Miss Lilly's name?"

"Because she'll love it. Think of all that free publicity. Look at all those likes already. Cool, hey?"

A stream of little hearts were popping up on the screen.

I said, "Hmmm."

A nursery rhyme was running round my head: *When it was good, it was very, very good, but when it was bad, it was horrid.* I decided not to read the comments, good or bad – but I couldn't help the little rush of happiness at all those people liking my watch.

* * *

Homework was way better with music in my ears. Two hours didn't seem so bad and soon we were heading to dinner. I wondered what I could find for the boy to eat. It wasn't going to be steak, that was for sure. I had mashed green stuff – I think it might have been broccoli – with C-plan. I'd have given him that but, firstly, I needed it – probably as much as he did – and, secondly, there was no way of me sneaking it out of the dining hall.

One of the other Blue House girls solved my problem. There was a note on Blue House door to go to the ODR. Someone was having a birthday and her mum had sent in a huge box of doughnuts. We sang a terrible version of "Happy Birthday" and lined up for one each.

Marsha was surprised when I joined the queue. "Didn't think you'd be able to eat this."

I shrugged. "I can lick the sugar off." I wrapped it in a napkin. "I'll save it for later."

All I needed was a bag to put it in so it didn't get wet in the rain and that was easy – there was some kind of waxed paper for wrapping food up in the kitchen drawers and a few string bags in the cupboard underneath.

Marsha said, "Want to come to my room for chats?"

I shook my head – I had a doughnut delivery to complete. "I think I dropped my—" I nearly said "watch" but that was still very visible on my arm. "Ring. When I was out running."

"When did you go out running?" Marsha said.

Keisha interrupted, "You aren't going out? It's pouring down outside."

"And what ring have you lost? I don't remember you wearing a ring?"

The stream of questions made me feel guilty, but once I'd started lying I felt I had to stick with it.

"It was my mum's. I don't know why I put it on, stupid really. I want to see if I can find it, before it gets too dark."

"I should come with you," Marsha said.

"Why? Don't be silly. I won't be long."

She made a face. "You sure you'll be okay?"

"Course. Don't worry about me. I want to get an early night anyway; I'm worn out."

I *was* worn out, but I needed to message Stacey when I got back from my mercy mission, and I didn't want to do that with Marsha around.

I ran down to the hedge. The ground was slippery with the fresh and falling rain and it was ridiculously windy. Running was hard work and I was breathless by the time I arrived. There was no sign of the dog or the boy. I didn't know what to do, so I hung the doughnut bag on a branch. As I did, I thought I glimpsed white fur through the bush. If Hedge Boy was there, he didn't want to see me. Well, that was fine. He was the poor kid stuck in the rain.

I tried to run back up the hill but the ground was slick and my legs were properly tired. I'd made it to the car park when I slipped and smacked down hard on my knee. I rolled over, clutching my leg and cursing. Blood flowed warmly from a gash where I'd landed on the edge of a broken flint. I squeezed my eyes shut and my hand tight over the cut while the initial shock passed.

Wincing, I inspected the damage – my hands were scuffed and covered in blood and the cut on my knee was pouring. I got up and hobbled back inside and straight into Madam Hobbs.

"Good Lord, girl, what have you done?"

"I slipped."

"Upstairs to the health centre with you."

She marched me up a narrow staircase and knocked on a door that said *Nurse*.

"Come in."

Madam Hobbs nudged me in and said, "Accident, Anabelle – Laura Henley, new girl. Leave you to it."

She left me with the nurse smiling up at me from behind a desk.

"Laura! How lovely to meet you. Oh…" She'd spotted my bloody knee. "Oopsie. Hop up on the bed. Right, let's clean you up and have a proper look. How did you do this?"

"I slipped on my way back from a run. I had permission."

She dabbed at my knee with antiseptic. "Good job all your jabs are up-to-date. I was actually just going through your records. You're due to come to see me on Friday for a check-up. It's quite deep this. I think you need a little repair job. Okay?"

I gritted my teeth and prepared for stitches. She finished cleaning the wound and then *glued* my knee back together before putting a dressing on it. She wiped my hands and checked them too.

"At least those are just a bit grubby. Okay, you'll do. No more PE until I've checked that knee again in case it bursts open. We can check it on Friday but if it gets sore, come back straight away. We don't want to risk an infection."

I hopped down from the bed. "Thank you. It feels better already."

"And how's everything else?"

"Fine. I've been eating a bit more. Actually, I was wondering, do you think it's okay to step up the solid food?"

"I don't see why not. Your tummy will soon tell you if you aren't coping. Any constipation?"

My cheeks burned; I shook my head.

"That's a good sign. What about your periods?"

"Not yet. Can I go now, Madam?"

"All right, but—"

"Thanks."

I didn't wait for any more embarrassing questions.

Marsha was coming out of my room when I got back.

"Hey, did you find it?" she said.

"Sorry?"

"The ring? Looks like you've fought a dragon for it."

I looked down at my leg – it was still a bit bloody and I had mud splatters all over me.

"Oh yeah – no. So annoying – I fell coming back. Did you want something?"

"Sorry?"

"You were coming out of my room?"

"Oh, just a chat. No worries."

I watched her go. She'd known I was out. I'd literally just told her. And if she'd wanted a chat, why was she going now that I was there?

I shivered, still wet from the rain. I needed a bath to warm up before I contacted Stacey. I ducked in my room to get my wash things and noticed my slate was active – Notitia-John was hovering above it.

Had I left it like that?

Marsha couldn't have been looking at it – she wasn't set up as a user. Besides, why would she? She had her own computer.

"Notitia, has someone else tried to use you?"

"I'm sorry, I don't understand the question."

"Has someone else used you?"

"Do you mean 'Has someone gained unauthorized access to this computer'?"

"Yes."

"No. There has been no unauthorized access."

I wrinkled my nose. I must have left it on. I grabbed my towel and a bottle of Miss Lilly bubble bath from the bag Mariya had given me and headed to the bathroom.

I poured the liquid soap under the gushing hot tap and delicious smelling steam filled the tiny cubicle. It reminded me of happy times at Blackhurst. I unwrapped the dressing from my knee and sank into the warm water. Careful to keep the wound dry, I wiped the mud and blood from the rest of my leg, then examined the cut. The glue seemed to be coming out. I touched it lightly and it just fell off. My heart skipped a beat. Where there had been a deep cut less than an hour ago, the skin was now clean and whole.

It was like my body had spat out the glue and knitted itself back together.

Deep down, I knew I should probably tell someone. But surely they were already aware of…whatever it was? This had to have something to do with my being frozen, didn't it? So why not tell me to expect it so it didn't freak me out? Urgh. I wasn't sure what to do. What if they didn't know? They'd make me go back to the clinic, wouldn't they? To investigate it? I couldn't bear to be poked or prodded any more. I didn't want to be a medical miracle. I just wanted to be Laura Henley. A normal, teenage girl. At Whitman's, with my new friends, it felt like I was getting there, and I didn't want to give that up.

I got out of the bath and put the bandage back on. It could wait. I'd mention it to Miss Lilly the next time I spoke to her.

Maybe.

chapter thirty-two
LAURA

Back in my room, I rummaged through my wardrobe for something cosy to put on. I pulled out the floppy-eared rabbit thing. It was ridiculous but so soft. I put it on and sat down to reply to Stacey.

I still wasn't sure what to say but I knew I wanted to be armed with all the facts. I steeled myself and asked Notitia-John to find the interview Stacey had given to the press. The one that had sent Mum and Ima running to France. It didn't take long.

FROZEN OUT!
Stacey Flowers tells our reporter how Laura Henley's lesbian mothers left her out in the cold when her best friend was put into cryostasis.

My stomach clenched like I'd been punched. Mum and Ima would never have done that. The report had a picture of me and Stacey when we were really young, before Alfie was born. We were sitting on a low wall in shorts and Aertex T-shirts, my scooter on its side at our feet. I was grinning a gap-toothed smile and she was sticking her tongue out.

Stacey *must* have given that to the paper. Who else could – *would* – have done that? Not Mum and Ima, that's for sure. And if she'd given them that photo, she was probably behind the Wikipedia picture too. She'd have only had to ask Mum and Ima and they'd have given her copies. They loved her nearly as much as I did. I couldn't bear to read any more.

I pressed my lips together. What should I say to Stacey? How could I explain how hurt I felt? How disappointed?

"Notitia," I said, "can you send this article as a link to Stacey Flowers?"

"Yes, I can do that."

I watched Notitia-John seem to suck up the report and throw it back into a message to Stacey.

A little pencil hovered over the message bubble and then her reply came straight back, like she'd been waiting all day.

That's not what it looks like. I was tricked, Lu.

Another message pinged in.

You have to believe me.

I wanted to believe her, but she must have given them the picture – there was no way that was a trick?

Laura? Please answer me.

I wrote back:

That interview pushed Mum and Ima over the edge. Did you know that's why they were in France? The coroner said they were distracted by recent events and that was why they crashed. I've got no one now.

You've got me, and Alfie – they're surely going to revive him too now?

Alfie – I had to take a steadying breath before I could type the rest – didn't survive.

The little pencil hovered and hovered. A message pinged in.

Are you sure?

Was I *sure?* She must know what had happened to the other cryopods in the fire. The fire caused by her and her friends.

I sat back. I had no idea what to say next. There was so much space between us – in time and place and in all the things that had happened. It was a vast and painful desert, which I had no idea how to cross. We'd always found it so easy to talk to each other before. I'd told her everything, *everything*.

Beads of rain dribbled down the window, pooling on the little lead ridges, then spilling over. Like tears.

Yes, I'm sure. They couldn't revive him. The kid who always wanted you to stay longer, who thought you had eyes like Batman and always saved cake for you – he died because you and your pals set fire to the clinic that was doing its very best to give him another chance at life.

My throat ached with tears.

I missed Alfie so much. I thought about all the things we'd never do together again. No playing football, no reading tractor books, no making sandcastles or eating ice cream.

The rain poured down the window, reflecting how I felt. Hedge Boy would be soaked to the skin.

No watching *Postman Pat*, no making butterfly cakes, no watching him open presents on Christmas morning.

My slate pinged with a message – not from Stacey, from Miss Lilly.

Hi Laura, hope you're settling in okay! I see you've updated your Instagram account – well done, 21st-century girl! You can post this if you like – she's a terror!

There was a video attached. I flicked it open. Batfink was sitting on the robotic vacuum as it moved around the kitchen floor. She was swatting at imaginary mice, then she fell off and scrabbled to her feet, pretending nothing had happened.

It made me smile. I messaged back:

The little minx got over her fear then? I miss her
furry face. x

Miss Lilly replied: And we miss you. x

I opened Instagram to see if I could work out how to post
the video. I was astonished to see the picture of my watch
had dozens of comments and hundreds of likes. There was
a message from Marsha:

Hey, Ice Girl. Come follow me.

I pressed on her name so I could see her timeline. There
were loads of pictures of her pouting at the screen. In some
she'd done something to the picture so she looked like a puppy.
I smiled. I scrolled back through her posts and was surprised
to see they didn't go back that far – pretty much only to when
she'd come to Whitman's. Maybe they didn't have Instagram
in Russia? Unsure of the etiquette but thinking you couldn't
go wrong by being nice, I'd started liking all her pictures
when a message blinked on my slate from Stacey.

Did you check?

What did she mean? Check what?

Did you check that she wasn't lying? That Alfie is
really dead?

I stared at it. What a horrible, horrible thing to say. Cold fury washed through me. How could she be so thoughtless? So *cruel*?

Another message:

This is making me nervous. Do you remember Spiditik?

Spiditik had been the code we used for secret notes. We just changed all the vowels to "i". It was a total joke; anyone could crack it.

Why?

We need a safer way to talk. Expect Spiditik.

I flicked the message away, my heart a pebble in my chest. To be so *heartless* about Alfie… I didn't know who that person was, but it wasn't Stacey. Not my Stacey. I wanted nothing to do with her.

At breakfast next morning, I was determined to eat porridge and start building myself up a bit. I persuaded Marsha to come to the canteen with me.

I stirred a big blob of jam into my bowl, making a red spiral. It tasted pretty good.

Marsha picked at hers, muttering, "I hate this muck."

Keisha sat down with a clatter of her tray. "Hey."

Marsha nearly exploded with rage. "Why do you have to make so much noise?" She got up and stormed out.

"What was that about?" I asked.

Keisha shrugged. "Marsha being Marsha."

I shook my head and raced out after her. "Wait, what's up? What on earth's the matter?"

"Nothing."

"Well, there's clearly something. You just bit your friend's head off."

"Keisha is not my friend. People like me don't have friends." She turned sharply away.

"What do you mean?" I caught hold of her arm.

"I mean..." She did a tiny stamp with her foot – for real, she actually did that. "My father wants me to leave. There is no point in me having friends, so if I was you, I wouldn't even bother talking to me."

"Leave?"

She walked swiftly away. I hurried to follow, thinking she'd head straight to our form room. She didn't. She ducked under the yellow tape and out of the side door and started walking in the direction of the bell tower. The dangerous ruin of a bell tower that we were expressly forbidden from going anywhere near.

I hovered beside the door. "Oh hell," I muttered. "Marsha, you idiot."

I took a deep breath, looked behind me to check I wasn't going to get into immediate trouble, and nudged the door open.

"Marsha?"

She was crouched by a wall. It looked like she was putting something into her pocket but before I had a chance to ask her what she was doing she got to her feet. "I just need some space, okay?"

"But it's dangerous out here."

She rolled her eyes at me.

I tried again. "Is there anything we can do? About your dad?"

She shrugged. "He snaps his fingers and I have to jump. I thought he might forget I was here. I hoped he would. Did you know he tricked me into coming here?"

I shook my head in disbelief.

"He told me I wasn't doing well enough at my Russian school and if I wanted to stay there, I had to prove to him that I was on a level with British girls my age. He made me sit the entrance exam and then, when I passed it, he sent me here."

"But why? If it proved you were doing so well?"

She shrugged again. "Maybe it was him – what do you say in English? – keeping up with the Smithses."

"Joneses."

"Whatever. Or maybe he didn't like my boyfriend back home." A sly smile crept up one corner of her mouth. "Yuri is not what you call a nice boy."

"But then it makes even less sense for you to go back."

"Please try not to be such an idiot. My father doesn't know about Yuri."

I frowned. Something about all of that didn't make sense,

but I was interrupted from puzzling it out by a crash as a piece of tower tumbled into the courtyard.

"Okay. Maybe you're right," Marsha said. "Maybe it is dangerous."

She slipped her arm through mine and said, "Come on. Let's go to form and begin the day's torture. Might as well get used to daily disappointment, that's what life is all about."

Something about the casual way she said that made me shiver. I could imagine the young woman she'd grow into if the people who were supposed to love her kept shipping her from place to place. Everyone needed roots, didn't they? Somewhere to call home.

I was so lucky to have a second chance at that. I gripped Marsha's arm just a little bit tighter and said a prayer of gratitude that Miss Lilly was looking after me.

chapter thirty-three
SHEM

It was time to go. I *had* to try and find somewhere half decent we could stay. I was just waiting for dusk, for gloom and quiet so we could slip away unnoticed, when the girl came back. I hid at the back of the bush, holding on to Scrag as she hung something on a branch. Scrag wriggled free but I caught him and pulled him back. Stupid dog. He had trust issues. He trusted everyone.

When I was sure she'd gone, I crept out. She'd left a bag. I almost didn't open it. It could have had anything in it – someone once threw a bag of fish heads at Bert.

I sniffed it. It didn't smell like fish. It didn't smell like steak and pizza either, but I took a risk. Inside was a doughnut, glistening in sugar. I was sick with hunger, actually drooling. I tore a bit off and gave it to Scrag and shoved the rest in my mouth in one go. It was so sweet, it filled me with a buzzing energy. I was sorry I'd been rude to the girl, but it was too late to fix that. I wiped my nose on the back of my stump. Time to go.

I headed back to the hole I'd made in the fence when I first broke in. It was hard to find in the dusk and I was just starting to worry that they'd fixed it when I spotted the gap. It looked smaller than I remembered but if I'd come in, I could get out. I watched for a bit, to make sure no one was lurking outside, then I crawled through, the wires snagging on my back. I called to Scrag to follow.

He wagged his stubby tail and came after me.

There was no point in going back to my burned-down shed. No point in going to the station. I decided to walk north and see where we ended up.

It took about two minutes to get to a proper road and almost straight away I had a *being-followed* ache between my shoulder blades. I looked behind me. There was no one there.

The feeling didn't go away but my shoulder blades had got it wrong. There was no one following me. They were in front of me. Waiting.

A shadow stepped out from behind a tree and shoved a bag over my head before I could do anything to stop them. It stank of something rotten. They clamped my arms to my sides. I kicked out, twisted and turned, fighting to get free. Scrag growled and barked.

My mouth filled with bits of dirt and God knows what else. I spat them out, shouting, "Get off, leave me alone!"

"Be a good boy now, Shem, and nobody gets hurt."

Someone kicked me in the back of the knee and I buckled to the floor.

Scrag snarled and I could hear from the change in his growl that he had his teeth in something.

"Get off me, you dirty…" the man said. I was tugged sideways as his boot lashed out. Scrag yelped and then… nothing.

"Scrag!" I struggled and fought and screwed my body every which way to get free of whatever was pinning my arms down, but then something was pressed tight against the cloth bag, right over my mouth and nose and I couldn't breathe, I couldn't…

chapter thirty-four
LAURA

We were halfway through a biology lesson when a Year Seven kid came in with a message for Marsha. My friend's face was white as she left the class. She didn't come back that lesson and she wasn't at lunch or afternoon lessons either. Just before prep I went to find her.

She was curled up on her bed, face to the wall.

"Go away."

"It's me."

"I don't care."

Keisha appeared from behind me. "Marsha, what's happened?"

"Did your dad call?" I asked.

"What do you care?"

"Don't take it out on us," Keisha said, hurt. "We haven't done anything."

Marsha rolled over. She looked awful. Her eyes were puffy and her face looked flushed and sweaty. She threw something small and hard at us and yelled, "I said, go away!"

Keisha caught the missile surprisingly neatly and held it out to me. It was a Cadbury Creme Egg. I hadn't seen one of those for, literally, decades. My mouth watered. Keisha dropped it in my palm and said, "You talk to her. I'm sick of her lies."

Marsha went pale. "I don't lie."

"Really? Then who's Yuri?"

Marsha looked away. "My boyfriend."

"You don't have a boyfriend. You don't have TouchTime. You *do* have a Creme Egg problem that would feed half of Russia."

Marsha sat up, fury bubbling off her. "How dare you? How DARE YOU?"

"That's better," Keisha said. "Far more Marsha."

Keisha opened a drawer that was completely full – I mean, COMPLETELY full – of Creme Eggs.

"Hang on," I said, "that doesn't look like a Creme Egg problem. That looks like Creme Egg heaven."

Keisha climbed up onto Marsha's desk and got a blue box file down from the bookshelf. She passed it to me. Inside, folded into hundreds of tiny parcels, were many, many – God knows how many – empty wrappers. She really did have a serious Creme Egg habit.

"Where do you get them all from?"

Marsha shrugged and took an egg from the drawer. "It's not hard – drone delivery. The teachers never notice."

"Oh." Those small flying robots. Maybe that's why Marsha was putting something in her pocket when we were in the quad.

"Have one if you like."

I hadn't eaten chocolate since I'd been brought back. I took one and peeled away the wrapper, drinking in the delicious scent. I bit the top off... Oh, that thick, soft crack. I let the gorgeousness melt in my mouth, coating my teeth, before chewing and swallowing and revelling in the glory of it. I tipped my head back against the wall.

"Heaven," I said. "Absolute heaven."

I stuck my tongue in the too-sweet centre and closed my eyes. Ravenous greed took over and I gobbled the whole thing down, licking the warm melted chocolate off my fingers. I slid sideways across the wall and lay on the floor, eyes closed. Eventually, Keisha shook me gently. I raised one of my sticky fingers to my lips and said, "Shh."

Marsha said, "She's chocolate drunk."

After a moment, the sugar hit. Heat flushed through me. I snapped my eyes open. I had to cool down. I went to Marsha's window and pushed it open, as wide as it would go, trying to lean out, letting the fresh sea air wash over me.

"How could I have forgotten my first love? Chocolate. How have I done without it for so long?"

Marsha said, "Watching you enjoy that was almost as good as eating it myself. Almost."

She peeled her own egg and bit the top off.

I was fighting the urge to jump up and down. Seriously,

what was going on with my limbs? I looked back out of the window – I wanted to run.

"Come for a jog with me?"

"Er, no. I think I've made it quite clear I don't do exercise," Marsha said, demolishing the last of her Creme Egg.

"You come then?" I said to Keisha.

"We've got prep, remember? School?"

No way could I sit in that room for two hours with all this…*juice* zinging round my body. I'd explode.

I pulled the window closed and as I stepped back I saw a note on Marsha's desk. On the front was a name:

Liiri Hinliy

My name.

In Spiditik.

"Marsha, where did you get this?"

She looked at the envelope. "In the quad."

"Why didn't you give it to me?"

"Why should I give it to you?"

"This is my name – it's meant for me."

She sat up and snatched the envelope from me, examining the writing. Her face went an even whiter shade of pale. Then she said, "That is the most rubbish code I have ever seen."

I took it back and stuck it in my pocket.

She said, "You can't have it."

"But it's meant for me."

"I found it."

"I don't care. It's meant for me."

Keisha interrupted our squabbling. "Who would be sending you a message? Who do you even know outside?"

"I…"

Marsha snapped all her attention on me. "Yeah, Laura, who do you even know?"

Part of me wanted to confide in them, but I was so taken aback by the sharpness in Marsha's voice, I didn't answer.

"Read it then," Keisha said.

I looked from her to Marsha and back again. The truth was I needed some advice about what to do, and they were my friends, weren't they?

I opened it and translated from Spiditik as I read out loud.

"Spidi2,

The car crash was her fault and you did not, do not, have never had cancer.

The flower is not who you think she is.

Spidi1."

I stared at the paper. A chill leached across my skull and down my spine. What?

WHAT?

What flower? Was she talking about herself? Stacey Flowers? Well, that was true: she definitely wasn't who I thought she was.

"What does it mean?" Keisha said.

"I don't know."

Marsha shook her head. "I know who it's from. It's that nutcase who set fire to the clinic, isn't it? Why are you writing to her?"

How did she know who it was from? How could she jump to that conclusion?

I said, "I'm not writing to her. She wrote to me…"

Keisha cut me off. "We have to tell someone, Laura. She sounds dangerous."

I shook my head automatically, jumping to Stacey's defence. "She just wants to talk to me. She'd never hurt me."

But she had hurt me. So much. And I honestly wasn't sure how much more she might hurt me if I carried on talking to her.

chapter thirty-five
SHEM

I came round in pitch dark, my heart racing and my head bouncing against a hard floor. My arms were pulled behind my back, my legs tied together. I could hear the faint electric hum of a vehicle and guessed I was in a car boot or something.

"Scrag?" I whispered, sensing his absence like my lost hand. I felt sick, but the stinking bag was still over my head. If I puked, the only place it was going was all over my own face. I wished I hadn't eaten the doughnut. I swallowed and swallowed and tried to breathe but the bag smelled rancid. My head was groggy, my thoughts a mess.

Where was Scrag?

I heard his pained yelp in my head, imagined his body flying through the air. I choked down a sob.

We stopped moving and a door clunked open.

"Get up!" someone shouted, tugging my arm. I fell out of the vehicle and landed heavily on my side.

They pulled me sharply to my feet. My arms were an

agony of pins and needles. They undid my legs and shoved me forwards. I tried to speak, to find out where Scrag was, but my throat was dry and tight and nothing would come out.

A door opened somewhere ahead, the floor changed to something flat and smooth. I guessed we'd gone inside.

Someone said, "Make sure he's completely decontaminated."

We turned right. I tried to listen for anything that might give me a clue as to where I was. We stopped and something sharp jabbed in my arm. They held me still until something said, *"Scan complete. Subject identified. Please wait."*

Another door shushed open. I was marched off again, through another door, then another. We turned right again and my hood was yanked off.

I blinked against the bright light. I was in a locker room. One end was screened off. Behind me, the cord around my arms was cut free. As it snapped apart, my shoulders fell back into place. The pain was shocking. I gasped and tucked my hand and stump into my armpits, bending double to try and ease the pain. A woman stood next to me. She was dressed in a blue papery suit, with a white mask covering the bottom half of her face. She was tall but I reckoned I could take her down.

"Don't even try," she said, as if reading my mind. "There are two guards behind you with Tasers. I presume you know what Tasers are?"

I nodded. Part of me was relieved there was no point

in fighting. I'd never liked physical violence. I always seemed to come off worst.

"Where's my dog?"

"There are no animals allowed here." She held out a yellow plastic sack. "Remove your clothes and place them in the bag, please."

"What?"

"Your clothes. Off. Put them in the bag."

"Why?"

"Just do it. You cannot enter the facility until—"

"What facility? Where am I? What do you want from me?"

"It's for your own good." She sighed.

"How is half suffocating me and nearly breaking my arms for my own good?"

"You shouldn't have resisted. Now, please remove your clothes."

"I am not stripping off in front of you."

"Fine."

I followed her gaze to the guards behind me. They were also dressed in blue paper suits but in a bigger size. A much bigger size. Enormous.

"The vagrant refuses to remove his clothes. Can one of you assist him, please?"

I backed away, holding my arms up. "You've made a mistake. I'm not a vagrant. I had a home. Seriously, I shouldn't be here."

The woman said, "We'll be the judge of that."

Judge, jury and... I didn't finish the thought in my head. I hit the wall of lockers behind me and slid along them until I was in the furthest corner of the room. She advanced towards me with her plastic bag and the guards beside her.

"Shoes first."

I was running out of options. I pulled one off and threw it at one of the guards. As he flinched, I ran past and yanked at the door. It wouldn't open. Of course it wouldn't.

They'd got me.

Whatever game this was, I'd lost.

chapter thirty-six
LAURA

Prep again. Two hours of science and maths. I pulled Stacey's note out and reread it.

How could she say that about the cancer? I'd been ill. I was *dying*. The only reason Mum and Ima did what they did was because there'd been no choice. Me and Alfie were going to die.

There was a time I would have trusted Stacey with my life, but now…? My mind bounced between the Stacey I remembered and this new version who said crazy stuff and set fire to…

A hand clamped my shoulder. "Laura, are you feeling okay?"

I looked up. Madam Hobbs was staring at me and at the note that I'd screwed up and smoothed out and screwed up and smoothed out. I had not written a single word of homework.

I shook my head. "I'm sorry. I feel really sick."

She took a step back. "You'd better pop up and see the nurse then."

I stood up and I genuinely felt a bit wobbly. I steadied myself against the table. "Better have someone go with you," Madam Hobbs said. "Keisha? Can you go with her, please?"

Keisha took my arm and led me up the corridor like an invalid. I had to know what Stacey meant. How could she think I hadn't been ill? She'd seen me when I could barely move. Did she think I'd faked being sick? That Alfie had?

Vicious layers of anger built in me. I wanted to have it out with her. I thought about Marsha picking up that message this morning.

"Keisha, those drone things...do people have to be nearby to use them to deliver stuff?"

"Depends on the sort of drone. Not the ones delivery companies use. Toy ones maybe. Why?"

Because Stacey might have been here. She might have dropped the note in the quad and still be about, hoping to see me.

I felt desperate. "I need to go out, I need some fresh air."

"You can't. I'm meant to be taking you to the health centre."

"Sorry, can't, need air." I found the nearest door and ran outside.

Absolutely no one was about. I tore down to the metal gates and looked through. There was no one there, not even any journalists, which was pretty lucky really. A picture of me peering through barred gates wouldn't look good on the news.

I climbed up the bank near the track and looked around. Stacey was nowhere to be seen.

I headed back to school, the wind blowing my hair everywhere even though it was tied back. As I scooped it away from my eyes, I heard a whimper. Tucked right up against the wall, tight in a corner and shivering violently, was Hedge Boy's little dog.

The dog looked hurt. One eye was smeared with blood and swollen shut. I wasn't sure if it was safe to go near him without his owner but there was absolutely no sign of the boy. I sucked my bottom lip for a second. The dog looked so sad I had to try and help. I walked slowly towards him, one arm stretched out so he could sniff me.

"Hey, little chap, what's your name? Scrag? What's up, Scrag? Where's your master?"

His tail wagged feebly and my heart lurched. I got closer. His eye looked awful but it was the way his tiny body was trembling that really got me.

"What's happened, little one? Where's your master?"

I crouched down. He cowered back at first and then sniffed my outstretched hand before giving it a tentative lick.

"You poor little thing."

I looked about for the boy, but he was nowhere. Had he abandoned the dog? Lost him? The little scrap seemed terrified. Very slowly, very carefully, I picked him up. His body squirmed in my arms and then relaxed. He lifted his head and licked my cheek.

God knows what I thought I was doing, but I took the dog inside, hoping, hoping, hoping no one would see me. Luck was on my side right until I got to Blue House corridor. I pushed open the door and Marsha was on the other side, in deep conversation with Madam Hobbs.

I turned around and went straight back out. I could not be caught with a dog. I headed for the nearest exit, the door to the quad. It was still light out but the courtyard was shaded from any sun in the evenings and was full of shadows. A bird, or a bat, or something fluttered right past me and I ducked. Scrag whimpered in my arms.

"I'm sorry. *Shh.* Please don't make any noise." I put him down gently and said, "I'll be back. Just wait here. I need to make sure the coast is clear."

I pushed open the door to Blue House – it was empty now but I was taking no chances. I pelted to my room and grabbed a towel before returning to the quad.

I was just about to safely leave Blue House corridor when someone grabbed my shirt.

"What are you up to?"

Marsha.

"You frightened the life out of me! Oh, Marsha, there was this boy…it's a long story…anyway, he's left his dog and…"

"A boy, here? A dog? Are you crazy?" she said, but glee played on her face. "Where are they?"

"It's just the dog. He's in the quad."

"Come on then. What are we waiting for? I'll get the dog. You can be lookout."

"No, he's injured. I'll get him. You can be lookout." I pushed open the door.

Scrag gave a little whimper when he saw me and got up slowly, clearly in pain.

Marsha crouched down. "Oh! He's so cute. What happened to you, boy?" He let her pick him up and push back the little fringe of hair that covered his bloodstained eye.

"We need to clean that up, don't we, little fluff ball? Looks like someone kicked you. Hold out the towel, Laura."

She was so gentle, so calm, so UN-Marsha like.

"What?" she said. "Come on, hold out the towel so we can wrap him up."

I did what she suggested and she placed him in my arms, saying, "I'll make sure the way's clear."

I followed her when she signalled it was okay. We made it halfway down Blue House corridor before we ran into Keisha and Susan.

"There you are," Keisha said. "You can't run off like that. I was charged with looking after you."

"Not now," Marsha said with a wave of her hand.

She stepped up her pace and I followed her all the way back to our rooms. She headed for hers but I'd found him. Scrag was coming to my room. I pushed the door open. Marsha followed me in but Keisha and Susan were right behind her. Scrag poked his head out of the towel.

Ruff.

"Shh…" I said.

Ruff, ruff.

"What's that?" Keisha said, as she and Susan made their way inside. "Are you mad?"

"Marsha, shut the door," I said. "Don't let anyone else in."

"Awwww," said Susan. "We can call him Elvis."

"Don't encourage them, Susan," Keisha said, exasperated. "Where...why...honestly, *how* have you got a *dog*? I literally left you, like, seconds ago."

"He's hurt," I said, as if that explained everything.

"Funny how he got hurt when your crazy friend was around delivering notes nearby," Marsha said.

"She wasn't around!" I said. "Why would you say that? She would never hurt a little dog."

"All right, I'm just saying. Two weird things happen in one day, it might not be a coincidence."

"Of course it is," I said, with more confidence than I felt.

chapter thirty-seven

SHEM

They shoved me into a shower and snatched a thin white curtain across the space. Roots of white-hot panic burrowed through me. I was sure it wasn't going to be a real shower. That's what the Nazis had done, wasn't it? Rounded up people they wanted to get rid of and gassed them in a pretend shower. I waited for the hiss of poison but, instead, water came on. Scalding. Almost too hot to bear. Only I was shivering as if it was ice pouring over me. I looked down at my shaking body.

I hadn't seen myself naked for years. I was thinner than I thought. And hairier.

The woman snapped, "There's soap on the wall. Use it."

"Why are you doing this? Who are you?" I asked.

"Can you just wash yourself? You'd think you'd be grateful. When was the last time you had a shower?"

I found a soap dispenser behind me. I squeezed some into my hand. It smelled like lemon and ginger and more weird thoughts crossed my mind – honest to God, I wondered if they were getting ready to eat me. I know, I know, but I was in full-on panic mode and nothing made any sense. I washed myself, thinking the longer it took, the better – the water ran grey around my feet. I kept going until it was clear. I had no idea what they wanted with me but the more time I spent in that shower, the less time they were spending doing something unimaginably awful. What was really strange was that I started to relax a bit. Even in that set-up, standing under the hot shower had some weird effect on me.

The water shut off and I was blasted with warm air. I was clean and I was dry but I wasn't leaving that cubicle until they dragged me out. Which they did.

"Put those on."

A grey sweat top and bottoms hung from a hook on the wall and all I could think was: *Prison. That's a prison uniform. I've been arrested. That's what this is.*

Something like relief swept through me. I'd get fed. I'd have a bed. I was so tired I could barely think – a bed, somewhere comfortable to sleep. And then shame nudged all that aside as my brain remembered what I was missing.

"Where's my dog?"

Nobody spoke to me but they spoke to each other.

"He's worried about his dog?"

"Yeah!"

And they laughed.

chapter thirty-eight
LAURA

"I'm going to get a bowl of warm water to clean his face," I said. "Marsha, please look after him."

I swept out of the room to the kitchen, trying to look like I knew what I was doing. Luckily no one asked why I was taking a bowl of warm water to my room. Marsha held it as I wiped gently at Scrag's fur with a wet tissue, cleaning the blood off his little face. He flinched when I had a closer look at the cut but it was more of a split than a deep wound.

"It might be bruised," said Marsha. "Be careful you don't press too hard."

He looked better when we'd finished. Then he dipped his head in the bowl and lapped some of the water up, splashing it over Marsha's lap. She smiled at him, a smile full of warmth, and curled a hand around his cheek.

"There you go, puppy. That's better, isn't it?"

He licked her hand and she put the bowl on my desk

before curling up on my bed with Scrag by her side. In moments, he was asleep.

Keisha interrupted the peace. "You can't have a dog here. Don't you realize what you're risking? If you get caught, exeat will be cancelled. Remember what that is? A precious day off. Me and Susan are going to the Pavilion – we've been planning it for ages."

"You'd better leave then," Marsha said to Keisha. "If you don't want to get in trouble."

"It's not that easy, is it? I know now." She scowled with fury and stomped out of my room. Susan shrugged and followed her out. I couldn't say I blamed them. As annoying as it was to admit it, I was an idiot to have brought a dog inside. Then I looked at Marsha, her eyelids drifting down as she began to doze, a soft smile on her lips. She was so peaceful curled up next to the dog. I couldn't bring myself to be sorry.

I sneaked to the kitchen and made some C-plan. Marsha was fast asleep when I got back, with Scrag nestled beside her. I made a towel nest on the floor and lay down quietly so I didn't disturb them.

I didn't sleep.

Stacey's message played over and over in my mind. *The car crash was her fault and you did not, do not, have never had cancer.* What did she mean?

Marsha and Scrag snored softly in harmony. I wished I could curl up with them and fall into blissful, empty-minded sleep.

* * *

Morning came and I was still staring at the ceiling. I needed the loo so I got to my knees, my back stiff after a night on the floor, and crept out. If there was enough time to go for a run, I'd take the dog with me and probably see Hedge Boy. I could return his dog and everything would be normal again. The dog part at least.

Back in my room, Marsha had crawled under my bedcovers and there was no sign of the dog, until he poked his head out.

"Want to come for a walk?" I whispered.

Marsha's arms tightened around him but he wriggled free and jumped down. He sat up, his stubby tail dusting the floor with wags.

"What are you doing?" Marsha murmured.

"Going for a run, the dog will need to pee."

"Oh, yeah, I guess." She looked at her phone. "God, it's only five a.m."

"Want to come with me? You can go ahead and be lookout."

She pulled the cover over her head, muttering, "Are you mad? No one will be up anyway. Use the Rabbit Run if you're worried."

I pulled the covers off her head. "What?"

"The Rabbit Run. There's a back door in the ODR – from there, the Rabbit Run crosses to Yellow House. There's a side gate partway along; it won't be locked. You can get out that way."

"No way," I said. "A secret passage?"

"Go away and let me sleep."

I tiptoed to the ODR with Scrag in his towel bundle. He wriggled his head free but there was no one in the kitchen so I let him peep out like a cute, furry baby. I eased open the back door. It led to a wooden walkway that crossed a small quad. There was a carved canopy over the top but the sides were open to waist height with wooden window frames filled in with chicken wire. No wonder they called it the Rabbit Run – it was just like a giant, Gothic bunny hutch. A bit creepy, but very cool.

I walked quickly along and completely missed the gate the first time I passed it. It blended in like it was camouflaged and creaked softly as I opened it. I crossed the quad to a short passage that opened out onto the car park. I set Scrag down and draped the towel round my neck. He pelted off around the side of the building. I hoped he'd caught a sniff of his owner.

I couldn't even see Scrag when I reached the corner. A little bit of me was relieved. Maybe he'd found the boy and I wouldn't have to worry about him any more. About either of them. I started to jog across the tarmac towards the fields and Scrag came bounding back to me.

"Oh no."

He had a rabbit in his mouth. A cute little baby bunny. I stopped running but within seconds he was dropping the poor dead thing at my feet. He sat down, his stumpy tail swishing the grass back and forward.

"Yeah, thanks but no thanks."

He lay on his belly and started to tear the thing apart. I ran on. Who needs to see that first thing in the morning? Mind you, I had wondered how it was he looked so well fed when Hedge Boy was practically a skeleton. I chewed the corner of my lip. What had happened to the boy that made him leave his dog? It was hard to believe Stacey could have had anything to do with it. Then again it was hard to believe any of the things she'd done.

With a sigh, I ran down to the bottom of the field. My legs were still weak and burned with the effort, but I felt alive. I gazed across the sea as the sun came up. All was calm apart from the odd seagull squawking and the rush of water over pebbles.

Why couldn't I just forget about Stacey? I had a new life and she was clearly nuts. But...

History. We had so much shared history – the things that had happened to me had affected her too. If I hadn't got ill and been frozen, we'd have just bumbled on with our lives. We'd have gone to college, found jobs, maybe both married a nice guy, had kids. She wouldn't have joined those activists. She wouldn't have been involved with the fire. She wouldn't have gone to prison. She wouldn't have lived so much of her life without me and made such a horrible mess of it.

I felt...responsible. Guilt bubbled inside me like a physical thing. I couldn't forget her because I loved her –

even if I didn't like her much right now. Stacey was like…I was going to say a sister but it was more than that. You don't choose your family, you choose your friends – you tie those bonds, you make them matter.

I knew who she had been and I owed that Stacey something. I had to see her. I had to look into her eyes and at least talk to her. Whatever she'd done, mad as it seemed, I at least owed her that. Maybe it was the only way I could draw a line under it all.

Scrag caught up with me.

The cut on his face looked okay. He could clearly look after himself, the little rabbit-murderer. If I left him outside, he'd be fine. I didn't *need* to take care of him. I had enough to worry about.

I headed back. He followed me.

"I can't look after you," I said.

He wagged his whole bottom and panted.

"You're obviously fine on your own. You can live off rabbits and run wild and free."

He wagged some more and sat back on his hind legs and offered me a paw.

"Seriously. I can't have a dog."

He rolled on his back.

What else could I do? I rubbed his belly and picked him up.

chapter thirty-nine

SHEM

They dragged me along a corridor.

The dragging was completely unnecessary.

I figured if I didn't fight them, they wouldn't fight me.

They keyed some numbers into a pad and opened the door to a long corridor of cells, each with a spyhole at eye height. I wanted to look inside, to see who was in there… if anyone. Maybe they were empty; it was very quiet.

The doors were locked with number pads that glowed a faint, sickly green. I watched them key the numbers into my pad: 07686. The door unlocked with a click and a firm hand on my back guided me inside. Somewhere deep in my foggy brain I felt something was missing from this whole process.

"Don't I get read my rights or something?"

The guard gave a grim shake of his head. "The doctor will tell you all you need to know."

He clanged the door shut and left me on my own.

I looked to the left of the door for the keypad.

Even I had to smile at my own stupidity. Cells didn't have locks on the inside.

And then I registered what he'd said.

Doctor?

chapter forty

LAURA

When I got back to my room, Marsha was still asleep. Scrag jumped onto my bed, completely at home. I tapped my slate to wake it up. I pinched the message icon and started typing before I could change my mind.

I niid ti sii yii. Cin wi miit?

As I waited for a reply, I started to freak out a bit that I was making a massive mistake. I had to talk to someone. I put Scrag near Marsha's head to wake her up. He licked her face until her eyes blinked open. I thought she'd go mad but she said, "You little scamp. Did you miss me, did you?"

"I did," I said. "Are you awake? Can I talk to you, about the note from yesterday?"

Marsha yawned. "The one from your mad friend? You know she went to prison. Look it up…"

"I know. I already have. Marsha, I need to see her."

"What?" She sat up. "Are you crazy? She's an arsonist! She could have killed you!"

"I know."

Guilt flooded through me again. This time for Alfie, who'd never got his second chance… Could I ever forgive Stacey for that? I pressed my fingers to my eyes but the tears leaked through.

I breathed hard until I was calm enough to try and explain.

"I need to understand what she did, Marsha. I need an end to it, one way or another. I mean, what if I bumped into her one day with all this stuff unsaid? I can't just…"

"Pass me your slate."

"Why?"

"What did she say? That you never had cancer?"

I handed it over. She typed a few things in and handed it back to me. "Look. There are literally a million articles on why you were frozen. It sounds to me like your Stacey has lost her marbles."

My slate pinged with a message.

Cin yii git ti brightin in sitirdiy?

Brighton on Saturday. It was exeat. It might just be possible. Was it a stupid idea? Meeting up with her?

Whatever she'd done, whoever she was now, I needed to see her so that I could let go and move on properly, without the dark cloud of her betrayal hovering over everything. Marsha peered at the message.

"Saturday?"

"Could I go, do you think?" I said.

"Are you crazy?"

"It's exeat, isn't it? So we get to do what we want? Keisha and Susan are going to the Pavilion, aren't they? Maybe I could go with them. Get Stacey to meet me there?"

Something strange passed across Marsha's face.

"Would the school let me?" I asked.

"Not without permission from your guardian."

I bit my lip. Then I told Marsha about my last trip to Brighton with Miss Lilly. "She'll never say yes, will she? Especially not if I tell her I want to meet up with Stacey. She doesn't trust her at all."

"With good reason," Marsha said. She thought for a bit. "What if you say you'll disguise yourself somehow? And that we'll go as a group?"

"We?"

"Obviously. Someone's got to look after you and it's not going to be those two idiots, is it? Anyway, I don't know how much longer I'm going to be here. I want to make the most of it. Maybe we could take the dog to the beach?"

I flung my arms around her. I couldn't help it. She was ace. Moody but ace. I crossed my fingers that Miss Lilly and school would say yes and sent Stacey a message:

12 iclick victiriis bidriim.

It was only later that I realized Marsha had used my slate

without Notitia asking for authorization. It was so clever, how it sensed me handing it over. The technology of the future really was amazing.

chapter forty-one

SHEM

I don't know how long I was left alone. I know I slept. It was light in the cell but I was so knackered nothing much could have kept me awake. I woke to a metallic clanging and my heart beating so hard it nearly broke out of my ribcage.

A doctor came in. At least, I think he was a doctor. He was wearing a short-sleeved white coat and pushing a metal trolley. I considered ramming it into him and making a run for it, but a couple of things stopped me. Firstly, he was about sixty and I didn't want to hurt him. Secondly, there was a monster of a man behind him who could easily have been the one who shoved me in the van and booted Scrag in the head. A little knot of anger tightened in my gut. I didn't do any trolley-ramming, but I crossed my arms and faced the wall.

"Come on, young man, nothing to worry about. Just roll up your sleeve and it'll all be over in a tick."

I looked at him.

"Your sleeve," he said again. "Pull it up, there's a good lad."

"Why?"

"Blood tests. Won't take a minute. Not scared of needles, are you? Big chap like you?"

I looked at the trolley. The top was loaded with sterile needle packs. What the hell was this place? I thought back over the last few days. Did they think I was an addict? Or was this a mental home? Had that girl at the school dobbed me in? Said I was a pervert or something?

My head was so cloudy I couldn't work it out.

"I know it's not pleasant but it'll be over in a jiffy if you just pop your arm out. Or, if you're really worried, I can ask Jimmy here to hold your arm steady?"

I could imagine what Jimmy-here holding my arm steady meant. I pulled up my sleeve and let him take my blood.

He patted a plaster over the little hole and said, "One last thing. A few pictures for the records."

That was the kind of thing you expected in prison. Mug shots. The doctor stepped back and another man came in from the corridor with a tripod and a camera big enough to film a Hollywood blockbuster. He made me stand this way and that and took loads of pictures before he was finally satisfied.

"Not too bad, hey?" the doctor said. "You see, a lot of fuss over nothing."

And they left me alone to stare at the ceiling.

chapter forty-two
LAURA

I popped back to check on Scrag before prep. He'd done a wee on my floor but I could hardly blame him for that. I mopped it up as best I could before sending a message to Miss Lilly. I worded it super carefully:

> Some of the girls are going to the Pavilion on Saturday
> – is it okay if I go with them?

Straight away she messaged back saying exactly what I'd expected:

> That sounds fun and I'd love to say yes but after our
> last trip to Brighton I'm not sure it's a good idea.

I typed: I thought about that. I have a plan.

Hold on, I'll Skype you…

I had no idea what that was.

What?

Just hit the green answer button when you're asked.

I bit my thumbnail while I waited.

My slate made a musical bleeping noise. I pressed the green phone and there she was, smiling at me.

"Hey! You look great, Laura. The uniform really suits you. What's your plan then?"

"We want to go to the Pavilion, me and a girl called Marsha and a couple of others. They're really nice."

"Marsha?"

"Yeah, she was the one who helped me lug my trunk to my room on my first day."

Miss Lilly laughed and just the sound of it made me smile. "I remember, the bossy one!"

"That's her." I smiled. "We thought if I braided my hair back and wore a cap, no one would recognize me, especially not in a group and without you drawing attention to us."

She laughed again. "You cheeky thing. I don't know, Laura. I'm not sure... I had wondered if you'd want to come home for a visit – you could bring a friend?"

I'd forgotten she'd suggested that. I bit my lip, worried I'd offended her. "Sorry, none of the other girls are going home. I didn't want to stand out."

"I understand but…"

"You know it was really you who got mobbed, not me."

"Hmmm…" She thought for a minute and I made a pleading face.

Then she said, "I suppose there are some things I can do to make sure you're safe… Okay, but you have to stick to my rules, all right?"

"Promise."

"The Pavilion only, no wandering off. And you get dropped off and picked up."

I felt so guilty. She was worried about my safety and she didn't know the half of it. What was I doing? I wasn't a risk-taker – I followed in the wake of trouble, I didn't seek it.

Miss Lilly said, "I'll send someone down to keep an eye."

"Who?"

"You won't even know they're there. I wouldn't embarrass you in front of your new friends. I'll write Madam Hobbs a message that I'm happy for you to go out with a surreptitious escort."

Someone tried to open my door; I'd locked it to stop anyone from walking in on Scrag. They knocked sharply. Scrag yipped at me. I put a hand on his muzzle so Miss Lilly wouldn't hear and said, "There's someone at my door. I'd better go."

"Okay, I'll make arrangements. I'm glad you're settling in. And don't go out without your phone."

"I won't! Thank you, you're the best."

Whoever it was knocked again and Scrag ran in a circle, yapping. I put my finger to my lips. "Quiet, little one."

I opened the door a tiny crack. It was Marsha, looking decidedly brighter than she had done earlier.

"I've been to see Madam Hobbs. Now you need to get your guardian to agree."

I grinned at her enthusiasm. "She just said yes – as long as there's a group of us. Do you think Keisha and Susan will mind?"

"They'll be delighted. Keisha will have us all organized with little backpacks and cucumber sandwiches."

"Miss Lilly is going to send some people to keep an eye on us. That might complicate things."

"Be grateful. If your long-lost pal turns out to be an axe-murderer, at least we'll have some muscle on our side."

I hugged her. I had *her* on my side and that meant the world. She was blushing when I let go, and then her face changed. She looked like I'd slapped her.

"I told you, people like me don't have friends. I'll be leaving soon, so don't rely on me, Laura." I felt even more guilty. Not just about Miss Lilly but because Marsha was trying to deal with her own stuff and was still willing to help me out.

I said, "Thanks, Marsha – for this. It means a lot. If there's anything I can do in return…"

"I'm only going for the dog," she said.

"Talking of which, I'd better take him out for a quick run."

Marsha raised her eyebrows. I knew it was risky, but he'd been shut in all day. It'd be another three hours until prep and dinner were done. Marsha wrapped Scrag in my towel while I checked the corridor was clear. Then she held court in the ODR while I slipped out through the Rabbit Run. I'd just put Scrag on the ground when a voice boomed across the car park.

"Is that a dog?"

The distinct tone and tracksuit of Madam Hoosier.

"Laura, isn't it? New girl?"

"Yes, Miss. Madam. I think he's lost."

"Oh right. Not yours then?"

"Of course not, Miss. Madam." Why couldn't I get that right? *Madam. Madam. Madam.* "I was going for a run and I just saw him."

"Before prep?"

"I got confused about the time. Sorry. Shall I take him with me, down to the field?"

"Absolutely not. Can't have dogs wandering around the place. I'll take him. Come on, little one, over here."

And Scrag, the treacherous little beast, trotted over to Madam Hoosier with barely a backward glance.

"Gosh. Lovely little fellow, aren't you?" She patted his head and said, "Off to prep for you, Miss. Go on now, and I'll pretend I didn't see you coming out of the Rabbit Run with a dog."

"Yes, Madam. Thank you."

Bum.

She watched until I'd gone back inside. Scrag gave one little yip but he seemed entirely happy to switch allegiance to my PE teacher. I knew I should have been pleased that I didn't have to worry about him any more but I felt like a little piece of our gang had gone. And I wasn't looking forward to telling Marsha she'd lost her furry pal.

I didn't have to. Not that night. I couldn't find Marsha all evening. She didn't reappear until breakfast the following morning.

"Where've you been?" I said.

She shrugged.

"How do you get away without going to prep?"

She shrugged again.

She wasn't in a good mood and I wasn't going to make it worse by telling her about Scrag. And then we passed Madam Hoosier on the way to form and with absolutely zero subtlety she said, "All sorted. He's staying with me. Pop up and see him any time you like."

I had no choice but to explain what had happened.

As predicted, it didn't go down well. When Marsha was disappointed she seemed to collapse in on herself, physically and mentally. Everything about her slumped. A flutter of butterflies released from my stomach.

"You're still coming to the Pavilion?"

"I said I would, didn't I? And I spoke to Keisha – she and Susan are fine about it."

chapter forty-three
SHEM

I was trapped, but somehow I didn't care.

I wasn't cold or wet. I wasn't being kicked or shoved around. Not most of the time anyway. I wasn't hungry. Food came in through a hatch in the bottom of the door. I ate it mechanically and immediately forgot what it was. Maybe there was something in it that made me numb. Maybe that in itself was a kindness. I didn't know. I wasn't that bothered.

Sometimes a tension built up in me and I paced the cell, counting the five steps from one end to the other. The walking calmed me down.

Lights came on, went off. When it got dark, I laid on the rubber mattress, my mind a fog. I missed Scrag. I missed walking and sunshine and cheese but...

A sort of blankness sat in my head, like I was suspended, waiting.

chapter forty-four
LAURA

I was up ridiculously early on the Saturday of exeat. I spent about an hour trying to decide what to wear.

At eight I went to wake Marsha but she wasn't in her room or the bathroom. That was both worrying and annoying. It was my first proper outing as a normal human teenager in this century and I really needed a friend to do all the friend things with. Primarily, outfit selection.

I could hear Ima in my head saying, *"It's not a fashion show."* How wrong she was. All of life is a fashion show and everyone knows it.

I'd plaited my hair in two tight braids and finally decided on black skinny jeans and my lemon sweatshirt, but I really needed a second opinion. I went back to my own room and changed my top, again, to a red gingham shirt Miss Lilly had bought me.

Maybe red was too bright to be inconspicuous. I took it off and put on Stacey's Benetton jumper. Only that might send the wrong message to Stacey.

I put the gingham shirt back on. With the plaits in my hair I did look a bit cowgirl but I took a deep breath and went to the dining room.

Keisha and Susan were eating toast and poring over old history books about the Pavilion. That was good. If they were completely engrossed in the history of the place they wouldn't notice me disappearing to find Stacey.

I was relieved to see they were both in black jeans – Keisha with a white shirt tied at the waist and Susan with a sort of weird patchwork sweatshirt, covered in cat pictures. She held out the hem of her top and said, "Do you think all these cats are related?"

We looked at her but I mean, seriously, what could you say?

Keisha said to me, "You look nice, is that a vintage top?"

"No, does it look it? I wasn't sure what to wear. Do I look weird?"

Keisha and me both glanced at Susan. Comparatively? No, I definitely did not look weird.

I was twitching with nerves though and very grateful those two were coming. Susan would definitely deflect any interest that might otherwise come my way and if Marsha didn't appear, at least I had them.

Susan flipped a page of her book and said, "Wow, look at this – isn't it the most beautiful room you've ever seen?"

She shoved the musty thing under my nose and showed me the ugliest room in the whole palace – it was orange with a crazy floral carpet – headache-inducingly bright. A rush of memory made me catch my breath.

My parents standing close together in that very room. Their little fingers hooked together, not quite a hand hold, not quite anything other people could comment on. And me, pushing my way between them, small enough to kiss each of their hands as I passed through – no Alfie yet, he hadn't been born. There was so much love in our family I could have taken a fistful of it and modelled it into a heart shape.

In that second, I felt the weight of all that loss. I was the curator of the museum of my family. All the responsibility to keep the essence of it rested in me and yet I still hadn't even asked about where they were buried.

I looked down at my porridge. I'd stirred blueberries in it so violently that it looked like a bowl of grey gloop.

"Hey? What's up?" Keisha said.

I blinked, suddenly aware of the tears on my lashes. I shook my head. "Nothing." I forced a smile. "Have you seen Marsha?"

Keisha shook her head. "I'll text her."

I should have thought of that. It wasn't a habit with me yet. "I'll do it," I said. Holding my phone under the table, I quietly sent a message.

Keisha said, "Eat up and we'll go get tagged."

"What?"

"Tagged. They won't let us out without knowing where we are, will they?"

I followed her, wondering what on earth they were going to do – put a luggage label on us like Paddington? *Please*

Look After This Laura. I sort of liked the idea that I couldn't get lost. If Stacey went crazy and tried to kidnap me or something, at least the school could track me down.

I did not want to be on the wrong side of Stacey's temper. I remembered when she'd been sort of seeing Michael Westerbrook, a kid in our class, and he'd got off with one of the Level-Johnson twins. Stacey went absolutely mad – she threw a chemistry lab stool at him and gave him a black eye. She'd been suspended for a week.

I'd expected we'd go to Madam Hobbs or reception but Keisha led the way to the medical centre. We climbed the stairs and she knocked on the door.

"In you come, girls. I'm ready for you. How's that knee doing, Laura? You were meant to pop in and see me."

"Oh, yes." I'd forgotten all about my knee, and my appointment. "Sorry, it's fine. The glue stuff did the trick."

"Excellent, I'd still like to check it though."

I looked down at my skinny-jean clad legs and she said, "Maybe when you get back. Let's sort this out first, hey?"

Keisha rolled her sleeve up and the nurse picked up one of three small metal tubes.

"What's that?" I said.

The nurse looked up. "Tracking serum. Nothing to worry about. A gentle push against your skin and it's done."

I swallowed. An injection?

Keisha held her arm out, palm up. The dark pink skin looked vulnerable and exposed but she didn't flinch when the nurse stamped her wrist.

"Can we go without it?" I said. "Marsha…"

"Oh, she's already been in. And no, goodness me, we need to know we can keep you safe, don't we?"

"But…"

She jabbed Susan and then turned to me. "It's fine. It's a benign virus carrying a code individual to you. It lasts about a week and then your body fights it off. You won't even know it's there as long as you stick to your exeat rules. I have you down as going to the Pavilion only with a six p.m. pick-up? Is that right?"

Keisha nodded and said, "Come on, Laura. We need to find Marsha."

I rolled up my sleeve. It didn't hurt, like she said. With just a tiny push against my skin, they could follow us wherever we went. I shuddered.

We found Marsha halfway back to Blue House corridor. She looked utterly miserable.

"Where were you at breakfast?" Keisha said.

Marsha shrugged.

I touched her arm. "Are you okay? Look, if you don't want to come, you don't have to."

"And abandon you in your hour of need? Of course I'll come."

As we walked back to get our bags, she seemed really down. I asked her where she'd been.

"Begging my father not to move me again. He's talking

about next weekend. He can't even wait until the end of term. He has a stone for a heart."

My mood sank with hers. I would really miss Marsha.

We went through the main door, signed our exeat slip and the receptionist held up a paddle to check the tracker virus was active and scan us out. It was kind of creepy but sort of reassuring at the same time.

A minibus was waiting to drive us to town but there was no driver and no guards. Other girls were getting on, with a lot of excited chatter about their plans for the day. I clutched at Marsha's sleeve; a great big ugly old ball of worry was growing in my gut. Marsha tapped away on her phone, not even acknowledging my pathetic clinging on.

The minibus stopped on the seafront and said, *"Alight here for Brighton and the Pavilion."*

We did and Keisha headed confidently away from the sea, Susan hurrying to keep up. Nerves held me back and Marsha was lost in her own thoughts until Keisha snapped her head round.

"Come on, you two. We haven't got all day. Don't you want to see the ice house exhibition?"

"Ice cream?" Susan said.

"No, ice house – where they stored ice for the palace. It's been fully excavated now – you can see it without any of the tech, just—"

"No," said Marsha, "we don't." Then she whispered to me in a voice that was definitely loud enough for Keisha to hear, "Honestly, does she do it on purpose? Idiot. As if after forty years in a deep freeze you'd want to visit another one?"

Still, when Keisha huffed off, we followed her because she did seem to know where she was going. She'd snapped her phone around her wrist like a chunky white bracelet and had a button in her ear that was probably telling her where to go.

I could soon see the beautiful onion-shaped roofline of the Pavilion. I scanned the crowd waiting to go in. Where were Miss Lilly's guards? Was Stacey here already? It was early. Too early probably.

Susan said, "Don't you think all buildings should look like vegetables? Like, a runner-bean tower block or a mushroom bungalow."

"Or a cabbage cottage?" I joined in.

She gave me the most enormous smile. "Yes! Or an aubergine apartment or a halloumi hovel."

I opened my mouth to ask what kind of vegetable halloumi was, but she seemed so happy that I just nodded.

We queued. Keisha buzzing with excitement, Susan quietly bonkers, Marsha still absorbed in her phone, and me ready to vomit. I was seriously questioning what I was doing. Maybe I should have just left well alone, ignored Stacey. Cut her out of my mind. I sighed. That was never an option. Not really. She would haunt me for ever – if not in real life, then in my head.

When we got to the door, an attendant explained that if we hired the AR glasses we could enjoy the company of King George IV or, if we preferred, Her Royal Highness Queen Victoria.

I nudged Marsha. "What's AR?"

Marsha poked her hand in the middle of the attendant – I mean, right through his stomach. He shimmered with static. My mouth dropped open.

She shrugged. "Holograms, Augmented Reality, but with the glasses, they seem to move about."

I stared at the attendant. "He looks so real."

She shrugged again as we went past. I was looking back at the attendant when Keisha tugged my arm.

"Do you want the glasses? Just tap there."

She pointed at a screen with a shelf underneath. I tapped it and a pair of glasses dropped into the tray.

"Where do I pay?"

"You already did, when you hit the button."

I looked at Marsha for an explanation – she held up her phone. "Airpay."

It was the most alien I'd felt since I came back.

"Do you still have actual cash?" I asked.

"Hmm, not many people use it any more," Keisha said. "It's dirty, isn't it? Disgusting, when you think about it. So many people handle it, it gets covered in germs."

By the time I'd finished being agog, we were in the pale green Entrance Hall being welcomed by a footman.

"Real?" I said to Marsha.

"Nope."

She put her glasses on so I did the same. The room was suddenly full of people in old-fashioned clothes, chattering to each other. I mean *really* old-fashioned clothes, not 1980s old-fashioned. I took the glasses off and the people disappeared. It was creepy. Totally creepy. But also kind of cool, even if the weird motion of it made me feel slightly sick. We walked through to the long gallery, me with my hands flapping about in front of me, struggling to work out what was real and what wasn't. I blinked at a short man in Chinese court dress and he started speaking to me. Convinced it wasn't a person, I reached forward to put my hand through him, like Marsha had done at the door, and stubbed my fingers on a statue.

"I can't deal with this," I said. "How do you know what's real and what's not?"

"You don't," Keisha said with that annoying superior tone in her voice. "That's the whole point."

"Haven't you been in the AR room at school?" Susan said, as we worked our way into the banqueting room.

"We have a room like this at school?"

"Since my grandma died, it's the only way I get to spend any real time with her," she said, smiling sadly. "And her giraffes."

"Giraffes?" I said.

"Don't encourage her," Marsha said, then more quietly, "Let's just go straight to the bedroom and wait. We don't want to miss your friend."

I felt properly jittery. What if I didn't recognize Stacey? She'd be so much older. I took the AR glasses off and checked the time. I had nearly an hour until I was due to meet her. I looked around. Without the glasses the room was so much emptier and I realized my friends had moved on. Even Marsha was heading through to the next room.

I watched the other tourists for a bit. It was strange watching them carefully navigating around non-existent Victorians, like the room was full of ghosts and I was the only one who couldn't see them. With a small shock, I noticed I could still see one, even without the glasses on. It was a woman in Victorian costume, her face in the shadow of a bonnet, who was definitely looking at me.

Could it be her? Could it be Stacey?

chapter forty-five
SHEM

Walls.

   White walls.

   Walking.

   And waiting.

   Was this it?

   Was this my life now?

   Why?

chapter forty-six
LAURA

We stared at each other, the invisible thread of our line of vision connecting myself and the woman. Her eyes had not a smudge of Robert Smith eyeliner, her skin was soft and doughy. I guessed she was in her fifties but I couldn't be sure. Anyone over forty seemed ancient to me. She didn't look like Stacey but why else would she be staring at me so intently?

My heart hurt. It seemed to be tearing itself in two with the simultaneous urge to run towards her and to run away. Unless... Could the woman be a journalist? Could she somehow have discovered that I was out for the day? Or maybe she was Miss Lilly's guard – if she was, I probably needed to shake her off before I met Stacey in the room upstairs. I needed Marsha's advice. I turned away, but before I'd taken two steps, the woman had crossed the room and caught hold of my arm.

I peered down at the hand holding onto me. It was blotched with freckles, the nails bitten to stubs, chewed and torn. Then I examined her face, really looked, and I knew her like I knew my own reflection. The breath I'd been holding escaped in a gasp.

Her eyes shone. "It's you, it's really you."

I nodded, unable to speak.

For a moment, all the betrayal, all the questions, everything fell away. She was Stacey, my Stacey. My past right here in my present. I threw my arms around her neck and hugged her.

She hugged me fiercely in return and then something changed – she stiffened and stepped back. "We need to get out of here," she said.

"I can't," I faltered. "I'm with –" I hesitated over saying "friends", it seemed too cruel, a reminder she wasn't one of them – "people."

"Get rid of them."

"I can't, they…"

"Do they know you're meeting me? Why did you take that risk? I told you…"

"What do you mean?"

"Keep your voice down."

Marsha put her head round the corner and called across the room. "Laura, catch up, will you?"

I wanted to call her back but she'd already gone. With the AR glasses on, Stacey blended in with the fake Victorians. Marsha wouldn't have realized. I was tempted to follow her, but Stacey put a hand under my elbow and swept me sideways, through a plain wooden door into a tiny hallway.

I pulled my arm away. "What are you doing?"

"We can't be seen," she said, and then, as if a switch had flipped, her face softened again. "Oh, Laura, I can't believe it, after all this time, I can't believe you're in front of me, real, solid, alive." She hugged me again, her bonnet biffing me in the face.

I hugged her back, but, hidden from other people, I was nervous.

As if she sensed it, she said, "This must be so strange for you. I'm so sorry about everything that happened."

"Your note, the things you said…"

Her face darkened and she gripped my arms. "You have to believe me, Laura. It was her fault, the crash – they were chasing your mum's car – her people. She wanted them dead."

"What? Who wanted them dead? What do you mean?"

"*Her*. Crisp."

My mouth opened in shock. "Miss Lilly? That's the flower you meant? In your note?"

"It's her fault, all of it…"

"Stacey, the coroner's report said no one else was involved in the collision, that Mum and Ima had been distracted by recent events, like you, writing in the paper – that's what caused them to crash. And what about the fire? How was that Miss Lilly's fault?"

"We don't have much time. I'm not supposed to be anywhere near you." She glanced over her shoulder at some stone steps that seemed to lead under the building. "Let's go down there, less chance of being overheard."

She must have read the mistrust on my face because a moth of disappointment fluttered across hers in response. She didn't act like my Stacey, but the pain in her eyes, I knew that and I couldn't bear it.

"Okay, lead the way," I said.

I let her go first, just in case she was a psycho and tried to shove me down the steps. I told myself to stop being weird. Whatever she'd done, she was still Stacey. She wouldn't hurt me, not on purpose, not physically at least.

At the bottom was a white tiled corridor, brightly lit and smelling of undisturbed damp.

She turned to face me, took my hand and said, "Crisp comes across as completely lovely, but she's a murdering, money-grabbing bitch."

It was so harsh, so bitter. I flinched.

"The things she achieves, they're not possible with legal treatments. I've done research."

I wasn't interested in Miss Lilly's achievements; there were more important things I needed to know. "Did you know we were there, Alfie and me, when you started the fire?"

She froze for a moment. "That was an accident. I don't know what happened but it wasn't... I didn't do anything deliberately – I don't know how it can have taken hold, I..."

She pressed the heels of her hands against her eyes. She was shaking, trying to get control of herself. Then she exhaled sharply and said, "She does this cryotherapy thing... not what she did to you, it's different – it's meant to freeze your cells and stop them ageing, but it's doesn't make sense. It works but it *can't* work – the science doesn't stack up. The elite, the rich, she can make them look twenty years younger – *literally* twenty years younger. How? There has to be something else behind it."

Stacey wasn't making any sense. Why would people use that horrible Ice Chamber I'd seen at the clinic if it didn't work? At least a bit? I tried to make her see what I saw.

"Stacey, Blackhurst Clinic saved my life."

She shook her head. "I've spent forty years researching what happened to you." She dropped her voice to a stage whisper. "I don't think your life ever needed saving."

"What are you saying? That I should have died?"

"No! But what if you were never really ill in the first place?"

"Stacey, you saw us, me and Alfie. We could barely function towards the end."

Her voice became sharper. "You remember the vaccinations at school? The TB vaccinations? That was all sponsored by her. Why?"

"Because it's a good thing to do?"

"No. So she could pick and choose her victims. She drugged them. And where are they now? All the others like you? The children who were frozen. What happened to them?"

My heart stopped. I didn't know much about the other people who were frozen but I knew what had happened to them at the end. "They died, Stacey, because of the fire –

the fire you started." It was too much. My throat tightened with sorrow. "I'm the only one left."

She held my arms so tightly her fingers dug into my flesh. "A child goes missing in the UK every three minutes – every *three minutes* – what happens to them?"

I pulled myself free. "I don't know, Stacey, but they aren't all in cryostasis capsules at Blackhurst!"

She slapped herself on the forehead, like she used to when she was frustrated with herself. "I'm not explaining properly. It's not…"

I was scared now; she wasn't right in the head. I tried to calm her down. "Think about what you're saying. That would be hundreds of thousands of kids. Where would she keep them?"

"They're hidden. You could find them. You have access."

I shook my head. I'd given her a chance but now I needed to get away. "Mum and Ima would never have done what they did if they hadn't trusted the clinic, would they? They weren't stupid."

"Not stupid but desperate. They were tricked. It was something to do with the TB jabs, I know it…"

"But Alfie didn't have the TB jab, Stacey. He was too young."

Stacey gripped my shoulders and glared into my face. "She did it. Whatever she says. It's her."

I jerked free from her grip. Her head drooped like it did before, like she was switching off and resetting.

"It's been so hard on my own."

A door opened above us.

"Is there anyone down here?"

Stacey stared into my eyes and I felt the power of her desperation. "I have to go. Please, Laura, think about what I've said. Think about Alfie."

I choked as I said, "I told you. Alfie died thanks to the fire. They were never able to revive him."

"Are you sure? Have you seen where he's buried? Or has he conveniently disappeared?"

The arrow struck. I had let that question slide from my mind.

The voice at the top of the steps called, "I can hear you, I'm coming down."

Stacey pressed a round flat thing like a compact into my hand and shoved me towards the stairs.

"It's all on there. Everything I found out. Watch it, then contact me."

She turned and disappeared into the cellars so fast it was as if she'd never been there. An old man was heading towards me with a heavy-duty torch, even though all the lights were on. I shielded my eyes from the beam.

"You gave me a fright, young lady."

"Sorry. I think I'm lost."

He shook his head. "Come on, this way."

I followed him up the stairs and he took me to the kitchens.

"You're back on track here."

"Thanks so much."

I hurried to find Marsha. When I caught up she said, "Where have you been? It's nearly twelve, come on, we need to go to Victoria's bedroom to meet your friend."

I let her drag me there, turning over the conversation with Stacey in my head. She hated Miss Lilly. I mean really *hated* her. Why? Miss Lilly was so lovely – everyone I met adored her. Was Stacey jealous? Or bitter about going to prison? Did she blame Miss Lilly for that? It didn't make sense – Miss Lilly was the one who should have hated Stacey, but whenever we'd talked about what had happened, she'd been nothing but understanding. Nothing but *fair*.

It was easy to dismiss most of what Stacey had said: kids went missing for all sorts of reasons and it wasn't like Miss Lilly could keep anything hidden even if she'd wanted to, with so many people working at the clinic. The only thing that stuck in me like a barb was what she'd said about Alfie. I should know where he was. I had to find him.

chapter forty-seven

LAURA

We reached the sunny yellow room that had been Queen Victoria's bedroom. Susan and Keisha were in raptures.

Marsha whispered, "Which one is she?"

"She's not here. I've already seen her."

"What? Without me? Laura! I got you here, I—"

"I know, Marsha, but it's not a game. Is there somewhere we can go for a cup of tea? My head is spinning."

"You… I can't believe you sneaked off without me. I…"

Marsha was angry. Really, truly, properly angry.

"I'll buy?" I said, trying to make it up to her.

"You don't understand, I…" She buried her face in her hands and then sighed. "Okay, let's go to the tea room."

I glanced across to tell Susan and Keisha but they were reading details about wallpaper so we left them to it.

* * *

I got Marsha a peppermint tea and me a proper brew. There was nowhere to sit so we crammed into a corner with a sort of shelf to rest our cups on and I told her what Stacey had said.

"She sounds mental," Marsha said.

"I know. But…"

But what? She *did* sound mental. But what she'd said about Alfie had got under my skin. It wasn't just the thing about where he was buried, it was what she'd said about him having "conveniently disappeared". He was hardly ever mentioned by anyone. All I'd seen of him on the internet was that picture on Wikipedia – and even that didn't name him. It was like he didn't exist in this world – like he'd never existed. He deserved more than that and he had to be somewhere. There had to be a physical place. Somewhere I could visit.

I said, "I need to call Miss Lilly."

"Why?"

"I just…I need to."

I dialled her number but she didn't answer. I tried again. Still nothing. It wasn't that far to Blackhurst from Brighton. I had all day. I could go and ask her myself. I'd been so wrapped up in my new life, in worrying over clothes and what my stupid teeth looked like and about Marsha leaving school – not even for her sake, for mine. I was disgusted with myself.

Alfie was only a little boy. There'd have been no one with him. He'd have been all alone at his own funeral, with not a single person that knew and loved him. A cold hand wrapped itself around my heart and squeezed. What was wrong with me? Was I really so selfish? He might even be buried near the clinic. There was a village nearby, maybe a churchyard. What if I could go there today? It was only midday. There'd be time.

"She isn't answering," I said. "Could I get to Blackhurst this afternoon?"

"Don't be an idiot."

"There's something I have to do. I don't know when I'll get another day off and Miss Lilly isn't answering her phone."

"Just try her later."

But the idea had lodged in my brain and wouldn't shift. I shook my head. "I need to go. It's not that far. The drive took less than an hour when we came to Brighton before. I could get a train or something? The minibus isn't due until this evening. I'd be back by then."

Marsha bit her lip.

I dialled the number again. *"This number is currently unavailable. Leave a message after the beep."* I hung up.

"Stacey asked me where Alfie was. I don't know, Marsha. My whole family are dead and I've never even asked where they're buried. What kind of daughter does that? What kind of sister?"

Tears leaked down my face. "I promised Alfie I'd always be there for him, but I haven't even said goodbye."

Other people in the tea room were watching us but I didn't care. Maybe it was the stress of the trip, of seeing

Stacey, of all the grief bottled up inside me, but the tears turned into hiccupping sobs I couldn't stop.

"All right," Marsha said. "All right. We'd better hurry up. We can get a train to the village but it's quite a walk from there and there won't be any taxis – Miss Lilly sends out private cars to pick up clients."

"You'll come with me?" I sniffed.

"Someone's got to keep an eye on you, you big idiot."

That made me cry even louder. We'd known each other such a short time but she took it for granted that she'd come with me. "Are you sure? We aren't supposed to go anywhere except the Pavilion."

She drained her mug, her eyes sparkling with determination. "You look so innocent but you're trouble really, aren't you?"

"I don't want to get you in trouble, Marsha. Your dad… it gives him more reason to move you."

"What's a reason to move her?" Keisha the stealth elf appeared from behind Marsha.

"Mind your own business," Marsha said.

"It is my business if you're up to something. We're out as a group, aren't we?"

I pressed my fingers against my eyelids. "Please, Keisha, can you just stay out of this?"

"Depends what *this* is, doesn't it?"

"Nothing. I just…I need to see Miss Lilly."

"You can't leave Brighton."

"I'm nearly seventeen. I can do what I want."

Keisha said, "No, I mean you actually can't. The tracking virus won't let you."

"What?"

"The tracking virus. It'll paralyse you if you travel too far."

She was so matter-of-fact about it. I just stared at her. "That can't be true. That can't be legal? Surely?"

"Why not? You signed an exeat agreement. If you don't break it, there's no problem. Anyway, it's only temporary. It'll have worn off after twenty-four hours."

"I don't believe you. You can't just paralyse people. What if one of us was actually kidnapped? You'd be incapacitated. That's stupid. Marsha? She's not right, is she?"

"It does something. I'm not sure what. Maybe not actual paralysis."

It couldn't. *I mean, seriously?* That was ridiculous.

I said to Marsha, "Wait. You knew something might happen and you were still prepared to go?"

She shrugged. "Why not? I'll try anything once."

Keisha stuck her hands on her hips. "I'll report you. Tell them, Susan."

But Susan was tucking into an eclair and said, "When you're paralysed, can you blink?" She blinked furiously. "I love blinking."

Keisha tried to reason with me. "What can possibly be so urgent?"

Because I'm so self-centred I didn't think to ask where Mum and Ima and my only brother were buried. Alfie, the person who meant more to me than anyone else on the planet.

I shook my head. Saying that to Marsha was very different to saying it to Keisha. Instead, I said, "Miss Lilly kind of wanted me to go home anyway. It'll be fine. If we're late getting back, just say you lost us in the Pavilion. Honestly, don't worry, you won't get in trouble."

Her little face went rigid with anger. "I'm not worried about me, you idiots. I'm worried about you!"

I shrugged. "We'll be fine, won't we, Marsha?"

"Fine or paralysed. One or the other."

My stomach squeezed. We wouldn't be paralysed. That was ridiculous.

"You can't," Keisha said. "It's a stupid idea."

I picked up my bag. Marsha followed suit and we left with Keisha shouting after us, "You're both idiots!"

I wished Miss Lilly had told me who she was sending to keep an eye out for me. I was half thinking we could ask for a lift but I didn't see anyone who looked like a guard I knew. Maybe they'd seen that I was fine and left. No one had mobbed us. Not a single person, apart from Stacey, had even recognized me.

We made our way to the train station – Marsha knew where everything was. When we got there I said, "What about tickets?"

"Just use Airpay."

I felt for my phone and had a surge of gratitude to Miss Lilly for giving it to me, swiftly followed by a punch of guilt.

I'd already betrayed her generosity by meeting up with Stacey – and now I was breaking my promise not to wander off. I tried to call her again – still no answer.

"Marsha, will school track us? Will they know we're not at the Pavilion?"

"Maybe. They don't usually follow people all the time, just if the alarm triggers."

"It will though, won't it? If we leave the Pavilion?"

"Who knows? It's like a magical mystery tour."

Not for one second did I imagine the virus really would paralyse us, but I was a bit worried someone would stop us. If I could just talk to Miss Lilly... I tried her phone again. Still nothing. Would she be mad at me? I didn't think so. A little part of me thought she might be secretly pleased that I'd gone home after all.

There was a train standing at the platform.

"Come on," Marsha said, tugging my sleeve. She went straight through the gate.

"But how do I pay?" I called after her.

"Just follow me, it'll pick up your phone and release the gate. Hurry up!"

I followed her straight through. It was easy. I felt a tiny bit smug about being so twenty-first-century. The train was busy. We walked down the carriage until we found two seats together. Marsha slumped into the window seat.

"Thanks for coming with me," I said.

She smiled sadly.

"Are you worried about your dad?" I said. "About leaving?"

"Laura, you are no psychologist." She stuck a button in her ear and closed her eyes.

I watched her for a bit. I liked Marsha – but I didn't understand her. Sometimes it seemed like there was something I was missing. I plugged in the earpieces she'd given me and listened to Frankie Goes to Hollywood's "Two Tribes" to give me a bit of courage.

We passed a field of sheep. Alfie had loved animals. I sighed and got my phone out to try Miss Lilly again but a vicious headache suddenly bit my brain and within moments I could hardly move.

chapter forty-eight
LAURA

Every jolt of the train was an electric shock through my head. I twisted to look at Marsha. Her face was white under a sheen of sweat. I tried to say sorry, but I couldn't speak. I'd done this. My impatience had caused this brain-crushing agony. She reached a hand across the seat and squeezed mine.

"Next...stop," she managed to say through gritted teeth. I tried to nod but every movement was crippling. When the train came to a standstill, we stumbled off, clinging to each other for support. Marsha was sick in a platform bin. We needed to cross a bridge to get out of the station. A cool breeze seemed to ease my pain but Marsha was getting worse. She could barely walk. I held her up, carefully navigating us towards the steps. By the time we were halfway up, my head was clearing but she was sweating and shaking.

There was no way Marsha could walk anywhere, and if we did, we'd be getting further from Brighton. For all I knew that would make it worse. I couldn't put her through any more of this.

"This is stupid," I said. "We'll go back. It's okay, Marsha. we'll go straight back."

She couldn't speak. I managed to get her across the bridge and steered her to a bench, then I looked to see if I could find out when the next train was.

An electronic sign said, *This is an unmanned request stop. Please press the button for a train. The next train to Brighton is in seven minutes.*

I pressed the button and went back to Marsha. She was huddled in on herself but I was feeling quite a lot better. I put an arm round her shaking shoulders.

"I'm so sorry, Marsha. It'll be okay. The train will be here soon." I stroked her back but that made her shake even more. I couldn't believe this was allowed. Whichever way you looked at it, this was not okay. It was like torture. It *was* torture. Marsha was sick again, all over the platform. She slumped against me.

"Marsha? *Marsha?*"

I shook her a little bit. Her head lolled to one side. This couldn't be right. I fumbled for my phone in a panic and called Keisha.

"Marsha isn't moving. What do I do? What do I do?"

"Oh God! Where are you? Get the next train back. You need to come back."

"I know that! The train is coming but what do I do now?"

Marsha slid further down the seat.

"Keisha, I think she's stopped breathing!"

"Put her in the recovery position."

"I can't – there's sick on the floor."

"Oh for goodness' sake… Is there a bench? Lay her on that."

I turned Marsha onto her side. She made a huffing noise that could have just been air getting knocked out of her lungs. I checked the clock. Four minutes until the next train.

I fumbled for my phone. "What next?"

"See if she's breathing – put your cheek next to her mouth. Can you feel breath?"

I leaned next to this girl who'd become my friend the instant I met her, and felt the softest tickle of breath. "Yes, yes. Oh thank God, she's breathing."

I heard Keisha let out a sigh of relief but that was all I heard because two people in green and yellow uniforms came running onto the platform.

"Okay, love, stand back. Paramedics. We've got this."

I watched them tear things from sterile packets, put a patch on Marsha's arm and slowly lift her into a sitting position. Her head was still a bit wobbly but she was coming round.

"An ambulance is here, Keisha," I said into the phone. "It's okay. She's going to be okay."

"The tracking virus must have triggered an alarm. Stay with her. I'll see you back at school."

The paramedics scanned Marsha with a hand-held paddle like the one they'd used at school. "Okey doke, this one's

Marsha Trifonova." They scanned me as well and then said, "Did you find her here?"

"No. I came with her, we were out together. I'm Laura Henley."

She waved the paddle at me again. "Nope, we're not picking anything up."

She tapped at the screen on the paddle and said, "Laura Henley was one of three girls with Marsha Trifonova who had a tracker administered this morning. That can't be you."

"It is me."

"That's not possible."

"But it is. I am me. I had a really bad headache on the train – maybe it just didn't affect me quite so much."

She scanned me again, checking the results.

"Are you sure you're Laura Henley?"

"Yes."

"More like they didn't administer the virus properly, lucky for you. What on earth were you thinking?"

"I didn't know what would happen…"

She shook her head. "Well, we'd better take you both back then, hadn't we?"

They drove us back to school in the ambulance. Marsha was groggy but awake. I held her hand. Pretty soon the back door of the ambulance was opened and the familiar wind on the cliff whipped through the air.

Madam Hobbs was standing on the drive, her face stony. She said to the paramedics, "Could you take Marsha to the health centre – Keisha will show you the way."

Marsha tried to say, "Laura…"

I made to follow but Madam Hobbs stopped me. "My room, I think, Miss Henley?"

I went with her, sick with nerves and regret.

In her office, Madam Hobbs said, "Close the door. I am not sure what you thought you were doing today. It was irresponsible in the extreme and a vast betrayal of trust. This school has high expectations of its pupils and today you did not meet them. In any way."

Shame flooded through me.

"So what did you think you were doing?"

I looked at the floor and muttered, "I needed to see Miss Lilly."

I heard her sigh and tap a pen on the desk. "Why did you not just call her? Or request a pass to see her? Why this elaborate ruse? Laura, you signed an exeat agreement, which you have broken. You were extremely lucky not to suffer the same unfortunate effects as Marsha."

"It wasn't a ruse. I'm sorry. I didn't think—"

"No, you didn't, did you? Not even for a minute. I am so very disappointed in you. Your guardian has been notified of your transgression. Now go to your room. You will be informed of any further sanctions in due course."

* * *

I sat in my room staring out of the window, waiting for someone to tell me that Marsha had brain damage or worse and for Miss Lilly to call me and tell me how ashamed she was of me. It seemed like hours before a message envelope appeared above my slate, blinking Miss Lilly's name. I watched it spin until I got the courage to open it:

> Sweetheart, what happened? I had five missed calls from you! I tried to ring you back but you didn't answer and now the school say you were trying to come home. Are you okay? Message me and let me know you're all right! I'm sending you something that'll cheer you up.

Below her message was a little video clip of Batfink sitting in the bath watching the tap drip, trying to catch the water splashes in her mouth.

Miss Lilly wasn't even annoyed; she was just worried about me. Stacey was so wrong about her. She had wasted her life trying to bring down a woman who was nothing but kind.

I chewed my lip. What could I say to Miss Lilly that would make up for what I'd done? Whatever she said, my behaviour must have embarrassed her. *I* was embarrassed of my behaviour. I wrote back:

> I'm so sorry – there's nothing wrong. I just realized I never asked about Mum and Ima and Alfie, about

where they were buried. I got a bit upset. I thought
Alfie might be near the clinic. I just wanted to say
goodbye.

She wrote back straight away:

Of course you did, darling girl. I am so sorry. This is
my fault. I should have told you. I scattered Alfie's
ashes where both your mothers are buried, in France.
It seemed the right thing to do. Just say the word and
I'll take you there. We'll organize the time off school.

He was with Mum and Ima. Relief flooded through me.
I wrote back:

Thank you. I'd like that.

As I sat back, a dark, pulsating cloud appeared on my
computer. I'd never seen it before. It looked poisonous. I
wanted to get rid of it, so I tried to pinch it closed but as soon
as I touched it, it expanded to fill my screen and burst open.

chapter forty-nine
SHEM

I still didn't know why I was locked up. After the doctor came, I thought they'd tell me what was going to happen to me. I cycled through panic and numb calm over and over. I fantasized about them sending me to a commune for homeless people, where we'd build our own shelters and grow our own veg. I'd get Scrag back and have a life. And then I started to think I'd be left in the cell for ever, just me, that I'd never hear another human. Never feel the soft fur of my dog's belly.

If I closed my eyes, I could imagine Scrag curled up next to me. I could bury my fingers in his fur and hear his soft snore-y breathing.

I closed my eyes and kept them closed.

chapter fifty
LAURA

Green letters scrolled across my screen:

This is an encrypted channel inside the Dark Web.
We're safe here. Have you played the recording
I gave you?

My hand went to my pocket. I'd forgotten about the little compact thing.

I fished it out.

Mum had had something that looked just like it, only hers had had powder in the bottom and a mirror in the lid. Between the two halves of this one spun a tiny glistening prism. I touched it with my finger, disturbing the image and prompting, *"Identify yourself."*

I snapped it shut.

The black cloud flashed with a little lightning bolt, another message:

Please, Lu. Please. I know this is hard for you, but imagine what it's been like for me. I lost you, my best friend, and none of it made sense. One minute you were there and the next you were gone and I didn't know if you'd be back next year, next decade or ever. No one spoke to me about it. Your mum and Ima, I loved them, you know I did, but even they closed up. No one understood. The only person who might have done was you and you were lost. So near and yet so far. I might have got things wrong but I swear I was trying to do what was right. You know me. You're the only person alive who really does. Please, listen to the recording.

I pressed my hands to my forehead. What was I supposed to do? How could I ignore a plea like that from my oldest friend? I pictured how she'd been when her gran had died. She'd huddled on her bed, her mascara silently laying black tracks down her face as tears puddled on her pillow and an unchanged record spun round and round on her turntable, hiccupping over grooves in the disc, scratching a rhythm from dust and distress.

I opened the compact.

"*Identify yourself.*"

"Laura Henley."

"*Your voice does not match our records. Please identify yourself by answering the following question: who was your year nine geography teacher?*"

I smiled. "Mr Gudgeon."

"*Access granted.*"

A grainy image of the older Stacey appeared, grey hair flopping across her face. She smiled briefly.

"*If you're watching this, I must have found you and you must be alive, which, believe me, are two things I doubted I'd ever live to see. God, I hope I do. Please listen to the whole of this message. Lu, all I can do is tell you the truth and hope that you believe me.*

"*After you were put into stasis, there was a lot of news coverage – your mum and Ima were the lesbo parents who gave their kids up for experimental treatment. Some of the papers said they'd been paid to hand you over. It was awful. The press made up whatever they wanted, and your mums wouldn't do any interviews. They wouldn't see me, they wouldn't see anyone. I tried every day and one time I arrived at your house to find it empty. They'd just gone. I was lost. I had no clue what to do.*

"*Do you remember PAFA? The activists we met in town? You were right about the skinny guy – Zappa – by the way, total creep. But after what happened to you, they picked me up, helped me through it.*

"*They were like a new family to me. I was young, I wanted to impress them, so I did all the stuff you'd have hated. Broke in places, smashed stuff up, released animals. We were always fundraising – activism is expensive – so Zappa suggested I did the interview about you to get some cash. I should never have done it. I've beaten myself up over it every day since but I can't change the past, no matter how bad I feel. And one good thing came out of it. A woman got in touch.*"

The recorded Stacey rubbed her face and then went on. *"At first, I thought she was just a nutter. She was an addict who'd had her kid taken away. She'd got clean and wanted the kid back but he'd run away from his foster-home in Brighton and no one had bothered to tell her. He was eight years old, Laura, and no one knew where he was. She scoured the streets looking for him and some homeless guy told her that he thought the kid might have been taken to Blackhurst Clinic. It didn't make a lot of sense but the woman was desperate for any clues. When she saw my interview, mentioning the clinic, she tracked me down to see if I knew what went on there. Somehow she'd got hold of some police records and realized that there was a string of kids who'd gone missing – kids of addicts, runaways, children blamed for their own disappearances. Kids the newspapers wouldn't shout about."*

Stacey blew her fringe out of her eyes. The hair may have changed but the gesture was pure Stacey.

"Two weeks after she got in touch with me, she was found dead on a railway line. The police said it was suicide but I knew she would never have given up on her son. Something had happened to her and I was sure it was to do with her investigations. I felt honour-bound to carry on her research, not just for her, but for you. I had to know if you were in any kind of danger. I had to get inside the clinic to see what was going on, so I persuaded PAFA we should break in.

"It wasn't hard. They knew there had been animal testing there, some of it pretty grim – search for it, you can still find stuff on the internet, buried under the weight of stories Crisp's

PR team put out to counter it…"

The image flickered and switched off.

I shook the compact. Closed it and opened it again. Was that the end of the message? It couldn't be. Maybe it was solar-powered like Miss Lilly's car? It was late but there was still a bit of sun coming in my window. I sat it in the light, hoping it would charge, and pulled my slate closer.

I typed in *Miss Lilly, animal testing*. A list of results came up: Miss Lilly judging a puppy competition, Miss Lilly investing in animal welfare, Miss Lilly opening an animal sanctuary, sponsoring a donkey, cuddling a kitten. I kept going through the list, just to be absolutely sure I wasn't missing anything and finally came to something horrible.

It was a poor-quality video of cages and cages of rabbits with bloodied eyes and bald patches of sore skin. My stomach lurched; it was revolting. Then I saw the date: 1982. I did a bit of maths in my head – Miss Lilly didn't even look as old as Stacey, so I reckoned she'd have been about twelve in 1982. Miss Lilly's dad must have been in charge then. She couldn't be held responsible for what her parents had done. Then I realized what else that meant – she'd have been so young when her parents died in that fire, when she had to take over the running of the business, she'd have been barely older than me. No wonder she felt a connection…

The compact flickered back into life. I snatched it up and Stacey started speaking, halfway through a sentence.

"*…left. They've been back recently. I think he's still at the clinic, Laura, I think Alfie is alive.*"

The message stopped, along with my heart. I held it in the sun, trying to fire it back into life, but it seemed dead as a dodo. That little hook of hope seemed like a cruel taunt. I threw it down and poked the dark cloud on my slate.

I sent Stacey a message:

What do you mean about Alfie? The fire made all the other pods unviable. I was the only one to survive.

I was tight with tension. I felt like Stacey had been dripping poison in my ear ever since I'd made contact – what if this was just another way to get at Miss Lilly?

A photograph pinged up on my slate. It was grainy but you could make out a series of silver pods. I'd never seen the capsule I'd been stored in – I hadn't wanted to – but I guessed that's what I was looking at.

These photographs were taken by a member of PAFA working undercover in the basement of the clinic. They are all occupied and working.

I stared hard at the image – there seemed to be lights on the front of the pods. The photo could have been taken before the fire. It meant nothing.

Another picture pinged up. It was the same one but zoomed in. A red circle was drawn around a date at the bottom of the photograph.

My breath caught in my throat.

It was six weeks ago.

Six weeks?

I couldn't believe it. *I'd* been there then. How would PAFA have got an activist in to take it? It wasn't possible, the security was too tight. Or was it? There'd been the photographer in the window. And the man who'd walked straight into the corridor when I was with Annie.

Stacey sent another message:

Alfie might still be alive. Isn't that worth being
sure about?

I didn't know what to think. I messaged:

If you really believe something's going on, why haven't
you gone to the police?

She replied:

The word of PAFA against Miss Lilly? There are
warrants out to arrest most of us.

Us. Was she still one of them? PAFA. The people who'd killed Miss Lilly's parents. The *murderers* who'd killed Miss Lilly's parents and destroyed my brother's chances of survival. Or had they? Could he really still be there? In the basement? Somewhere on those two floors of *storage*?

Stacey messaged:

She tightened security recently. There's no way any of
us will get in there now. You could though. You could
see if Alfie was still there. You could get more
evidence.

Us. Us. Us. She was manipulating me like they had
manipulated her. Only the image of those undamaged pods
wouldn't leave my mind. *Six weeks ago?* And if I did go back and
check, PAFA couldn't make me do anything I didn't want to.

No. Why was I even considering it? Miss Lilly wouldn't
lie to me. She wouldn't.

Lu? Are you still there? I know you're finding it hard to
process, but the photo proves there is something
worth investigating, doesn't it? You should go now.

What? She wanted me to go back to the clinic now?
I messaged:

I can't just go. I'll try and look when I'm back there
next time.

What did she expect me to do? Run away from school? I
was already in trouble up to my ears. I pulled on my braids
until my scalp hurt. It was nonsense, all nonsense.

Another message:

I think they might be testing stuff on children. Have

you noticed anything strange about your skin since
they brought you back?

I froze. My super-fast-healing cuts. How did she know?
I hadn't told anyone. I typed:

That's just the body's response to being frozen.
It's not an experiment.

She replied:

Isn't it? Can you be sure? I don't know how it all fits
together, only that every minute we delay could be
putting another child at risk. Experiments have
casualties, Lu – you remember the bear bile pictures,
from years ago? How would you feel if that was Alfie?
How will you feel if you leave it too late to save him?

She'd got me. The photograph, my weird skin, Stacey's
suspicions... Fear and hope hooked their dual claws deep
inside me. Because if there was a chance – a single chance
– that she was right and my brother was alive, alive and *at
risk*, then I had to do something. Maybe there wasn't a bank
vault for a small country in the Blackhurst basement. Maybe
there was something far more precious down there. I had to
know and I could only trust what I saw with my own eyes.

I checked my watch – it was nearly eight in the evening.
No one had been to see me for hours. I guessed they were

leaving me to stew on what I'd done. I felt another stab of guilt that I was thinking of betraying the school that had embraced me as one of them. I picked up the pasta-framed picture of my family and kissed Alfie's face.

"If you're still there, I'm coming to find you."

I stood up, grim determination overriding every sane thought. I put on my running stuff. No one would question me going out for a run. Actually, they might. Madam Hobbs had told me to wait in my room. I glanced at the window. The drainpipe. I could climb out and go down that way. A wave of panic made me dizzy.

Just get on with it, girl. Don't think, just do. My running stuff was meant for summer and it might be cold later. Apart from uniform I didn't have any warm dark tops, so I stuffed the fluffy onesie in my backpack. My stomach growled. I had to eat before I went – and I needed to lay a false trail. I grabbed a bottle to fill up with water and went to the kitchen to make up some C-plan before I left.

There were a few girls in the ODR. They looked up when I went in and then looked away. I could see they blamed me for Marsha and why not? It was my fault she was lying in the health centre barely conscious. I drank the milkshake, wiped my hand over my face and said, "I'm going to have an early night. See you tomorrow."

There were a few murmurs and sullen head nods.

Back in my room, I put my bag on my back and stuffed some clothes in my bed to make it look as if I was in it sleeping. I locked my door and opened the window carefully.

It was dark but I could just about see down the drainpipe. It seemed like an easy climb. It was gloomy outside and no one seemed to be about. I got on the desk and put my leg over the ledge before I could change my mind. I rattled the drainpipe before I trusted it with my weight. It seemed pretty solid so I eased myself out.

It *was* easy. I went down, hand over hand, letting my feet slow me. I was on the ground in seconds. Drippy Issie had been right to worry about intruders.

I ran along the drive and within moments I was at the gates. I'd forgotten I'd have to climb over them. Not only that, there were headlights coming towards me. I threw myself flat on the grass as tight to the fence as I could. Nettles stung my bare arms and legs as the gates opened, and a car slid through. It was a chance I might not get again. I waited a few seconds and, just before the gates closed, I darted through and ran down the road. No point looking back. If I'd been seen, they'd catch up with me soon enough.

I ran slowly towards the city lights. When the streets got busier, I hugged the shadows, trying to find my way to the station. I remembered Keisha using her phone to find the Pavilion. I tried to figure out how to use mine to navigate but every two minutes a stupid advert popped up, reminding me that white teeth were a sign of good health. I shoved it in my bag and started to look for road signs instead.

I nearly turned back half a dozen times. What was I doing? What possible reason had I to doubt Miss Lilly? Why would she lie to me about Alfie? It made no sense.

And yet…there was just enough doubt to keep me going. Or maybe I was just stubborn and stupid. I was also sick with nerves, and started panicking that I was having a delayed reaction to the tracking virus. At last I saw the curved roof of the station. I held up my head, crossed my fingers that no one would recognize me, and walked in.

I checked the departures board. I'd only have to wait about ten minutes.

As I boarded the train, my insides were torn apart by two opposing thoughts – that there was no reason to doubt Miss Lilly, and that there was. Because if there was, it might mean Alfie was still alive. And that's what was driving me. I wanted that so badly I'd have given anything for it to be true. Even my new life.

chapter fifty-one
LAURA

It was chilly on the train. I pulled my onesie on over my running kit. I still thought it was a weird thing for people to wear but it was warm and Marsha said loads of people had them so it couldn't be that weird. I pictured Marsha's face when we'd taken this journey earlier and hoped desperately that she was feeling better now. I didn't want to miss the stop so I sat, hyper alert, watching everything flash by, hoping the tracker virus wouldn't try and kill me again. When we pulled into the station closest to Blackhurst, I couldn't get off fast enough.

The train left, and I was alone in the dusky quiet, my stomach churning with anxiety. All I could hear were night noises – they made me think of Ima. When the Perseids meteor shower had come by, we'd put blankets out and had lain on the grass late into the night watching for shooting stars, just me and her. Ima explained the screeching of an owl or the eerie scream of a vixen, until one of us spotted a white streak in the sky and threw a hand in its direction. *"There! Did you see it? Did you?"*

I shivered and adjusted the bag on my shoulders. How had my life come to this? Saturday afternoons listening to the radio with Stacey, lunchtimes at school gathered around the drama studio TV to watch music videos our teacher had taped for us, racing Alfie up and down our street on a space hopper – all gone.

I gave myself a pep talk. I was a big sister and that meant something. That meant responsibility. I missed my Alfie so much I had a hollow place inside me that nothing else could fill. I'd have done anything to have him back and that hope overrode any last flicker of good sense telling me to turn back.

I rubbed my face hard with my cold hands, pulled up my hood and got my phone to work out where the clinic was.

After walking for about ten minutes a huge lorry rumbled towards me and I stepped up the bank into a bramble bush. It snagged at the onesie, and I had to yank myself free. At least the inky colour kept me a bit hidden. It was probably good that it was dark but it was so creepy. The road was creepy. The bushes were creepy. And it didn't get any less creepy when I saw the barbed-wire fence around the clinic grounds – how had I not noticed that when I was living there?

When I spotted the little white guardhouse on the drive, I realized I didn't have a plan for getting into the clinic.

I pulled up my rabbit hood and headed towards the gate, hoping I could sneak in or that some genius idea would dawn on me before I got there. The old man on duty was fast asleep, his head nodding on his chest. I ducked under the barrier and crept across the grass towards the building that sat squatly ahead, gleaming in the moonlight. A guard walked around the corner of the building and every ounce of courage I'd summoned deserted me. What was I doing?

I threw myself behind a straggly shrub that couldn't have hidden a real rabbit let alone a stupid girl dressed as one. I forced myself to breathe.

My phone vibrated in my bag. I pulled it out as quietly as I could. It was Miss Lilly. My heart tripped a bit but I answered it: "Hello."

"Laura," Miss Lilly said, her voice flat. "Someone is coming out to fetch you." And she hung up.

I was the worst spy in the world. I barely had time to ask how she knew I was there before a pair of booted feet were standing in front of me. The guard offered me a hand and pulled me up.

We went straight to the apartment. Annie was waiting for me by the front door. Without a word, she led me to Miss Lilly's office. She was sitting behind the desk, her hands pressed to her mouth as if in prayer. She wasn't looking at me, she was staring at the window. It was night outside; the glass made a black mirror reflecting the room back at her.

Miss Lilly was deep in thought, and they didn't look like happy thoughts.

I felt like a complete fool. I pulled the hood of my onesie down so at least the rabbit ears weren't flopping over my face. Eventually she turned to me and lowered her hands.

"Laura."

I tried to lick my lips but my mouth opened with a dry suck that sounded like a kiss. I was so not cool.

She said, "How am I supposed to explain this to the school? On top of your dangerous escapade on the train this afternoon? This is embarrassing for me, Laura. Highly embarrassing."

I bit my lip.

She swung around in her chair, stood up, and walked over to perch on the edge of her desk. She had her sheepskin slippers on. That touch of homeliness made my heart squeeze with guilt. She made it worse by saying, "Why aren't you happy, Laura?"

"Sorry?"

She looked like I'd kicked her. "I've done everything. Given you everything I can. Money, gadgets, I'm paying for your school. Haven't I been kind? Haven't I done everything possible to give you a good life here? What more can I do?"

"Nothing. I mean, I'm grateful, I love the school and everything." I felt like I'd let her down by wanting something more. I could imagine how hurt she'd be if I asked about going down to the basement. She'd told me where Alfie was. I should just trust her.

The phone rang on her desk. She wrinkled her nose with a *this conversation isn't over* look before picking it up.

"I see. Okay. Yes, well, I don't think we need any more complications. I'll come down."

She smoothed out her skirt, stepped towards me and cupped her hand around my cheek. She smelled delicious, of lime and blossom and something softer, like baby powder. It was almost...hypnotic...my nose just wanted to follow the smell.

"I'll be back shortly. Don't go anywhere. Please."

She left me on my own.

I replayed the conversation in my head. Why wasn't I happy? It was a weird thing to ask. I'd lost my whole family. Of course I wasn't happy. Not deep down inside. I mean, I thought one day I might be okay – I had moments that were really pretty good but...my life had been devastated. No amount of new clothes or new gadgets were going to fix that overnight.

The longer Miss Lilly was gone, the more uncomfortable I felt about what she'd said. It was like she thought I should forget about my family. Like the new life she'd given me should just replace them. Maybe that's why Alfie wasn't ever mentioned in the press, because she wanted me to put him firmly in the past and move on. Maybe she'd done a deal with the journalists like she had over my interview, not to report his time at the clinic – the loss of him – at all.

Or maybe it was because he hadn't been lost and he was still here, underneath me somewhere. I could feel the basement under my feet, a vast, unanswered question. A question I had to answer.

I tried the door. She'd locked me in.

Why? Did that mean she really was hiding something?

chapter fifty-two
LAURA

There was a keypad beside the door. I needed one of those card things that Annie had given me when I first moved into the apartment, but mine was in my room. I checked the desk drawers but they were locked. Stacey had once shown me a little trick to get around that. If you could get at the base of the drawer and push it up at the back, the bolt part can drop down enough to release it. I kneeled down and tried. It took a couple of goes and quite a bit of heaving but, unbelievably, it worked.

There was only one thing in the drawer. A key card.

I held it up to the pad and the door clicked open. I scraped my teeth over my bottom lip and opened the door a crack. There was a guard at the end of the corridor – in the apartment, *our* apartment – a guard. That was weird. Suspiciously weird.

I didn't have a pocket so I slid the card into my bra and closed the door quietly. My insides were a horrible stew of worry. I kneeled down to reverse the process of opening the drawer. When I'd got it back into place, I looked around the office. It was so sparse there was nothing in it that might give me a clue as to whether my brother might still be here. Miss Lilly's desk had a glass insert in the top, which I guessed might be some kind of computer. The logical thing would have been to try and find something on that but computers were still a bit of a mystery to me. I didn't even know how to switch it on. So what else was there?

A huge map covered one wall. I ran a hand over it, bumping softly over several large flower pins that, I guessed, marked out all the places Miss Lilly had been. Or maybe all the places where there were Miss Lilly enterprises.

I wondered if there was another hidden lift in here, like the one in the kitchen. I felt a bit ridiculous even thinking it. Like I was playing at James Bond. Next I'd be expecting bookshelves to spin around, revealing a nuclear bunker. Or a trapdoor that would send me to a crocodile-infested pit and a bitey death. The door opened behind me.

"Admiring my empire?" Miss Lilly said as she came back in. I could hear the pride in her voice and the germ of an idea took root. I felt bad being so sneaky, but I thought if I could get her to talk about the clinic, maybe I'd pick up some clues or something.

So I said, "It's amazing. Do you have clinics in all these places?"

She crossed the room and stood next to me. "There are only a couple of clinics – Blackhurst and another in

California. Most of these are production sites and distribution centres. Impressive though, isn't it? I wish my parents had lived to see it."

"They'd be so proud."

A tight, sad smile flashed up and was gone. "Maybe. Look, Laura, what happened to my parents was sad but it hasn't blighted my life, no more than the loss of your parents should blight yours. I want you to be part of this. More than that, I want us to be a family. You and me. Come and sit down."

I followed her to her desk. The room smelled very familiar now she was back. It reminded me of the happy times we'd had together, watching movies and hanging out. Someone knocked on the door and Annie came in with a cup of hot chocolate that she put in front of me.

Miss Lilly smiled and tipped her head to one side. Her hair gleamed, black and silky.

"We have a bond, don't you think, Laura? Look at you, such a poppet in your little rabbit outfit. You're a survivor, a fighter, just like me. You have real potential to be someone. But your friends…"

My mouth went dry as unbuttered toast as guilt bubbled to the surface. "Marsha?" I said.

Miss Lilly laughed. "No, not her. The other one, Stacey. She's been in touch, hasn't she?" She slid the hot chocolate closer to me.

How did she know about Stacey?

"I can't tell you who to be friends with, Laura, but I'd

hoped…" She looked at the floor and then whispered, "You know what she did."

I swallowed. The fire.

I felt so bad. I wanted to say something comforting, but embarrassingly my stomach grumbled loudly instead. I blushed like the great big idiot I was, sitting there in my stupid onesie with my stomach gurgling like a baby.

Miss Lilly laughed. It was like a light being turned on. "Oh, Laura. Can't we leave the past in the past and just move on?" she said, all reasonable loveliness in the face of my idiocy. "Drink your chocolate – that'll help with your growly tum."

As I drank she said, "Why don't you stay tonight? I'll call the school and we'll get a car organized to take you back in the morning."

The warmth of the chocolate, the scent of the room, the promise of a happy future – it was all so lovely and comforting and real. Of course Alfie wasn't still in the basement, his ashes had been scattered with Mum and Ima. And one day, maybe soon, Miss Lilly would take me to say goodbye.

"You look wiped out, sweetheart." Miss Lilly put an arm around my shoulder and said, "Come on, let's get you up to bed."

Batfink was in my room. It was lovely to see her but I was so exhausted and my bed was so comfortable… I sank into the lavender-scented sheets and went out like a light.

chapter fifty-three
SHEM

I lost track of time. I lost track of everything. I was forced to open my eyes by the doctor coming back and my imaginary Scrag dissolved into the bright lights of the cell. I swallowed a sob. The doctor was flanked by two armed guards, like they were expecting me to fight. What had I got to fight for? Scrag was gone. I'd never find him. I was warm and dry and not hungry. I was existing and that was all I could hope for.

Hope.

What was the point of hope? There was nothing for people like me. No chance, no help, no hope.

"Follow me, young man," the doctor said, so I did.

We took a lift down and I was pushed into a small room with a desk and two chairs.

"Just a few things and then I can hand you over to my colleagues."

A spark of fear ignited against my will. My mind didn't want to care, but my body had other ideas. It must have shown on my face because the doctor laughed and said, "No, not the guards, my nursing colleagues."

"Nursing? I thought this was a prison."

He laughed again, not unkindly, and asked me to sign some forms.

"What are they?" The writing was tiny and close together and my head was too fuzzy for my eyes to focus.

"Just sign on the bottom there. You can write, can't you?"

As I tried to make sense of it, I remembered one of Bert's stories and said, "It's not a contract for me to hand over my kidneys, is it?"

I was sort of joking but the doctor didn't deny it.

Was that what this was? Seriously? They wanted my kidneys? Just when I thought I'd lost everything, they found something else to take. I started to shake but not out of fear. A new emotion was flaring inside me: the flicker of a flame of a fight.

When the door opened and a nurse put his head around it, I shoved my chair back and tensed.

chapter fifty-four
LAURA

I was woken by a soft paw batting my face.

My head was groggy, my thoughts sluggish and confused. For a moment I couldn't remember where I was, then Batfink meowed loudly at me.

I sat up too quickly and my head spun. I tried to shake off the feeling that I'd had too many snakebites. It was probably hunger. When had I last eaten? I vaguely remembered drinking something before I went to bed. Why was I so confused?

I pushed the covers back and found I was still wearing my clothes from the night before. Batfink meowed again.

I stumbled to the bathroom for a pee and felt something sharp inside my bra. I pulled out the key card and vaguely remembered taking it from Miss Lilly's desk. I scooped up my kitten and headed to the kitchen. There was no one around but there was a note on the white marble counter: *C-plan in the fridge with strawberries and some banana. When you're ready, call my office, M.L. x*

I fed Batfink and had my own breakfast, hoping food would clear my head. I downed the C-plan and turned on the cold tap, splashing water on my face until the world started to make sense.

The photograph. The picture of the basement.

Alfie.

I'd come to Blackhurst looking for Alfie.

And I'd just abandoned my mission. Rolled over and gone to sleep. My phone rang. I snatched it up. A message in Spiditik played across the screen.

I'm it thi clinic. I'll privi it ti yii, Liiri.

I'm at the clinic. I'll prove it to you, Laura.

Stacey was here. My breakfast threatened to come back up.

chapter fifty-five
SHEM

I backed into a corner and tried to threaten them with the chair. I couldn't even lift it up, I was so weak. They took it off me and one of them tried to punch something into my arm. I pulled away and felt liquid dribble down my skin. I thought I'd stopped them jabbing me with whatever it was, but I can't have, because I slid to the floor and the next thing I knew, I was on a bed and someone in blue was sliding thin needles into my elbows. It didn't hurt, not really – fogginess clouded everything. I tried hard to think, fighting against my sluggish brain. Because even through the fog, I knew this wasn't any kind of prison I'd ever heard of.

I lay as still as I could while I tried to figure out what to do. They wiped my face with some sharp-smelling stuff, and one of them pressed their rubber-covered fingers against my temple and around my eye socket. My heart thudded painfully against my ribs and when they brought one of those long, thin needles near my eye, I freaked out.

I jumped off the bed, stumbling into the woman in blue, knocking her sideways. I pulled the other needles out of me with fumbling fingers, all the time searching for an exit. I could see a couple of doors at the other end of the room but the nearest way out was a lift behind me.

The nurse was looking at me with horrified eyes. She shuffled on her bum to get away from me. I didn't wait for a second chance, I darted towards the lift and pushed the button to call it. The nurse got to her feet and hit an alarm next to the bed I'd been in. The noise near deafened me.

A man came out of one of the doors at the end of the room. He looked stunned for a second and then said, "Why isn't he sedated? He should be sedated."

"He was! I don't know what happened."

My gaze went from one to the other.

The man held his hands up and said, "Now then, you're very sick. You need to stay calm."

"I'm not sick."

"Yes, you are. You don't know it but you need our help."

"I am not sick. That's sick," I said, waving at the machine with all the tubes and needles coming out of it. And then I noticed the other beds.

The shadowy outline of dozens of other people lying under white sheets. Tiny, thin…children. They were all children, little husks of humans. Tubes and needles trailed from their joints into machines like the one next to my bed. Sick rose up my throat as I focused on the face of one of the people. I couldn't tell if it was male or female, but needles stuck out from behind blankly staring eyes. That's what they'd been trying to do to me! I swallowed a scream, and banged desperately against the lift button.

The blue-suited woman moved towards me. "This is a pioneering programme – you are very lucky to be part of it."

"But I'm not sick," I said. My voice was tight, high-pitched. "I was hungry, I was knackered, but there was nothing wrong with me until you dragged me here."

The man stepped forward. "The delusions are part of your illness. You need to stay calm."

"You come any closer and…" What? What could I do? The alarm stopped ringing and I felt the lift drop to a stop behind me. That trickster *hope* made me think I might make it, but the ward door opened and a guard filled the doorway.

chapter fifty-six
LAURA

I'd come back for a reason – I had to get into that basement. I stared at my phone, cold sweat sliding down my spine as I tried to think. I didn't want Stacey at the clinic. If she was wrong, Miss Lilly would think I'd taken sides and... A terrible, pounding alarm rang through the building and shutters slid down over the windows. Batfink panicked and climbed up my leg onto my shoulder, her sharp little claws spiking my skin. Stacey must have broken in.

Panic gripped me. She didn't know I was here. What if she set fire to the place while I was trapped inside?

I held onto Batfink and ran to the kitchen door – it was locked. I rattled the handle. Nothing. I tried the windows. The shutters wouldn't budge. I was trapped.

Okay. Think. The lift?

I pressed the button to call it but then realized it wouldn't help – I didn't want to go up or down, I was on the ground floor. I just needed to get out. *Use your brain, Laura.*

I messaged Stacey back:

Don't do anything crazy. I'm inside.

Spiditik?

Stacey, please, just don't do anything stupid.

I watched my phone.
Come on. Message me back…

Don't trust her, Lu, please. I'm going to prove it.
Alfie's alive, I'm sure of it.

Oh God.

I can't get out of the kitchen, everything has locked
down. Have you triggered an alarm?

There was a pause before she messaged.

Not me. I'm not that close. I need to find a way in past
the fence.

Was she lying? I had no way of knowing.
I messaged Miss Lilly:

I'm trapped in the kitchen.

The reply was almost immediate.

We have a security breach. As soon as I know what's going on, I'll be there.

They must know about Stacey. They must.
There was a whining noise behind me. The lift was moving.

chapter fifty-seven
SHEM

My insides turned to liquid.

There was no way out unless the lift behind me miraculously arrived in time. I should have gone for the door. Why had I thought waiting for a lift was a good idea? I was done for. I never had the luck. Never. I was screwed – three against one.

I stepped back as far as I could, pressed right up against the lift door. For a minute, they were frozen, the woman on the floor, the man and the guard in the doorway – they just stared at me. Then they all moved, as if a switch had been flicked. I'd had it.

They headed towards me but like a wonderful electronic miracle the lift doors opened and I fell backwards into it. I scrambled to my feet and hit a button, willing it to close and quickly.

The big, ugly guard sprinted towards me but he caught

his foot on one of the beds and went flying forward, skidding across the floor. As the lift doors closed, he was looking up at me like he'd kill me if he could.

chapter fifty-eight

LAURA

The lift whined its way towards me. It was a chance to go down and see for myself what was there. I could tell Miss Lilly I panicked because of the alarm. I swallowed as the doors slid apart, ready to step in, only the lift wasn't empty. The homeless boy I'd seen at Whitman's spilled out onto the kitchen floor. He'd cut all his hair off, shaved it close to his skull, but it was definitely him. Hedge Boy. Right there, in Miss Lilly's kitchen.

"You?" I said. "What are you doing here?"

He stared at me, his eyes wide, terrified. Something glittered near his temple. I reached for it but he scuttled back against the wall and it dropped to the floor.

It was a long, thin needle.

We both looked at it.

"Why? What…?" I was so confused I couldn't even form a question.

"Doughnut Girl? Where am I?"

"My guardian's house. Blackhurst Clinic."

"Where's my dog?" he almost growled.

How did he know I'd found his dog? Why was he here? What was going on? "He's with one of the teachers. This is a clinic. A hospital."

"If you've hurt my dog, I swear I'll…"

"He's not hurt. He's fine – he's at school."

The boy seemed to collapse a bit, his thin shoulders jerking with silent sobs. I had an urge to hug him, to try and stop his tears, but the kitchen door opened and Miss Lilly strode in with two nurses.

She came straight to me. "Laura, sweetheart, are you okay?"

Hedge Boy shrank away, his hands grasping for something to defend himself with. There was a cupboard behind him; he edged it open.

"I'm fine," I said. "I think this boy got lost, didn't you?"

Miss Lilly squeezed my shoulder gently. "This young man is here for rehabilitation but, I'm afraid, doesn't know what's best for him. He'll be fine though. Once we get him back down to the ward."

The next few seconds unfolded like a comedy spy movie. The nurses stepped towards Hedge Boy and he pulled a container of something out of the cupboard and smashed it, first in one face and then the other. When he hit the second nurse, the container opened and dried peas went everywhere. They clattered to the floor, bouncing up and down, and in the moment that followed, a tiny whine started up as the robot vacuum appeared to suck them up.

Miss Lilly stepped between me and Hedge Boy and began guiding me away, but not before I saw the nurses grab him, twist his arms up behind his back and force him to the floor so hard I heard his head hit the ground with a thud.

I cried out, "No! Don't! He's not well."

"We're aware of that, Laura," Miss Lilly said. "Please let my staff do their job."

Something felt so wrong. I squirmed out of her grasp to see one of the nurses kneeling on Hedge Boy's back, holding him still. He looked at me with enormous dark eyes. Dark, terrified eyes.

"Stop it!" I yelled. "You're hurting him."

Miss Lilly took my face in her hands and her perfume radiated towards me, so familiar, so soothing. Something clicked in my head. I remembered the night before, the smell of home, the hot chocolate, how I'd got into my lavender-scented bed and fallen so soundly asleep I could hardly remember where I was when I woke up. Had I been drugged?

I tried to pull away, but Miss Lilly kept her hands firmly in place and said, "Darling girl, compassion is a wonderful thing, but when it's misplaced it can do more harm than good."

Was it misplaced? Why was Hedge Boy in the clinic? How had he got separated from his dog? I couldn't fit any of the threads together, but I knew one thing: I needed to work it out for myself. For whatever reason, I'd been bumbling along, letting other people make decisions for me, about me. After everything I'd been through, I'd felt like I needed someone to take care of everything – that I deserved it even. I hadn't really questioned anything. But you can't live like that for ever, can you? When something feels so totally wrong, you have to question it.

I pushed my shoulders back and said, "Tell me why he's here. What's wrong with him?"

A flicker of something passed over her face. It was so fast I couldn't read it. Irritation, anger, impatience?

"Telling you that would break patient confidentiality, Laura. I will tell you that some of my patients have been sectioned under the Mental Health Act. I'm afraid they can be dangerous. Sometimes you have to be firm."

"But—"

"Laura, it's my job. I know what I'm doing. Now, I think it's high time you went back to Whitman's. Can I trust you to stay here while I make some arrangements?"

Something snapped inside me. I was done with other people making decisions for me. I had Stacey telling me one thing, Miss Lilly another. School organizing me, Marsha organizing me, even flipping Keisha organizing me. What was the point of having my life back if I was going to let other people control it for me?

I made myself say yes as the nurses pulled Hedge Boy to his feet. Miss Lilly kissed my cheek but I stared at Hedge Boy, willing him to understand that I was going to try and help him. He glared at me as if I was worse than the nurses.

I nearly called out as they dragged him into the lift – the betrayed look in his eyes was almost unbearable. One of them pressed the button and the door slid shut.

They were going down. That's what Miss Lilly had said earlier. *Down* to the ward. Down to the basement where Stacey's picture of all the working cryogenic pods was taken.

Once they'd gone, she turned back to me.

"Time to return you to school. I've got one or two other things I need to do but I'll ring Whitman's first. We'll soon have things back to normal."

Stalling for time, I scooped up my cat and said, "No rush. I haven't seen Batfink for ages."

"Hmm, I think someone might be trying to avoid lessons."

She didn't sound like she was hiding anything, but I *felt* something was wrong. The image of Hedge Boy with that needle dangling from his head played over and over in my mind. I didn't have any idea how that fitted with the photo Stacey had shown me, or my weird skin, but I was going to find out.

As soon as I was alone, I kissed Batfink on the head and put her down. A kind of crawling menace mingled with hope in my veins. What if Alfie *was* down there and they were treating him like Hedge Boy?

I tried to call the lift but it didn't respond. I pressed the button a few times but they must have locked it or something. Why would they do that if it wasn't to keep me out? I'd have to find another way.

I headed to the internal door that connected the

apartment to the clinic. Miss Lilly's key card opened the door. Now I just needed to find a way down to the basement. My heart raced as I hurried along the corridor. I was sure I'd run into someone and I did. Two people – nurses I guessed, from their blue scrubs and hairnets – came out of a side room. They nearly walked straight into me. I thought they'd demand to know what I was doing but they just smiled and walked past. I guessed they'd got used to seeing me about the place while I was recovering. Once Miss Lilly realized I'd gone from the kitchen and got everyone searching for me, that wasn't going to be quite so helpful. If everyone recognized me, they'd find me in seconds.

I peeked into the room they'd just left. It was a changing room. Lockers lined one wall and there was a giant laundry bin in one corner, a canvas thing on wheels. I had the maddest idea that I could get in it and somehow wheel myself around until I found whatever it was I was going to find. Like a laundry basket moving by itself wouldn't attract attention all. That was the kind of genius idea Susan might come up with.

A sensible disguise might help though. I tried one of the locker doors. Locked. Obviously, it was a locker. Anyway, that must be where their day clothes were kept. Staff probably had to change into fresh scrubs whenever they came in. Which meant somewhere there must be spares.

I found a bigger locker with a key still in it. It was full of clean scrubs. I shoved my onesie behind the laundry bin and put a suit on over my running kit. There was a pile of disposable hairnets too. I pulled one on, shoving my braids inside. It wasn't a great disguise but…well, it was a hundred per cent better than my rabbit onesie – or wheeling myself along in a bin.

I walked briskly along the corridor, trying to look like I had purpose. I caught a drift of scent, orange and pepper. I remembered what Miss Lilly had said about using aromatherapy to help people feel calm. Well, I didn't want to be calm. I wanted to find out what was going on.

At the end of the corridor was a set of double doors and through them, stairs. Stairs! I pressed the card against the keypad and it unlocked. I headed straight down two flights to another set of doors. The card worked again. Surely if there was really something terrible down there, it wouldn't be that easy to get in? Unless I'd pinched some kind of master card. I went through, turned left and bumped straight into a guard.

"Jesus, you gave me the fright of my life!" he said.

Would he recognize me?

"Sorry," I said. "I was miles away."

He smiled, held his own card to the pad behind him and opened the door. "No problem. The others are already in. Guess you got held up by the alarm. He's back now, it's all sorted."

I croaked, "Okay," and walked through.

Tentacles of fear stroked my spine as I took in what I saw. There were no cryogenic pods but two rows of beds running down the sides of what looked like a normal hospital ward.

Normal apart from two things: the lighting was extremely dim and most of the beds seemed to be occupied by unusually small and creepily still bodies under thin white sheets. My brain froze with shock as I processed what I was seeing. They were *children*. Wizened children with thin needles sprouting from their elbows and behind their eyes. My hand went to my throat. It was like something from a horror film.

A noise at the end of the room snapped me out of my stupor.

Two nurses were supporting Hedge Boy. He seemed completely limp and his head flopped around as they manhandled him onto an empty bed. One of the nurses noticed me. I tensed – I wasn't sure in the gloom if it was one of the nurses who'd been in the kitchen. He pulled down the mask that was covering his mouth and came over.

"First day?" he said, confusion on his brow.

He was acting like everything was completely normal. I nodded, trying to give the impression I was just a new colleague on a normal workday.

"Sorry, nobody told me you were starting. Okay, well, gloves and masks are in the sluice." He indicated a door on my right. I went into the tiny room.

Maybe they were so confident in their security they would never have imagined an intruder? Or maybe they actually did have nothing to hide. Was all this really some kind of treatment? What for? How could I find out? Did Benjie and Mariya know about this part of the hospital? Should I go and find them? Ask them? I scanned the shelves in the sluice and found a box of gloves. I fished out a pair and the door opened. The nurse stuck his head in.

"We don't need help on the ward, now the newcomer has calmed down." He waved at a pile of instruments by a machine that looked like a dishwasher. "You might as well stay in here. All that needs sterilizing – it's a standard unit. Can you get started with it?"

"Okay."

"You don't say much, do you?"

I forced a smile. "What's this ward again?"

"Weren't you listening in induction training? This is the extraction suite."

He shook his head and shut the door sharply. Extraction suite? What the hell…? I poked through the things waiting to be sterilized. What was it all for? Miss Lilly had said something about the Mental Health Act, so what were they extracting? Bad thoughts? From children? You didn't treat mental health by sticking needles in kids and leaving them to wither. There wasn't a single toy on that ward. Not a poster, not a teddy. I couldn't figure it out.

There were so many questions spinning round my brain. How did any of it link together? What could they be doing to those kids? And Hedge Boy? What was he doing here? *Was* it rehabilitation of some sort? Was there a connection with the missing children Stacey had talked about?

My mind galloped to work it out but I just came up with more questions. What about the pods in Stacey's picture? How did they fit in? I hadn't found them yet – could Alfie really be in one? Were the pods somehow connected with the children on the beds? A new thought hit my brain with a white-hot explosion: what if Alfie was still alive but not in a pod – what if he was in one of those beds?

My mind sketched an image of my brother, deathly still, under one of those white sheets. I started to shake as I pictured him staring blankly at the ceiling, needles dripping from his body, from his eyes… I was sick. Right there, all over the floor. Milkshake and strawberries splashed up the walls and down my blue-clad legs.

"Oh my God, oh my God, oh my God."

I had to see. I had to know.

I opened the door and took two steps back onto the ward before the nurse grabbed me by the arm.

"Look at the state of you! What did you do? Are you sick? Didn't you fill in a health questionnaire before you started work? The contamination risk! Out. Get off the ward and don't come back into work until all your symptoms have been clear for forty-eight hours."

He glared at me. I tried to look behind him, along the ward, but he shoved me towards the door and I was too nauseous and trembly to resist.

"Don't touch that keypad without gloves. I'll let you out." He pushed me through the doors before I could protest.

The guard outside said, "In trouble already?"

I was sure I looked guilty, like I knew I shouldn't be there. I was sweating, shaking and desperate – I had no idea what to do next. I managed to splutter, "The nurse said I needed to get changed but I can't remember where the locker room is."

The guard said, "End of this corridor, up two flights, through the double doors."

"Thanks."

"No problem. This place is like a maze – took me weeks to find my way around."

How could they all act as if everything was fine? It was like some horrible dream where reality was warped and distorted. I desperately needed help but I didn't know who to ask. Were they all in on it? Whatever *it* was?

chapter fifty-nine
LAURA

I needed help. I wanted my phone but I'd left it in my onesie behind the laundry bin. I tried to get back to the changing room as quickly as I could but after about five minutes, I was completely lost. Then the key card stopped opening doors.

I pulled the stupid paper hat off my head and leaned against the wall. Panic made me teary and I was gulping back sobs when I heard Miss Lilly's heels come tap-tap-tapping down the corridor towards me. I wasn't even surprised.

She had a guard with her.

"Laura, for goodness' sake! You had me so worried. I got back to the apartment and you'd disappeared."

I swallowed and looked at the floor.

"And why on earth are you wearing scrubs? You've been sick? Are you unwell?"

I looked up at her. I was so confused. If she was behind

some horrible scheme to test products on little kids, how could she also just be...nice? It didn't make any sense. Unless I was going mad? Was this how it felt to go crazy?

"Let's get you back to the apartment, shall we? I've organized a driver to take you back to school but it looks like you need a shower."

I nodded. I didn't know what else to do. I followed her, trapped in my nightmare.

She patted my back lightly and said, "If you keep disappearing, we'll have to get you fitted with a permanent tracker."

I hoped she was joking. My thoughts were all over the place. And suddenly the question bubbled up and out of my mouth before I could stop it. "I've been downstairs. I've seen that ward with all the children. Is Alfie down there? In one of those beds?"

"No! What on earth made you think that? Of course not. You really are poorly, aren't you, sweetheart? Come on. I think we need to get Benjie to check you over. Maybe you need a few days in bed."

I shook my head. "I'm not poorly. I just want to know what's going on."

"Nothing is *going on*. The people on that ward have a condition where their body overproduces certain chemicals – the process they are undergoing removes the chemical."

Extraction.

"Even Hedge Boy?"

"Hedge Boy?" She seemed amused. "Is that what you call

the young man who broke into our apartment? Yes, even him, but it's very complicated, Laura. I'm not sure—"

"What chemical?"

Her jaw tightened for a moment. "Like I said, it's complicated. If you really want to understand, this corridor is hardly the place for a complex science lesson."

Was she telling me the truth?

I said, "Stacey—"

She cut me off sharply. "Stacey Flowers? Is that what this is about? You've been listening to her? After everything she's done?"

I was swamped with guilt but I had to know – there was no other way now. I needed answers. "She showed me a picture, a recent picture. The pods we were stored in, they're still active. You said they were damaged, that no one else survived. You told me—"

"I…"

"I have to see for myself. I want to see the pods."

"There are no pods!"

"So show me. Let's go down there now and I'll never mention it again."

She turned away and when she looked back, tears beaded her lashes. She leaned against the wall and when she spoke, she looked so small and sad that my heart melted.

"Laura, sweetheart, I think I've made a terrible mistake. I wanted to save you from pain. I wanted you to be able to move on with your life, to start afresh."

"What do you mean?"

She shook her head. She was finding it hard to talk. Eventually she whispered, "I lied to you."

I had to put a hand on the wall to steady myself.

"It was a stupid thing to do," she went on. "I see that now. I'm so sorry. Your brother's pod *was* damaged...but we were able to revive him."

Hope surged through me.

"Alfie is alive?"

chapter sixty

LAURA

Miss Lilly looked at me with those big violet eyes and said, "Barely, Laura – there was irreparable harm to his brain. He's in a permanent vegetative state."

I hardly heard her. My brother was alive. Alive and alone. "I could have been with him. I…"

A cold lump of rage lodged in my chest, radiating anger into every cell of my body until my hands clenched into fists. I wanted to shake some answers out of her.

"Where is he?" I hissed.

She held a hand up as if to ward me off. "Laura, it was for the best. I swear we've been taking good care of him."

I felt like the floor was moving under me.

"For the best? You lied to me."

I couldn't take it in.

"I want to see him."

"Of course. Yes. You'll need to get cleaned up – the infection risk… And, Laura, you need to understand, he's not…he can't talk, he—"

"I don't care. I'll get showered but I'm not leaving this building until I've seen him."

Maybe not ever. If he needed me, I was staying right by his side for as long as it took.

We went back to the apartment. I was shaking as I got showered and dressed in clean clothes. Batfink wanted to play but I paced my room, nerves building as I waited for Miss Lilly to come and get me. I was desperate to see Alfie. To hold him in my arms, to smell the top of his head. By the time Miss Lilly came back, I was tense as a bowstring pulled tight, ready to release an arrow.

She didn't say a word as we walked to a small room in a part of the clinic I hadn't seen before. It was empty apart from a couple of chairs and a huge mirror on the left-hand wall.

"Where is he?"

Miss Lilly waved at the mirror and our images dissolved to reveal a room beyond. And there he was.

Alfie.

My baby brother.

He looked so small, lying absolutely still under a neat hospital blanket. A machine seemed to be breathing for him. I pressed my hands against the glass; a deep, growl of pain came from somewhere inside me. I wanted to hug him so much my arms ached.

"I need to hold him."

"His condition is very unstable—"

"But if he hears my voice—"

"You vomited, Laura. I know you've showered but if you have a sickness bug, it could make your brother very ill."

I leaned against the glass, desperate to be closer. All the times I'd longed for him, Alfie had been in the same building. The guilt I'd felt about not visiting his grave, the shame of failing him, and all the time, I could have been by his side. I covered my mouth, trying to control the overwhelming flood of sorrow that threatened to drown me.

"Can I just stand by his door? Please. I could talk to him from there."

"I don't think so, Laura, we don't want to take any risks. He's in total isolation for his own protection."

"But he needs me. I can help him get better."

She shook her head. "I'm so sorry. The truth is, he won't even know you're there. I wanted to spare you this pain because it's unlikely he'll ever recover. I'm so sorry."

I willed Alfie to turn and look at me. To show some sign that he knew I was there. It seemed so unfair. That my body could heal itself so easily but his…

"Wait, the brain is an organ in the body," I said, "so why isn't it fixing itself?"

"What do you mean?"

"My body, it heals faster than it should. Why doesn't his too?"

"Ah. That. It's a side effect of the process used to revive

you but it only works on new injuries…the fire meant Alfie's brain was damaged before we attempted to bring him back."

I was so tired. So…wrung out. All I wanted was to sit by Alfie's bed and hold his hand. The cold hard glass of that window was a poor substitute for my warm cuddly little brother. It was unbearable to be so close but unable to touch him. Maybe Miss Lilly had been right not to tell me. It crushed me, but I didn't want to leave. If this was all I could have, I wanted it. I drank in every tiny detail of Alfie and his room.

Miss Lilly put a gentle hand on my back, but as she did so, I realized there was something *off* about what I was seeing. There wasn't a door to the room. There was no way in.

"Where's the door?"

"What door? What do you mean?" She followed my gaze and then the window silvered over, erasing everything from my view.

"Bring it back, make it work again." I tried desperately to peer through the glass, but all I could see was my own confused face.

"Please, can't you clear it again?"

"Sweetheart, I think you should just let us look after your brother now. You need to go back to school. You have to get on with your life. I don't want to sound harsh, but there's nothing you can do for Alfie."

There was no door on this side of the wall and I was sure there hadn't been one in that room. Which was impossible.

I ran out of the room and along the corridor to the next

doorway. It led to a waiting area, not Alfie's room. It was all wrong.

I ran back into the corridor in case I'd missed something.

Miss Lilly caught hold of me. I tried to pull away. "Where's the room? This should be his room. I thought it was a two-way mirror... Where is he? Where's Alfie?"

"I understand you're upset, but you really need to control yourself. This is a hospital, you can't just run around willy-nilly."

"Where is he?" I demanded.

She blinked. "It isn't a mirror. It's an image projected from a different part of the hospital. I knew you'd find it hard not to go into the room if we were near it. I'm sorry, but you've proven me right, haven't you?"

She sounded so convincing, but there was too much that felt *wrong*.

"So let's go to him. I swear I won't do anything, I'll stay back from the door, I won't touch anything..."

"Not everything is about you, Laura! Alfie needs protection."

"Not from me!"

Her face turned stony. Very quietly, she said, "And what, exactly, do you mean by that?"

This was a Miss Lilly I had never seen. She felt... dangerous. I was scared. Properly scared. I didn't know what was going on but I knew it wasn't good and I was absolutely sure that somehow it involved my brother. I had a horrible feeling that what she'd shown me wasn't him at all, that he was two floors down in that basement with all the other children. Somehow I had to check, but there was no way she'd let me go and look now. I needed her to believe I still trusted her.

I said, "Sorry, I'm upset, I wasn't thinking straight…"

And she flipped back, just like that – her face softened into an understanding smile. "It's okay. I understand. Let's say no more about it. Let's get you back to Whitman's before they change their minds about having you!" She laughed gently.

I let her steer me away but I had no intention of going anywhere until I knew what was going on.

I thought fast. If I contacted the police, would they come? What would I say? What had I actually seen? Were those children really in danger? Would the police believe me, when I wasn't sure what I believed myself?

That was when I realized we weren't going back to the apartment – Miss Lilly was leading me straight out to a car.

"I need to get my things," I said.

"The car is waiting."

"Please, I need my bag."

"Well, quickly then."

As soon as we were in the apartment I ran upstairs, pulled out my slate and messaged Marsha and Keisha:

I'm at the clinic…something isn't right…I don't know what to do.

Miss Lilly came in. I shoved my slate in my bag.

"Batfink!" I said. "I haven't said goodbye."

My kitten wasn't in my room. I thought I could use looking for her as an excuse to buy some time.

"I'll check the kitchen," I said.

"Laura, the car!"

I ran to the kitchen, my brain buzzing.

Batfink wasn't there either. I called her, all the while trying to make a plan. I *couldn't* get in that car and drive away.

"Come on, Laura, this is getting silly now. Batfink has probably gone out. I'll give her a hug from you when she comes in."

I was desperate. I didn't know what else to do, so I cried. I know, pathetic, but worth a shot.

"Don't send me back, please. I want to stay here. I'm being bullied, they call me names. Everyone hates me."

She frowned. "You seemed so happy."

"I covered it up. I didn't want to disappoint you."

"Come on now. I'll speak to the school, everything will be fine."

Annie came in with my onesie in her arms. "They found your clothes in the laundry, your phone was with them. Here." She handed the pile to me.

Miss Lilly said, "Shall we go?"

What could I do? I couldn't physically fight her and run to the basement, the guards would stop me in seconds. She smiled at me encouragingly. I backed away, chewing the side of my thumb, accidentally tearing a big strip of skin away.

I winced as blood filled the cut, but I instantly felt the wound begin to knit itself back together.

A sob rose inside me. Everything was wrong. I looked at my guardian, wanting answers, but I didn't even know how to ask the questions. She smiled that gentle smile again and led me firmly by the arm, out of the kitchen, out of the apartment, to the waiting driver.

What to do? What to do?

One way or another, she'd lied about Alfie, manipulated me – or tried to. We were crossing the drive to the car now and I still didn't know how to stop all this. Panic bloomed in my chest. Miss Lilly kissed me goodbye and with a firm hand, eased me into the back seat and shut the door. I heard the locks click down. I was trapped. I felt like I was going to faint, I was breathing so hard and fast.

The car crunched along the gravel, telling me to strap myself in.

No.

I couldn't go. I had to look for Alfie, whatever it took. "Stop the car!" I shouted.

The driver turned in his seat, letting the car drive itself. "Sorry, love, no can do. Instructions are to take you straight back to school."

"I'm going to be sick," I said, trying the door.

"No point. They warned me you're an escape artist. There's a sick bag in the back of the seat."

I was pulling at the door as the driver said, "What the…!"

I looked up just as Stacey stepped in front of the car.

We should never have hit her. The cars of the future had sensors that were meant to prevent a collision, but the driver's instinct took over. He grabbed the wheel to take control and swung the car sideways. Instead of avoiding her, it clipped Stacey's side. I saw her buckle and drop as we went the other way into a tree. Air cushions deployed, the bonnet crumpled and when I looked back, Stacey was sprawled across the drive.

chapter sixty-one
LAURA

An avalanche of icy shock spread from my skull to my feet.

The driver was just as stunned. He stared at his own hands gripping the wheel. Everything was silent, like we were in a bubble. I shook my head, forced myself to move and tried the door – it was still locked.

"Open the door! She needs help!" I said.

The driver didn't move. I grabbed his shoulder. He turned slowly and blinked.

"Let me out of the car!"

He didn't respond. I reached over him, fumbling at the stupid dashboard that had not a single recognizable knob or button on it.

"My friend is hurt. UNLOCK THE CAR!" I screamed in his face and finally he pressed a palm to the centre of the steering wheel and the car unlocked. I scrambled out and flung myself on the ground next to Stacey.

"Stace, Stacey, oh my God, Stacey!"

She gazed blankly at the sky; a small pool of blood darkened the gravel behind her head. I didn't know what to do. I looked around desperately. The old man from the gatehouse was shuffling as fast as he could up the track.

I yelled, "Get help! Call an ambulance!"

Someone in the clinic must have seen the accident because two nurses were running towards us. Instead of relief, I panicked. I wasn't sure who I could trust. A police car turned into the drive. I barely had time to question how they'd got there so fast before two officers were kneeling by Stacey's side.

I whispered, "Please be okay."

One of the officers stood up and I grabbed her arm. "Don't leave her here. Don't let them take her into the clinic."

"An ambulance is on its way. She'll be going to Worthing General, they'll look after her."

My breath was ragged. "Promise me? There's something not right here. I don't know what but…"

She nodded and said, "We had an anonymous call saying there'd been a break-in and someone had been injured. Don't worry, we'll be checking it out."

Who had called? Maybe Stacey, knowing that she was going to do something drastic? It didn't matter – I was wasting time, this was my chance.

The old man from the gate nodded towards Stacey. "That's Stacey Flowers. There's an injunction to keep her away from here."

The policewoman turned her attention to him and said

something about calling it in and checking the injunction, but I didn't have time to wait for them to investigate Stacey. I had to get back inside. I ran to the clinic.

I fished the key card out of my bra and pressed it against the door pad. It didn't work. I threw it on the floor. Frustration sent pulses of anger zipping through me. I looked at my thumb where the cut had healed so quickly and I looked at the window next to the door and, with a sharp breath in, I punched my fist right through it. Glass crashed to the floor and an alarm ripped through the air as pain sent shockwaves up my arm. I pulled my hand into my stomach, blood dripping from my knuckles. I glanced back – one of the police officers had seen what I'd done and had started running towards me. At almost the exact same time, Miss Lilly appeared behind the door, staring at me with her mouth open. "Laura! Have you gone mad?"

I dived through the window, breaking the rest of it as I went; splinters of glass tore chunks from my skin. There was blood everywhere. I yanked some of the bigger shards out, flinging them aside. I stood square in front of Miss Lilly, rage powering my determination. "Where's my brother? Where's Alfie?"

Her mouth opened and closed but no words came out.

"Fine, I'll find him myself."

She glanced over my shoulder and I knew there was a police officer right on my heels. Miss Lilly tried to block my way and keep me out but I spun past her.

I got lost again – so many doors were blocked. I wanted

to scream in frustration, but I kept going and eventually found myself back at the apartment. I rang the bell. Miraculously, Annie answered. I shoved past her, pushed her into the corridor and slammed the door to keep her out. I dragged a chair over and jammed it under the handle to stop it being opened. I'd use the lift in the kitchen to get down to the basement.

My fingers left bloody prints over the wall as I frantically pressed the button, trying to get the lift to respond. It still wasn't working. I cried out, "I just want to call the stupid lift!"

"Would you like to call the lift?"

The room answered me. THE ROOM.

I yelled, "Yes! Yes, I'd like to call the lift."

"Thank you, Miss Lilly. Lift approaching."

I barely registered that the lift had mistaken me for my benefactor, I just cried with relief when the door opened: "Take me down."

It rumbled its descent and I got ready to dash out as it bumped to a stop. A nurse was standing there when the doors slid open. He turned around, took one look at my bloody clothes and said, "You again? And now you're covered in blood!"

"The police are here," I said. "Whatever you're doing, it's over."

I don't know what I expected him to say but he just looked really confused. Over his shoulder, I could see Hedge Boy on a bed, still as death, tubes draining from his eyes, his elbows and God knows where else. I gulped down horrified sobs. Miss Lilly had said they were overproducing some chemical and this process was to extract it – but he looked half-dead now and he'd been fine before. Skinny, but fine. And he'd been so frightened when they'd taken him from the kitchen.

I had to look for Alfie. I stepped forward but the nurse grabbed my arm. I tried to see the next bed. There was a little kid in it about Alfie's size. My heart thundered in my chest. The man tried to twist my arm back, but before he could get a decent grip I sank my teeth into his hand and wrenched myself away. I stumbled to the bed, my knees giving way.

The boy was so tiny, barely a shadow under the white sheet that covered him. His hair was shaved, his skin dry and wrinkled and he had those tubes sticking out from behind his eyes… My hand trembled above his forehead, afraid to touch him but desperate to.

"Is it you, baby boy?"

The nurse pulled both my arms back, saying, "Don't touch him."

Tears dripped down my nose. The nurse dragged me away but I couldn't tear my eyes away from the child. It was gloomy in the room, but as I looked at that little boy, his face like a shrunken elf's, I could see he didn't have a little mole over his right eye. It wasn't Alfie. Disappointment crashed through me.

Arguing voices filtered through the main door of the ward. One of my arms was tugged painfully higher.

"You can't go in there," Miss Lilly was saying. "There are very sick people here. There are procedures to follow."

"A credible source has reported unauthorized activity in this facility. Could you unlock the door, please?"

"Don't you dare unlock that door! On the word of a woman who killed my parents? This is an outrage. There's an injunction against her. You can't do this!"

The nurse holding me tightened his grip further, unsure of what was happening. Then the door opened and Miss Lilly and the police officer who'd followed me up the drive were framed in light spilling from the corridor. I opened my mouth but Miss Lilly spoke first. "Laura…"

I lost my tongue; I scrabbled for words to make the policewoman see that this had to be wrong, whatever this was, and Miss Lilly had to be behind it. Why else would she lie and lie? But no sensible words would come. All I managed was, "That boy, the one on the end, I know him. There was nothing wrong with him and now he's got needles in his head."

Miss Lilly seemed to collect herself a bit.

"Laura has a traumatic history," she told the police officer. "You may have heard about it in the news? Laura Henley? Sleeping Beauty? I'm her guardian. I'm afraid we had an argument this morning and now she's punishing me."

She turned to me. "That's quite enough now, Laura. You are endangering these patients with your behaviour. It's totally irresponsible."

The police officer finally seemed to clock that my arms

were being yanked off by the big bully behind me. "Perhaps we could release the young lady?"

The nurse hesitated but Miss Lilly nodded and he let go. The sudden rush of blood made my fingers throb.

"Well," said Miss Lilly, "this room is now going to require a full decontamination. Perhaps we can leave my staff to get on with it."

She was so calm it was throwing me off track. Maybe I'd got it wrong? Then I looked down at the child that wasn't my brother, at the other beds filled with other tiny bodies – any one of them might be Alfie. I struggled for something that would make the police officer listen to me.

"They're just children," I tried. "Why are they on their own down here in the dark? Where are their families? Why aren't there any pictures, any toys?"

The police officer's radio sent out a scorch of static. She said, "They're trying to get hold of me. Why don't we all head upstairs. Perhaps if we could just take a look at the paperwork for these patients, we could clear all this up?"

"Of course," Miss Lilly said. "Though I do need to be sure Laura is taken care of. She ran away from school last night. I was trying to return her when Miss Flowers flung herself in front of the car Laura was in."

The policewoman said, "Understood, and I think the young lady could do with some medical attention."

I looked down at my blood-splattered clothes. "It looks worse than it is. I'm fine."

"My doctors will sort Laura out," Miss Lilly said.

"Until we clear up a few things, I think it's best if the paramedics do that."

I wasn't leaving that room without searching for Alfie. "I have to check the beds, my brother…"

Miss Lilly said, "I think you've disturbed things down here quite enough."

The police officer said, "Perhaps, if she doesn't touch anything, we could let her look, put her mind at rest."

I went from bed to bed. The children seemed to be all different ages, all thin and wizened, all with shaved heads. All tiny except for the last bed. The one with Hedge Boy in it.

Alfie wasn't there.

I had hoped *so much* and I was crushed. Tears slid down my face. I wanted him so badly. I wanted Mum and Ima. I wanted my old life back. But it was all gone and the new life I had was built on a raft of lies.

chapter sixty-two

As soon as we were out of the basement, the crackles from the policewoman's radio turned into voices asking her to report in. She radioed back asking for a medic and saying there were some things she wanted to check. Miss Lilly argued that my own medical team should look after me but the police were having none of it.

"I'm sure the paramedics can cope with a few cuts and bruises."

"You don't understand. Laura has been through a lot. Her body—"

The officer cut her off. "If the professionals run up against anything tricky, they can radio for assistance."

The policewoman led me back to the ambulance on the drive. On the way out we crunched over the mess of broken glass and splatters of my blood over the floor where I'd broken in with so much determination. Stacey was gone and I felt defeated.

"Have they taken Stacey to the hospital?" I asked. "Will she be okay?"

"I should think so, on both counts."

I pictured my friend stepping in front of the car, her body jerking backwards as we hit her. What a stupid, overdramatic, absolutely typically Stacey thing to do. My heart lurched. I still might not know what was going on here, but I was finally certain of one thing: she loved me. I knew it.

"Hand out, Miss."

I let them swab away the blood on my hands and waited for the surprise.

"Oh."

They swabbed my arm.

"How odd. Is this someone else's blood?"

I didn't want to deal with their questions while I had more important things to worry about so I said, "It might have been Stacey's – she smacked her head."

"You've no injuries then?"

I shook my head.

"We'll just check your stats before we let you loose."

Another policewoman was waiting for me when they'd finished.

"What will happen?" I said. "What's going on with those children in the basement?"

"We're looking into that. Try not to worry."

I was taken back to the apartment kitchen under police supervision.

"We need to search the hospital for my brother.

Somewhere in the basement there are the pods we were frozen in; he might be in there. We should—"

"Laura, I understand you're anxious but you need to leave things to us now."

"Where's Miss Lilly? I think she knows more than she's saying, we—"

"If there has been anything untoward going on, we need to gather evidence. It would be helpful if you could just wait here."

"But the basement, those children—"

"Laura, you can trust us to do our job."

I clamped my jaw shut. Everyone, always, just took over. I'd found my own way here, I'd discovered the people in the basement, and now they expected me to sit here and wait quietly?

"I could help."

"Seriously, Laura, we know what we're doing. It's safest for everyone if you let us do our job."

But I had to do something. Maybe I could sneak upstairs and search Miss Lilly's room. I said, "Can I go find my cat? I haven't seen her this morning."

"Okay, but stay in the apartment, please."

When I got to the top of the stairs I called, "Batfink!"

I was only saying it for effect, but then I heard a faint *meow* in response. I expected her to come tumbling along the corridor but there was no sign of her. I called again.

"Batfink?"

I heard another muffled *meow* back, but she still didn't

appear. I thought I'd better find her in case she'd got stuck somewhere. I checked my room but I couldn't even hear her in there. I went back into the hallway and followed the sound of meowing to Miss Lilly's room. The door was open – I went in and called again. Batfink's meow was definitely louder but I still couldn't see her. I thought I could hear scratching coming from Miss Lilly's wardrobe.

"Batfink?"

She answered me with a faint cry from behind the door. How had she got in there? I tried the handle. Locked. It was an old-fashioned keyhole. I looked around for a place you might hide a key and then remembered what Mum always did – top of the door frame.

I put my hand up and felt the hard metal shape. Miss Lilly had hidden a key right where anyone could find it. Anyone used to twentieth-century security anyway.

I slid it in the keyhole and it opened with ease.

The smell of her clothes was intoxicating. My head actually spun. I ran a hand across the familiar jackets and a fresh explosion of scent filled the tiny room. Frantic scratching made me focus.

"Batfink?"

Where was she? I pushed through the clothes to get to the back.

"Laura?" The policewoman had come to find me. "Are you in here? Laura?"

I stood up sharply, banging my head on the clothes rail. As it bounced up, I heard a click and the entire back wall of the wardrobe swung away from me.

With a loud *meow*, Batfink bowled into me.

"What the…!"

"Laura?"

"I'm in here," I called. "In the wardrobe."

I picked up Batfink and peered into the hidden room. I ducked into the tiny space and lights flickered on. The policewoman followed me through.

"What's this?"

I shook my head. "I don't know."

But I suspected. The room was full of filing cabinets, the kind of thing we had in 1986, the kind of thing no one had any use for now. I put my cat down, pulled open a drawer and picked out a file. On the front it said:

Subject: Abigail Stone
Origination: Homeless runaway
Age on intake: Approx. 13 years
Project: Cryopreservation
Outcome: Fail

I took out another.

Subject: Ksenia (surname unknown)
Origination: Child refugee, alone
Age on intake: Approx. 9 years
Project: Cryopreservation
Outcome: Fail

I was shaking as I pulled out another one and this time I opened it. A photograph of a little girl was paper-clipped to a sheet of information.

Parents: Father absent, mother drug addict
Social situation: Weak support
School: Southwold Primary
Suitability: Good
Health: Historic injuries – broken arm, two broken ribs;
no vaccines

The policewoman said, "Let me see?"

I handed her the file and reached in the drawer for another. Then my hand stopped. What if we were in there? Me and Alfie. I looked for "H" and found my file straight away.

Subject: Laura Henley

My head swam...

Origination: Isolated parents
Age on intake: 16 years
Project: Cryopreservation
Outcome: Success
<u>Second Phase</u>
Project: Cell regeneration (special circumstances,
no extended research)
Outcome:

Inside, there was my picture, clipped to a sheet of paper. My hand trembled as I read:

Parents: Mother, artificial implantation (Blackhurst 1969); father, specimen 7X0; egg donor LC
Social situation: Isolated
School: St Andrews Secondary
Suitability: Excellent
Health: Good

I could barely take it in. "But I was sick... This says my health was good."

I handed the file to the police officer.

How was that possible? Was Stacey right? Had we never had cancer?

Alfie.

I searched for his file. As I picked it out, a photograph fluttered to the floor – Alfie's little face looked up at me.

I read his notes:

Name: Alfie Henley
Origination: Isolated parents
Age on intake: 5 years
Project: Cryopreservation
Outcome: Success

Success?

He was alive!

So where the hell was he?

I read down:

Second Phase
Project: Cell regeneration
Outcome: Project interrupted

What did that mean?

I handed the file to the police officer, my voice shaking with hope and panic in equal measure. "This is my brother. He's five years old. He has to be here somewhere. We have to find him."

She answered by calling on her radio: "We've found something of interest. Can the DI come to the apartment?"

chapter sixty-three
LAURA

The officer in charge looked through the files and said, "Okay, let's get forensics in here. Post someone on the door. Can we get a family liaison officer for the young lady, please?"

I was whisked back to the kitchen with Batfink. A whirlwind of people came in. A youngish policewoman called Melody was introduced to me.

"I'm here to help you, Laura. Anything you want to know, if I can tell you, I will."

"What's going to happen? To Miss Lilly, to the people in the basement?"

"Miss Lilly will be taken in for questioning. The rest, I'll tell you as soon as I can."

"Can I help look for Alfie now?"

She smiled sadly and shook her head. "Things need to be done carefully. We can move you to a hotel if that would make the waiting easier?"

I cuddled Batfink and shook my head. I wanted to be nearby.

"We're going to need your phone and anything else Miss Lilly has used to communicate with you on, I'm afraid."

"Really?"

"Sorry. They'll check them ASAP and give them back. You aren't under any suspicion."

As I handed them over, I remembered the photo Stacey had sent of the pods with the lights on. I showed it to Melody in case it was helpful. Someone came to take my statement. Melody stayed with me while I told them everything I knew. They took some blood from me and scraped a weird stick around my mouth.

After they'd gone I was stuck in the kitchen with Melody. I sat at the table playing listlessly with Batfink and a feather on a string. Every now and then Melody went to the kitchen door to whisper softly to another police officer. Sometimes she came back with news.

The paperwork in the hidden room showed that Miss Lilly had taken children from the streets and from their families under false pretences. Children who didn't have a strong support network. The most vulnerable. I wanted them to go down to that basement and pull all the tubes and pipes out of those poor kids but Melody said they couldn't do that until they fully understood what was being done to them in case it caused more harm than good.

The nurses were no help. They knew they were extracting

something but claimed they didn't know exactly what or why. I found it hard to believe.

I asked Melody if I could see Benjie but he was being held as a suspect. I could not fit the Benjie I knew – or Mariya or any of the others – with the monstrous thing that had happened below us all. But Benjie had told me my cancer had been cured. He was my doctor – he must have known I'd never been sick. My brain was in turmoil. I wanted to talk to Marsha but with no phone that wasn't possible. Vera might have helped to make sense of the mess in my head but, you know, *suspect*.

Batfink curled up on a chair and went to sleep while I paced the kitchen. Someone else came and whispered to Melody. She returned looking serious and sad and told me the photograph Stacey had sent of the cryo-pods was an old one that had been doctored to make it look more recent. There was a PAFA member undercover at the clinic but it wasn't Stacey. It was Annie. She'd handed herself in straight away and was helping as much as she could. She had told the police Stacey had nothing to do with them since she'd come out of prison.

For about a minute, I was furious with Stacey for lying to me. And then I realized she'd just been trying to show me something that would make me take notice.

"There's something else," Melody said. "The basement search *has* revealed a number of rooms containing occupied and functioning pods."

"Is Alfie in one of them?"

"We can't say right now. We're working our way through records that we hope will tell us. It's all on paper, so it's taking quite a long time to cross-reference everything."

Twenty-four hours passed while they searched every inch of the clinic. I barely slept. I put my head down on the kitchen table and dozed fitfully, my neck cricked, Batfink sprawled out next to me, purring in my face. I had no idea what time it was when I was woken by Melody muttering to someone in the doorway. I sat up, hope igniting in my chest, but she looked over and shook her head. "Nothing yet, but they found the room you were in with the screen showing your brother. They traced the source of projection. I'm so sorry, but what you saw was definitely a computer-generated image. It wasn't real."

"It wasn't Alfie?"

"I'm sorry."

Even though I'd suspected it wasn't really him, it was a blow. My throat was too full of tears to speak for a moment. "What about Miss Lilly? Has she told them anything yet?"

Another shake of the head. "So far she's refusing to speak at all."

She knew where Alfie was. The fact she wouldn't tell us sat like a rotten lump inside me. I was so angry, so hurt, but there was a strange part of me that felt a thread of connection with Miss Lilly that I didn't understand. She had been kind to me. We'd had some really good times. It was like there were two Miss Lillys. The one I knew and the one who'd done…whatever it was she'd done.

"What will happen to her?" I asked. As I said the words, another thought echoed in my mind: *What will happen to me?*

"I can't say for sure right now. Until we know more, she's being held on suspicion of false imprisonment based on the information you provided about the young man you call Hedge Boy."

Part of me felt guilty, like I'd betrayed her, even after everything she'd done. I was overwhelmed for a moment – it was all such a mess.

Sitting in the kitchen, just waiting, was driving me insane. I scooped Batfink into my arms and stood up. "Can I go to my room? I'm really tired." At least it would be a different four walls to look at.

Melody nodded and followed me upstairs.

"I thought I wasn't under suspicion?"

"You're not."

"Can't you give me half an hour on my own then? Please? Maybe you could try and find out if there's any news on Stacey? I'd be really grateful."

I don't know what she thought I was going to do. I couldn't exactly interfere with evidence – paper-suited people were all over the apartment. One came out of my room.

To her credit, Melody said, "Can Laura have a lie-down on her own bed?"

"Sure. We're done in there."

I closed the door behind them both. Through my window I could see what Melody called the "major incident centre" being set up – a giant white marquee on the lawn. It looked like a village fete was going on, staffed by police and scientists. All it needed was a cake stall and a coconut shy and they'd have nailed it.

I put Batfink on my bed and lay next to her, hoping I might sleep. I was staring blankly at the ceiling when Melody knocked on my door. Instead of news of Stacey, she held out a letter from Keisha.

Dear Laura,

I've been trying to find out what's happened but no one will tell me ANYTHING. And you NEVER ANSWER YOUR PHONE.

I had a burst of anxiety that she'd think I'd been ignoring her until I remembered I had a cast-iron excuse: my phone and slate were still being examined by the police. I unfolded the rest of the letter, grateful that I could reply in my own good time. It felt a lot less demanding than the insistent ping of a phone.

There's loads of rumours going round about Miss Lilly – been a bit of a scandal really. The school relies on her money for all the scholarships so not sure what's going to happen. I'm not blaming you, just a bit of a worry.

Marsha's gone, her dad must have pulled her out but I

didn't even get a chance to say goodbye and she's not answering any calls either. I think she was okay though, no lasting damage from the tracking serum, Madam Hoosier said.

Hope to see you soon,

Keisha and Susan

PS Susan says meditation is good if you're feeling stressed. Try sticking your tongue out really far and opening your eyes really wide.

What a mess. At least Marsha was okay, even if she had left the school. I put the letter down and went back to staring at the ceiling.

Melody came back again later, this time with my phone and slate. I wasn't sure I really wanted them.

"They found tracking devices in them," she said matter-of-factly, "but nothing unusual."

"Seriously?"

She shrugged. "Most parents consider it their responsibility to track their kids. Be weirder if they didn't have tracking devices. They've cleaned your slate up a bit. You had quite a few registered users on there. That's not good for security, you know, Laura – especially letting your school friends register."

"I didn't. None of my school friends were registered. Only Benjie, I think, and Miss Lilly."

"There's definitely more than that. Not to worry, just a suggestion really."

I was puzzled by who else it could be. Then I remembered the time when I walked in on Marsha and my slate was awake and the time when I handed her the slate and it worked for her – could Marsha have installed herself as a user? Why would she have done that? *How* would she have done that?

Melody said, "You'll doubtless be thrilled to know that your school have sent some work over for you, but try and get some rest. It can wait."

She left me to it.

I called Marsha but it went straight to a recorded message: *"This number is no longer assigned to your contact."*

I tried again. Same result. I threw the phone on my bed and woke up my slate. There was literally a ton of messages from Keisha, but absolutely nothing from Marsha. No word at all. I skimmed through Keisha's messages. They mostly said Message me! in a gazillion different ways.

I thought I should probably reply. I typed:

Hey, Keisha. Have you heard from Marsha yet?

Her reply was instant:

OMG, you're alive. Thank God. I was beginning to wonder. Don't know about Marsha. She's just gone, not answering her phone or anything. It's crazy here,

they're saying school might have to close. About half
the girls have scholarships that are paid for by Miss
Lilly and she's been arrested! You probably know that
already but look at this...

She'd attached a link to a news headline.

I didn't really want to read malicious reports about the
wreckage of my new life. None of them would tell me where
my brother was.

I stared at her message for so long that my slate switched
itself off. Batfink crawled into my lap and nudged her head
against my hand. I sighed. I was probably going to see all the
headlines eventually; why not do it with a cute little fur ball
on my knee? I stroked her head and re-activated my
computer, pinching up the link that Keisha had sent.

chapter sixty-four

LAURA

FROZEN KIDS KEY TO
KILLER LILLY'S CREAM

A fistful of gnawing piranhas swam in my gut as I read:

In a shocking twist to the fairy-tale story of real-life
Sleeping Beauty Laura Henley, police have uncovered
horrifying scenes in the basement of Blackhurst Clinic.
Famed for its unrivalled beauty treatments, Blackhurst
has many celebrity clients, including regular patients
Iggy Foundling and Sasha Green, winners of this
year's Love Idle. They must be looking in the mirror
this morning and wondering about the real cost of
their glowing complexions.

Unnamed sources allege that Crisp, known
throughout the world as Miss Lilly, has been running a
battery farm in the basements of her buildings,

extracting the highly prized chemical hyaluronic acid from unwilling donors. Even more shockingly, the victims of this appalling crime are children, some as young as six years old.

Hyaluronic acid has been synthetically reproduced for use in the beauty industry for many years but no other brand has been able to replicate the extraordinary results of Miss Lilly's treatments. Experts are unsure why the extracted HA seems to achieve such startling results. Current theories suggest that the process of reviving the body from cryopreservation encourages the growth of super-healing cells, similar to those that are responsible for the regeneration of limbs in some reptiles.

According to Annabelle Rush of the Institute for Paediatric Dermatology, removing the hyaluronic acid from these children is like removing lubricant from an engine. "They are likely to suffer from swollen and stiff joints, as well as premature ageing and some may even have been blinded by the process of harvesting…"

I stopped reading. Images flashed through my mind: the children in the basement; the beautiful tiny-waisted women strolling the corridors of Blackhurst; those yellowed files in the hidden room – *Phase 2: Cell regeneration*. Alfie and me, all those kids in the beds, we were bears in a bile farm. I ran to the loo and was sick until my throat was sore. I slumped against the bath, exhausted. Batfink rolled around next to me, pushing her little feet against my leg.

The woman who had been so kind to my face, so warm and loving…she was Dracula. Sucking youth out of her victims for a face cream. Destroying lives so rich people could look younger. And why wasn't I being pumped for my super-healing cells? Why had Miss Lilly plucked me from her vampire programme? What made me special? I pictured our evenings on the sofa together, pressing our fingertips together like ET, the pamper day we'd shared. Oh God, I'd had a massage – had they used that stuff on me? I felt dirty, tainted, disgusting. I tore my clothes off and got in the shower and washed and washed until my skin was raw.

The more I thought about her smiling, deceiving, betraying face, the more I wanted to confront her. The rotten lump inside me hardened into resolve.

I picked up my slate and went to find Melody.

She was in the kitchen, making coffee. "Do you want one?"

I shook my head. "Have you seen this?"

She read the article. "How the hell…? Someone has leaked this."

"You knew about it?"

"Some. But I've only just been told."

"I want to see Miss Lilly."

"I don't think that's a very good idea."

"I want her to explain how she can have done what she's done. And I want her to tell me what's happened to my brother."

"As far as I know, she's refusing to speak to anyone," Melody said – and then, as if she realized it might actually be useful, "but maybe she'll speak to you. I'll see what I can do."

chapter sixty-five
LAURA

That afternoon we left the grounds of Blackhurst through a throng of journalists – cameras, reporters, more cameras. I ducked down in the back of the police car. It was the same outside the prison where they were holding Miss Lilly. I was ushered in, surrounded by burly bodies as security.

I thought Miss Lilly would have swung it so she'd have some kind of hotel suite, but we met in a small, square room that smelled of sweat and vomit. There was a metal table with one chair on her side and two on mine. A camera watched our every move, as did the stone-faced prison guard standing behind Miss Lilly.

She was as neat and beautiful as ever, but in a grey sweatshirt and leggings, she didn't have quite the same impact as she had on the outside. And then I realized what was actually missing – it wasn't her clothes.

It was her smell.

She didn't smell of anything; she just blended into that sweaty room.

The guards made us sit down. Miss Lilly reached a hand out to me. "Darling girl, I'm so glad you came. I have something I must tell you…"

Ignoring her hand I said, "Is it about Alfie?"

She shook her head. I knew the best way to get her to talk was to stay calm and reasonable but anger and frustration bubbled up inside me and I blurted out, "How could you do it? All those children in the basement – you took their lives for a face cream?"

"Face cream? Is that what they're saying?" She shook her head. "We were working on more than face cream – that just helped to pay the bills, sweetheart. Don't be too angry with me. Sometimes you have to make difficult choices; *sometimes* the end justifies the means."

"You can't be serious? What ends could possibly justify what you did?"

"There's always a cost in medicine."

"Medicine? You run a cosmetics empire."

She tipped her head to one side and smiled. "It's not just that."

"What do you mean?"

She leaned forward, her eyes even wider than normal. "We discovered that the revival process after cryogenic preservation stimulates the production of macrophages – cells that are critical for the immune system, for the healing process of the body. With so few effective antibiotics available today, the benefits of that are immeasurable."

"Benefit to who? Not to those kids in the basement."

She sat back. "You know what you can do, Laura, what your body can do. You fought off a tracker virus in minutes. Your body can regenerate new flesh. If we can extend that, we could patch up brains riddled with dementia, grow new bone, nerves, any kind of tissue – if they'd let me carry on with my research the potential is limitless."

I could see her passion, her obsession. She was so convincing I could *almost* see her justification. But the *reality*… What she'd done to human beings. To children. To Alfie.

"Where's my brother?"

"You don't need him."

"How can you say that? My family…"

She leaned forward. "Yes, your family. That is what I want to talk to you about. Won't you take my hand?" She was looking at me like she was about to give me a wonderful surprise.

I edged away from her.

"You think you lost your family, but you didn't. *I* am your family."

I stared at her. Had she completely lost it?

"You are my daughter. It was my egg that was implanted when your parents came to me for fertility treatment. The woman you knew as your mother was just a womb to carry you."

Shock sent freezing roots burrowing through me.

I shook my head, trying to get the confusion out. "No, I don't believe you."

"Yes. Blackhurst was at the forefront of IVF technology. No other clinic was even close to success when your parents were looking to conceive you. They jumped at my offer of a trial attempt and were quite happy to be sworn to secrecy. It was a simple thing to implant one of my fertilized eggs instead of your mother's. DNA records will prove it."

I felt sick. I looked around for Melody. She seemed as shocked as I was. When she realized I was staring at her, she gave herself a shake and said, "Do you want to leave?"

Miss Lilly reached for me but the guard put a heavy hand on her shoulder and sat her back. For a very brief moment, her face rippled with displeasure before her gentle smile was back in place.

I didn't want to believe her but she said, "You know it's true, don't you? We actually look a little alike, I think. And we sound almost identical."

I remembered the lift in the kitchen responding to my voice, mistaking me for Miss Lilly. I was trembling but I had to hear the whole story. "Why? And what about Alfie?" I said.

She shrugged. "Insurance. You had measles when you were nine, do you remember? I was a little worried I'd put all my eggs in one basket, so I offered them another free round of IVF."

I was struggling to make sense of what she was saying. "You tricked Mum and Ima? So Mum would carry your children? But why? Why not pay a surrogate?"

"I didn't need to pay them. Their reward was sixteen years of you. What other surrogate gets that?"

"But hang on…" I did some quick maths in my head. "That can't be true. I was born in 1969, you'd have been a young child yourself."

"I know when you were born, Laura. I'm not an idiot. Let's just say I'm a little older than I look."

"A little older? You'd have to be thirty years older."

She smiled and shrugged. "How old do you think I am? Fifty? Fifty-five? You assumed I was a child when my parents died, but I was twenty-five when you were born, Laura. Which makes me, crumbs, how old? I've not thought about my real age for a while…eighty-three?"

I stared at her, astonished. It wasn't possible.

She went on, "Sadly, while I can hold back the years on my skin, I've had less success with my internal organs. My team have worked hard but even they can't perform miracles. Not yet. My time on earth is limited, Laura, and I want you to take over the business. I want you to carry on the work I've been doing."

She said it like she was handing me a golden chalice, not a poisoned one. I wanted to shake her. Hurt her. Make her see what she'd done – because she seemed to have no idea. No comprehension that she had wrecked countless lives. I was almost blinded by the fury that flooded my body.

"Don't be cross with me, sweetheart."

I searched for something to say, something to shock

her like she'd shocked me. "If you wanted a baby so much, why didn't you bring me up?"

She rolled her eyes. "I didn't want a *baby*. I wanted an heir. And I didn't have time to raise a child. You had an excellent upbringing and I kept an eye on you from a distance. I was busy, Laura. Besides, I took great care selecting your parents. Leaving you with them was good for all of us. A child couldn't run my empire – I needed a young woman, and here you are."

"So why freeze me? Why not just wait for me to be old enough? Why put my parents through all that pain?"

"Sweetheart, think about it. I was only in my forties when you were frozen. I had years ahead of me then and I knew, if I kept you young, when the time came, you'd have years ahead of you too. I was confident the cryogenic process was safe. We'd done trials and we hadn't had a death in months. It made perfect sense."

She said it like all her plans had been an excellent idea.

"You're mad. You're completely mad."

She rolled her eyes as if *she* was disappointed in *me*.

I was raging inside. I wanted to storm out of that room and never speak to her again, but she was the only one who could tell me what had really happened to my brother. I had to find a way to coax it out of her.

"How did you make it seem like we were ill?" I asked. "Stacey said you poisoned us with the TB jab."

Miss Lilly shook her head. "That girl really is useless. I was so disappointed you chose her for a best friend. You completely ignored all the girls I placed at that horrible school to befriend you."

I felt a pang for Stacey and crossed my fingers that she was getting better. Miss Lilly might have been disappointed I'd chosen her, but I knew I couldn't have chosen better.

"We did sponsor a national programme for TB," she continued, "it was getting quite out of control – but that was nothing to do with you."

"How then?"

"It was the vitamins. We told your parents there were concerns that IVF babies couldn't retain crucial elements needed for proper development. Given our involvement in your conception, it was natural for us to provide the solution."

The vitamins. Mum and Ima had made us take them every day – a tablet for me, half a tablet for Alfie.

"But we'd been taking those for ages before we got ill."

"Honestly, Laura, will you use your brain? If you'd started taking them and then keeled over, suspicion would have fallen on the tablets straight away. I needed you to keep taking them – in fact your parents had to think you needed them even more because you were ill. I hadn't planned on giving them to Alfie, your foster-parents took that upon themselves."

"Don't call them that."

"Once you were in hospital, it was easier. I had someone working there who administered the drug through your IV line – it wasn't hard. Security in state hospitals was very lax in those days. It made you ill enough that your foster-mothers—"

"Don't call them that!"

She carried on. "I contacted them when I 'heard' you were sick. The local hospital was struggling to identify your illness and loosely, and usefully as it turned out, diagnosed a rare cancer. You were already too weak for the only real effective treatments they had for cancer then. They had nothing else to offer so I suggested bringing you here."

"You could have killed us," I whispered, shocked to the bone that she could tell me all this so calmly.

"Of course not. The dosage was carefully calibrated and easily reversed if you knew what it was. We have excellent chemists at Blackhurst."

Miss Lilly turned elegantly in her seat and asked the guard if she might have a drink. Melody tapped my shoulder and asked if I wanted one too. I must have nodded because someone came back with two paper cups of lukewarm water. I felt disconnected from everything. It was all so mad, so unbelievable, I barely knew what to ask next. I said, "You could have let Alfie get better. It was me you wanted."

She shook her head. "There would have been too many questions if your mystery illness didn't follow the same trajectory."

I closed my eyes and whispered, "So you kept him for your child farm."

"Child farm? Where on earth did you get that phrase from?"

"What else would you call it? You were harvesting chemicals from them, destroying their bodies…"

"Do calm down, Laura."

"Calm down? You took everything from me, from my parents!"

"But I didn't. You were never really theirs to lose, don't you see?"

She smiled and held her hands out towards me again.

Even then. Even after everything I knew, I still wanted to hold them. I still wanted her approval. I sat on my own hands to stop them betraying me.

"Did you have Alfie killed?"

"Oh for goodness' sake, what kind of monster do you think I am?"

"You really don't want me to answer that. Are you going to tell me where my brother is or not?"

Silence.

"Okay. Melody, I want to leave now."

I got up and walked away slowly in case she decided to tell me, to stop me leaving. Instead she said, "I tried to do my best for you."

I nodded. In her own crazy way, she had. But the cost of her actions…it was beyond anything I could comprehend.

Outside, I asked Melody, "Where are they keeping Stacey?"

"Worthing General."

"Can we go? Now?"

Stacey was in a room on her own. Her whole face lit up when she saw me and I glimpsed an echo of the girl she'd been, before age and grief had remapped her features.

"Lu!" She tried to sit up, but pain flashed across her face.

I said, "Hey, how are you doing?"

"Hey, yourself. Bit of a headache."

I said, "Stacey, I'm so sorry I didn't believe you. I should have…"

She shook her head. "Don't be sorry. You've done nothing wrong. I can't imagine how weird this is for you."

We had years to catch up on, but I could only think about one thing. My eyes filled with tears. "I don't know what to do, Stace. No one knows where Alfie is. And the only person who does won't even tell me if he's alive. Do you have any clues?"

She shook her head. "I kept trying after I got out of prison, but she had an injunction against me. I had to be careful. Prison was so hard, Lu. I didn't want to go back. If I broke the injunction, I knew I might get another custodial sentence."

It hit me then – really hit me – just how much she'd given up for me, how much she'd lost and how much she'd risked.

"But you sent letters to the clinic, after I was revived."

"Things changed when I knew you were awake. It was worth the risk to try and make contact. I had to make sure you were okay. I was scared but prison seemed less important than you…"

"I'm so sorry, Stace. For not believing you. For not being there. For all of it."

She held her arms out and I hugged her. She patted my back and shushed me like a mum would do and I wondered if she had even given up her chance of being a mother because she was looking out for me.

Tears of guilt came then: hot, heavy, sorry tears.

Eventually, we both stopped crying. I picked up her hand and said, "Thank you… Your whole life…you did everything you could."

She sniffed. "You'd have done the same."

I wasn't sure I would have done. Not then. But I think I would now.

I said, "When you get out of hospital, we'll make up for it. We'll listen to The Cure. Phone some random boys."

Her bottom lip wobbled. "I think I might get arrested again if I start phoning teenage boys."

chapter sixty-six
SHEM

I woke up in a room on my own in a proper bed. It was like sleeping in a cloud. Light streamed over me and I thought I was dead. That I must be in heaven. Until I moved and found a tube draining out of my arm. I sat bolt upright and felt something tug in a place nothing should tug. I looked under the cover – disappearing into a pair of pyjama bottoms was another tube shoved into my thing. I yanked it out, gasping with pain as I did – but, jeez, what kind of nutcase wants someone's wee?

I pulled the one out of my arm too. Blood trickled down the inside of my stump but I knew that would stop soon – I'd always been a good healer. Only some sensor had triggered an alarm and just as I was getting to my feet, a woman in white blocked the doorway.

I looked around for something to throw. The bag of wee was trickling itself empty on the floor – fat lot of use that would be. I backed around the bed, putting it between me and her while I tried to think.

"Shem, it's okay. No one is going to hurt you. I'm a nurse. I'm looking after you."

"I don't need your kind of looking after, thanks."

A man appeared behind her. My heart nearly thudded its way out of my chest.

He held his hands up. "It's okay. Shem, you are free to go whenever you want, but you've been through a lot and we'd like to take care of you for a bit."

"You put a tube in my thing."

The nurse said, "A catheter – you've been unconscious for a couple of days."

I let that sink in before I said, "I can go?"

They nodded. "But the police would be very grateful if you'd give a statement first. Would that be okay?"

I shook my head. I wasn't talking to no police. "I just want to leave."

Someone else came in. Another woman. I felt cornered, panicked. There was a window in the room but I couldn't see how to open it. Maybe I could just dive through it and run? My legs were wobbly and weak but it was amazing where you could find the strength if you dug deep.

The new woman whispered something and the nurse said to me, "We'll leave you to think about it. If you need anything, you can call me with the buzzer by your bed."

They went, leaving the door open. I looked around the room for my clothes but all I had were the blue pyjamas

I was wearing. I pulled the blanket off the bed and wrapped it round my shoulders. I peered out of the door.

The corridor was empty apart from one nurse sitting at the end, tapping on a computer. She smiled at me and went back to her work. Could I really just leave?

I stepped out. Just walked down the corridor. There were other rooms, all with kids in, some with nurses sitting by their beds. No one stopped me.

I got to the end of the corridor and sped up, my legs threatening to give way any second. There was a door ahead and through it, the outside. I was sure it would be locked but it wasn't. I glanced back to see if I was being chased – there was a nurse watching me but she just nodded. I was free. Really free. I opened the door and went outside. The sun felt good on my face. I looked around to get my bearings.

Across the grass was a massive white tent. Someone strode out of it – a bulldozer of a woman with a beautiful white dog on a lead. A white dog that nearly pulled her over when he saw me.

"Scrag! Oh my God, Scrag."

I dropped the blanket and fell to my knees. She unclipped him and he flew at me. I caught him up. He licked my face, whining and yipping and wagging at the same time.

"Scrag, you're alive. You're alive!"

He wriggled out of my arms and rolled on his back. I rubbed his belly – he was so white, even his tummy was white.

"You look like a little prince. How can I call you Scrag now, hey?"

The woman who'd had him on the lead stopped near us. I looked up at her and said, "This is my dog."

"I know. I've been taking care of him."

She gave me his lead. Like he'd need that again. Still, I didn't forget my manners.

"Thanks, thank you."

"My pleasure. I'd happily keep him. Delightful dog. Clever too."

"You can't—"

"It's okay. I know he's yours. Laura, the girl who found him, she explained everything to the police. Besides, anyone can see he's your dog. Got somewhere to go when this is all over?"

I shrugged. Back on the streets, I guessed, but I never said that.

She stuck out her hand. It took me a minute to realize she wanted me to shake it – it had been so long since anyone had treated me like an equal. Except maybe that girl.

"I'll leave him with you then," the woman said. "I'd better get back to my pupils – they're waiting to see Laura. Perhaps you'll let me say goodbye to this little chap later?"

"If I'm still here," I said.

A man came out of the tent. I struggled to my feet. He kept his distance and said, "Shem, hello. My name is Adam, I'm a police officer here. I've been assigned to make sure you're looked after. If you're up to it, we'd be very grateful if you'd give us five minutes of your time? It would really help with our enquiries here. Perhaps you'd come into the marquee?"

I shook my head – I wasn't getting trapped anywhere. I had all I wanted now I had Scrag back. I just wanted to leave.

"What if we talk here?" he said. "I don't need to come any closer? We could get you some clean clothes? Something to eat maybe?"

Something to eat would be good. And maybe a coat and some shoes. Before I got back on the road.

So I nodded. "Okay, but right here. And you don't touch me, or my dog."

chapter sixty-seven

LAURA

Back at the flat, Melody came with me to the kitchen. There were papers all over the table and officers poring over them.

One of them smiled at me and said, "Laura, we found something that belongs to you. Letters from your parents."

"Letters?"

He nodded. "This box is full of them, for you and your brother. They must have been written while you were in cryostasis."

He pushed the box across the table and I glanced inside. It was almost full; I recognized Ima's handwriting on the top one. I touched the letter but I couldn't take it out. I couldn't read about their pain. I just couldn't bear it.

I looked up at Melody. "I can't. Not yet."

"I understand. Do you mind if we read them? There might be useful evidence in there. We'll keep them safe."

I nodded. "I can have them back though? To read another time?"

"Of course."

I didn't know when that time would be. I couldn't imagine ever climbing out of the pit of loss I felt in that moment. And knowing that Miss Lilly could put me out of a tiny bit of that misery if she wanted to...it dug the thorns of sorrow even deeper into my skin.

I just wanted to know where Alfie was. Even if he was dead, I just wanted to know.

chapter sixty-eight
SHEM

"Did you know someone called Marcus Berthald?" Adam asked.

I shook my head.

"You might have known him as Mark maybe?"

"Never heard of him."

"Shem, your blood tests show that you have a number of the same traits as some of the other children found here. Do you have any idea why that might be?"

"No. What are you trying to say? I've done nothing wrong."

"We know that. No one is accusing you of anything. Laura tells us that you were brought in very recently. We're just trying to understand why – you're considerably older than some of the other victims."

"They said I was a vagrant, which I wasn't because I had a place until they burned it down."

"How did you come to be homeless?"

"I wasn't homeless! I told you, I had a shed."

"Yes. Sorry, I'm just trying to establish your history so we can figure out why Miss Lilly was so interested in you."

Someone came out of the tent with a handful of papers and said, "I think we've got confirmation."

Adam said, "Will you wait? While I see what they've found?"

"You said you'd get me something to eat."

"I will. Anything you want."

"Fish and chips and a sausage for my dog."

He smiled. "I'll get on it right away."

chapter sixty-nine
LAURA

I was sitting on my bed, numbly waiting for one minute to pass into the next, when Melody called me from downstairs.

"Laura? One of your teachers is here. She brought the little dog you found and a couple of your friends."

Marsha?

I ran down. In the hall stood Madam Hoosier, Keisha and Susan. Susan was holding a balloon in the shape of a carrot. Keisha flew up the stairs and nearly knocked me over with a hug.

"You're okay!"

"Yes, I'm fine."

"We've got so much to tell you! The school is on emergency measures or something. The police are saying it might have been funded from criminal proceedings. We don't know if it's even going to stay open!"

Madam Hoosier barked up the stairs, "Keisha!"

I said, "What about Marsha? Have you heard anything?"

Before Keisha could answer, Susan said, "I got you a present." She bounced the carrot up and down, saying, "Squawk, squawk, I'm a carrot parrot."

I don't know why, maybe the exhaustion had made me hysterical, but I started laughing. Then Susan let go of the balloon. It drifted upwards and bumped to a tinkling stop against Miss Lilly's crystal chandelier and my laughter turned to tears.

chapter seventy
SHEM

Adam took ages with the food. I nearly left, but I had nowhere else to go and it was sunny and warm and I had Scrag so I waited.

Eventually he came back with a bundle of fish and chips wrapped in paper. I could smell the vinegar and my mouth watered but I didn't want him to come too close.

"Put them down there."

He laid the package on the floor before backing away.

Scrag sat to attention as I collected the package warily and fished out the sausage for him.

"Thanks," I said.

Adam said, "Shem, some years ago a man worked here. His name was Marcus Berthald."

I mumbled through a mouthful of chips, "I told you, I don't know him."

"He left here with a child. A five-year-old boy who'd lost his arm. We think that child…"

My hand stopped halfway to my mouth. "You think it was me?"

"We believe so."

I forced myself to swallow. "Marcus Berthald... Bert."

He nodded.

"We think Marcus..."

"Bert."

"Bert...was trying to rescue you." He gave me a sad little smile.

I stared at him and said, "So what was I doing here? Who am I?"

chapter seventy-one

LAURA

I cried on both my friends until Susan said, "I'm sorry I let go of your balloon." Like it was that that had made me cry.

I laughed through my sniffling and said, "Don't be silly, it was so kind of you to bring it, thank you. Come on, let's go down."

At the bottom of the stairs I said, "Madam Hoosier, I'm so sorry about running away."

"Shows great resource and courage, Laura. I completely understand."

"Will you come back to school?" Keisha wanted to know.

I said, "Even if they'd have me back, I've no one to pay my fees now."

"Mountains turn into molehills," sighed Susan.

To which there was obviously no answer.

Madam Hoosier said, "Take heart, girls, the governors are looking for new sponsors and if they succeed, there is no doubt there'll be a place for you, Laura."

Even without Marsha, I knew I wanted to go back. It was the nearest thing I had to normal.

Keisha pulled her slate from her bag. "I've got something to show you. It's a message from Marsha."

We sat on the bottom step and she pinched an icon up to play a video.

Marsha smiled sadly at me from the screen. She pushed her hands into her hair so it stood up in a ginger Mohican. Someone said something behind her and as she turned around I saw a woman in a medical bed. A medical bed in a tiny living room.

Marsha said, *"I know, Mum, just give me a minute."*

She didn't sound right. There was no trace of a Russian accent. She sounded British.

She said, *"Okay, so I haven't been entirely honest with you."* She dashed a tear away and clenched her jaw. *"This is so embarrassing. I don't know where to start. My dad isn't a Russian zillionaire. I don't even see him. I live in Worthing with my mum. She's got motor neurone disease and needs twenty-four-hour care. I was barely getting to school at all until Miss Lilly found me and offered me a chance to go to Whitman's."*

She pressed her fingers against her eyelids and took a breath before saying, *"This is so hard. Ah well, out with it, Marsha. I was paid to keep an eye on you. I got to go to Whitman's and I had enough to fund Mum's care at home."*

My jaw dropped open.

"Miss Lilly placed me at school the term before you. Time to bed in while you recovered from being in stasis. It was a well-

thought-out plan. I'd be your best friend, looking out for you…"

She broke off. I could see her lip trembling.

I said, "Oh, Marsha."

"That day we went to Brighton, she wanted me to trap your friend. I didn't want to do it, Laura. I liked you, I really did. Miss Lilly threatened to abandon my mum and pull me out of school if I didn't. Her people were waiting in Victoria's bedroom, where you were supposed to meet, and then you saw your crazy friend without me. I didn't know what to do. I don't even know why I agreed to go to Blackhurst – maybe to show Miss Lilly that you weren't as pliable as she seemed to think you were. And then the tracker kicked in and…I'm sorry. I wish we could have been proper friends. I told you though, people like me don't get to have proper friends."

She leaned forward and clicked the camera off. I stared at the empty space.

Stunned.

Susan put her arm around my shoulder.

I didn't know what to say. I should have been angry but I just felt so sorry for Marsha. She'd done what she did for her family. She hadn't even known me when I first arrived at school. She probably thought it was a great opportunity, until the person she was betraying became a real human being.

"Laura?" Melody came in. "Sorry to interrupt. Can you come with me – to the marquee?"

Keisha said, "We can wait here," and then to Madam Hoosier, "Can't we?"

Madam Hoosier said, "If Laura wants us to?"

I said, "Yes, please."

I followed Melody out of the door.

chapter seventy-two
SHEM

I listened as Adam told me what they knew of my story.

"What happened to my hand?"

"We think it was amputated to see whether it would regenerate. They have records that show they had some success with toes on other patients – it's not such a leap to a hand. It seems that was the point at which your Bert decided to get you out."

"I lost my hand for an experiment?"

"I'm so sorry."

I stared at the empty space where the rest of my limb should have been. All those stories that Bert had told me about how I lost it – I never thought the one about the mad chef might turn out to be so close to the truth. That's all I had been worth to someone – a collection of body parts.

·Then I imagined the kid I must have been and something cracked inside me. That little boy was five years old – what kind of monster could do that to a child? No wonder Bert had been paranoid about me being captured again.

Bert. He'd saved me. God knows what he'd given up – his job, his home. Who knew what else. He might have looked like a tramp on the outside but on the inside, he was a hero. My hero. My insides seemed to swell up with tears. I didn't want anyone to see me cry so I muttered, "Right, thanks. Well, we'll be off then."

I sniffed. Stood up. No clue what I was going to do now.

"There's something else you should know. Can you wait five more minutes? I won't force you to give a statement but some important information has come to light and we think you should hear it."

As we walked around the building Melody said, "We believe we've located Alfie."

She said it so calmly it took a moment for it to register but when it did, everything in me soared. "What? Where? Where is he? Is he okay? Oh my God, I can't believe it!"

"He's not going to be what you expect, Laura."

"Is he in the tent? Are we going there?"

Before she could say anything else I was running. I raced around the building, but she caught up and pulled me back.

"Laura, listen to me. He's changed. He…"

Hedge Boy was sitting on the grass with his dog and a big packet of fish and chips. I was pleased to see him looking better but I didn't have time to stop. I raised a hand to him but said, "Come on, Melody."

"Laura, stop. Alfie isn't in the tent. He was revived twelve years ago. He's a young man now. A young man who's been through a lot."

"A young man?"

Melody nodded.

I tried to realign the picture of Alfie I had in my mind – twelve years ago? My little brother was seventeen? Older than me?

"Where is he?"

Melody turned and looked at the skinny boy on the grass with close-cropped hair and gaunt cheeks.

I shook my head. Hedge Boy? Hedge Boy was Alfie?

In my dreams of our reunion, I scooped him into my arms and snuggled his head. I promised to read him *Thomas the Tank Engine* and make him hot chocolate.

"How do you know?" I said.

Melody said, "Blood tests – your DNA matches."

I didn't really understand what she was saying but as I looked at Hedge Boy, I didn't need to.

He was looking at me with that defiant tilt to his chin, his bottom lip sticking out but steady. The look I'd seen when I first saw him, that had seemed so familiar because it was.

I knew him.

My little brother was my big brother.

And he was staring at me as if I was an alien.

chapter seventy-four
SHEM

I had family.

A sister.

Had she known?

Was that why she was nice to me?

Adam said, "This is Laura, Shem."

She was hovering about twenty metres away. Nervous.

I stood up and Scrag saw who I was looking at. He galloped off, the little flirt, and flung himself at her feet, wriggling on his back. She bent down to rub his tummy. Then she walked slowly over to me.

Her hands were in tight little fists and I thought, for a minute, she wanted to hit me. Then her face crumpled and she started crying. Man, she looked ugly when she was crying, like a big sobbing pug. It made me smile.

"Why are you laughing?"

"I'm not! You just…your face looks funny."

She cried even more and then ran at me, flinging her arms around my neck so tight I had to prise her off.

As soon as he said it, I broke.

"Your face looks funny."

It was such an Alfie thing to say.

I flung myself at him, spluttering, "I don't care how big you are, I've got you back. I'll take care of you, Alfie, I swear I will."

He eased away from me and said, "My name's Shem, and I look after myself."

I sniffed and nodded. "Shem. Okay, Shem. It's…nice."

I looked at his too thin face, at the little mole over his eye. I couldn't resist reaching out to touch it but he pulled away. I was getting it all wrong. I didn't even know how to speak to him. But I had my brother back and I *was* going to take care of him. Decades ago, I'd made him a promise. A sister promise. And one way or another, I was going to keep it.

chapter seventy-six

EPILOGUE

It's been a year since I found Alfie.

Shem.

Hedge Boy.

My brother.

A sulkier, more tetchy person I've never met in my life. But, it's fine, he's had a rough ride and I've got a thick skin. He's living here, at the school, but he won't stay inside. He says it makes him feel trapped. We built him a shed in the grounds. He lives there with Scrag and Batfink – she can't live with me in the school itself because too many of the girls are allergic to cats. I see her all the time though and she and Scrag are super sweet together.

Shem is sort of being a caretaker's assistant – he's brilliant at fixing stuff, and he gets some tutoring from Madam Hoosier. She's the only teacher he talks to. He has to because Scrag and Batfink are very fond of visiting her – she keeps a cooked chicken in her fridge for furry visitors, so her kitchen is a very popular destination for those two little beasts.

When I look at how far we've come in the space of a year, it's hard to believe all the stuff that happened before. There was a period after Miss Lilly's arrest when they found shocking thing after shocking thing. The graves were the worst. It breaks my heart to think about all those lost children. The police are still trying to identify some of them. I can't bear it that we don't know who they are. They need to have their names back so they can always be remembered. Shem thinks we should plant a tree for every child that died at Blackhurst. I think it's a beautiful idea.

Then there were the pods. Seventy-two of them were occupied. All the occupants have been revived. Some of them were frozen quite recently. Others, like me, are adapting to life in a different time. They're doing better than the children who were on the extraction ward though. Some of them will never recover properly. We were lucky Shem wasn't there for too long.

There's the money too – a whole lot of it. Miss Lilly did own the school building, but she'd put it, and the clinic, in my name the day I was born. She'd been very careful to keep legitimate earnings away from anything that could be considered the proceeds of crime, and she'd put it all in trust for me. It was like she was convinced that having her blood in my veins would make me some kind of mini version of her – she never doubted that I'd run things exactly as she wanted. She got that wrong.

I tried to refuse the money at first. It was blood money – however she'd earned it, I thought it would always be tainted. Stacey made me see things differently. She said I should think of the money as compensation and use it to put things right, not just for myself, but for all the other survivors from the clinic.

So I accepted the money and set up a foundation for the school and another for The Ark. That's the clinic. We've turned the building into a true rehabilitation centre. It's a home for any of Miss Lilly's victims who need it. Miss Lilly absolutely hates it.

Her case hasn't come to court yet – they're still going through evidence – but she's likely to get a life sentence. They've put her in a high-security wing for her own safety. She's been attacked by other prisoners more than once. Almost all the clinic staff have been charged as accessories to her crimes. From my team, only Vera and Edna didn't seem to know the full extent of the horrors in the basement. I was devastated when I heard. How could Benjie and Mariya behave so normally when they knew what was happening two floors below their feet? Did they think that they weren't responsible because they didn't actually work on that horrible ward? How could they have done nothing to try and stop it?

Stacey spent her life trying to find out what was happening there and she didn't even know the half of it. She's pretty much physically recovered from the car accident now, but she's got something called post-traumatic stress disorder. She's getting a lot of help and I think she's going to be okay. It's her birthday soon and I wanted to do something for her, to make up for all the ones I've missed. So we're having a party, here at the school. Keisha, me and Susan are organizing it – Susan is in charge of the decorations. They're going to be vegetable-themed. I know. Totally weird, but what does it matter? I'm just letting her get on with it, with a bit of mild interference from an exasperated Keisha.

Guess who we've booked to play?

The Cure.

Well, it's not actually them, it's a holographic version of them but they're so good it's easy to believe they're the real thing. It's pretty expensive but I quite like that I'm spending some of Miss Lilly's money on Stacey – her arch-enemy. It's definitely going to be worth it. When I told Stacey she was going to see Robert Smith nearly live, she just about peed herself with excitement. She bounced around the grounds squealing and nearly put her back out.

I'm hoping Marsha will come. She's having a hard time dealing with how ashamed she feels. I genuinely don't hold any grudges – I like her, I really do, and I get why she did what she did. I'd love it if she came back to school, if she'd let me pay to take care of her mum – she just won't hear of it. I don't know, it's complicated, but I'm working on it.

Shame is a weird thing. There was such an odd response after the story of Blackhurst became public. Nobody wanted to believe that the cream they'd been putting on their faces, that worked so well, contained cells extracted from children. They didn't want to give it up, so they just ignored the evidence right in front of their noses. I swear, if we hadn't got rid of the stock, people would still be buying it today. We destroyed all of it. Cleared out every last warehouse. I wanted to be sure it was over, that no one would ever benefit from what had happened to those children.

I couldn't destroy the research though. That was taken, along with all Miss Lilly's papers, by the police. I think it's entirely possible it will end up being used somehow – we need new methods to manage infection because of the antibiotic shortage. I really don't know what to think. Does it mean the suffering wasn't wasted? Or should it be obliterated because the methods of discovery were just too horrendous? I don't know. I really don't.

Keisha thinks I'm crazy, but I'm still in touch with Miss Lilly. Well, I was. She stopped speaking to me when we shut down the clinic. She was furious and said I'd betrayed her, that she'd trusted me with everything and I'd let her down. Still, when Miss Lilly's ready to speak to me again, I think I'll visit her. It's partly because I want to understand her, partly because there are still things I don't know – like what really happened to Mum and Ima – but mostly it's because I don't want any dark corners left inside me. She's being punished. I have to think about myself. No hate. No bitterness. No turning her into a monster. She's just a deeply disturbed woman who cannot hurt me any more.

There's one important thing I have left to do and I'm heading to Shem's shed to do it. I'm wearing my *Choose Life* T-shirt as a badge of honour and as a promise to Mum and Ima, who chose life for us. Me and my brother.

I knock on Shem's door. Scrag yaps as it opens, and he skips around my feet when he sees me. I look up at my brother and smile. He's grown over the last year, and filled out. I miss the little boy he was but I've got quite attached to the grumpy teenager he is.

"Come in then," he says, still awkward but trying hard not to be. He takes the box I'm carrying and sets it down. I sit on his bed where Batfink is curled up. She stretches out her front paws and yawns widely before padding her way onto my lap. I kiss her soft warm head. Shem's kettle whistles on the tiny stove that serves as his kitchen.

"I thought you'd want tea," he says.

I nod but I can't speak because sometimes it just feels so miraculous that I'm in the same room as him, my heart puffs up in a cloud of contentment. When he's handed me my tea, I say, "Ready?"

"Ready."

We've got some letters to read, and we're going to do it together. It's going to be hard but it's part of our story. The part we never got to live. There's a cold corner inside of us, where Mum and Ima should be, and it needs warming up.

I learned a few things from Vera's book, *How to be Calm in The Midst of A Storm*. You *can* live your life with a partly frozen heart, but ice cracks under pressure. Far better to melt it gently, even if it hurts you. Even if it scares you.

I pick up a letter.

Our beautiful babies, today we walked by the pond in the park. There were two swans circling on the water, their heads dipped together to make the shape of a heart. They reminded us of you. Everything reminds us of you...

ACKNOWLEDGEMENTS

No book is an island, and I have a few thank yous for those that helped in the creation of this one.

Emily and Archie, try not to be sick when I say this, but seeing the bond between you two has been one of the greatest privileges of my life. I hope I've shown a fraction of that in this book. Also, thanks for endlessly answering my synonym questions. If you can think of another way of saying, "You're the best," it definitely applies to you.

Nick, you turned your life upside down while I was writing this book and I know it was partly to make more space for me. Thank you. I am so glad you lives wiv me.

Dr Blood, Helen Peters and the girls of Roedean School. Thank you for sharing so much with me. I genuinely couldn't have written this book without your help – my school experience was so very different. Your generosity with your space and stories was invaluable. You gave me a cloth to embroider; I hope you don't mind the liberties I took.

To my hairdressers, Buzby and Blue in Chichester, where much of this book was written, especially to Albert Pascal, Kate Gibson, Sophie Yates – you're all FABULOUS, darlings! And Kate, you so inspired Susan's random sayings…I had to cut the "Did I blink or was that a power cut" line though – my editors didn't believe anyone would actually say that.

To all my SCBWI pals, especially my original online critique gang who met Laura and Shem a gazillion years ago in a very different story. You know the truth, it never would have happened without you.

To every librarian that was, is and ever shall be. Unappreciated so much of the time, you change lives. We need you and not just for biscuits.

Endless thanks, always, to my agent Sophie Hicks. Your faith in Laura and Shem made this story live.

And finally, thanks to all at Usborne but particularly Will Steele for the glorious UK cover of this book and always, always to all my editors, but most especially Sarah Stewart and Anne Finnis, whose input is at least half the value of anything good I've ever written. The rhubarb gin is on me!

ABOUT THE AUTHOR

Kathryn Evans has been an actor, a waitress, a celery cutter and a newspaper deliverer – she's even scrubbed the decks of the *Mary Rose*. Now she combines being an author with being a mum, running a farm, volunteering as a co-regional advisor for SCBWI, dancing and fencing competitively. Kathryn's debut novel *More of Me* was nominated for the Carnegie Medal and won the Crystal Kite Award, and also won the Edinburgh International Book Festival First Book Award – the first YA novel ever to do so.

IF YOU ENJOYED
BEAUTY SLEEP, DON'T MISS

kathryn evans

MORE
OF ME

Twelve girls.
One identity.

The world must not know about our freakery...

Teva's life seems normal: school, friends, boyfriend.
But at home she hides an impossible secret.
Eleven other Tevas.

Because once a year, Teva separates into two, leaving a
younger version of herself stuck at the same age, in the
same house...watching the new Teva live the life that she'd
been living. But as her seventeenth birthday rolls around,
Teva is determined not to let it happen again. She's going
to fight for her future.

Even if that means fighting herself.

"Weird, wonderful and utterly fabulous." Teri Terry

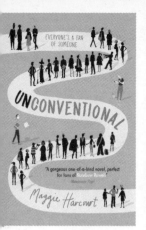
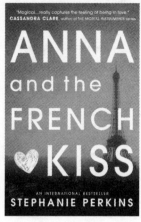

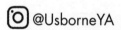